THE WILDCAT OF BRAETON

To: Amy —
Keep Reading!

[signature]

THE WILDCAT OF BRAETON

CLAIRE M. BANSCHBACH

TATE PUBLISHING
AND ENTERPRISES, LLC

Published by Tate Publishing & Enterprises, LLC
127 E. Trade Center Terrace | Mustang, Oklahoma 73064 USA
1.888.361.9473 | www.tatepublishing.com

Tate Publishing is committed to excellence in the publishing industry. The company reflects the philosophy established by the founders, based on Psalm 68:11,
"The Lord gave the word and great was the company of those who published it."

Book design copyright © 2015 by Tate Publishing, LLC. All rights reserved.
Cover design by Niño Carlo Suico
Interior design by Gram Telen

Published in the United States of America

ISBN: 978-1-68097-981-7
Fiction / Action & Adventure
15.02.23

To my parents, who have always supported and encouraged me not only in writing but in life. I wouldn't have gotten this far without you.

Acknowledgements

Firstly, I would like to thank all my siblings for their support, encouragement, and general harassment when they find out I have a new story.

To my sister Sarah, who once again saved my life with her editing. You'll probably always be my fist editor. I hope you're ready for that burden.

To my sister Jocelyn, who demanded that Emeth have his own story and for condescending to illustrate again. You will never be paid except with my undying love.

To Catherine who assisted with the pronunciation guide and spent several late nights helping me go through the manuscript one last time. I hope I can convey adequate gratitude.

I want to thank Mary Kaylyn Miller for the fully awesome map and for agreeing to make another version. I can't ever thank you enough for bringing my world to paper.

To the parental units who have always fostered a love of reading and who have shown unending support and encouragement through the publishing process. And for demanding to read my other stories now that they know I write. It's like they love me or something.

I'd also like to thank my beta readers for agreeing to read this story and giving me some needed feedback.

I also want to thank the terrific folks at Tate Publishing for working with me a second time.

Pronunciation Guide

c: hard as in *cat*–e.g., Corin, Celyn, Cimbria, Cyndor, etc.

ae: long *a*–e.g., Braeton

ll: *l* rolled on the side of the tongue–e.g., Llewellyn, Lleu

í: long *e* as in *meet* when used in Calorin names–e.g., Hamíd. (sometimes *i* is long in last syllable as in Karif, Hosni, etc.)

j: sounded like soft *g* as in *gentle* when used in Calorin names– e.g., Jaffa, Janzori

g: hard as in *great*–e.g., Gavin, Gelion

I: pronounced as *e* for Aredorian names only–e.g., Iwan (Ew-an) Ivor (Ee-vor)

y: sounded like short *i* when used as a vowel in Aredorian names– e.g., Colwyn, Celyn

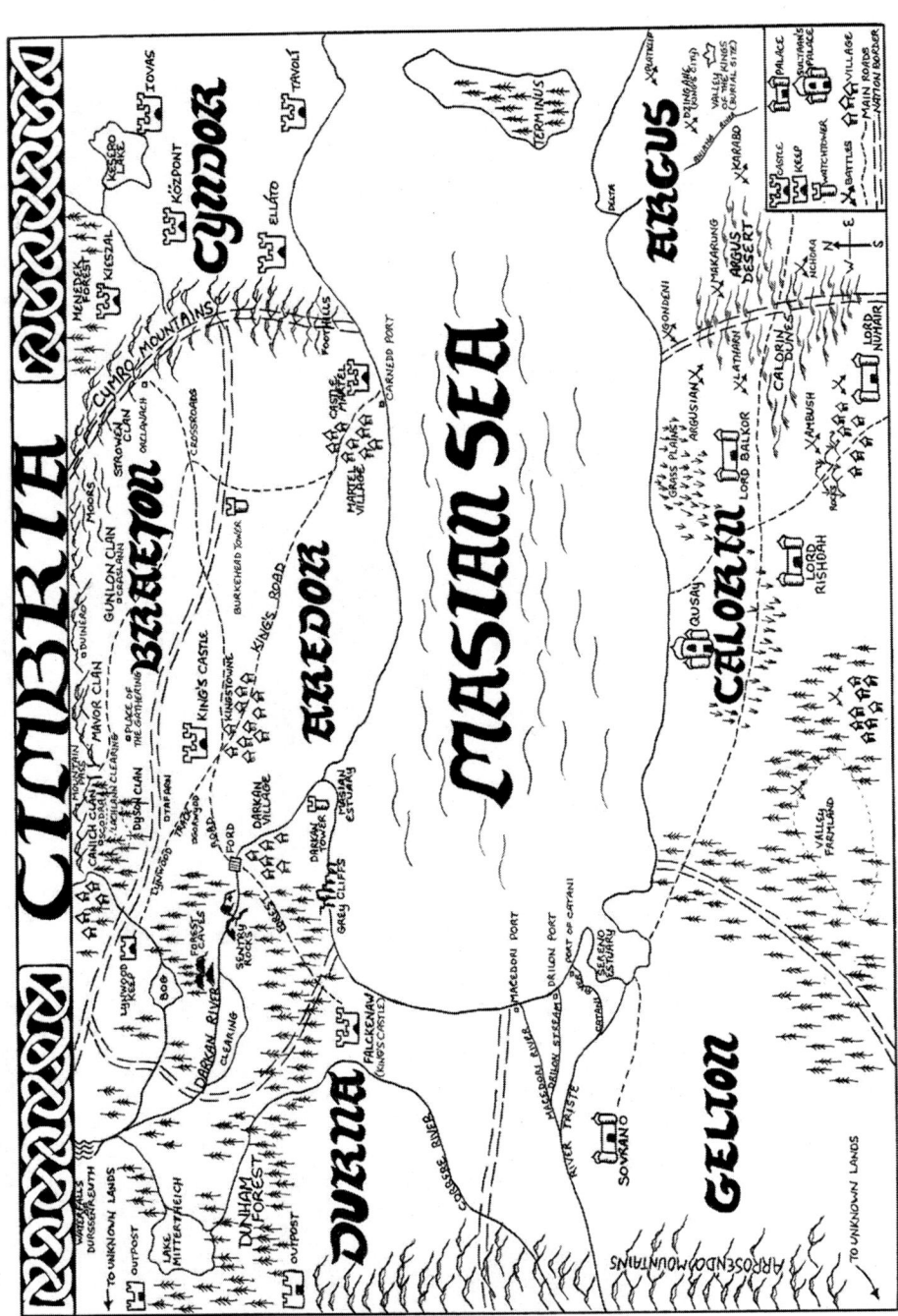

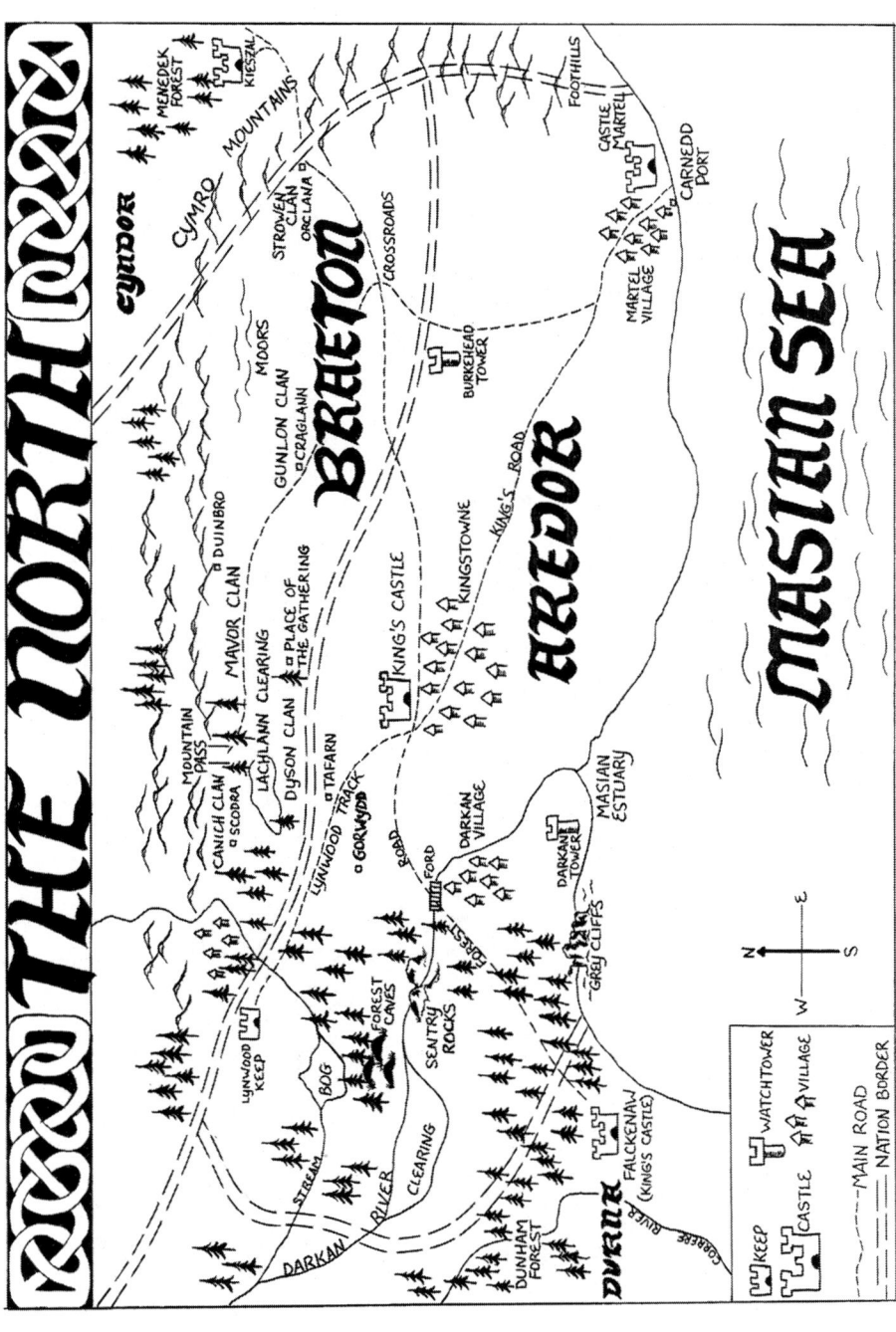

Death in front of me
And death to the sides.
But I cannot go back.
They fall by tens of hundreds,
My brothers who trusted me.
Can I now lead them out?
Who can survive this reckless advance?
Will we yet all perish?
But faithful till the end
When death comes for all.
They follow by tens and tens of hundreds
My brothers who trusted me.
Light shines in their eyes,
They hope to follow me
And defy Death to the end.
Yes, by tens and tens of hundreds
We stop the advance.
By horses-our speed
And spears-our strength
The sword will guide us home.
Death comes not today.
A victory for me,
A victory for my brothers,
Yes, a hard-won victory.
But no rest-the enemy is powerful.
We can but fight-even to the end.

Book 1

Return to Scodra

Chapter 1

Two men trudged down a dusty road. The hot Calorin winds ruffled the grassy plains around them. They were dressed identically in black and red uniforms. A phoenix was emblazoned on the front of their tunics and mail coats glinted beneath the leather. Black belts held an array of weapons. One carried two swords across his back in addition to several knives. The other's hand rested easily on the handle of a scimitar and he also carried daggers within reach. But beyond the uniforms all resemblance ceased.

The second man was a Calorin—dark skinned, slender, muscular. His companion's fair skin stood out in sharp contrast. Green eyes glinted dangerously beneath his dark hair. And if he slipped back into his native northern tongue, the strong accent of the Clans of Braeton would be heard.

Emeth stopped for a moment to take in his surroundings. The flat, grassy plains of Calorin stretched in all directions as far as the eye could see.

"You're not going to miss the incredible scenery, are you?" his Calorin companion asked with a smile.

Emeth laughed. "Maybe for a day or so," he said, glancing at the position of the sun as he adjusted his double swords. "Come on, Ahmed, pick up the pace! I want to get back to camp before dark."

"Shut up or I'll make you carry the pack," Ahmed threatened.

"You're the one who didn't want to take the horses!" Emeth shot back.

"We've been over this! It was only a short scouting trip."

Still arguing, the two companions continued down the dusty road. Within an hour their camp came into view. They passed the sentries unchallenged and headed toward the tent of their commander, Lord Rishdah. They were met at the entrance by a Calorin dressed as they were in the uniform of the Phoenix Guard.

"Nicar," Ahmed greeted him. "Where's Lord Rishdah?"

"He went to meet Ismail on the west road," Nicar replied. "Did you two find anything?"

"We found Khalid's camp," Emeth said.

For the last two years, there had been unrest on the Calorin borders. Lord Rishdah was one of the Sultaan's most trusted generals so he had been given the task of settling the uprisings. And so, once again, they were encamped along the eastern border by the desert country of Argus.

Khalid, a renegade general, had been stirring up the Argusians against the Calorins despite the peace treaty that existed between the two countries. Khalid now commanded almost five hundred men, a mix of Calorins and Argusians. His camp lay only a day's march from Lord Rishdah's army. After giving their report, Emeth and Ahmed were dismissed to go rest.

The Phoenix Guard's tent was pitched next to Lord Rishdah's. Sleep, however, eluded Emeth. He lay on his cot and stared at the ceiling. Emeth had come to Calorin nearly eight years ago after running away from his home in the North. He quickly came into the service of Lord Rishdah and swore seven years to his service in the elite Phoenix Guard. Those years were now complete. But he had decided to stay until the trouble with Khalid was finished and then he would be free. He had avoided all mention of leaving for Ahmed's sake. The two of them were as close as brothers and it was for that reason Lord Rishdah had sent them with his only living son Ismail when the Sultaan had ordered him to Aredor.

That nightmarish year they had spent in the northern country, then under Calorin rule, was the closest Emeth had been to his home in years. They had been in Aredor when the Calorins were driven out by an army of rebels and Braeton Clans. Ismail had not told his father the part they had played in the events surrounding the deciding battle although Emeth had a strong suspicion that Ismail's wife, Nadirah, knew what had happened.

Watching Corin, an Aredorian and former slave, leave the Phoenix Guard four years ago was harder on Emeth and Ahmed than they would admit. So was meeting Corin in the forests of Aredor as the leader of the outlaws. And now Ahmed was going to be left behind again. Captain Azrahil was trying to find a replacement to take Emeth's place. Lord Rishdah depended heavily on his Guard in missions and battles, allowing them a certain familiarity with him and his family. Only the best were allowed in the Phoenix Guard and Emeth was determined that his replacement would ably fill the hole left by his departure.

Dawn came quickly and the camp bustled with activity as the army prepared to move out. Emeth helped Nicar pack the Guard's few belongings and their tent and then he began to saddle his distinctive black and white spotted stallion. The horse nickered softly, butting Emeth's chest and looking for treats. Emeth pushed him away.

"Sorry, Narak, I don't have anything today," he said.

The captain of the Guards came to find him.

"Lord Rishdah wants you to accompany Ismail. Scouts brought word in that Khalid is on the move," Captain Azrahil said.

"Yes, sir. Find out his position so we can head him off and finish this blasted campaign," Emeth said. Azrahil flashed a quick smile.

"More or less," he said. "And, Emeth? Try not to get caught."

Emeth saluted. "Yes, sir. I don't really feel like having a chat with Khalid anyway," he said. Any reply that Azrahil would have made was cut off when Ismail rode up.

"Ready?" he asked.

"As I'll ever be, sir," Emeth replied as he mounted. Gathering up the reins he cantered after Ismail.

They rode for an hour before finding the first signs of Khalid's army. The plains of Calorin rolled into hills before reaching the sandy borders of Argus. With ease born of practice, they guided their horses through the hills, taking care to remain unseen.

"They're a ways from their camp, sir," Emeth said. Ismail nodded as he watched the enemy force.

"Khalid is taking them west and right toward us. If we hurry we can meet them out on the open plain," Ismail said. Turning their horses, he and Emeth raced back to camp.

A few hours later, Emeth guided Narak to his familiar place by Ismail on the front battle line. The stallion moved nervously, sensing the upcoming conflict. Emeth stroked Narak's neck gently. All along the line of Ismail's cavalry men were also performing the same familiar motions of soothing anxious animals.

"Not much longer, boy," he said in his own language. "If only these Calorins didn't love to take any chance to hack at each other, we'd be home by now."

"Emeth, you forget I speak Rhyddan," Ismail reprimanded, not taking his eyes from the advancing army.

"Sorry, sir," Emeth said, not very contritely.

Ismail smiled faintly. "You are not the only one who wants to stop fighting and go home. I've barely been back in two and a half years."

"Yes, sir. How are your boys doing, by the way?" Emeth asked, reverting to the Calorin tongue.

"Castimir gives every indication of being exactly like his namesake. Sharif is crawling now and getting into everything," Ismail said, laughing at a memory, and Emeth smiled. A horn sounded, announcing that Lord Rishdah and the main army were in position. Ismail gave the signal and the cavalry moved forward as one. Emeth and Ahmed settled in on either side of Ismail as the horses lengthened stride, flying toward the enemy. Emeth unsheathed a sword as he heard the pounding of hooves and the war cries around him. The warrior spirit of the northern Clans arose and he plunged fearlessly into battle.

Once the cavalry successfully engaged the front lines, Lord Rishdah advanced. He divided his forces and brought them in from the sides in a pincer movement. Caught on three sides, Khalid's forces fought to the death. When the sun sank, it was on a bloody plain.

Emeth awoke in darkness. Once his vision cleared, he realized he was looking at a night sky filled with stars. The next thing he realized was that his legs couldn't move. Panicked, he sat up, his aching head protesting at the sudden movement. Gradually he became aware of his surroundings. He lay on the battlefield. Torches flickered as men searched for survivors. Groans of the wounded and the dying seemed to echo in the night air. Finally, he turned attention to himself.

He was half trapped beneath a dead horse. He dimly remembered getting thrown from Narak while a mounted Argusian moved in to attack. The rim of the shield had clipped his forehead, creating a bloody gash. He had killed the Argusian but a spear had pierced the horse, causing it to fall and pin him to the ground. Emeth carefully pulled himself out from under the horse. Apart from his head and the usual cuts and bruises, he was unharmed. Groping in the darkness, he found his swords and sheathed them. As of yet, he had no indication of how the battle had ended.

Shakily he stood. Torchlight flared behind him and a hand reached out to steady him.

"I thought for a minute we had lost you."

"Ahmed!" Emeth said in relief. "I guess this means we won?"

"Barely. Khalid surrendered a little over an hour ago. Both sides lost almost half their men and I still haven't found Ismail," Ahmed said worriedly.

Together they began the gruesome process of searching the battlefield. After a few minutes, Ahmed pointed. "There!" he cried.

Ismail lay draped across the body of his slain stallion. At first glance they thought him dead, but closer inspection showed him unconscious and wounded.

"Now what?" Emeth asked, noticing for the first time the bandage around Ahmed's arm. "Between the two of us, I don't think we're taking him anywhere."

Ahmed shouted and signaled with his torch. Within minutes stretcher bearers came and carried Ismail back to the camp. Ahmed and Emeth walked slowly after them as Emeth's legs were still stiff after being trapped for so long. Azrahil met them and helped Emeth to a cot before Emeth lost consciousness again.

Chapter 2

"Hold still, you big baby!" Nicar exclaimed.

"If you would stop trying to finish taking my head off, I would!" Emeth replied as Nicar washed the cut on his forehead. "Are you trying to drown me now?" Emeth complained as water trickled down his face into his collar.

"Well, if you had let me take care of it when you came in, but no! Look at you now! Blood all over!" Nicar retorted.

"You two ladies almost done over there?" Ahmed asked from across the tent.

"I would be if *someone* would stop moving," Nicar said. Emeth muttered vague threats as the healer washed away the dried blood that was caked around the wound.

"Once you're done, Azrahil wants to see you both," Ahmed said.

A few minutes later, Nicar finished tying a light bandage around Emeth's head. Emeth stood, swaying a bit unsteadily.

"What did you do? Put a turban around my head?" he asked, feeling the bandage. Nicar tossed him his swords. Emeth caught them deftly and buckled them on.

"Oh, stop moaning!" Nicar said. "You're worse than anyone I've ever treated."

Chatting companionably, the three Guards left the tent and went to meet the captain.

"Finally!" Azrahil said as they came up. "Emeth, I need you to do some tracking. Ahmed and Nicar, stay with Lord Rishdah," he ordered.

"Where are we going, sir?" Emeth asked.

"To find Khalid," Azrahil said grimly. "One of his generals posed as him last night and surrendered. Khalid escaped."

"Brilliant," Emeth said. A troop of thirty soldiers rode up leading two extra horses. Azrahil mounted his horse and Emeth looked quizzically at the captain as he took the reins of the second.

"Ah, we couldn't find Narak. He wasn't on the battlefield or anywhere around here," Azrahil said. "I'm sure if anyone had found him we would have heard about it." He smirked.

"It's not my fault he bit that groom!" Emeth exclaimed as he mounted. Narak could be rather ill-tempered which was perhaps why he and Emeth got along so well together.

"You keep saying that," Azrahil said.

"Which way are we going, sir?" Emeth asked.

"East. That's where he was last seen."

It was late in the day when Emeth raised the trail. Dismounting, he led the troop through the tall grass. The sun was setting when they came to a small river. Emeth found more tracks in the muddy bank.

"Looks like he has five men with him, all mounted, sir." He broke off suddenly, studying a set of hoofprints. "Unbelievable!" he said. "That man is riding my horse!"

"How do you know?" Azrahil asked.

"You remember those horse thieves a few years back?" Emeth asked. Azrahil nodded in remembrance. "Once we got our horses back, Hamíd and the blacksmith put a small mark on all of the left hind shoes."

Azrahil bent to study the track. Inside the print of the horseshoe there was a small circle with a slash through it.

"You're sure it's Narak?" Azrahil asked.

"As far as I know only seven horses were fitted with marked shoes, and they're all accounted for except Narak," Emeth replied.

"So you will be able to track them anywhere?" a soldier asked.

"Mostly, but we'd better hurry. Khalid is taking them toward Argus. That marked shoe will be useless in sand," Emeth said.

"How far ahead are they?" Azrahil asked.

Emeth studied the prints again.

"Half a day," he said.

The troop stopped a few minutes more to water the horses and then Emeth led them on, leaning over the neck of his horse to keep an eye on the trail left by Khalid.

The night was well advanced when they halted and made camp.

"How's your head?" Azrahil asked Emeth as he rubbed at the bandage.

"Horrible," Emeth admitted. "Whatever Nicar drugged me with wore off hours ago."

Azrahil handed him a small bottle.

"Here, Nicar gave this to me. A few sips should help," he said. Emeth drank and felt the throbbing in his head recede. "Get some rest. We're not stopping tomorrow," Azrahil said.

"How did I know you were going to say that?" Emeth muttered, wrapping himself in his cloak.

Dawn broke a few hours later and the camp stirred into motion. Emeth cast about for the trail. Once he found it, the troop mounted and followed. Hours passed as Emeth followed the tracks carefully. The troop made good time and he reckoned they were only a few hours behind Khalid.

The ground began to change, becoming sandy and dry as it began to rise into dunes. Emeth snorted in disgust. He had lost the trail among the shifting hills. Dismounting again, he searched along the edge of the grasslands and into the desert without luck. He pushed up the bandage around his head irritably. Then a thought struck him. He searched left and right as he walked back along the tracks. Azrahil watched curiously but knew better than to say anything. Emeth gave a yell of triumph: tracks split off heading south.

"You sure they went that way?" a soldier asked.

"Yes. Look, three different prints lead off to the south and one of them is marked. Two more lead into the desert. Those two are leaving a decoy trail which almost worked," Emeth admitted. "I have a feeling they will all meet soon along this trail."

He proved right and they were again following the tracks of five horses. By nightfall, Emeth called a halt.

"Sir, I can't keep going," Emeth told Azrahil. "If it were a full moon we could go on, but it's on the wane and I might miss something. Torches would just alert them to our presence," he said.

Azrahil reluctantly agreed and the troop made camp once more. At dawn, they continued again. Midmorning, Emeth signaled for a halt. He dismounted and continued up the trail for a half mile until he saw a small copse of trees surrounding a pond of water. He crouched and made his way closer until he heard the soft murmur of men talking and the movements of horses. Keeping flat, he wormed forward until he saw the shapes of the men. Two were Argusians; the others Calorins.

"Are you sure they followed the false trail?" one asked.

"Yes, my lord. I've seen no sign of anyone following us," a soldier replied.

"You'd better be right, Rafiq!" the first man sneered.

"My lord Khalid, where shall we go from here?" one of the Argusians asked.

Emeth did not wait to hear the reply. He worked his way backward quietly until he was out of sight and then ran back to the waiting patrol. Azrahil divided the troop in half. They would ride out in a wide arc and close around the enemy.

"How do we know they're still there?" a soldier asked.

"I'll go in first and give the signal," Emeth said. Azrahil nodded approvingly.

"How will you do that?" the soldier asked. Emeth swung into the saddle.

"I'm going to get my horse back," he said. "You coming?"

The troop broke into smiles and chuckles.

"All right, let's move out," Azrahil commanded.

Khalid and his men looked startled as Emeth walked through the trees. Drawing their swords, they leapt to their feet.

"You said no one followed us!" Khalid snarled.

"Sorry to prove you wrong, mate, but the false trail didn't work," Emeth said.

"What do you want?" Khalid asked. Emeth smiled disarmingly.

"I just want my horse back," he said.

"I don't believe you," Khalid said. "Are you alone?"

"Sort of," Emeth said.

"Kill him," Khalid ordered. Emeth put his fingers to his mouth and whistled sharply. Azrahil and his men stepped from the trees, encircling the enemy. In a panic, two of Khalid's men charged in an attempt to break free. They were cut down instantly.

"Throw down your weapons unless you want to join your comrades," Azrahil ordered.

"Don't," Khalid told his men. "He'll kill you as soon as you're unarmed."

Azrahil sighed. "If I wanted you dead I wouldn't have wasted my breath. Lord Rishdah wants you alive, Khalid," he said. Azrahil signaled his men forward. Weapons were taken from Khalid and his men. They were bound and forced to mount their horses.

"Excellent job, Emeth," Azrahil commended the young guard.

"Thank you, sir."

"Let's go home."

"Three words I've been longing to hear for months, sir," Emeth said with a smile.

With Khalid's army routed and its leader captured, Lord Rishdah ordered his forces home. Emeth's spirits rose as he beheld the familiar walls and turrets of the castle. Lord Rishdah and Ismail rode ahead to greet their waiting families. No man begrudged their eagerness. Every soldier in the army awaited the dismissal order so they might return to their own homes.

The four Phoenix Guards rode through the gates. Old friends and soldiers left behind called out greetings. Grooms came forward to take their horses. Emeth unbuckled his saddlebags and took them to the barracks.

As was his custom, Lord Rishdah dismissed his guards, allowing them two days of rest after returning from a campaign. Emeth would spend it as he usually did: sleeping.

Bathed and dressed in clean clothes, he first went and visited Castimir's grave as he always did after returning home.

"I survived another, mate," he said softly. "Last one for a while, I hope. We take Khalid to the Sultaan in a few days and I leave for home."

Emeth sighed. Castimir might have been Lord Rishdah's son, but he had been friends with the younger guards, especially Corin. Castimir had always been curious about the North and was continuously pressing Emeth and Corin with questions. Corin had always been reluctant to talk about Aredor for he feared he would never return there.

If things had worked out differently, Corin would be standing beside him, Emeth thought. Of course if things were different, Castimir might be alive too, he thought sadly.

Do not mourn for me. My time had come, Castimir had told Corin in a dream. It did not make it easier for Emeth or Corin. They had both been with him in the ambush when he died and they both still felt like they had failed him and Lord Rishdah.

"I thought I might find you here," Ismail's wife Nadirah said, coming up behind Emeth.

"Yes, m'lady. Just paying my respects," Emeth said. Nadirah smiled.

"Once Ismail has rested, we will come here with the boys. He wants to give them a memory of an uncle they will never know," she said. Emeth glanced at the gravestone. A bundle of wildflowers lay in front of it.

"It must be comforting to know that you're remembered after you're gone," Emeth said.

"I don't know if Castimir would appreciate the flowers, but it helps his mother," Nadirah said. Emeth smiled.

"Believe me, every warrior hopes to lie in a grave marked and decorated," Emeth said.

"Does it make the thought of dying easier?" Nadirah asked curiously.

"Honestly it's more a matter of pride. We leave the world with a monument to our names," Emeth replied, laughing. Nadirah laughed with him. They turned and left the quiet graveyard together.

"I heard Lord Rishdah say that you are leaving in a few days," Nadirah said.

"Yes, ma'am, my term of service is up. I'm going home, for a while at least."

"Do you have much family there, Emeth?"

"My parents and three brothers, and I might even have some nieces and nephews by now."

"Any girl waiting for you?" Nadirah teased.

Emeth laughed. "No, ma'am, I never really paid much attention to girls before I left."

"What will you do once you get home?"

"I don't know. It might prove to be too quiet and I'll wander off again. Maybe travel to different parts of the world."

"Well, don't forget us and come back to visit," Nadirah said. "And if you see him, give greetings for us."

"Yes, ma'am, I will," he replied, knowing of whom she spoke. Corin had touched almost everyone's life in Calorin.

Emeth returned to the barracks, tumbled into his bed, and slept until supper. After the meal, he played the customary game of cards with Nicar and Azrahil, Ahmed having gone to visit his family. Ahmed had lived on Lord Rishdah's lands all his life. His father tended to the Lord's horse herds. Rishdah had offered Ahmed a place in the army when he was younger. After seeing him fight, Lord Rishdah made Ahmed part of the Guard.

Nicar had joined the Guard only a few years before Ahmed. No one seemed to know where he came from. But the hole in his ear convinced Emeth and Ahmed that he had either been a pirate or he was part of the roaming bandit tribes. Azrahil had always been with Lord Rishdah. He had been made Captain of the Guard after a battle had killed two of the Phoenix Guard years before.

As they played, they talked about anything but Emeth's departure. He made no effort to bring it up. It would be hard on all of them. Sometimes he thought it wasn't fair that he knew so much about them and hadn't ever shared much about himself. They knew his real name, Aiden, and where he was from, but he had never wanted to tell them anything else. Corin had been the same. He had gone by Hamíd during his time in Calorin and it wasn't until they received the news that the Calorins had invaded Aredor that Emeth had learned he was actually a prince.

Nicar won as he usually did which drew colorful oaths from his companions. Azrahil threw down his cards in disgust as Nicar calmly gathered together his winnings. Emeth tossed his cards down. He had stopped trying to catch Nicar cheating a long time ago. Corin had beaten Nicar once but Corin and Nicar had both cheated so badly it could hardly be called a fair game. Emeth turned in again shortly after the game ended.

The next few days were busy. Azrahil tested soldiers for the Guard, finally deciding on a man named Fakhir. He was a friend of Emeth's from the army and he had referred Fakhir to Azrahil. The morning they were to leave to take Khalid to the Sultaan, Emeth packed his bags. He said farewell to Ismail and Nadirah as well as the few other friends he had. Lastly, he paused again at Castimir's grave. Giving a salute, he joined Lord Rishdah and his Guard. Mounting Narak, Emeth fell into formation as the soldiers took their places around Khalid who was bound and mounted on a horse.

Lord Rishdah signaled and they rode forward. Emeth passed under the gates for the last time as a Phoenix Guard. The company turned north toward Qusay, the city of the Sultaan.

Chapter 3

This is strange, Emeth thought as he packed his saddlebags. He had laid aside his uniform but out of habit had pulled on the coat of chain mail. A plain leather tunic replaced the embossed one of the Guard. The day had come for his journey home.

Emeth went down to the stables and began tacking up Narak. As he finished, the doors opened and Lord Rishdah entered.

"I meet with the Sultaan in a few minutes but I wanted to say good-bye," Lord Rishdah said.

Emeth came out of the stall. "And I wanted to thank you, my lord, for helping me out of that mess when we first met, and for giving me a place," Emeth said.

"I think I made a good decision that day. You have given me seven long years of service. Thank you," Lord Rishdah said. "But before you go, there is something else I wish to speak to you about."

"Yes, sir?"

"I know you are returning to the North, so I will send a warning with you. The Sultaan is again preparing for war. I do not know when or how, but it will come," Lord Rishdah said.

"Why are you telling me this, sir?"

"Because I think it is foolish. He did not learn from the first failure. You Northmen are a stubborn lot and I do not think you will look kindly on a second attempt."

Emeth had to smile. Lord Rishdah was right about that.

"There are rumors that we negotiate with Durna. And it is also said that not all is right in Braeton. Be careful where you go, Emeth. You may think me a traitor to my people, but I will not send you blindly into danger. The Sultaan will no doubt tell me more but that is all I will say. Prepare yourselves."

"Thank you, my lord."

"Best of luck to you, lad," Lord Rishdah said, extending a hand. Emeth clasped it firmly. After Lord Rishdah left, Emeth met the other Guards in the courtyard.

"Are you fully equipped?" Azrahil asked.

"Yes, sir," Emeth replied, hiding a smile. "I'll take the north road to the coast and pick up a ship to Gelion. I have a friend there who can get me passage to the North," he said. Azrahil nodded approvingly.

"You did learn something after all," he remarked.

"Thank you, sir. I'll miss you too," Emeth said. Azrahil gave one of his rare smiles and shook Emeth's hand.

"Good luck, lad," he said.

"Try not to get into too much trouble, Emeth," Nicar said.

"You know me, Nicar. Trouble seems to find me anyway. But I'll try and be careful." Emeth grinned.

"Well, that's reassuring," Nicar said. "Greet an old friend for me?" he asked.

"Yes, sir." Emeth shook Nicar's hand.

"Take care of yourself, Emeth," Ahmed said as they embraced.

"I will," Emeth said. "And I'll come back and visit when I can," he promised. "I'll pass on greetings for you too."

"Thanks," Ahmed said. They clasped hands and Emeth reached out to the newest member of the Guard.

"Good luck, Fakhir. Don't let Nicar cheat you out of too much money," he said.

Fakhir laughed. "Good luck, Emeth," he said.

Emeth mounted Narak and with a last wave of farewell he rode from Qusay.

The merchant walked the docks of Drilon port in Gelion. He was headed to inspect his ship one last time. They were to leave with the morning tide. He was halted by the sound of two voices arguing. The merchant smiled as he recognized one of the voices.

"You said five silver pieces when I boarded and five more when we arrived. Not ten more!" Emeth said.

"Yes, but I must repair the damage caused on the voyage. By you, I might add!" the Calorin merchant said. "Be grateful I am not charging you more!"

"Grateful!" Emeth spluttered. "You should be grateful I stopped those pirates from looting and destroying your ship!" he said.

"You smashed two barrels of my cargo!" the merchant persisted.

"Right! Because I'm sure the pirates would have let you keep all your precious merchandise and your life just because you would ask them to please leave!" Emeth said angrily. "You're lucky *I'm* letting you live!"

"Seven silver pieces," the merchant backed down slightly.

"I'll only pay you what we agreed on which was five," Emeth said.

"I can have you arrested!" the Calorin threatened.

"I'd like to see you or any of these fat, overdressed guards try!"

"Habib! You know very well you're being unreasonable!" The Gelion merchant decided it was time to step in. "It sounds as if you are in this man's debt."

"You know nothing of this matter, Mustafa!" Habib said angrily.

"I heard enough," Mustafa said. "This man owes you nothing or I'll make sure you never trade again."

Habib backed down at this statement and walked away, muttering angrily.

"You're welcome, Aiden," the merchant said in Rhyddan. Aiden smiled to finally hear his name again.

"I had it handled, Mustafa," Aiden replied.

"I could tell," Mustafa said. "But enough of this! What are you doing here?" he asked.

"Going home," Aiden said. "I'm trying to find a ship going to Aredor."

"Well, you're in luck. I leave tomorrow for the North. I can give you passage," Mustafa said. "For free."

"I'll take you up on that," Aiden said. "Thanks."

"Stay with me tonight. I even have a place for your horse. You can tell me what you've been up to for the last few years," Mustafa said.

"Again, thank you," Aiden said. They walked away from the docks together with Aiden leading Narak. They wound up the streets until they came to Mustafa's villa. Aiden quartered Narak in the roomy stables and followed the merchant inside. A servant led Aiden across the tiled entryway to a small chamber.

"There's hot water and towels through there, sir," the servant said, pointing to an adjacent door. "Supper will be in an hour."

"Thanks," Aiden said, throwing his bags on the bed. The room was richly decorated giving evidence of Mustafa's success. The merchant was Argusian by birth but had run away to sea at a young age. He had settled in Gelion and married the daughter of a merchant. Having a good mind for trade, he had worked his way up the ranks of his father-in-law's business.

Years ago, he had met Aiden in Aredor and gave him passage to Gelion. Mustafa found Aiden work in the city as a squire to the men-at-arms in the governor's palace—a job that appealed to a young, adventurous boy. There, Aiden put aside his claymore and learned to use the double swords. Living in a port town, he saw many people from foreign lands. His curiosity was aroused and Aiden decided to travel again. Mustafa again helped, taking Aiden with him on a trip to Calorin. There, Aiden struck inland and Mustafa went back to the sea.

After he had washed and dressed in clean clothes, a servant came and escorted him to dinner. They passed rooms with merchandise from many countries: fine rugs from Argus, vases and incense from Calorin. The floors were tiled in mosaics in the tradition of Gelion. Tables and furniture were made from the finest wood of Durna and Mustafa wore an ornate dagger of Aredorian make.

Aiden greeted the merchant's wife, a beautiful woman with the wavy dark hair and olive skin of Gelion. The couple's four children ate with them and the boys stared in fascination as Aiden related story after story over a meal of fresh fish, bread dipped in olive oil, wine, and melon, all grown in the lush, green hills of Gelion.

The house rose early the next morning to bid farewell to their master. Mustafa would be gone for weeks trading all along the northern coast from Durna to Cyndor. Aiden bid farewell to Mustafa's wife, thanking her again for her hospitality. He and Mustafa walked down to the harbor where Aiden took Narak aboard the ship and settled him in the hold next to several other horses Mustafa was transporting. He made his way back up to the deck as the sailors prepared to cast off.

Unlike other ships, Mustafa had no soldiers. His sailors all carried weapons, for Mustafa was, as he put it, a fighting merchant. A fresh wind sprang up, filling the sails and propelling them out into the Masian Sea. Aiden took a deep breath of the tangy salt air and smiled. The wild forests of the North called. He had had enough of flat plains and deserts. He was ready to go home.

Chapter 4

Corin led his men along the Lynwood Track. They had just finished a circuit patrol through Dunham Forest and were headed home to Kingscastle. It had been over a year since the Calorins had been driven out of Aredor but the country was still trying to rebuild.

Corin was also reconstructing the Hawk Flight, the warband that he had formed in the war. They had been Aredor's last warband and under his leadership had fought the Calorins. Their secret cave in the forest was seldom used but was kept fully provisioned in the event of another attack that Corin felt sure would come eventually.

Lynwood Keep, the forest castle, could not yet boast a full garrison so the Hawk Flight helped to run regular patrols through the forest. Lynwood Keep was not the only garrison short of men. The war had taken its toll on Aredor and they were desperately short of warriors. Many had survived and had lived in hiding in the villages and towns, but they were not enough to bring the warbands back to their former strength. The Calorins had killed every officer they could find during the invasion and Corin and his brother, Darrin, were hard pressed to replace those men.

As Kingscastle came into sight, a lone figure rode to meet them.

"Kara," Corin greeted the rider. A cheerful young woman dressed in the uniform of the Hawk Flight saluted.

"Captain, Prince Darrin wants you tae meet him on the training grounds, sir," she said.

"Did he say why?" Corin asked.

"No, sir, not really," Kara replied.

Corin scowled. "I hate it when he does this," he grumbled. "All right, I'm on my way."

"Permission to come along, Captain?" a lieutenant asked.

"Granted, Martin. Flynn, you're in charge," Corin said to another lieutenant. Corin and Martin broke away from the warband and followed Kara around the town and across the river to the training grounds on the east side of Kingscastle.

The three riders threaded their way around groups of men training with broadswords, longbows, spears, and on horseback. Kara led them toward the center of the grounds where a group of men stood.

Prince Darrin stood with Tristan and Trey, the brothers from Castle Martel by the sea. They greeted Corin and Martin as they rode up. During the war, Darrin and Corin had shared command of the warband and Martin, Tristan, and Trey had held places as lieutenants.

"Anything to report?" Darrin asked.

"No, it was quiet," Corin replied. "But I don't think you asked me out here to talk about the patrol."

Darrin sighed. "You're always too direct, Cor," he said. "Truth is, Tristan wanted to ask you a favor."

Corin turned questioningly to Tristan. The brothers' father had died in the war and Tristan now wore the ornate golden belt of a lord across his chest.

"There's a minor lord whose fief isn't far from Castle Martel," Tristan began. "He was one of the lords whom the Calorins allowed to remain in control of his lands in the war. He has one son, his pride and joy. It's his wish that his son fight in the King's warband—most specifically, the Hawk Flight. He seems to think that his son will come home with high honors because of that, and maybe erase the fact that he served the Calorins," he continued.

"Well, what's the young man like?" Corin asked.

"Like a gigantic thorn in your foot!" Trey said. Martin raised an eyebrow. Trey was not known for his patience but, as his close friend, Martin put some stock in Trey's opinions.

"Ah, yes. I sent Andras with Trey on a coastal patrol and, um, Trey almost killed him," Tristan said.

"No, I suggested maiming for life," Trey said darkly. Martin laughed.

"Sounds horrific, but I still don't think anyone could be that bad," he said. Trey gave him a haunted look.

"Tristan, why don't you call him over and introduce him to the captain?" he said.

Tristan signaled to two young men who stood some distance off.

"There's another young man that Andras forces to go with him. You'd do me a big favor if you could take them both off my hands," Tristan said to Corin.

"It's about time! How long did you expect me to wait?" a dark-haired young man asked. Corin looked him up and down. He was no more than twenty-one years old. He wore clothes of the finest make and carried a sword with a decorated hilt. Brown eyes stared haughtily from his finely chiseled features. His companion was dressed more simply and carried a serviceable sword. He seemed about the same age as Andras, but less sure of himself.

"Well?" Andras demanded. Corin shot a sideways glance at Darrin who raised his shoulders as if to say "He's all yours, brother."

"What's your name, boy?" Corin asked.

"Andras, son of Cadoc," Andras answered proudly.

"Never heard of him," Corin replied coolly. Trey and Martin grinned knowingly at each other.

"And yours?" Corin asked the other young man. Andras began to answer but Corin cut him off. "I asked him," he said.

"Evan, sir," the man stammered, seeming surprised at being addressed directly. Andras glared angrily at Corin.

"Now, let me introduce myself," Corin said. "I am Prince Corin, commander of the King's warbands and Captain of the Hawk Flight. Lord Tristan has asked if I will take you into my warband. That decision will come after you both pass the training courses. You two are dismissed. Lieutenant Marc!" Corin called.

A grizzled warrior wearing a silver-buckled cross belt came up and saluted.

"Assign them separated bunks in the barracks. See that they know the rules and are out here early tomorrow morning with Flynn," Corin ordered.

"Aye, sir," Lieutenant Marc saluted again. "This way, lads," he said, pointing to the castle.

"I protest! I won't stay in the barracks!" Andras said. "My father wouldn't allow it!"

Corin nodded at Marc, who faced Andras.

"I don't care who your father is, boy! No one does here. You're in the army now and you'll address those higher in rank by 'sir.' The barracks will be your only home from now on. Don't get smart with me or I'll have you flogged!" Marc bellowed in his best parade-ground manner. He led the two men off toward the castle.

"Nicely handled, Corin," Darrin said. "I think that was hero worship in Evan's eyes."

"I will permanently resign if Andras gets put in my patrol," Martin told Corin.

"Told you, didn't I?" Trey said.

"I fully believe you!" Martin said. "Come on, Trey. I need a drink!"

"You owe me!" Corin threatened Tristan.

"It will be good for him, Corin, and you know it," Tristan said. "He needs to become a man, and he will with some stern discipline."

"If he survives that long," Corin said.

Darrin laughed. "I still need an official report from both of you," he said. "Father will want to hear it too," he said.

They left the training grounds and headed toward the castle. Corin was glad of the walk. His right leg had been wounded during the time he had spent in Calorin. He had saved Ismail's life by fighting off an attacking lion and he now walked with a pronounced limp. He'd always refused to let it stop him, but it was a little stiff after the day's ride. As they entered the courtyard, one of Corin's men approached.

"Can I take Zephyr for you, sir?" he asked.

"Yes, thank you, Ian," Corin handed him the reins.

"A stranger arrived almost an hour ago. He said he knows both of you," Ian told Corin before leading Zephyr away. They continued up the broad stone steps and through the great oaken doors of the keep. Corin and Darrin went first to find their father. King Celyn was troubled by an old wound from the war that had never fully healed during his imprisonment by the Calorins. He still ruled as king but Darrin had taken over many of the duties of state and Corin was given control of the warbands.

They still reported to him as if he were a commanding officer. King Celyn's body might have been ailing but his mind was a sharp as ever before. Corin was still unused to the duties now entrusted to him and he sought his father's advice often. He was like his father in many ways. They both had blonde hair, unusual among the darker headed inhabitants of the North, and Corin and his siblings had all inherited the King's piercing blue eyes.

King Celyn met his sons in a smaller council chamber.

"I don't know if I would have done the same, Corin," King Celyn said when they mentioned Andras. "I would have sent that young man off to Burkehead Tower on the border."

"I'd almost rather keep him under my eye," Corin said. "It'll be an interesting next few months."

"I think that's a bit of an understatement," Darrin said.

"Be glad we're at peace right now. He'd be insufferable on a campaign," said King Celyn.

Corin shuddered at the thought. "Anything interesting happen while I was gone?" he asked.

"Nothing out of the ordinary," King Celyn said. "But a young Braeton came in today. A very interesting young man. He said he wouldn't stay very long."

"Did he come in from the South?" Corin asked.

"Yes, how did you know?" his father asked.

"Just a guess," Corin said with a grin. He excused himself and went to find Aiden.

As Aiden walked through the great hall of the castle, he looked at the tapestries hanging on the walls. The last time he had been in the castle the tapestries had been torn down by the Calorins.

"They make for an interesting study, don't they?" someone said behind him.

Aiden grinned. "You still sneaking up on people?" he asked.

Corin laughed. "One of many habits I haven't broken," he said.

Aiden turned around. "That doesn't surprise me at all," Aiden said. "It's good to see you, Corin."

"You too," Corin said. They embraced and Corin stepped back. "Are you finally headed home?" he asked.

"For a while, at least."

"Come on, things have probably changed by now."

"If you're trying to get me to look on the bright side of things, it won't work," Aiden warned. Corin only laughed.

"Well then, you can tell me what happened over the past year at dinner. I have to change. I might be a prince, but I can't show up dirty to the table," Corin said.

"Are you still patrolling?" Aiden asked. Corin nodded.

"I'm not entirely convinced that the Sultaan won't attack again," he said.

"I might have some news for you then," Aiden said. "On my way back my ship stopped in Durna at one of the main trading ports. We docked next to a Calorin vessel. I recognized her flags and markings, one of the Sultaan's. And there's more." He told Corin what Lord Rishdah had confided in him.

"An alliance with Durna could bring the Calorins over our western border. We'd have a bit of a problem on our hands then," Corin said thoughtfully.

"I hate to bring this kind of news," Aiden said.

"Aye, but we'd best prepare for anything," Corin said.

Aiden hesitated slightly before speaking again.

"I don't suppose you've had much contact with the Clans?" he asked.

"Mainly with Clan Dyson and Clan Gunlon," Corin answered. "We don't have much to do with the others right now. I wish I could tell you something about your family."

"That's all right. To tell the truth, I'm a little nervous about going back," Aiden admitted with a sheepish grin.

"I wouldn't worry. It's probably only gotten quieter and more peaceful since you left," Corin said. Aiden laughed as Corin strode off but deep down he felt that something was not right at home. He needed to get back.

Corin went to his room and dressed in clean clothes. Seeing Aiden again brought back more memories. They had become close friends in Calorin after Lord Rishdah found Corin. When he was twelve years old, Corin had been kidnapped and sold into slavery in Calorin to a Lord Balkor. His family had found no trace of him and thought him dead but Corin had managed to survive under the cruel lord. When he was twenty, Lord Rishdah bought him and, seeing something in him, had Corin trained to join the Phoenix Guard. It was there that Corin had gained experience in the art of war. He served for three years before Lord Rishdah gave him his freedom.

But by then, Aredor had already been invaded by the Calorins and Corin had returned to a strange home. He became an outlaw and used his knowledge of the Calorins to fight against Lord Balkor. The war neared an end when Corin was captured one day. Unwilling to see him die, Ismail, along with Aiden and Ahmed, sought out Darrin and the outlaws and, with their help, the Aredorians were able to retake their country. That had been the last time Corin had seen Aiden. He had missed Aiden's company. The young Braeton had helped him transition into the Guard and had helped Corin learn to trust others again. He also felt that Aiden understood him more than Trey, Martin, or Liam ever could because he knew what Corin's life had been like in Calorin.

A grey hawk landed on the windowsill. It shook its wings and began preening.

"Karif, where have you been all day?" Corin asked the hawk in the Calorin tongue. He had found the hawk in Calorin. Its wing had been injured and after Corin helped nurse it back to health, the hawk remained by his side. It was Karif's companionship that had led to Corin being called the Hawk. He had to laugh every time he heard that. That had been Castimir's nickname for him in Calorin.

The hawk chirped at him and settled down on his favorite perch by Corin's bed.

"Aye, I'll see you later," Corin said.

At supper in the hall, Aiden sat next to Corin at the main table and related the events of the past year. Almost unknowingly they lapsed into the Calorin tongue. After eight years Aiden was still unused to speaking primarily Rhyddan and they both spoke more quickly in the southern language. They noticed the looks given them as others heard the strange tongue and they lowered their voices. Many recognized it as Calorin and muttered a curse in remembrance of the years spent under Calorin rule. But no one dared to challenge Corin on his use of the language.

"Tristan says you owe him a story," Corin said.

"Aye, I promised him I'd tell him why I was with Ismail during the war. I guess I should have known he wouldn't forget," Aiden said.

Corin laughed. "Tristan never forgets. And you might have a bigger audience; neither Trey nor Martin likes to be left out," he said.

"Just so long as you trust them not to tell everyone who I am. I'd rather the whole North not know that I was here with the Calorins," Aiden said. "I don't think anyone else has recognized me yet, except Tristan and your brother."

"You don't have to worry about them," Corin reassured him. He took no offense at Aiden's comment. He knew how it looked but Aiden had chosen to remain with Ismail and Ahmed and then to return to Calorin after the war had ended. Anyone who did not know Aiden and the part he had played would see him as a traitor.

After the meal had ended, Corin and Aiden met the others in a secluded room. Aiden was reintroduced to Trey, Martin, and another man he remembered as Liam. He knew they had all been lieutenants in the warband at the time and therefore knew of his involvement. Aiden told his story as he promised: how he ran away from home, his journey to Calorin, how he met Corin, and of his service in the Phoenix Guard.

The others listened with few questions, finally satisfied at uncovering at least part of the mystery of Corin's friend and those who had helped in the war.

"Are you sure you don't want to stay awhile?" Tristan asked. "You've got more experience than half our warbands combined."

"Maybe someday." Aiden smiled. "So, you're a lord now?"

"Aye, our father died in the war, so I've taken over Castle Martel. But not a day goes by that I don't wish I was back with the Hawk Flight," Tristan said.

"That's why I've always been glad to be one of my father's younger sons. I don't have to worry about being any sort of leader," Aiden said.

"Lucky dog," Corin muttered and Aiden grinned. He knew full well that Corin hated his newfound responsibility.

"Completely carefree, that's me," he said.

"Shut up," Corin replied. "Nobody cares."

Aiden only laughed.

Chapter 5

The next morning Aiden joined Corin, Trey, and Martin on the training grounds across the river from the castle. He became better acquainted with the others as Corin stopped to talk with different men on the training grounds.

Martin was highly skilled with a blade and had earned the title of Blademaster of Aredor. As such he was always curious about new weapons and questioned Aiden extensively on his double swords. Stopping in an open area, they unsheathed their swords and Aiden showed him various maneuvers he had learned abroad. Within a short time a ring of spectators had gathered and a warrior challenged Aiden. He readily accepted and a few moments later the warrior was defenseless with Aiden's sword at his throat. Another challenge was thrown out and accepted. Two more men were defeated in short order.

"Anyone else care to try their luck?" Aiden asked.

"I think I might," Corin said, stepping through the circle and unsheathing his scimitar.

"You might want to step back a bit, lads," Aiden told the onlookers while giving his swords a twirl. Corin fastidiously inspected his blade.

"You ready?" he asked.

"When you are," Aiden replied and they slowly began to circle each other, searching for an opening. Suddenly they clashed. Those who watched could barely keep track of the combatants' swords. Corin managed to send one of Aiden's blades falling to the ground. Undeterred, Aiden kept fighting. Then twisting his remaining sword, he brought it up against Corin's side at the same moment Corin laid his scimitar against Aiden's neck. Cheers broke out as they drew back from each other.

"Every time I think I have a chance, you beat me with that same move," Corin said as he returned the fallen sword to Aiden. He grinned as he took it.

"That's how I beat Azrahil for the longest time," Aiden said.

"I fully understand why he hated those swords!" Corin laughed.

As they prepared to leave, Martin caught sight of a young soldier coming toward them.

"Corin, I have a pressing need to be at the other side of the grounds right now," he said.

"What—" Corin began and then saw Andras. "Denied. Martin, you can deal with this," he said.

"What does he want now? He's only been here a day!" Trey moaned.

"Captain?" Andras asked haughtily.

"What?" Corin growled.

"How long will I be forced to train and live in these conditions?" Andras asked.

Aiden saw Corin's jaw clench and Trey's hand close longingly over his dirk handle and he decided to step in.

"May I?" he asked Corin in Calorin.

"Please!" Corin replied.

"Straighten up at attention when you address the Captain! You'll be here as long as we bloody well please! Let me tell you, laddie, 'conditions' will only get worse! Be grateful I'm not in command or where I come from I'd force march you through the desert on short rations. Any more questions?" he barked.

"No, sir!" Andras said stiffly.

"Good! You are dismissed! And clean that sword! It's filthy! A disgrace to your warband!" Aiden said sharply. After Andras was gone, Martin turned to Corin.

"How much would it take for Aiden to stay? I just had a wonderful vision of someone else dealing with Andras," he said.

"A forced march through the desert?" Corin asked Aiden.

"It was the first thing that came to mind," Aiden said. "That horrible blighter deserves worse though!"

"I liked the bit about his sword. That really stung him! You sure you won't stay, Aiden?" Trey asked.

"Sorry, Trey, I have many talents, but putting up with people like him is not one of them," Aiden said.

As it was, Aiden only stayed a day longer and then, laden with fresh provisions, he resumed his journey north to Braeton. He was anxious to get home. Lord Rishdah's words had remained in his mind since the day he left Calorin. He hated to bid farewell to Corin so soon, but he knew he was always welcome in Aredor.

He traveled quickly across the border and was soon looking over the fertile lands of Clan Gunlon. He spent one night in a small settlement among the Clan of the Unicorn. After that he only saw solitary Clan members tending their herds of horses. By midday of the fourth day, he was at the eaves of the forest that sheltered the peoples of Clan Canich. Another day's ride through the forest would bring him to Scodra, house of the Wildcat Lords.

Aiden made camp beside a small stream as the sun began to set. Wrapping his cloak around him, he sat against a tree and stared at the dancing flames of his fire. As he had travelled he had heard more rumors of trouble in Clan Canich. He had realized in Aredor that he was tired of fighting. He wanted to rest. But it seemed there were more battles to be fought.

Rolling up his left sleeve he looked at the tattoos he had kept hidden for almost ten years. The wildcat tattoo took up most of his upper arm. The wildcat bared teeth and claws as it balanced on hind paws. The tattoo marked him as the Chieftain's son. The Laird and his sons were the only men to have the clan emblem marked on their left arm. Below it on his forearm was the four pointed star of the Clan. A *C* was inscribed in the middle to mark his bond with Clan Canich. Every member of the Clan bore the same tattoo.

When he was young, he had discovered that he could imitate almost anyone. As a result, he could perfect any accent he chose, or more importantly, disguise the thick brogue of the Clans. He had hidden his tattoos and his accent in an effort to forget where he had come from as he sought a new life away from the Clan. Even now, back in Rhyddan-speaking countries, he refrained from his full accent out of habit and the unsurety of a welcome upon his return.

Maybe this isn't a good idea, he thought. He wasn't expecting a warm welcome from his father after running away and now returning practically a stranger. So far he had no idea what he was going to say to his father. They had been constantly at odds with one another ever since Aiden could remember, due largely to their matching hotheaded personalities. The Laird's heavy-handed tactics when it came to his obstinate and rebellious young son was, in part, what had prompted Aiden to run away when he was sixteen. His oldest brother, Ranulf, was the only person to whom he had said good-bye when he left. Ranulf had caught Aiden in the stables as he prepared to leave. It was mainly for Ranulf's sake that he promised to come back one day.

He was almost frightened now that he didn't know what awaited him. The thought of his home and family being in trouble was worse than anything else he had been through. A restless night passed and as sunlight first streamed through the branches of the trees, he turned onto a familiar path. In a few hours he would enter into the valley that sheltered Clan Canich.

Aiden led Narak along the forest pathway, brushed most of the dirt from his clothes, and straightened his cloak and weapons. He had groomed Narak until his coat shone softly and Aiden's saddlebags hung from a well-polished saddle.

There was a rustling in the undergrowth and a young hunting dog tumbled onto the path. It saw Aiden and bounded toward him, its tail waving joyously. Aiden knelt and began stroking its ears. As if this weren't enough, the hound fell onto its back. Aiden laughed and began scratching its belly as the dog beat its tail against the ground. Footsteps announced the arrival of the dog's master. Aiden stood to greet him.

"Sorry about that. I had him on the hunting run this morning and he goes off chasing squirrels. I can'nae figure it," the man said. "Maon, come!" he commanded. The hound ran to the man's side where he remained for a few seconds before bounding off down the path.

"He's friendly enough. He came right up to me," Aiden said.

"Och, I think he'd rather sit and chat with the deer than chase 'em," the man said with a smile. Another whistle brought Maon back to his side. He ruffled the dog's ears in a gesture that brought back a memory to Aiden.

"Jamey?" he cried. "Jamey, it's me, Aiden!"

Recognition broke over Jamey's face.

"Aiden! I never thought I'd be seeing you here again!" he said, clapping Aiden on the shoulder as they embraced. "Where've you been?"

"I've been traveling all over Cimbria. There's always some battle to fight," Aiden replied. "What about you? How's your father?"

"Father died a few years back. Our banishment was harder on him than he let on. When he died, I went tae Scodra tae tell Laird Gòrdan. Everyone expected him tae pardon me then but he never did, so I'm on my own now," Jamey said.

"I'm sorry to hear about your father," Aiden said. "I'd have liked to see him again."

"Aye, and he'd have given you another lecture for running off tae the forest tae visit us again," Jamey replied.

"To be fair, I was only caught twice," Aiden said, then turned more serious. "Jamey, do you know how my brothers are?"

"Sure. I get most of my news from the settlements," Jamey said. "Ranulf's as serious as ever. There's some hope that your father might pass the torc tae him soon. Young Tamhas is turning intae the finest bard a Clan could ask for."

"What about William?" Aiden asked quietly.

"He left almost two years ago. There's been no word since. *He* claims that Will is a traitor and went tae turn the other Clans against us, but no one believes it," Jamey said.

"Who said that?" Aiden asked.

"His name is Adalwulf," Jamey sighed. "I'm afraid you'll find things changed since you left."

Jamey and Maon accompanied Aiden down the road until they came to the edge of the valley. There Jamey stopped.

"I can'nae go any further," he said. "Be careful, Aiden, and if you can get away, the house is still open tae you."

Aiden smiled. "I'll try and take you up on that."

Jamey returned to the forest and Aiden faced the valley which spread out for more than a mile. In the distance the clear, blue waters of a lake glistened in the sun. Around the shores of the lake and throughout the valley were fields tended by the Clanspeople. On the nearer side of the lake, a huge three-storied wooden fortress rose up. It was surrounded by many smaller houses and dwellings. A vast circular wall made of rocks and timber encompassed the structures. More than half of Clan Canich lived in the Scodra valley while the rest lived in other towns and settlements scattered throughout the forest.

The valley seemed peaceful enough until Aiden realized just how quiet it was. He walked down the road leading Narak.

He saw some of the fields were overgrown and the few people working there looked up in fear as he passed. The gates to the fortress stood open and he entered. The vast compound was quiet and empty of ordinary daily activity. As in the fields, only a few Clanspeople moved about, gazing at him mistrustfully. Aiden realized how he must have looked dressed in southern clothes, carrying strange weapons and leading a fine Calorin stallion.

Several dark figures who lounged on the stairs of the fortress arose and walked toward him. The obvious leader of the group swaggered forward. He was dressed in foreign clothes but wore the blue plaid cloak of Clan Canich. He had long, blonde hair pulled back in braids and carried a battle-axe which suggested he was from Durna.

"Who are you?" the man demanded rudely in a clipped accent.

"You're no Braeton and yet you wear the plaid, so maybe I should be asking the questions," Aiden returned.

"Save your insolence or you'll answer for it when you come before Adalwulf!" the man said.

"Och, it's not Adalwulf I want tae see," Aiden said in irritation, finally relapsing into his thick brogue. "I'm looking for Ranulf."

"All strangers must be announced before Adalwulf. He will decide if you may stay," the man said arrogantly.

"Last I heard, it was Laird Gòrdan who ruled here and not this Adalwulf!" Aiden said, becoming angry. "Now get out of my way!"

The Durnian was shocked that Aiden dared to stand up to him. He moved to grab Aiden and bring him inside but Aiden took hold of the man's arm, twisting it behind his back and forcing the man to his knees. Another Durnian moved to help his leader but froze as the point of Aiden's sword hovered at his throat.

"I've no intention of being bullied about. I'll come and go as I please and if you try and stop me again, it's your arm you'll be losing," Aiden said, his voice dangerously low as he spoke to the captain. "Now, where is Ranulf?" he asked.

When the man did not answer, Aiden twisted his arm harder.

"Inside!" the man groaned. Aiden glanced up to see a young man staring open-mouthed at the proceedings.

"You there! Get over here!" Aiden called. The young warrior came over.

"What's your name?" Aiden asked.

"Alec, sir," the man replied.

"Take my horse tae the stables and see he is well cared for. If he's not, I'll take it out on you personally," Aiden said. Alec nodded and led Narak away. Aiden gave the Durnian's arm one last twist and released him.

"The same goes for you two as well," he threatened the other soldiers. Sheathing his sword, he stepped through them and up the stairs of the fortress.

"Impressive, but you just made a powerful enemy out of Torsten," said a tall, lean man standing by the huge oaken doors.

"It's a talent I have of offending all the right people," Aiden replied. "That great windbag will think twice before next time."

The man laughed.

"Still as cocky as ever, eh, Aiden?" he said. Aiden saw part of the wildcat tattoo under the man's rolled up sleeve and he smiled.

"Afraid so, Davy." He used the brothers' inexplicable childhood nickname for Ranulf. Bounding up the remaining stairs, he wrapped his brother in a rough embrace, returned affectionately by Ranulf.

"So you finally decided tae come home then?" Ranulf asked.

"Aye, I promised I would," Aiden replied. "Just like I promised you I'd find you first."

Ranulf stood back and crossed his arms.

"I can'nae tell you how good it is tae see you again!" Ranulf said. "Where have you been?"

"Everywhere," Aiden said. "I've been tae the South, Gelion, and spent time in Aredor. But that's not important. Ranulf, what happened here?"

"I think it's best if I tell you in private," Ranulf said. "Let me find Tamhas first."

A fire blazed on the hearth in the middle of the great hall. Benches were shoved against the walls out of the way. Sunlight shone through the few windows, illuminating the hall and casting shadows among the heavy ceiling beams. Despite the fire and the warm afternoon, the hall was cold and empty. At one end of the hall on a raised dais stood an empty, ornate wooden chair draped with a wildcat skin. Aiden stared at it for a moment, half expecting to see his father sitting there and glaring angrily at him.

"Here he is now!" Ranulf said. "Tam!" he shouted at a figure crossing the other end of the hall. Tamhas acknowledged Ranulf's hail and came over to them. Aiden studied his younger brother curiously. A young man of twenty-three now, he had the same green eyes as the rest of the brothers. Tousled black hair framed an open face with a puckish grin. He was slim and muscular and carried himself with an easy grace.

"What's happening? Torsten stormed through here looking for Adalwulf," Tam asked Ranulf.

"Our new arrival managed tae upset him a little," Ranulf replied. "You'll now have tae deal directly with Adalwulf. He's not easy tae bargain with," Ranulf told Aiden.

"I'm not worried, Davy. I've always preferred being announced," Aiden said.

"That's grand, but Torsten won't rest until he's killed you," Tam told Aiden.

"Don't fret, Tam! I've faced worse than that scoundrel," Aiden said cheerfully. Tam looked startled.

"Do I know you?" he asked.

"Och, it's a sad day when you can'nae recognize your own brother!" Aiden said.

"Unbelievable! Aiden, you're back!" Tam exclaimed, stepping into an embrace.

Ranulf forestalled the flood of questions Tam was about to unleash by saying, "Let's go tae our old meeting place and we'll tell you everything."

The brothers ascended several flights of stairs into one of the tall wooden towers of the keep. Pushing open a trapdoor they climbed up into the chamber of the tower. Ranulf sat on a stool, Aiden leaned against the wall, and Tam settled on the floor.

"It all started about two years ago," Ranulf began. "Mother died that spring. I'm sorry, Aiden," he said.

Aiden bowed his head in grief at the news.

"Father took it hard, as did we all. He became strained and more and more angry. That summer we went hunting after a wild boar that was tearing up the fields. Adalwulf had arrived a few weeks before, claiming tae have been driven out of Durna. He went with us on the hunt. That day was unlucky as the boar turned and would have gored Father tae death if Adalwulf had not stepped in and killed it.

"After that, he was ever at Father's side and began tae advise him. Will mistrusted Adalwulf from the start but nothing he said would deter Father from the smooth words of Adalwulf. You know Will's temper. He almost killed Adalwulf, but Father intervened. The argument they had was enough tae bring the hall down around us. The next morning Will left. Tam and I saw him off but we don't know where he went." Ranulf said. "When Will left, Father secluded himself in his room for days. All he would say was 'I have driven off and lost another son.' He began tae rely on Adalwulf even more and that's when Adalwulf's true nature revealed itself. He claimed that Will had gone tae turn the Clans against us and before we knew it, he began tae set the warriors against one another. Last year they began tae leave. Those with young families went tae the settlements. Most went tae Clan Mavor where there's always some battle going on they could join. A small group went tae Clan Dyson.

"I tried tae convince them tae stay but they refused tae come back as long as Adalwulf had favor with Father. Tam and I stayed tae keep an eye on things. Then last winter, about three score Durnians showed up and they have controlled the valley since. There are hardly any warriors left. Adalwulf now rules through Father," Ranulf finished the frustrating tale.

Aiden stood silent, thinking over what had been said.

"Have you tried tae raise warriors from the settlements?" Aiden asked.

"We tried, but Adalwulf threatens a larger Durnian invasion if any resistance shows. The people won't take up arms and the warriors won't return either," Tam said.

"Bloody cowards!" Aiden exploded angrily. "They disgrace their own Clan. I can'nae believe it!"

"They won't listen and I'm ashamed tae say that I've almost given up hope. You and Will could have taken this valley back singlehandedly," Ranulf said to Aiden.

"Since Will is not here, we'll do the best we can," Aiden said. "I've spent the last seven years fighting in one war or another and I'm not about tae let this Adalwulf destroy our home. He'll have tae kill me first!"

"I'm glad you're back, Aiden. But for now, don't do anything rash. Our best chance is tae catch the Durnians unprepared." Ranulf said. "Now that you know everything, you should go visit Father."

Aiden hesitated. "Is that a good idea?"

"You'll have tae see him sooner or later. But, Danny, just know that your leaving grieved him more than he let on. And also be warned that he has changed, and not for the better," Ranulf said.

They descended from the tower and Ranulf led the way to the chamber where Laird Gòrdan spent most of his time. Aiden took a deep breath and entered the room. Laird Gòrdan stood at the window, gazing out toward the lake.

"Tam, is that you?" he asked absentmindedly.

"No, Father, it's Aiden. I've come back," Aiden said. Laird Gòrdan did not turn.

"What kept you? Your mother is dead yet you were not here. Did you not love her?" he asked abruptly after a silence.

"No, sir, I did very much! Ranulf only just told me she was dead," Aiden stammered.

"Ranulf!" his father mocked. "Ranulf telling tales, trying tae tell me what tae do, just like William! Trying tae steal the torc!" He whirled around. "And now you! Skulking around, joining those who plot against me!" he accused.

"No, Father! I would never plot against you! You know that!" Aiden protested.

"Do I?" his father asked. "You were always lying and disobeying me!"

Aiden listened in silence, cut to the heart by the change in his father. Despite their arguments in the past, he did love his father. Now it seemed Laird Gòrdan hardly remembered his son and took a strange delight in accusing him.

"What? No answer? I though as much!" Laird Gòrdan said.

"Father!" Aiden pleaded. "Please, what happened tae you? You know me! I would never hurt you like that!"

"Would you? Because of you, my wife died before her time and I lost another son. You ran away tae spite me. I do not know you." His father said. "Leave me."

His vision blurred by tears, Aiden stumbled to the door. Before leaving he turned to his father again, but Laird Gòrdan had turned back to the window. Gathering himself, Aiden stepped into the empty hall and leaned wearily against the wall. After the events of the past hour, his world seemed twisted and shaken and devoid of any color.

Tam found him a short time later sitting by the shores of the lake.

"How did it go?" he asked Aiden as he sat down beside him. Aiden shrugged noncommittally, not willing to talk about it.

"Davy didn't tell me everything, did he?" Aiden asked suddenly.

Tam sighed and shook his head. "I'm afraid not," he said.

"Tell me."

"Aiden, hasn't your day been bad enough without hearing the rest?" Tam protested.

"Come on, Tam. At this point it can'nae get any worse," Aiden said, tearing a grass blade apart.

"When Will left, he said he was going tae try and find you. After he was gone, Adalwulf convinced Father that Will was a traitor and tae banish him from the Clan. He had riders proclaim it all over Braeton. William won't be coming back. Ranulf tried talking Father out of it, but when he started trying tae bring the warriors back Adalwulf accused him of trying tae take the torc. Father won't speak tae Ranulf anymore."

"What about you, Tam? Anything I should know?" Aiden asked.

"No, I haven't threatened Adalwulf in any way yet. Although I'm sure he could get rid of me whenever he wants," Tam said.

"Are you carrying a weapon?" Aiden asked.

"Adalwulf has forbidden the Braetons from carrying swords, but Ranulf and I both carry knives," Tam said.

"Good," Aiden said, relieved that at least they were armed. He unbuckled his swords and laid them on the grass beside him.

"Where did you get those?" Tam asked.

"In Gelion. I traded my claymore for them."

"What did you do in Gelion?"

"I served as a squire in the governor's palace for two years. One of the men there taught me how tae use them," Aiden said. With Aiden's permission, Tam took one of the blades and unsheathed it. There was a gash on the handle near the pommel.

"What happened here?"

"That happened in a fight with an Argusian. I nearly lost two of my fingers," Aiden said.

"What's that mark on your vambrace?" Tam asked as he returned the sword to the sheath.

Recognizing his brother's attempt to get his mind off the events of the day, Aiden answered, "A phoenix; in Calorin I was part of a Lord's personal bodyguard known as the Phoenix Guard. It's on most of my gear." He pulled a dagger from his belt and showed it to Tam. On one side of the blade was a rising phoenix and on the other was engraved a word in Calorin. Tam looked at the flowing script.

"What does it say?"

"Emeth. That's the name I went by in the South. It means 'faithful,'" Aiden said.

Tam slowly repeated the strange word.

"It suits you," he said.

Aiden smiled. "After a while you get used tae it," he said. "Our captain had the knife made for me."

"How long were you in Calorin?"

"I swore an oath of service for seven years."

"That's a long time," Tam commented.

"Aye, I guess it was. But it was good for me. I changed somewhat while I was there," Aiden said thoughtfully. They sat in silence for a few minutes watching the waters of the lake lap gently against the shore.

"Well, we can'nae stay out here forever and I want tae see how well my horse was taken care of," Aiden said. They rose and Aiden buckled his swords back on. Tam noticed a dagger held in a sheath on one of the cross belts.

"How many knives *do* you carry?" he asked.

Aiden grinned. "Depends on the day, but usually four," he answered. Tam shook his head in disbelief. "You wouldn't believe how often a few extra knives come in handy. There was one time I was tied tae a tent pole—"

"What—"

"It's a long story. They thought they had taken all my weapons but I still had one hidden in my boot. After some maneuvering I managed tae get it out and cut myself free," Aiden finished.

"So did you escape?"

"Ah, no," Aiden said. "I got caught again, but the next day I was present during some 'negotiations' and returned tae the Guard in time for a battle."

"One day I'll get all of your stories from you and put them in a song," Tam said.

"Well, then, I'll only tell the ones in which I played hero," Aiden said with a grin. Tam laughed.

"And as bard, I'll take creative liberties," he said.

"You have a deal," Aiden said.

In the stables he found Narak had been well quartered in a stall and supplied with hay and water. Despite his full trough, Narak nosed at Aiden. He slapped the stallion's nose and Narak blew gently in his face. Aiden picked up his packs from nearby and the brothers walked back to the hall. As they entered, an imposing figure stopped them.

"You must be my Lord Gòrdan's son who just arrived," the man said, addressing Aiden.

"Aye, I am, but who are you? I haven't had the pleasure," Aiden said.

"Your pardon. I am Adalwulf," he said. Aiden inclined his head.

"An honor. My father spoke highly of you," Aiden said.

"I thank you." Adalwulf said. "We eat in an hour, would you join me?"

"Again, you honor me," Aiden said with a disarming smile. As soon as Adalwulf was out of sight, Tam turned to him.

"Aiden, what are you doing?" he asked.

"It'll be easier if he's not trying tae kill me. Torsten might be a problem, but I'll assure Adalwulf that it was a harmless mistake."

"You? Harmless?" Tam snorted.

"What? You don't think I could pull it off?" Aiden accused.

"Well, the fact that you're practically a walking armory had me convinced otherwise," Tam said.

"Have some faith, laddie!" Aiden said, smacking him on the head before bounding up the stairs.

Ranulf met him halfway up.

"There's hot water and I had some of Will's clothes laid out. You'll have tae wear his until some are made for you," Ranulf said. Aiden nodded his thanks and continued on until he came to his old room. Pushing open the door, he slowly entered. He was relieved to see that nothing had changed since the day he had left.

Aiden laid his packs on the low bed covered with a deer skin. On the chest of drawers that sat by his bed was a wooden box. Inside were the small carved warriors that had waged many a war on the floor. Aiden reached in and took out his favorite one. A solemn-faced warrior wielding a spear sat astride a prancing horse. The figurine had played a prominent part in his games. Setting it upright on the top of the drawers, he took off his cloak and hung it on a peg by the door. He hung his bow and quiver alongside it with his sword belts. His leather tunic and chain mail he left on the overstuffed armchair by the fireplace. Pulling black pants, a blue shirt, and a soft leather tunic from the pile, he went to the adjacent room, bathed, and then dressed.

The clothes fit well, although Aiden was unused to the softness of the cloth after the rougher garments he had worn in Calorin. He felt light without his mail and swords. Pulling on his boots and buckling on his vambraces, he picked up his daggers and slid them into place. Two hung in plain sight in his belt, the smallest fit into his boot, and the last, which usually stayed on his sword belt, he put into a sheath under his tunic where it sat unseen against his ribs.

Feeling less than ready, Aiden left the room and went downstairs. The great hall had been changed. Tables had been set up and benches pulled away from the wall. Fresh torches blazed in sconces on the wall. The people who remained in the fortress all gathered in the hall for supper. Quiet murmurs of conversation filled the hall as Aiden glanced around the room. Adalwulf had not yet arrived, but several Durnians already sat in the hall.

Aiden noted where each Durnian sat, automatically memorizing their location and the weapons they carried.

Just relax! he told himself as he prepared to meet his enemy. He tried to tone down his reactions, heightened by his years in the Phoenix Guard. Unfamiliar footsteps sounded behind him and his hand went to his dagger. Ranulf eyed him suspiciously.

"Are you about tae stick me with that?" he asked.

"Sorry, old habits," Aiden said.

"Be careful. Torsten will be keeping a close eye on you through dinner. He usually stays close tae Adalwulf," Ranulf told him.

"Lovely!" Aiden muttered. "I hoped I wouldn't have tae see him for a while."

The brothers made their way to the main table which sat at the top of the hall in front of the Laird's chair. They seated themselves to the left of the chair as Tam entered and joined them. New whispers broke out as people began to recognize Aiden as the Laird's son who had finally returned. Everyone had begun to sit as Adalwulf and his guards entered. The Durnians stood as their leader passed, but the Braetons remained seated, scowling sullenly. Adalwulf seated himself familiarly to the right of the throne. Aiden rose as he came to the table and greeted him politely. Aiden had purposely chosen his chair so he was close to Adalwulf.

Ranulf looked surprised and Tam shot him a look that said "don't ask."

"My Lord Gòrdan, regrettably, will not be joining us," Adalwulf said.

"Ah, indeed a shame! Tell me, how is my father's health?" Aiden asked.

"I wish I could give you good news, but he is gradually fading. The years have been hard on him," Adalwulf said, looking properly distressed.

"It must be a great comfort tae him, and tae all, that you have helped so considerably with matters of the Clan," Aiden said.

To his left, Ranulf choked on the contents of his tankard and Adalwulf's eyes narrowed. But he could catch no trace of sarcasm in Aiden's face.

"May I offer you some wine? It's Durna's finest," Adalwulf asked. Aiden accepted, watching him carefully as he poured wine from the flagon on the table.

"I hear you have traveled much," Adalwulf said, handing him the glass.

"You heard right. I am somewhat restless. I never stay long in one place," Aiden answered half truthfully.

"You have been many places?" Adalwulf asked.

"I have travelled the South extensively and I lived in Gelion for a short time. I have never been tae Durna though. What is it like?" Aiden asked.

"Petty and small minded. People are afraid to take control, to rule as a country should be ruled! I had plans, ideas, but they drove me out!" Adalwulf said. "But I digress. Will you stay long?"

"As I said, I never stay long in one place. There are a few people I wanted tae see again. One lives in a neighboring settlement. I assume it would be no trouble if I visited for a few days?" Aiden asked.

Adalwulf again scrutinized his face carefully, and then deciding he had nothing to fear from the young man, he said, "No, not at all."

Aiden rejoiced inwardly. He had a way out if needed and he was safe for the moment.

The next few days passed uneventfully, but Aiden felt on edge. The Durnians had complete control of the valley and everyone was afraid of them. Ranulf and Tam wanted to be rid of them, but didn't know how. Aiden saw that neither of them had the experience to stage a war or rebellion, especially Tam. The

Durnians did not threaten Aiden. Adalwulf only ruled because of his intimidation. After the wars he had fought in, this seemed like an insignificant infestation to Aiden but he could not see a clear solution yet.

He racked his brain for any plan, and then one night, it came to him. He lay awake most of the night, fine tuning it, and then he began to pack. He needed to visit Jamey.

Chapter 6

Corin remained at Kingscastle for two days after Aiden left. He had passed on the news to Darrin and his father of another Calorin invasion and their possible alliance with Durna. They agreed not to spread this news in order to avoid undue panic, but Corin still took the Hawk Flight to strengthen the border.

Even though he now bore the responsibilities of the General of the warbands, he was not yet officially named to that position. He was fighting the promotion as well as he could. He didn't want it. Corin felt that he didn't have enough knowledge or experience for the task. He would be content to remain Captain of the Hawk Flight. But, in addition to the Hawk Flight, he now had another personal command of forty men called a deugain. He had personally selected the men for the deugain as well as replacements for the Hawk Flight. To both bands, he had imparted some of his own training, turning them into some of the best fighting forces in Aredor.

Martin had been content to remain a lieutenant in the Hawk Flight rather than take the bronze-buckled cross belt of a captain in the King's warband. The Hawk Flight did not use the distinctive cross belts of the warbands to mark their officers and instead used small silver brooches in the shape of a feather to identify the lieutenants.

The entire Hawk Flight met at the caves and Corin gave his men the news.

"It looks like you were right about the Calorins trying again, sir," Flynn said. With the departure of Tristan and Trey to Castle Martel and to the southern warbands, Corin had promoted Flynn to lieutenant.

"Aye, but I would rather have been wrong," Corin said.

"When do you think they'll attack?" Liam asked. In the war, Liam had been Corin's second-in-command in his patrol, but now held his own command. A man named Llewellyn was Liam's replacement.

"I don't know, but this time we'll be ready," Corin said. "I don't want word of this getting spread around just yet. We'll start patrolling like we did in the war. Most of you know the routes, so make sure you teach the new members everything you know about our ways here. The lieutenants and I will arrange for you all get leave time regularly. We'll be settling back into the caves as quickly as possible and then start out on patrol."

There were no questions. The stories told of the Hawk Flight during the war and the captain's reputation as a fighter and strategist gave even the newest warriors reason to trust Corin implicitly. They dispersed into the secret caves of the Hawk Flight. The warband was larger than it was during the Calorin War, now numbering almost eighty strong, but the caves were able to hold them all easily. Before Corin went in he gave a sharp whistle. An answering call came from the sky and Karif swooped down and landed on his arm.

"It looks like we have more hunting ahead of us, my friend," Corin said. In answer, Karif shrieked his challenge to the sky.

The next morning, Corin rode out with ten men on a patrol. Midmorning they halted.

"Sir, do you smell that?" a man named Dylan asked. The unmistakable smell of wood smoke lingered on the air. Corin signaled and they dismounted. With the hoods of their dark cloaks drawn well over their heads and masks bound about their lower faces, Corin and his men crept forward silently. They spread out to encircle the clearing where the fire burned.

A man crouched by the fire accompanied by a dog. They were the strangest pair Corin had ever seen. The man was short and stocky with dark hair pulled back in a braid. His eyes slanted curiously in a browned face covered in a scruffy beard. A fearsome double-bladed axe was strapped to his back. His was clearly alone except for the dog, so Corin gave a low bird call to signal his men and stepped into the clearing.

The man rose alertly at his appearance. Corin saw his clothes were a mixture from different lands. A scar cut across his cheek giving him a startling look. The dog also rose, growling softly. It was grey and white, its thick fur making it look larger than it was, and its blue eyes watched Corin cautiously.

"Who are you and what do you want in Aredor?" Corin asked.

"My name is Skive. I am only travelling through to find a new home," the man replied in a strange accent.

"You travel alone?" Corin asked. The man nodded.

"Except for Illyria," he gestured to the dog, "She is my only companion." Skive asked in return, "Who are you?"

Corin pulled down his mask and pushed back the hood. "My name is Corin. My men and I watch these borders."

"Corin, I mean no harm here," Skive said. Corin studied him for a moment.

"We will let you continue on. But tell me, where are you from?"

"I once lived in a far land beyond the country called Gelion. My wife and daughter were killed one day by evil men. My quest for vengeance took me far and wide. When I finished my search and destroyed my enemies, I could not return home so I traveled again. I have been searching since then for a place to live," Skive said.

"Where will you travel?" Corin asked.

"My heart tells me to go north," Skive said.

"As I said, we will not stop you. If you continue north, you will cross over into the country of Braeton within two days. Maybe that is where your journey ends," Corin said. "I wish you luck, Skive."

"I thank you. May the stars always shine on and guide you," Skive said. Corin raised a hand in farewell and left the clearing. Moments later, Skive heard more bird calls and slight rustles in the undergrowth and then the forest was silent again.

"Do you think he's telling the truth, sir?" Llewellyn asked.

"I think so. Dylan and Bran, follow him just to make sure," Corin ordered. Dylan and Bran saluted and remained behind without their horses as the patrol moved on.

Corin went back to Kingscastle a few days later to report and check on the newest recruits and to face an office filled with paperwork. He arrived around noon and went to the training grounds where he met with a Captain Pedr.

"What's the verdict?" Corin asked him.

"Well, sir, the King's warband is back to its old form. I only wish we had the same numbers as we did before the war. The recruits are almost fully trained. I should expect to let them join the army in a matter of weeks. Those men you wanted for the Hawk Flight are progressing quickly. They will be able to take the oath soon," Pedr reported.

"And our two newest members?" Corin asked.

"Evan is coming along well despite the fact that he holds back so as not to pass Andras," Pedr said.

"Dare I ask how that terror is doing?" Corin asked.

"He is actually quite talented. Discipline has improved him slightly. Of course, I also encourage him strongly not to open his mouth in my presence," Captain Pedr replied and Corin chuckled.

"Are they out here? I should watch for a few minutes," Corin said. Captain Pedr led him across the field, past other groups of soldiers. Finally, they arrived where the prospective members of the Hawk Flight trained. The men broke off training to greet the captain. Corin returned their greeting and drilled them in a series of maneuvers. After they finished, Corin chose two men.

"You are to report to Lieutenant Llewellyn tomorrow. You'll get uniforms and join him when they leave for patrol," Corin told the two warriors. They were congratulated by their companions. As he dismissed all the men, Corin gestured to the young man who stood slightly off to the side.

"Evan, I want you to try again, this time against me," Corin ordered. Evan obeyed, hesitantly unsheathing his sword. Corin drew his scimitar and they closed on each other and a few seconds later, Evan's sword flew from his grasp.

"Pick it up. Again," Corin said. Evan did and again Corin disarmed him.

"Don't hold back, Evan. Again," Corin said. This time the fight lasted longer before Corin disabled him.

"Better, but I want to see you again tomorrow," Corin said.

"Yes, sir," Evan said as he returned his sword to the sheath.

"Evan, tell me something. What brought you here?" Corin asked.

"Andras's father thought it would be good for me to come, and so here I am," Evan said.

"Do you even want to be in the warband?" Corin asked. "Tell me truthfully."

"Yes, sir. My father fought in the Martel warband. I've always dreamed of being like him," Evan said.

"I can send you back there if you want, or you can become part of the Hawk Flight," Corin said.

"What about Andras?" Evan asked.

"Let me worry about Andras. You don't answer to him. Where would you rather be?" Corin asked.

"Well, sir, we've all heard stories about the Hawk Flight. My father died in the invasion and I figure I can best honor his memory by serving under you," Evan said.

Corin watched him thoughtfully.

"You're proving to me that you belong there," he said. Evan only nodded.

"I won't let you down, sir," he said. Corin followed his glance back to where a figure stood waiting.

"Like I said, let me worry about Andras," Corin said. "Keep working hard and you might be taking the oath sooner than you think."

Evan saluted and left as another captain came up to speak with Corin.

"What did he say to you?" Andras asked.

"Nothing much," Evan said.

"Tell me!" Andras commanded.

"I don't have to," Evan said. Andras fairly spluttered in shock.

"I'm the reason you are here!" he said. "And I don't see why you think he's so impressive."

"Maybe because he saved us from the Calorins," Evan suggested.

"We would have eventually freed ourselves," Andras huffed.

"I think you're the only one who believes that," Evan said.

"I am not! And don't speak to me like that, you forget your place!" Andras said. Evan shrugged and quickened his pace, outdistancing Andras. The captain's words had significantly boosted his confidence.

Corin left the grounds and went back to the castle. He went to the room by the barracks that acted as his office. Sitting down at the desk he began to sort through the mess of papers that were heaped the table. This was one of the reasons he didn't want to be General: the never-ending stream of reports and papers on the country's garrisons and armies. He'd rather face an Argusian berserker than the cluttered desk.

An hour later, Corin's sister Amaura entered.

"I heard you were back, so I went to the kitchens and Jenny sent your favorite," she said setting a tray on the table.

Corin looked up from a report and smiled at her. "Thanks, Amaura."

"Come on, Cor, take a break!" she said, taking the paper from his hand.

"Maurie, it has to get done!" he protested but she withheld the paper.

"It won't go anywhere," Amaura said. Corin relented and Amaura sat down opposite him. "Are you staying very long this time?"

"Depends," Corin answered, taking a sip from the mug of brown ale.

"You work too much," Amaura complained. "You're always gone to the forest or to some garrison I've never heard of. I feel like I've hardly seen you, not since you were hurt." She referred to the injuries sustained by Corin in one of the final battles against the Calorins the year before.

"I know. Believe me, I thank our genius brother every day for giving me this post," Corin said.

Amaura giggled. "You should be glad to know that I'm making you and Darrin take the day off tomorrow. We're going for a ride, just the three of us, down to the river like we used to," Amaura said.

"I'll be at the training grounds in the morning," Corin warned.

"Well, you have to be done by lunch," Amaura said. "You can't get out of this. Father said it was a good idea."

Corin shook his head in mock despair. "All right, I'll come," he said.

"Good, and you *will* change out of your uniform before," she said.

Corin laughed and managed a tug at her hair before she left the room.

The next morning, Corin directed the training session for the men. He noted with satisfaction that Evan was doing better than the day before and seemed more sure of himself. Some of the younger men stared in barely disguised awe as Karif came to land on Corin's shoulder, as if they still couldn't believe that Corin was the Hawk.

"Captain, the men from Cadan will be arriving this afternoon. Will you be there?" Llewellyn asked.

"No, you can get their report. Leave it on my desk somewhere I can find it. I'll speak with them later," Corin said. "My own sister is kidnapping me this afternoon."

"Good, it's about time you and Prince Darrin took a break," Llewellyn said.

"Does everyone think this?" Corin asked.

"Aye, sir, and the princess asked me personally to escort you if you tried to get out of it," Llewellyn said.

"Why don't we make her commander then?" Corin complained good-naturedly.

Llewellyn laughed. "I asked her that myself," he said.

As the noon hour approached, Corin hurried back to the castle where he changed into fresh clothes and went to meet Amaura. She was waiting in the courtyard with Darrin. Their horses had been saddled and brought out for them.

"You, brother, were almost late," Amaura said to Corin.

"Well, dearest sister, you can thank Llewellyn. He performed his job admirably," Corin said.

"Good, I wasn't the only one threatened," Darrin said. "Huw took entirely too much pleasure out of this whole thing."

Amaura laughed.

"Oh, come on, you two! You know you want to go," she said, swinging easily into the saddle. Her brothers followed her lead and mounted their Calorin stallions. They rode from the south gate and turned east toward the mountains. Darrin turned his stallion in a small circle.

"I bet I can still beat both of you to the fir tree," he said, grinning. Amaura and Corin exchanged smiles.

"If I win, you give me your dessert," Amaura enacted their old bargain.

"Deal," Corin replied. With that, all three spurred their horses into a gallop. It was half a mile to the fir tree which had been riven by lightning many years before. As they neared it, Corin and Darrin exchanged a wink and eased up slightly on their mounts allowing Amaura to pull ahead.

"You didn't lose on purpose, did you?" Amaura asked suspiciously as they settled down to a walk.

"Do you think we would ever lose willingly to a girl?" Darrin asked with an offended expression. Amaura glared at Corin.

"I try never to lose when dessert is on the line," Corin replied.

"You two are hopeless," Amaura said.

A few minutes later they came to the river. It wound its way slowly down from the mountains and foothills until it came to the wide lands surrounding Kingscastle. Trees grew along the grassy banks providing many a sheltered spot. They picketed the horses nearby and brought out lunch from the haversacks. They talked and laughed over many a childhood memory at that place as they ate. Amaura relented and shared out the sweet cake in three equal parts even after Corin caught and tossed a frog at her. After lunch, Darrin had to return to the castle but Corin and Amaura stayed a while longer at the water's edge.

"Corin, did anything happen to Trey during the war?" Amaura asked tentatively as she dangled her feet in the water.

"What do you mean?" Corin asked.

"Well, he is more reserved than he used to be," Amaura said.

"It was hard on everyone and it changed a lot of men," Corin said.

"Like you changed?" Amaura asked.

"It was more than the war that changed me," Corin said gently. "But when I first came back, Martin, Trey, and Liam were the only ones who were still free. Trey had been the first to make it to the forest after Darrin was captured. He blamed himself for that."

"I didn't know that," Amaura said.

"He also thought he had lost Tristan until, almost by chance, we found out Tristan was alive. Living in the forest was not as adventurous as it sounds. Imagine being hunted every moment of every day. We lost many good men, our friends and brothers," Corin said.

"That helps a little," Amaura said. "At first I thought it was me. After you disappeared and we got older, Darrin became busier. When Tristan and Trey visited, Trey would always find some time to talk to me. I thought at first he was only being polite, but we struck up quite a friendship. I admit, I think I was in love with him," Amaura said, blushing a little.

"What about now?" Corin asked.

Amaura shrugged. "I don't know. He's busy and when we do get to see each other, he's always so frustratingly polite and distant."

"Well, he'll kill me for saying this, but I think he still likes you, Maurie," Corin said.

"Really?" Amaura asked hopefully.

"Aye, you can tell," Corin said. "I'm sure you can find some way to tell him that you feel the same way."

Amaura stared at the flowing waters for a few minutes, not hearing the teasing tone in Corin's voice.

"Have you ever been in love?" she asked.

Corin looked up from the apple he had begun to cut.

"Yes," he said.

"What was she like?" Amaura asked curiously.

"She was a beautiful chestnut mare," Corin began, his face serious, but Amaura saw the twinkle in his eyes.

"Corin, I'm serious!" she cried, splashing water at him.

Corin laughed. "Truthfully, no," he said, handing her an apple slice.

"Would you ever get married?" she asked as she bit into the fruit.

Corin shrugged. "I don't know. Who'd want to marry someone like me? Like you said, I'm gone all the time and I've got a rather frightening past. They wouldn't be happy."

"There are lots of young women who would die to marry you," Amaura giggled.

Corin smiled. "A fact Mother likes to remind me of rather frequently," he said. "I'm still trying to get used to castle life again, and now I'm trying to learn how to direct warbands and guard against a potential invasion. I don't have the time or inclination for that right now."

Amaura took another apple slice and sighed. "Do you ever think about what would have happened if you had grown up here or if the Calorins had never invaded?" she asked.

"Sometimes," Corin replied. "Life would be very different," he said. They remained on the bank in silence, watching the water flow by endlessly. Eventually, they rose and packed the bags and rode slowly back home, savoring the ending of the day.

Chapter 7

As soon as his bags were packed and he was dressed and fully armed, Aiden went to the kitchen to pack provisions. Outside, he was confronted by Torsten.

"Leaving so soon?" the Durnian asked suspiciously as he eyed Aiden's bags.

"Aye, but don't worry, I'll be back before you can miss me." Aiden gave a perfect imitation of Torsten's accent. The Durnian's eyes flashed.

"I've had enough of your insolence, boy!" he snarled. "You'll leave only if I let you!"

"Last time you tried stopping me didn't end so well, did it?" Aiden asked with a dangerous smile.

"You'll pay for that!" Torsten choked with anger. The tension was broken by the arrival of Adalwulf.

"What is going on here?" Adalwulf asked sharply.

"Torsten was just saying good-bye. I'm off tae visit my friend," Aiden said smoothly. Torsten glared angrily at him.

"How long will you be away?" Adalwulf asked.

"A week at most. Jamey has some of the finest hunting hounds in the Clan so we'll be spending most of our time out on the hunting runs," Aiden said.

"Ah, I am an avid hunter myself. I wish you luck," Adalwulf said.

"I thank you," Aiden said. "But if you'll excuse me, I am anxious tae be on my way."

As Aiden continued to the stables, Torsten turned to his master. "Do you think he tells the truth, Lord?"

"He seems harmless, but if he causes trouble, a few words in the right places will get rid of him forever," Adalwulf said coldly.

Aiden tightened the girth of the saddle around Narak.

"All right, boy, you've spent the week in a stall. You ready to run?" Aiden asked softly in Calorin. The stallion nickered in reply. "That's good enough," Aiden said, arranging his packs on the saddle. He heard someone come up to the stall door.

"You're not running again, are you?" Ranulf asked.

"Not yet," Aiden replied. "Listen, Davy, I've got an idea. I'll be gone about a week."

"Where are you going, Aiden?" Ranulf asked.

"Tae visit Jamey first, and as far as anyone else is concerned, that's where I'm staying."

"Jamey? The outlaw's son?"

Aiden led Narak out of the stall. "You know my opinion on that one," he warned.

"You know what his father did!" Ranulf protested.

"I know what they said he did!" Aiden snapped. "You think Niall was the only one there that day? I saw what happened! Jamey's father is not a murderer. But I couldn't go against Niall and Father, not when they were already set against him. But I never gave up on Jamey."

"Aiden, be careful. If anyone, especially Father, finds out about you visiting Jamey—"

"He'll what? He can'nae do anything he hasn't already done!" Aiden said harshly. He saw the look on Ranulf's face. "I'm sorry," Aiden said. "After the second time I got caught visiting them and the Laird and I fought…I'll just say that's when I decided tae run away."

"Aiden, I'm sorry," Ranulf said.

"It's not your fault," Aiden said. "I need tae go. I'll be back in a few days, I promise." He mounted and left the fortress. Cantering easily down the forest paths, he soon came to the clearing where Jamey lived. His friend came out of the low house at Aiden's call.

"Aiden, what are you doing here?" he asked in surprise.

"Jamey, how many men went tae Clan Dyson?" Aiden asked abruptly.

"About two score," Jamey said. "I saw them go myself. You're not thinking about going after them, are you?"

"That's exactly what my plan is," Aiden replied. "We need men and they're the closest. I want tae stay off the main road. What's the quickest way there?"

"Aiden, if Adalwulf finds out, he'll bring in a bigger army, destroy us, and take the Laird's chair," Jamey protested.

"All I've heard since I got back is 'can't' and 'too dangerous' and I'm sick of it! And if Adalwulf thinks he can kill me, then he's going tae get the fight of his life!" Aiden said.

Jamey finally relented and told Aiden which paths to take. He travelled quickly away, riding all day and well into the night before he stopped to rest Narak and sleep. He rose with the sun and continued his journey.

When he knew he was close to the border of Clan Dyson's lands, he stopped. If he was going to convince the men of Clan Canich to come back, then he had to look the part of a Laird's son. Drawing clothes raided from Will's wardrobe from his bag, he donned a black shirt without a left sleeve to show his tattoos and a blue tunic over which went the plated brigandine of the Clans. Finally, he drew out the blue plaid of the Clan, wrapping it around his shoulders and fastening it with a circular brooch bearing a wildcat head. Making sure his vambraces and weapons were securely in position, he again mounted and rode on.

His plan was rough, but he figured Clan Canich's warriors would be in the main city of Lachlann. He would have to convince them to come back to Scodra. Once they had men on their side, it would be easier to bring the other clanspeople back.

Claire M. Banschbach

Lachlann was teeming with life as Aiden rode in. If possible, the town and wooden fortress were larger than Scodra. He caught glimpses of the blue plaid of Canich amongst the green of Clan Dyson. He halted Narak in the courtyard in front of the keep.

"Excuse me," a man said to Aiden. He wore the blue plaid. "You're from Clan Canich as well?"

"Yes, sir, I am," Aiden replied. The man saw the wildcat on Aiden's arm.

"You're one of Laird Gòrdan's sons!" he exclaimed.

"Aye, I'm Aiden," he said.

"I beg your pardon, my laird. My name is Eanraig."

"Och, you don't have tae call me laird," Aiden said. "I'm no good with titles."

Eanraig smiled. "Well then, Aiden, may I be of any service?"

"I was told some of the Clan was here. I thought I might stay for a few days," Aiden said.

Eanraig nodded understandingly. "I'll introduce you tae Laird Dandin then," he said. A stable boy took Narak as Eanraig led Aiden to the keep. "You're the one who ran off?" Eanraig asked.

"Aye, that was me. I wanted tae get away and see what was beyond Braeton," Aiden said.

"And did you?" Eanraig asked.

Aiden nodded. "Aye, this world's a big place. I've seen a lot in the past few years."

Eanraig greeted the guards at the doors as they passed. Inside, the hall was large and roomy. Light streaming in from multiple windows barely illuminated the tall ceilings. Stairs and hallways wound away from the great hall to the rest of the keep. To the left, wide stairs led to the upper floors and a balcony looked down over the main hall. At the end of the hall on the raised dais, sat Laird Dandin holding an audience. Eanraig and Aiden waited until they were signaled forward to speak to the Laird.

"Eanraig, what can I do for you?" Laird Dandin asked, rising. He was well built, a stag tattoo reared on a well-muscled arm, and on his forearm were two circles, one inside the other, encircling a *D* for Clan Dyson. Green plaid was carefully folded across his shoulders and around his neck hung a silver torc.

"A visitor you might like tae see, sir," Eanraig said gesturing to Aiden. Laird Dandin recognized Aiden as one of Laird Gòrdan's sons.

"You must be Aiden," he said, descending the steps and extending a hand. Aiden clasped it firmly.

"Aye, sir. It's been a few years," he said.

"Indeed it has. Though the scrawny, rebellious youth I last saw you as is long gone," Laird Dandin said.

Aiden laughed. "Not completely, my Laird."

"What brings you here, lad?" Laird Dandin asked.

"I've just returned tae Braeton and found Scodra under some...rather interesting circumstances," Aiden said. Dandin saw the look in Aiden's eyes and understood. He led Aiden away from the hall and to a private room.

"Ranulf came here too. I would have sent men, but we were in the middle of helping the Aredorians with the Calorin War," Dandin said. "And now this Adalwulf threatens Durnian invasion if we send men. Forgive me for saying, but I think Laird Gòrdan would only see the Clans coming tae help now as an attack on him. There would be war in Braeton."

"I understand," Aiden said.

"So what are you really here for? I know you don't want sanctuary," Laird Dandin asked.

"I have no patience left," Aiden said. "I'm going tae stop Adalwulf. But I can'nae do it on my own. We need the Clan back."

Dandin sat at the table.

"How is your father?" he asked.

"My father..." Aiden paused. "He is controlled by Adalwulf. He banished William and has almost disowned Ranulf and myself," he said.

"I didn't know it was so bad," Dandin said.

"My Laird, I'm not asking for your help. I just need tae know how many of Clan Canich are here," Aiden said, leaning forward on the table.

"I'd say around forty," Dandin said. "You're going tae raise the Clan?"

"That is my intent, although it never should have come tae this."

"The men here obey the command of a man named Artair. Convince him, and you'll have your men," Laird Dandin said. "But I warn you, that will be no easy task. You are welcome here for as long as you need."

"Thank you, sir," Aiden replied gratefully.

At the evening meal, Aiden was seated at the main table. He was placed beside a jovial man slightly older then himself. The man was shorter and heavier but bore a strong resemblance to Dandin. Aiden was not surprised when the Laird introduced the man as his brother Conan.

"So you're just visiting, then?" Conan asked with a wink, indicating he knew the real reason behind Aiden's visit.

"That's right," Aiden grinned. It was impossible not to like Conan. As they ate, Aiden noticed Eanraig talking closely with another man. Conan followed his gaze.

"That's Artair," Conan said.

Aiden studied the man carefully. He was well built and had a presence that commanded respect from Eanraig.

"What's he like?" Aiden asked.

"Well, he's a good leader and his men respect and admire him. He can be hot-headed and stubborn at times, but what Braeton isn't? Once you win him over tae a cause, he'll stick by it tae death. It'll take some doing though," Conan said.

"What of Eanraig?"

"He acts as the second-in-command."

"Any suggestions?"

"Typical of Clan Canich! Rushing in headfirst without a plan," Conan muttered.

"I have a plan!" Aiden protested.

"Sure you do," Conan said. "I will say that if nothing else works, the Clans do have some very strict traditions concerning these things."

"Typical of Clan Dyson, always talking around the subject," Aiden replied.

Conan laughed. "Let me know if I can help in any way."

The next morning Eanraig found Aiden.

"Are you here tae raise the Clan?" he asked boldly.

"Do you want tae know or does Artair?" Aiden asked in return.

"I do, sir. What other reason does a Laird's son have for being here?" Eanraig asked.

"Maybe I'll answer if you tell me why it was you left in the first place," Aiden said.

"Adalwulf," Eanraig replied. "Once Laird Gòrdan favored him, things got bad. True, William tried tae stop it, but after he was banished no one would say anything openly for fear of suffering the same fate. Before we knew it, rumors began spreading. Some said Ranulf would try and seize the torc, others that the other Clans would take over Canich. The warriors became divided. Any who opposed Adalwulf or Laird Gòrdan were forced tae leave and most of the others followed them. No one would follow Ranulf for fear of what would happen if he failed. That's the truth," he finished.

"I'm here tae find those men willing tae help me overthrow Adalwulf," Aiden said in turn. "Are there any that would go with me?"

Eanraig thought for a long moment as he studied the man in front of him. Every inch of his compact and powerful form radiated quiet confidence. Eanraig immediately knew that Aiden had been to war and back, maybe even more times than he or any of Artair's followers had.

"You seem different from your brothers. Something tells me that you might succeed. I, for one, will go with you. There are a few others who would listen tae me," Eanraig said.

"Thank you," Aiden said.

As Eanraig left, Aiden went to visit Narak. The stallion had been placed in one of the best stalls and was resting after their quick journey. Aiden left the stables and noticed a dog had begun to follow him. Aiden paused to look at the huge, shaggy animal. Blue eyes peered intelligently back at him. Aiden reached out his hand and the dog allowed him to stroke its thick coat.

"You're a pretty thing," Aiden said to it. The dog solemnly proffered a paw. Aiden smiled.

"Where'd you come from, eh?" he asked.

"From the land of snows," a voice replied. Aiden looked up to see a short, stocky man standing beside him. "Her name is Illyria."

"Is she yours?" Aiden asked. The man nodded as the dog looked up adoringly at him.

"My name is Skive," he said. Aiden introduced himself as well.

"Have you been here long?" Aiden asked.

"Two days," Skive replied. "I will not stay much longer. I continue to journey north in search of a new home," he said. "But you are not of this Clan?"

Aiden shook his head and briefly explained the circumstances that had brought him there.

"I understand your need to fight this man. May the stars shine on your endeavor." Skive made a curious bowing motion and left with Illyria.

"I see you've met Skive," Laird Dandin joined Aiden.

"Yes, sir. He's a bit different," Aiden replied.

"He said he came from beyond the mountains of Gelion. He has an unusual quest."

"Aye, but I think we both understand each other a bit," Aiden said. "I have also searched for a new home."

"Then maybe you will be able tae help each other somehow," Laird Dandin said. "Meanwhile, we go on a hunt today. Will you join us? I heard Captain Artair is coming."

"Yes, sir, I will!" Aiden jumped at the chance. It would be a good time to study his likely opponent.

As they prepared to ride out, Eanraig approached Aiden with another man.

"My Laird Aiden, this is Artair." Eanraig introduced his companion. Artair and Aiden sized each other up briefly.

"Sir," Artair made a slight mocking bow. "Eanraig has informed me of your intentions."

"And what have you tae say on the matter?" Aiden replied to the challenge in Artair's voice.

"I have yet tae decide. However, this is not the place for this discussion. I will speak with you later," Artair replied.

"Very well, tonight," Aiden said, forcing an agreement from the captain. Artair led his horse away while Eanraig remained with Aiden.

"Some of the younger lads want tae meet you," he said. "I doubt you'll have any trouble convincing them." He waved three men over.

"This is Douglas," he introduced a man with red hair. "And Dillon and Blair, born exactly a year apart. That's the only way you can tell them apart," Eanraig said. The two brothers stepped forward to greet Aiden. They looked identical in almost every way except Blair was shorter.

"May we ride with you, my Laird?" Douglas asked.

"Only if you call me Aiden," he replied.

"Sure, I think we can manage that," Dillon said as they swung into the saddle. Hunting horns rang out and the party moved into the forest to the head of the hunting trails.

"Did you hear what we're hunting today, lads?" Douglas asked.

"All I got was rumors," Eanraig said.

"Bear," Douglas said. Excited grins spread over the faces of his companions.

The hounds began barking and straining at their leashes as they found the scent. The handlers released the dogs and they ran down the hunting runs deeper into the forest. The hunting party shouted and spurred their horses after the dogs. They soon came upon fresh tracks and followed them to a small river. There the dogs lost the trail. The tracks entered the water but did not reappear on the other side. Men searched downstream to no avail.

Aiden turned Narak upstream and found what they were looking for some distance away. He called the rest of the party over.

"Those are still wet," he said, pointing to the scratches and gouges on the opposite bank under some bushes. "The bear passed only a few minutes ago."

"We'll follow your lead then, since you found them," Laird Dandin said.

Aiden urged Narak into the river and onto the opposite bank. Dismounting, he began to follow the tracks. Dillon took hold of Narak and Blair tossed Aiden a hunting spear. Suddenly, the bear plunged out of the bushes straight toward Aiden. He tumbled backward, jabbing out with the spear. It caught the bear in the leg as it swept past. Snarling in pain, it turned on Aiden, swiping with its massive claws. He dodged away as two dogs came bounding in to attack. While the bear was distracted, Douglas ran to Aiden and helped him stand. The bear half turned toward them, but fell as it was pierced by two hunting spears.

"Aiden, are you all right?" Laird Dandin asked in concern.

"Aye, my Laird. Just startled a bit, that's all," Aiden replied with a shaky smile, drawing a few chuckles.

The hunting party arrived back at Lachlann just before the evening meal. Aiden took some good-natured joking from members of the hunt at the main table.

"Why, you could have been killed!" Dandin's wife exclaimed.

"I was too busy rolling out of the way for that," Aiden replied lightly, prompting more laughter.

"It worked in our favor, for I'm sure if Aiden had stayed on his feet, we wouldn't have gotten a chance at that bear," Laird Dandin said.

"That's funny. I've never felt more like bait in my life," Aiden said.

Talk slowly turned to other matters. Aiden listened with interest as the Laird and the men at the table began recounting previous battles, particularly those in the Calorin war. As the meal ended, Eanraig approached him.

"Captain Artair will speak with you now," he said quietly. Aiden followed Eanraig up the stairs and into a large chamber where Artair and the other members of Clan Canich were gathered.

"I keep no secrets from my men and this concerns them all," Artair said.

"Fair enough," Aiden agreed.

"Lads, this is Aiden, Laird Gòrdan's third son, as most of you may remember," Eanraig introduced him. As visitor, Aiden had the right to speak first.

"I returned home not long ago tae find a stranger ruling in Scodra and her warriors gone. So I have travelled here tae find some men willing tae fight back for our home," Aiden said. Addressing Artair, he asked, "I'm asking you, Captain, if you will help me?"

"I say no," Artair replied. "We are only a few against many. We'd be cut down by a Durnian army. Why risk our lives for an impossible cause?"

"Once a few stand up, more will follow. I've seen it before," Aiden said.

"Your brother was here before and promised us the same. How do I know that you can do what he could not?" Artair asked.

"You don't, but know that I never give up," Aiden said.

"Brave words, but my answer is still no. I will not return tae a place where I have been insulted and degraded as a traitor," Artair said and his men murmured in agreement.

"So you would remain here feasting at another Laird's table while an enemy rules your own? You can'nae wait it out either. You speak of an invasion if we strike back but Adalwulf will soon grow tired of his games. He will kill Laird Gòrdan and my brothers and seize control. Scodra will become part of Durna and Clan Canich will be no more. He will spread through Braeton like a disease and find you in the end!" Aiden argued. "Lleu's hands! Where is your pride?"

"Pride? You are the one here begging! You accuse us of fleeing but we are not the only ones here who were driven away!" Artair glanced meaningfully at Aiden.

"I ran, yes, but I also returned and am willing tae fight for what is mine. I remember a time when insults were avenged at the point of a sword. Maybe Adalwulf truly has nothing tae fear for I see before me only cowards willing tae sacrifice everything for the sake of their lives!" Aiden said.

The men would not meet his angry gaze and Artair leaped to his feet. "No! We will not go!" he shouted.

"At least let those willing tae go, go!" Aiden argued.

"No!" Artair replied again, striding to the door. Aiden suddenly remembered Conan's words.

"Then I challenge you in combat for the leadership of these men!" he said.

Artair stopped and turned. He could not refuse in front of his men.

"I accept! We meet tomorrow morning at dawn!" he gritted out before leaving the chamber. Aiden followed, still seething with anger. Dillon ran after him.

"Aiden!" he called. Aiden stopped. "What you said in there, most of us agree with. Just know that Blair and I will be there with you tomorrow," Dillon said. Aiden only nodded his thanks and went to find Conan.

"I've challenged Artair," Aiden said. Conan smiled in satisfaction.

"I knew you would understand eventually," he said. "Did he accept?"

"Yes. We fight tomorrow at dawn. I've come tae ask you tae oversee it," Aiden said.

"Gladly," Conan replied. "You won't be able tae use your double swords though. It's tradition tae use a claymore not your own."

Aiden cursed interiorly, but at least Artair would also be disadvantaged by a strange weapon.

- -

Aiden spent a restless night, worried not only by thoughts of the duel but also by concerns about whether Adalwulf still suspected nothing in Scodra.

He rose well before dawn and dressed and armed himself. His left arm remained bare and he wore the armored tunic. Dillon and Blair met him in the silent hall and escorted him outside the fortress. They halted some distance into the forest in a large man-made clearing. Artair was already there, also attended by two men. The other men of Clan Canich gathered around and Conan stepped forward.

"You've both asked me tae marshal this fight and as such, I choose the rules. You will both fight with claymores chosen by myself," Conan said. Aiden and Artair stepped forward and laid their own weapons on a low table.

"The fight shall be until first blood or until one of you yields," Conan continued. "You must stay within the boundaries or forfeit. The winner will take command of the Clan members here. In order tae have a secondary witness, I've asked Skive here tae witness the duel. That's all, lads," he finished.

Aiden and Artair stepped inside a ring carved into the earth. Dillon handed Aiden a claymore and Eanraig did the same for Artair. The sunlight grew stronger and the sun rose. Birds began to sing in the trees. A sunbeam glanced off a sword blade, making it sparkle. But all of this was lost on the men in the clearing who watched with bated breath as the two contestants closed on one another.

The glade was filled with the clash of steel on steel, frightening the birds into silence. Aiden struggled at first with the heavy claymore and Artair pressed his advantage. But Aiden was not easily pushed back. Around and around the ring they fought until they both reeled away from each other. Blood flowed from a slash on Aiden's arm. Conan leapt in and called a halt.

"Artair has first blood," Conan began.

"Not so fast, Conan," Aiden said, holding up his sword. The edge was streaked with blood. "Check the underside of his arm."

Conan ordered Artair to lift his arm, revealing a small wound above his wrist.

"There is no clear winner. The fight continues," Conan ruled. Aiden and Artair began to circle each other warily. Aiden feinted and Artair lunged. They both gave full strength to their blows, trying to wear down their opponent. Aiden stumbled backward and Artair closed in. As he came closer, Aiden fell to the ground, swinging out with his leg and knocking Artair's legs out from under him. As Artair fell, Aiden sprang up and rammed a foot into Artair's chest, pinning him down. Aiden's sword point rested at his throat and Artair knew he was defeated.

"I yield," he said.

Aiden stepped away. As victor, Artair's command and weapons now belonged to him. He struck his claymore into the ground and went to the table. He picked up Artair's claymore and turned back to where Artair now stood. Aiden held the sword out to him.

"It's yours, as are these men," Artair said in confusion.

"I know, but I could use your help," Aiden said.

"Well, now you've got me convinced of two things. First, you might be able tae overthrow the Durnian. And second, I'd rather be on your side than against you," Artair said.

Aiden smiled. "Likewise, brother," he said, extending a hand. Artair clasped it and the men burst into cheers.

"You are a strange people. One moment you are fighting each other, and the next you are friends," Skive said to Conan.

The burly clansman laughed. "So we are, and so it shall ever be, I'm afraid," he said. "But now young Aiden has his men and a powerful ally in Artair. I only wish I could go with them."

"I will go with him to help in this fight. I fear I know something of the trial he will face," Skive said.

"What do you plan from here?" Artair asked, sitting at a table in the main hall.

"We need tae get back as soon as possible," Aiden said, sitting on the table itself. "I told Adalwulf I was visiting a friend in a settlement tae throw him off my trail. I don't know how well it worked. Our best chance is tae take the Durnians by surprise before they can send for reinforcements."

"Who knows you're here?" Eanraig asked.

"No one except for Jamey," Aiden replied.

"Rowan's boy?" a warrior asked. Aiden nodded.

"That's good. He's well out of Adalwulf's way," the man said.

"How long will it take tae get back?" Dillon asked.

"Depends on how fast we can travel. I made it here in less than two days," Aiden said.

"And we'll do the same. Lads, be ready tae leave tomorrow morning at first light," Artair ordered.

Heavy clouds gathered during the night. Thunder growled ominously as they prepared to leave. Laird Dandin's mother stopped Aiden as he descended the stairs.

"Your mother and I were close friends. She understood why you had tae leave," she said.

"I wish I had been here when she died. I never really told her good-bye," Aiden said.

"She told me that she thought you were always afraid you would turn intae your father. But you have more of your mother in you than you think," she said. "She'd be proud of you right now."

"Thank you, my lady," Aiden said, bowing. Then he turned and stepped outside.

The men of Clan Canich stood waiting by their horses. A horse was led out for Skive who looked at it with distaste.

"I prefer my own feet for travelling," he said.

"Why walk when you could ride?" Eanraig asked.

"I have walked many great distances. If there were not such a need for haste, I would do the same now," Skive said. He slowly mounted as Aiden brought Narak from the stables. The big stallion snorted and pranced in the cool morning air. Skive watched distrustfully.

"Is that safe to ride?" he asked.

"Of course," Aiden said. "You just feel good this morning, don't you, boy?" he asked the stallion. Narak whinnied and bobbed his head as if in agreement.

"You can'nae argue with that, can you?" Artair said with a laugh. They sprang up into the saddles as Laird Dandin joined them in the courtyard.

"I wish you the very best of luck, lads," he said. "I hope you'll not hold it against me that I can'nae help."

"This is not your fight, my Laird," Aiden said. He bowed with a clenched fist over his heart. He turned Narak and rode from the courtyard followed by the rest of the men.

They retraced Aiden's path and travelled quickly despite the heavy rain that began falling on the second day. As they neared Jamey's house, Aiden saw a movement on the path through the rain and they halted. It was Maon. The hound was bleeding from a cut and limping badly. When he saw Aiden, Maon started barking wildly and turned down the path, stopping only to look back at them.

"Something's wrong with Jamey!" Aiden said to Artair. Aiden drew a sword and spurred Narak after Maon.

Chapter 8

Corin sighed and flicked rainwater from his collar. It had been raining for three straight days and still showed no signs of abating. Dylan and Bran had returned to report that Skive had crossed over into Braeton. And so far, all patrols had been quiet.

Karif perched sulkily on Corin's shoulder and shook himself from time to time to rid his feathers of extra rainwater.

"Not much longer and we'll be home," Corin told the hawk. Corin was returning with his patrol to Kingscastle. He tired of the constant travel back and forth and wished he could stay in the forest. As the towers of the castle came into view, blurred through the rain, Karif took off from Corin's shoulder and flew toward them, choosing to fly in order to find a dry perch more quickly. The men of the Hawk Flight urged their horses on, also eager to get out of the rain.

Corin refused the services of a stable hand in the courtyard as he preferred to care for Zephyr himself. As he finished rubbing the stallion down, a groom came up to him.

"The mare foaled while you were away, sir," the groom said. "A fine young colt that looks to take after its sire," he said, rubbing Zephyr's forehead.

"That's good news. Where did you put them?" Corin asked.

"Down at the end, sir," the groom replied.

"Thank you," Corin replied, stepping out of Zephyr's stall and making his way to the large stalls at the back of the stables. As he neared, he saw a figure standing at the stall door. It was Martin's sister, Mera, one of the castle healers. She looked up, surprised, as Corin came up quietly.

"Sorry if I startled you," he said apologetically.

"No, it's all right," she reassured him. "I've been hearing about the colt from all the children and this was my first chance to come see him."

Corin leaned on the door. The mare stood quietly at the back of the stall and the colt lay on a pile of hay, fast asleep.

"He'll grow up into a fine horse," Corin said in satisfaction.

"What will you do with him?" Mera asked curiously.

"With his size, he'll make a good warhorse," Corin said.

"A warhorse," Mera mused. The reminder of war was never far away. "I do not mean to pry, sire, but do you think there will be another war?" she asked hesitantly.

"It's very possible, but there have been no signs so far," Corin said.

"But you are worried?"

"Do I read that easily?" Corin asked with a grin.

Mera smiled. "I have plenty of practice with Martin," she said. "How was your patrol?"

"Fine, up until the last few days, and we haven't been able to keep dry," Corin replied. "Your brother sends his greetings. He'll be back sometime next week."

"Thank you, sir," Mera smiled.

"Please don't call me that," Corin said. "You make it sound so solemn. And we have known each other since we were children."

Mera laughed softly. "All right then, Corin."

"That sounds better," he said. Karif landed between them on the stall door. "There you are! I thought you abandoned me for someplace warm and dry," Corin said to the hawk. Karif pecked gently at his hand.

"Oh, I'm so sorry! I've kept you out here! You must be tired and—"

"I'm all right, really. I won't drop of exhaustion any time soon," Corin stopped her with a laugh.

She laughed with him as they turned to leave the stables. Pausing at the doors, Mera drew her cloak around her and prepared to step out into the rain.

"You can't just walk out there!" Corin said. Mera looked surprised. "Nothing but a straight run will do," Corin asserted.

Mera saw the twinkle in his eyes. She looked at the courtyard filled with pools of water and a sudden smile spread across her face. "I concur," she said.

"Well then, shall we?"

They took off running at the same time, splashing through numerous puddles, until they arrived breathless and laughing at the foot of the stairs. Corin gallantly offered his hand to help Mera up the slippery steps. Bounding up the last few stairs, they stepped squarely into a pool of water. Mera covered her mouth, aghast. Then Corin's shoulders began shaking and he was laughing uncontrollably. She couldn't help but laugh helplessly with him. They entered the castle and shed wet cloaks.

"My lord?" a soldier addressed Corin.

"Yes, Andras?" Corin replied, regaining control of himself. Andras clearly disliked the fact that he had to carry the message.

"There is someone here who requested to see you, sir," he said.

"Does he have a name, Andras?" Corin asked.

"I was not told, sir," Andras replied.

"Has he been here long?"

"Since this morning, sir."

"Tell him I'm sorry to keep him waiting. I'll see him as soon as I am able," Corin said. Andras gave a reluctant salute and hurried away. Corin turned to Mera.

"If you'll excuse me, ma'am," he said.

Mera curtseyed. "Of course...sir," she replied. They both laughed again.

"You haven't looked that happy in a while," Amaura said to Mera as Corin left.

"What do you mean?" Mera asked.

"Well, you just don't laugh as much as you used to. Even when Martin is here," Amaura said.

"I suppose we just don't get to spend as much time together anymore," Mera said.

"I know what you mean," Amaura agreed forlornly. "Corin and Darrin are always busy. And I'm just getting to know Corin again. It's not fair!"

"What about you and Trey? Have you talked to him yet?" Mera asked. She and Amaura had grown up together and were as close as sisters and so Mera knew of her dilemma.

"No, Darrin said Trey will be here tomorrow, so I suppose I can then," Amaura said.

"You sound so solemn!" Mera laughed.

"I just don't know what to say!"

"Too bad you're not a warrior. You could just point a sword at him and make him talk," Mera suggested. Amaura laughed.

"You've been around Martin too long. I should just have you do it then," she said. "Maybe Kara will lend me her rapier."

At that moment, the young woman in question was walking into the barracks. It was after the evening meal so most of the men were inside. Kara pushed back the hood from her cloak as she returned greetings. She and her twin brother, Kieran, were half Braeton, born into Clan Gunlon. He had been with their father in Aredor when the Calorins invaded. After hearing nothing from them for a year, Kara began to train with an older warrior. When she was seventeen, she ran away from their aunt in Braeton and went to Aredor where she met the Hawk Flight and found her brother. Corin had allowed her to stay with the warband and she and Kieran became the Hawk Flight's message runners, a function they still performed.

She was returning from an outpost not far from Kingscastle with dispatches for the Captain and letters for the men of the

Hawk Flight whose families did not live in Kingstown. They looked up expectantly as she took the letters out of the pouch slung over her shoulder.

"Here, Ian," she handed him a letter. "I might have one more in here for you. What's her name again?" she teased. He only smiled and took the letter from his family. Ian had quickly befriended Kieran and Kara during the war. After the war ended, most people thought that Kara and Ian would settle down together but they saw each other as brother and sister. As such, they never lost the chance to tease each other.

"I can only tell you that she likes to fish," Ian smirked. Kara laughed and punched his arm lightly. She distributed the rest of the letters to the men while she joked with them. Andras watched, frowning. He didn't believe that she could ride with the Hawk Flight. He pushed over to where Evan sat, reading his letter.

"Do you really believe she was in the war?" Andras asked.

"You don't?" Evan asked.

"She's a girl!" Andras protested.

"Have you seen her ride?" Evan asked. "She's better than anyone I've ever seen."

"Thank you, Evan," Kara called. Both men looked up, surprised that she had heard them. She only grinned. "Just a little trick I learned from the captain in the war," she said. Laughter greeted her comment, but Andras glowered when he saw that Evan was also smiling.

"How could he teach anything? He can barely walk. I don't understand the blind devotion," Andras said. The room fell silent.

"You'd best think carefully before you continue," Bran said. Andras swallowed a bit nervously. Bran was one of the best bowmen in the warband and was not usually known for a calm temperament. "You've never seen him out there, so you don't know. He can do anything, and let me tell you, laddie, he's the only reason that we're standing here free men," Bran said.

"Thank you for that speech, Bran," Corin said. Even some of the seasoned veterans flinched at the sound of his voice. Another quality the captain had was being able to appear without warning. Corin leaned against the doorway, his arms crossed. No one was sure how much he had heard.

"Anything you need, Captain?" Lieutenant Llewellyn asked quickly.

"Kara apparently missed one letter. Andras, this is for you from your father," Corin held up a letter that had been given to Darrin by mistake. Andras rose a little shakily and went over to the captain. In person, the captain looked more intimidating than Andras remembered. Corin held the paper out.

"Just a warning this time, Andras. Just watch what you say around here. As Kara so aptly illustrated, you never know who might hear," Corin said.

Andras flushed. "Sorry, sir," he mumbled.

"Like I said, just a warning this time," Corin said. There was no hardness in his voice, but Andras did not dare look into his eyes. "And some advice—you might want to start trying to make a few friends around here. You might need these men someday," Corin said. He had kept his voice low so that no one else could hear them, hoping that it would affect Andras more than a lecture. He still didn't know how to deal with the young man and at times wished that Trey had carried through on his threat. Andras barely nodded again, and Corin left to find the stranger who waited for him.

The man was in the great hall. At first glance, Corin thought it was Aiden, but a closer look proved otherwise. The stranger was taller, more broad-shouldered, but with the same wavy black hair as Aiden.

"You're the one they call the Hawk?" the man asked.

"Aye, my name is Corin," he said. The stranger clasped Corin's proffered hand.

"I'm William," he said.

"You are from Braeton?" Corin said, noting the man's accent.

"Aye, that I am. Clan Canich was my home," William said.

"How can I help you, William?" Corin asked.

"Och, you can just call me Will. Everyone does," he said. "I came here because I thought you might be able tae help me. I'm looking for my brother. He's been gone a few years now. I've been through Braeton and east across the mountains tae Cyndor. I've heard you've been across the sea and figured you might have seen him there."

"What's your brother's name?" Corin asked, even though he already knew.

"Aiden," Will replied.

"Aye, I know him. In fact he was here a few weeks ago," Corin told him. "He was on his way home."

"That's good and bad news," Will said. "Danny, I hope you're not planning on doing anything rash!" he said partly to himself.

"What do you mean?" Corin asked. "Couldn't you stop him?" Will shook his head.

"It's not as simple as that," he said.

"Why not?" Corin asked. "Is Aiden in trouble?"

"I don't know," Will said. "Looks like you want an explanation," he said. Corin nodded and led Will over to a more secluded part of the hall where there was a table with benches. A servant brought two beakers of ale and Will waited until the man had left before he began.

"Aiden's been gone ten years now. You might think it's a little late tae be looking for him but things changed in Clan Canich. A stranger came and divided and scattered us. My father banished me almost two years ago. That's when I decided tae go looking for my little brother. I figured if anyone could help put things right it would be him. He never takes 'no' for an answer."

"Aiden should be back by now. And if I know him, he won't stand for anything. But he'll play it smart," Corin said.

"How do you know him?" Will asked curiously.

"We fought together in the South for a few years. He told me a little about why he left," Corin responded.

Will nodded. "I'm afraid we're both very alike. That's why I'm worried about him going back. If he loses his temper, he'll end up getting himself killed."

"He's changed over the years, Will. You might be surprised at what he can handle."

"I hope you're right, sir."

"What will you do now if you can't return home?"

"I'm not sure yet," Will shrugged.

"You're welcome to stay here. We can find a place for you in the warband," Corin said.

"Thanks, I might take you up on that," Will responded.

"Take as long as you need, Will. There's nothing I wouldn't do for a brother of Aiden's," Corin said seriously.

Chapter 9

Aiden thundered down the forest path after Maon. He burst into the clearing that sheltered Jamey's dwelling. Hearing his approach, two men ran from the house, leapt on their horses, and galloped away. Aiden saw by their clothes and weapons that they were Durnians. Jumping from Narak, he ran into the house.

Jamey lay half-conscious on the floor. Aiden knelt by him and tried to staunch the blood flowing from a gash on Jamey's chest.

"Jamey, don't move," Aiden said as Jamey feebly tried to sit up. Artair stepped in and looked around. Furniture had been overturned and Jamey still clutched a bloody claymore.

"What happened here?" Artair asked.

"I don't know yet," Aiden replied sharply. "Right now Jamey needs help."

Artair stepped outside. "Any of you know about healing?" he asked his men.

"I do," Skive replied.

"Get in here then," Artair said.

Skive entered and crouched next to Aiden. Aiden moved his hands away and Skive opened Jamey's shirt to expose to wound.

"I need some water to wash it," Skive said. Aiden rose and took a pitcher and drew water from a barrel by the door.

"It's not a deep cut," Skive reassured Aiden when he came back. Skive washed the cut and then took some powder from his pouch, poured it into the water, and mixed it until it formed a paste which he then spread over the wound. Aiden helped him put a bandage over it all.

"I've sent two scouts down tae Scodra and assigned a few more tae patrol here tae make sure we're alone," Artair said as Aiden washed his hands.

"Good," Aiden said. "I'm about tae talk tae Jamey."

Jamey had come fully awake and Skive helped him sit up against the wall. Aiden crouched in front of Jamey. "What happened?" Aiden asked.

"I guess Adalwulf got suspicious. Two of his men managed tae track you here a few days ago. I saw them coming and made sure I wasn't here. They didn't stick around long. But then they surprised me today. Since there was no sign of you here, they didn't give me much of a chance tae make anything up. Thankfully you got here when you did."

"I'm sorry, Jamey. I should have been more careful," Aiden said.

"It looks like your crazy plan worked though," Jamey said.

"For now," Aiden said. "We might have just gotten intae worse trouble."

"You're probably right, sir," a warrior said as he entered the house. "Scodra is in an uproar. Those two Durnians saw all of us before they scampered away. But we managed tae catch one of them."

"Bring him in," Artair ordered. Two Clansmen brought in a struggling Durnian. Aiden grabbed the man's tunic and shook him.

"What is Adalwulf planning?" he asked. The man's mouth tightened as he refused to speak. "Bad idea, laddie," Aiden said softly. "I know how tae make you talk."

The Durnian took one look into Aiden's eyes and decided he meant it.

"Don't hurt me, please!"

"That depends on what you tell us," Aiden said.

"Something changed a few days ago. Lord Gòrdan wanted to see you and when Lord Adalwulf said you weren't here, the lord flew into a rage. Obviously he was right about you bringing men back. Adalwulf believed him for once and sent to Durna. Our army will be here by tonight," the man told Aiden.

"Has he done anything tae my brothers?" Aiden asked.

"I don't know," the man said.

"Has he?" Aiden shouted.

"No, not yet!" the Durnian replied frantically. Aiden let go of the man and he fell to the ground.

"Artair, we need tae leave now. We have tae get down tae Scodra," Aiden said.

Artair nodded in agreement. "What do we do about him?" he asked, gesturing to the Durnian. Aiden shoved the man out the door. The Durnian whimpered in fear as Aiden laid a shaft on his bow.

"I'll only use this if you're still in my sight in five seconds," Aiden said to the man. "One…"

The man leaped up and dashed from the clearing as fast as he was able and Aiden returned the arrow to his quiver and went back inside the house.

"Can Jamey ride?" he asked Skive.

"Yes," Jamey replied instead. "Braith is in the pen," he said. Aiden strode out into the rain again and through the trees. A pen was constructed between four trees behind the house and a bay mare stood inside. Aiden slipped the halter on and led her back to the house. Artair threw the saddle and bridle on the mare. Jamey sheathed his sword and slowly mounted.

The rest of the company mounted and Artair turned to Aiden. "What would you have done if he hadn't talked?" he asked curiously.

"You don't want tae know," Aiden replied grimly and spurred Narak into a canter.

They rode into Scodra valley a few minutes later. The gates of the fortress were wide open and they rode to a halt in the courtyard. There was no sign of the Durnians. Ranulf appeared at the doors and ran down the steps.

"Aiden!" he cried. "Adalwulf is gone."

"Not for long," Aiden replied. "He'll be back with an army by tonight."

"What's your plan, Aiden? Between us and the few warriors here we can'nae defend these walls," Artair said.

"You're right. We need more men and you are going tae get them," Aiden told him.

"What?" the captain exclaimed.

"Our only chance tae defeat Adalwulf is if we have our own army. Most of our clan is with Clan Mavor. You and Ranulf will go get them. Take a few men with you," Aiden ordered.

"What do you think you're going tae be doing here?" Ranulf asked. Aiden shielded his eyes from the rain and looked up at the structure rising before him.

"We don't have tae defend the walls. We just need tae hold the keep. Two score determined men could hold out in there for a few days. Or until you get back and save our lives," Aiden said.

"Are you sure, Aiden?" Artair asked.

"We don't have much of a choice, do we?" Aiden said.

"I'll need a horse. The Durnians turned ours loose," Ranulf said.

"Take Narak. I won't be going anywhere," Aiden said. Tam ran out of the keep.

"Ranulf! Father's hurt!" he cried. "I just found him. Adalwulf tried tae kill him!"

"Skive!" Aiden called but Skive had already joined Tam. Aiden stopped Ranulf from following.

"Davy, you have tae leave now. We don't have time," Aiden said.

"Let me get my sword," Ranulf said and ran inside. Skive sent Tam back outside where Aiden briefly told him what was happening.

"You can go with Ranulf," Aiden said.

"No, I'll stay here," Tam said decidedly.

Ranulf reemerged with his weapon and mounted Narak. He nodded a short farewell and he and Artair clattered out of the gates on horseback with three other men. The people who remained at Scodra gathered in the hall as Aiden told them what was to happen. The women gathered their children close and the warriors stepped forward.

"You can leave for the other settlements but I don't know how far you will get. And we need anyone who can fight tae stay," Aiden said. An old man stepped forward to speak for the Clan.

"It's safer here," he said, his voice raised in determination. "And together we might just see this through."

Murmurs of agreement ran through the hall.

"Bring everything you can inside: weapons, food, and water. And hurry, we don't have long," Aiden said grimly.

"I see them! They're coming!" a warrior yelled, running through the gates. His cries halted all activity.

"Dillon, keep them working on those windows!" Aiden called. "Gareth, where do we stand on the provisions?"

"Almost all in, sir. We only need a few more minutes!" Gareth replied. Aiden grabbed the reins of a horse still standing in the courtyard.

"I'll be back. Be ready tae close the gates!" he ordered as he rode out. The rain had slowed and he could see the first ranks of the Durnians breaking through the trees at the far end of the lake. Aiden spurred toward them and halted on the shores of the lake. Adalwulf saw him in the dim twilight. He raised his hand and his army stamped to a halt.

"I'm impressed! It didn't take too long for you tae figure out that I was double-crossing you," Aiden called, leaning on the pommel of the saddle.

"Your father had some choice words to say about you, Aiden. I regret not having my men deal with you when you arrived," Adalwulf replied.

Aiden chose to ignore the first comment. "You shouldn't blame Torsten. He was obviously less than up tae the task!" Aiden laughed.

Torsten's face darkened in rage. "I will enjoy watching you scream as I kill you!" he shouted.

"I'm sure I will too. Just make sure our places are not reversed," Aiden warned.

"Do you wish to surrender, Aiden?" Adalwulf asked.

"It hadn't really crossed my mind. I was just seeing how long I could stall you," Aiden replied.

"Kill him!" Adalwulf screamed. Aiden wheeled his horse as archers stepped forward. Arrows flew all around nearly hitting him. Aiden kicked his right foot out of the stirrup and held himself onto the left side on the horse as it galloped back to the fortress. Archers lowered their crossbows in confusion as suddenly they had almost no target.

Aiden's warriors slammed the gates shut as he tore through them. There was a dull thud as the locks were slid into place.

"Blair, get up intae one of the towers and keep an eye on them," Aiden ordered as a soldier took the horse to the stable. "We ready?" he asked Dillon.

"As ready as we'll ever be," Dillon replied. "We've got everything inside. All the windows and doors are boarded and barricaded, except for the front and very top."

"Good work," Aiden said, clapping Dillon on the shoulder. "Let's get inside."

The heavy wooden doors were closed and bolted and the warriors took up their assigned positions at the windows in the great hall and the second level of the keep. The women and children who were not fighting were huddled in an adjacent chamber where there was no danger of them being hit. Besides the thirty-seven men left in his command, Aiden had found another fifteen old men and boys, as well as a few women, who could fight.

Tam came to stand by Aiden at the doors.

"How is Father?" Aiden forced the words out.

"Skive thinks he'll be all right," Tam replied. "He's still unconscious but we brought him down here. Ailsa's looking after him."

"Good." Aiden nodded.

"Danny," Tam said softly.

"Not now, Tam," Aiden said shortly.

Aiden stared out the open window at the rain still pattering down in the empty courtyard. Blair had reported that Adalwulf's army was sitting at the gates. The wooden walls surrounding the town rose up twice the height of a man and each log sharpened to a point at the top making them near impossible to scale and so Adalwulf had sent for a battering ram. The wooden gates were over a foot thick, fire hardened, and reinforced with iron bars. It would give a valiant resistance to the ram they could hear pounding away. The night was passing quickly but Adalwulf would not stop. The Durnians would break through by the morning.

He left the window and went around checking on the sentries. He stopped at the window at the far end of the hall where a young woman stood guard. "It's Rona, right?"

"Yes, sir."

"How are you holding up?"

"Fine, except for that infernal banging on the gates," Rona replied. Aiden had to agree. The dull thumping had begun to grate even on his nerves.

"Your relief should be here shortly. You should rest while you still can," he said. Rona nodded briefly and Aiden turned upstairs.

Jamey sat in a chair by a window in the long hallway of the second floor defenses. Maon sat faithfully at his feet.

"You sure you're up for sentry duty?" Aiden asked him.

"Aye, I don't know what Skive did but I can barely feel that cut," Jamey replied. Aiden stroked Maon's ears as he looked out of the window.

"We've got a good view of the Durnians here. Why don't we take advantage?" Jamey asked.

"I've thought about it," Aiden said. "But they can move out of range and the ram carriers can just as easily shield themselves. We'd best save our arrows. We don't have enough tae spare."

"What's your plan once they break in?" a warrior named Cai asked.

"We'll let Adalwulf make the first move. I want tae see how he plans tae fight," Aiden said.

An hour later the sentries were changed. Aiden made his rounds again and found Skive on duty.

"I think I got you intae more than you were expecting," Aiden said apologetically. Skive tested the edge of his battle axe.

"Nothing is ever as we expect, is it?" he replied. "I do not regret following you here."

"I need tae thank you also for looking after my father," Aiden said. Skive simply inclined his head.

"He is a strong man. The Durnian used his axe handle to strike his head. It might be some time before he regains consciousness. Will you visit him?" Skive asked. Aiden shook his head vehemently.

"Not now...not yet," he said.

Skive said nothing. He had heard enough to begin to understand the young man standing beside him.

Aiden slept little that night. Just before dawn, the Durnians broke through.

Chapter 10

Adalwulf marched through the ruined gates and stood gazing through the rain at the silent keep as his army filed in behind him. Aiden found himself standing beside Rona again. She wore the brigandine and had found time to pull her hair back into several intertwining braids. She grasped a spear she had taken from the extra weapons piled at every station. Tam and Blair stood to his left, hastily eating breakfast.

"When do you think he'll attack?" Blair asked.

"Well, it's commonly known that there's nothing like a dawn attack tae get your day off tae a wonderful start," Aiden replied. Tam saw the slight smile on his brother's face and grinned.

"Have you done this often, sir?" Rona asked.

"You mean barricade myself in with dangerous, spear-carrying women? No, this is a first," Aiden replied. His smile was impossible to resist and Rona smiled.

"No, defending places like this?" she specified.

"A few times. Don't worry, it's easier than you'd think," came Aiden's cheerful, if slightly false, response. But his words had the desired effect as the defenders within earshot straightened and grasped their weapons with renewed confidence.

"Aiden, I know you're in there! Come out and talk!" Adalwulf shouted.

"Ah, Adalwulf! I would love tae but I'm just finishing breakfast," Aiden called back. Tam and Blair grinned over their own meal, though they knew Aiden hadn't touched food since the day before. Adalwulf caught sight of Aiden leaning on the sill of the window.

"I come to offer you one last chance to surrender," Adalwulf called.

Aiden appeared to ponder this statement before answering, "I'm still not interested. Surrender is not really my style."

Adalwulf smiled thinly.

"Even so, how long do you think you can last? You do not have many men. Look! You are reduced to having women fight!" he pointed at Rona.

"What's the matter, Adalwulf? Jealous you didn't think of it first?" Aiden retorted quickly, prompting laughter from his men and even a few smiles from the Durnians.

"Last chance, Braeton! March out here and I will spare your lives," Adalwulf said.

"I don't think so," Aiden replied. "I like it fine in here. Did I mention that it's dry?"

"I will not ask again. Even if you beg for mercy I will not hear it!" Adalwulf thundered.

"Pity. I was really beginning tae enjoy our talks," Aiden said smiling, but Adalwulf could see the cold resolve in Aiden's eyes.

"How is your father, Aiden?" Adalwulf asked, matching his smile. Aiden stopped Tam from giving an angry reply.

"He's fine. He doesn't send his love if that's what you were wondering," Aiden said. The careless smile was still there but Adalwulf felt a chill. He stepped back and raised his hand. When he brought it down, the Durnians charged forward.

"Archers, fire as quickly as you like!" Aiden called. Jamey relayed his order to the men upstairs. "Cai, watch for any that try tae come around back!" Aiden said.

The front rank of Durnians had raised their shields to protect themselves. The defenders angled their bows so their arrows would pass over the shield wall and into the ranks behind it. Despite the confusion, Adalwulf's men advanced steadily.

As the Durnians reached the windows, they were forced to drop their shields to attack which left them open to the thrusting spears and claymores. The warriors on the second floor kept a steady hail of arrows raining down on the Durnians.

Midday, Adalwulf drew his men back, having met with little success against the solid walls and their defenders. The clanswomen not fighting made the rounds, giving food and drinks to the warriors. Aiden also went around with Skive as the burly warrior tended to the wounded. As the afternoon passed quietly, Aiden relieved half the defenders. He appointed Cai, with three other men and a woman, to patrol the upper floors and towers. They would have a clear view around the fortress from the unblocked windows and apertures while remaining out of range of the enemy.

The night also passed uneventfully and as the next day dawned it became apparent what had kept the Durnians busy. The enemy advanced again while bearing rough ladders in their midst. The ladders were placed against the second floor windows as fresh forces assaulted the lower level.

"Dillon, take seven men and reinforce upstairs. See if you can get rid of those ladders!" Aiden shouted as the Durnians began to scale the wall. A badly wounded warrior reeled back from a window. Aiden drew one of his swords and sprang to take his place.

Adalwulf pressed the attack all day long. Dillon and his men managed to dislodge one of the ladders. It snapped in half as it hit the ground. The Durnians withdrew as night fell, taking the two remaining ladders with them. Aiden took count of his warriors, finding that three were dead, two were mortally wounded, and many others were hurt in some way, including himself. The dead were wrapped in clean plaid cloaks and laid in an adjacent chamber with their weapons.

Aiden saw Rona sitting on a bench by the hearth, trying to clean a cut on her cheek.

"You look like you could use some help," he said, going over to her. She blushed a little but handed him the cloth. He tilted her face toward the light and dampened the cloth. After cleaning and wiping the blood from her face, he gave her a clean cloth that she pressed against the cut.

"Are you hurt anywhere else?" Aiden asked.

"Nothing bad. I'm all right, unlike so many others," Rona answered. "You?"

"Och, I'm fine," Aiden said. "And no, you don't get tae ask me if that's really true."

Rona smiled as she took the cloth from her cheek. "I thought you might say that," she said. Aiden only smiled and walked away.

Later, Tam came to relieve Aiden on sentry duty. He was just in time as he caught his brother stifling a yawn.

"Aiden, when was the last time you slept? Or ate, for that matter?" Tam asked.

"Sometime yesterday." came the reply. "You all right?" Aiden asked as he stifled another yawn.

"I think so. This is my first battle. I'd rather be singing about it," Tam said.

"Believe me, brother, I wish you were too," Aiden said before stumbling off to snatch a few hours of sleep.

The next morning, Cai reported that a few Durnians had been seen circling the fortress, but nothing had happened. The enemy made no attacks that morning. Aiden was relieved as it gave him a chance to reposition his men.

"Aiden, are you hearing this?" Jamey asked. They looked out of the second story window to see Torsten strutting in front of the Durnians.

"Braeton! Where are you hiding, coward?" Torsten shouted.

"I'm here, scum!" Aiden shouted back. Torsten smiled as he gazed up at Aiden.

"We have yet to meet in battle, Braeton. My axe waits to greet you," he said.

"Tell your master tae call off his men and we'll face each other alone," Aiden replied.

"I am not here to deliver challenges," Torsten said. "Only to tell you that we caught the one called Ranulf as he ran. I slew him myself."

Aiden was caught off guard and stood in silence.

"We will meet again, Braeton! Fate decrees it!" Torsten sneered.

"Then you had better hope she's on your side," Aiden said. He turned from the window to confront the stricken faces on the defenders.

"Aiden, do you think it's true?" Dillon asked.

"I don't know. Adalwulf might be bluffing. Get ready, they're going tae attack again," Aiden said as the Durnians began to advance while beating their shields with axe blades and bearing the ladders.

Aiden sent more men upstairs as he rushed to help the lower floor. This attack lasted well into the night before Adalwulf called his men off. Four more Braetons lay dead but Dillon and his men had destroyed the remaining two siege ladders. As everything quieted in the fortress, Aiden heard his name called. A young woman pushed toward him and he recognized Brighde, Ranulf's betrothed.

"Is it true? Is Ranulf dead?" she demanded, tears filling her eyes. Aiden saw that everyone had gathered to hear what he would say.

"I think he's still alive. Torsten offered no proof that he had actually killed Ranulf. Adalwulf must have figured out that Ranulf is gone because he hasn't been seen here. They didn't say anything about Artair or the men with him either," Aiden said. The hall sighed in relief at his explanation. Brighde thanked him and gave him a quick hug.

"How long until Ranulf and Artair can make it back?" Blair asked worriedly.

"It would take at least two days tae reach Clan Mavor," Dillon said.

"Add two days at least for them tae raise the warriors and another two tae return," Aiden said. "We've already held out for three days. They could already be on their way back. We only need tae last a few more days," he said.

"Do you believe that we can?" Tam asked after the others had left.

"We have tae. There is no other way," Aiden replied.

Adalwulf sat by a blazing campfire. The sun had broken through the heavy clouds the day before and the ground had finally begun to dry. But the remaining dampness was the least of his concerns. His bluff earlier had seemed to affect the Braetons somewhat, yet they still held firm. He had lost almost a third of his force and still gotten nowhere. He was fairly sure that Aiden had tried to send for reinforcements but he was confident that his still large army could handle it.

But there was his main problem. He needed to get rid of the stubborn young Braeton. Once Aiden was out of the way, the defenders would crumble. He watched Torsten prowl on the other side of the fire and suddenly a solution came to him.

"Torsten!" he snapped.

"My lord!" Torsten came to attention.

"Do you think you can defeat Gòrdan's son in combat?" Adalwulf asked.

"I know I can, sir!" Torsten snarled. Adalwulf sniffed.

"You will get your chance, but first, I will make certain precautions before we challenge. Here is what I intend to do."

No attack came at all the next day. Aiden doubled up the warriors. One rested while the other stood watch. He himself didn't rest. He wished Ahmed or Corin were there with him. Then he wouldn't feel as burdened with the hopelessness of the situation. As night fell again he sat by the doors, sharpening his swords and striving to stay awake. He sheathed his last blade and a new wave of weariness swept over him. His eyes closed against his will and he slept.

Sometime later, he heard someone calling his name and was shaken awake. He opened his eyes with an effort and saw Tam.

"Aiden, we've got a problem," he said. Aiden rubbed his eyes as Cai came up behind Tam.

"We saw two groups of Durnians start tae come around the keep. It looks like they're going tae try the side doors," Cai reported.

"Tam, take eight men and take one door. Dillon, take another eight and get tae the other door. Do whatever you can tae stop them!" Aiden ordered.

Dillon hastily unbarred the door and risked a glance outside. The Durnians hadn't arrived yet. He sent his men out into the darkness to wait. The Durnians came around the corner of the fortress and came to the door. They turned at the faint ring of steel behind them and saw themselves surrounded by the cold-eyed Braeton warriors.

Tam and his men also removed the barricade protecting their door. The leader of the small group of Durnians tested the latch. To his surprise, it swung open. As the last soldier stepped inside, the door was slammed shut and guarded by Skive and a snarling Illyria. The Durnians had no choice but to face Tam and his warriors.

The main gates also came under attack. A sentry reported that enemy soldiers, well sheltered behind shields, were laying up wood and brush against the doors. Aiden called Jamey and Blair over and explained his counterplan.

Adalwulf watched as the soldiers laid the last of the wood at the doors. There was a chance that this plan, coupled with the attacks from the sides, would work and he could drive the Braetons out to him. As a warrior bore the torch forward to light the fuel, the doors swung open and three figures leapt out. Adalwulf hastily ordered more men forward.

Aiden sprang down the steps to engage them as Blair and Jamey dragged the wood inside. As they finished, two warriors stepped forward and fired the defender's last arrows at the Durnians, allowing Aiden to retreat. But as he turned up the steps, a crossbow bolt whistled from the darkness. The sword fell from his right hand and he staggered. Jamey bounded forward and dragged him inside.

By skill or luck, the bolt had hit between two metal links high on Aiden's right shoulder. Outside, Adalwulf smiled. He had seen Aiden take the arrow. He could almost taste victory.

Jamey pulled the arrow from Aiden's shoulder and then helped him take off the armored tunic so that Rona could bandage the wound. Aiden pushed her hand away and stood as he saw the other men return and the body they bore.

Chapter 11

Dillon lay on the floor with his chest torn open by a battle axe. Skive knelt by Dillon but Aiden knew the young man was dying. Blair pushed forward to kneel beside his brother. Blair grasped Dillon's hand as he choked out some words. Blair understood and took Dillon's sword from one of the men and wrapped his brother's hand around the hilt. A smile spread over Dillon's face and a few seconds later he died.

"We took care of the Durnians. The doors are locked and barricaded again," Tam said quietly to Aiden. Then he noticed Aiden holding his shoulder steady. "You're hurt!" he exclaimed.

"It's not bad," Aiden replied.

"It won't be if you let us bandage it," Rona put in. She and Jamey took Aiden over to a bench and forced him to sit down. Jamey helped Aiden pull off his shirt as Rona cleaned and bandaged the wound. Aiden winced as he pulled his shirt back on. He saw Blair, dry-eyed, beginning to sharpen his claymore. Aiden knew the look in his eyes; Blair would have his revenge.

Blair quietly unboarded a window. He had just finished when a figure moved beside him.

"How long were you watching me?" Blair asked.

"Long enough tae know that you're about tae do something stupid," Aiden said.

"Don't stop me. I will avenge my brother," Blair said.

"I won't stop you. I'll just follow tae bring your half-dead body back and finish the job myself," Aiden replied.

"You're the one who said we should fight and avenge ourselves!" Blair argued.

"I said we should stand up for what is ours. You know that. Are you doing this for Dillon or for you?" Aiden asked.

"I only need tae find one man," Blair said.

"Out of three hundred still out there? You'll be killed, Blair! We've lost too many men already. Don't make us lose another," Aiden said.

"What would you have me do?" Blair demanded.

"Wait. You will get your chance, I promise," Aiden said.

"You had better be right," Blair warned. They blocked the window again and returned to the hall.

Adalwulf ordered another dawn attack to test the resolve of the defenders. It was well into the afternoon when he strode forward and halted in the center of the courtyard.

"Aiden!" he shouted. His enemy appeared at the window.

"I thought we weren't talking, Adalwulf. Or are you here tae surrender?" Aiden called.

"Unfortunately, I do not surrender either," Adalwulf replied. "I come to discuss another matter. So far you and your people have held against me. I wish to avoid this pointless bloodshed by offering you a challenge."

"I'll listen," Aiden replied. Adalwulf smiled.

"A duel between our best fighters: Torsten and yourself. Do you accept?" he asked. Aiden was tired, hungry, and wounded and he saw from Adalwulf's smile that he knew that. But here was a chance to end it.

"Under what terms?" Aiden asked.

"You fought in the South. You know their arrangement," Adalwulf answered.

Aiden knew too well. He thought it over and then said, "I accept, Adalwulf. But on the understanding that there is a truce between us until the fight," Aiden replied.

"I accept. You will meet tomorrow at noon where I stand now," Adalwulf said. Aiden nodded his understanding and they withdrew.

"What were the terms?" Tam asked.

"Total surrender. We fight tae the death," Aiden replied.

"But, Aiden, you're hurt!" Jamey said.

"I know, but he challenged me. I had tae accept under those terms," Aiden said. Realization dawned on Jamey.

"He knew! That was his plan last night!" Jamey exclaimed and Aiden only nodded.

"At least I have until tomorrow. I need tae find a new sword," Aiden said. His comrades saw the empty scabbard hanging over his shoulder as he strode off. Jamey cursed roundly.

"He'll be crippled with that shoulder and having tae use a different weapon!" Tam said. "What do we do?"

"Keep calm for now," Blair said. "He wouldn't have accepted if he couldn't do it."

That had to be enough reassurance for the others and they gradually dispersed.

Ailsa came to find Aiden in the early evening.

"Sir, Laird Gòrdan is awake and asking for you," she said. Aiden fought away the feeling of dread that came over him. He didn't think he could handle another outburst from his father but he turned and made his way slowly to the end of the hall where Skive treated the wounded warriors.

He found Laird Gòrdan sitting up on the rough pallet. A bloody bandage was wrapped around his forehead. Aiden crouched beside him.

"You wanted tae see me, sir?" he asked.

"Yes, but I didn't expect you tae come," Laird Gòrdan replied.

"Well, I'm here," Aiden said a little sharply.

"Aiden, I called you here for several reasons. The first is tae say that I misjudged you earlier. I've made too many mistakes over the past few years. It is ironic that it takes a good whack tae my head before I begin tae see things more clearly, isn't it?" Laird Gòrdan said wryly. Aiden said nothing. He hadn't expected those words from Gòrdan. His father was a proud man and it must have taken much for him to speak that way.

"Where is your other sword?" Laird Gòrdan asked.

"There was an incident outside the doors last night. I lost it, sir," Aiden replied.

"Tam has told me much of what has happened. You are tae fight Torsten?" Laird Gòrdan asked.

"Yes, sir," Aiden said.

"Have you a sword?" the Laird asked.

"Not yet. I haven't found one that suits me," Aiden replied. Laird Gòrdan reached over and picked up a long sheathed blade that Tam had brought down to him.

"I want you tae take mine. Go on, try it and see what you think," he said as he held it out.

Aiden took the sword and stood. He drew with his left hand and swung it experimentally. It was well balanced and fit his hand well. Dropping the sheath, he grasped the handle with both hands. His wounded right shoulder immediately protested the movement.

"You're hurt?" his father asked as he saw Aiden wince.

"My shoulder. But I can fight with either left or right hand, so it doesn't matter," Aiden said as he sheathed the sword. "It will serve. Thank you, my Laird," he said. He made to leave but Gòrdan caught his arm.

"Aiden, I'm…be careful," he said, his gruff voice softening.

"Yes, sir," Aiden said and strode to the far end of the hall where he began to put a new edge on the claymore.

"Father gave you his sword?" Tam asked. Aiden nodded, not taking his eyes from his task. "Dinner is ready and Skive wants tae take a look at your shoulder," Tam said.

"I'll be along in a minute," Aiden answered. Tam left him alone. His brother had been quiet all afternoon. Aiden was plainly worried about the next day and that frightened Tam more than anything.

Rona watched Aiden as they sat at the table. He only picked at the stew in front of him, his mind completely preoccupied. The claymore leaning on the bench beside him was a subtle reminder of his worry. A bold young boy of about seven years scooted down the bench until he was sitting in front of Aiden.

"So you gonna fight tomorrow and beat that big, mean man?" the boy asked.

Aiden smiled faintly. "You think so?" he asked.

The boy, Brannan, nodded emphatically. "Oh, yes! You gotcha a big sword, don't you?"

Aiden turned to Rona. "I can'nae beat his logic," he said.

Rona laughed. "Did you finish your dinner, Brannan?" she asked.

Brannan made a face. "Don't like it. It doesn't taste very good," he said. Apparently he wasn't the only one as rumblings of agreement came from the other small children seated nearby.

Aiden leaned forward conspiratorially. "I don't like it much either. What do you think they put in it?" he whispered.

"I tink dead leaves," said a girl of five years. Rona saw the children move closer to contribute.

"Squished frogs," a boy said.

"Probly bath water," another said.

Aiden took a bite, pretending to choke as he swallowed. "You forgot crinkly bee wings," he said. The children broke out in giggles and followed his example, throwing out more suggestions as they ate.

"What about Jean's shoe that she lost the other day?" Tam asked as he sat down next to Brannan with his own food. More laughter greeted the newest addition to the stew. The grownups smiled as they watched the brothers' ploy to get the children to eat.

"Nothing like the old Gamble Stew trick, is there?" Tam asked quietly.

"You have tae get it down somehow, don't you?" Aiden replied.

"You two are horrible! That soup was very good," Rona said.

"She probably ate everything in front of her when she was little," Aiden said. Rona couldn't keep a straight face, dissolving into helpless laughter with the brothers.

Jean left her place and scrambled onto Tam's lap.

"Singus a song! Please!" she pleaded. Tam was good natured and had a vast store of songs which made him a firm favorite with the little ones.

"Please! It's been about fifty months since you sang for us, I tink!" another boy chimed in.

"Has it really been fifty months?" Tam exclaimed. There were emphatic nods all around from the children. Tam obliged with a lively song about a young boy and a mockingbird. Aiden leaned forward on the table and listened to the old song. It was the first time he had heard his brother sing. Tam had a pleasant tenor voice that carried throughout the hall. As Tam finished, Brannan requested his personal favorite, the "Song of Taran" in which the warrior Taran had to defeat a fierce dragon.

The quiet hall was transformed as it filled with song and laughter. Everyone joined in, their troubles forgotten for the moment. Aiden slipped away unnoticed. He visited the few sentries still posted. Despite the truce, Aiden did not trust Adalwulf.

Skive finished putting a fresh bandage on Aiden's shoulder.

"Get some rest now, Aiden," Skive said as Aiden pulled on his shirt and the thick leather tunic that had replaced the brigandine.

"I can't. The sentries change in a few minutes," Aiden replied.

"I'm afraid you're outvoted on this one," Jamey said. "You need tae sleep. Let us worry about things tonight."

"You won't be of any use tomorrow if you don't rest," Blair put in. Aiden gave in, not unwillingly.

Everyone else in the hall was turning in. They left a place for Aiden by the hearth.

"You wouldn't mind one more song, would you, Tam?" Ailsa asked as she struggled to put the children to bed. Tam pulled out a small pipe from his pouch and began playing a soft melody. The children quieted instantly as the quiet notes of the lullaby floated through the air.

Aiden lay down on the pallet and wrapped his cloak around him, listening to the music. By the time Tam finished, he was asleep.

Brighde watched Aiden. He lay on his side with the claymore resting in the crook of his arm. Tomorrow this young warrior would decide their fate. The fire burned lower and he shivered in a dream. For generations her family had woven the plaid of the Clan. She gently spread a blanket over him. That night, Aiden slept in peace under the blue plaid of Clan Canich.

Chapter 12

Andras found himself in trouble again. He had come in from the training grounds and was stabling his horse when he was confronted by an angry young woman.

"What do you think you're doing?" Kara asked.

"Umm…Putting my horse in his stall," Andras replied, slightly puzzled.

"This is Delyth's stall," Kara said as she gestured to her gelding. "*Everyone* knows that." She stressed the word.

"This was where I was told to keep Emil," Andras argued. He knew her status in the Hawk Flight but was not going to back down. Kara's temper got the better of her and she began to tell Andras just exactly what she thought of him and his horse. Darrin and Will happened into the stables at that point. They had met each other once before the Calorin War and had struck up a new friendship in the few days that Will had been at Kingscastle. They watched openmouthed as Kara and Andras argued. Darrin didn't know whether to laugh or not as Kara used some choice words in Calorin.

Just then they were interrupted by a stern voice. "What, exactly, is going on here?"

Everyone turned to see the latest arrival. Corin stood in the doorway of the stables, papers in hand.

"Sorry, Captain, but he's trying tae take my stall!" Kara pointed to Andras.

"Kara, I have those orders for Lynwood ready to go. You have ten minutes," Corin said. Kara shoved Delyth in the stall and ran off to change. Corin caught sight of some grinning stable boys loitering nearby and guessed what had happened.

"Andras, I believe that Captain Pedr assigned you stall 17C. It's in the next row over, a common enough mistake if you don't know your way around and if no one helps you like they should," here he shot a glare at the stable boys who scurried quickly off. "While you have Emil out you can deliver these to Dyffryn outpost. The garrison captain there is a little abrupt so try and be polite," he said.

Andras wasn't sure if he should be offended at that but he relished the chance to be the one to deliver the letters. Corin handed the dispatches to Andras and the young man rode from the stables.

"Well done. You were almost nice to him, Corin," Darrin said.

"He hasn't been quite as irritating recently. And it saved me from hunting down Bran to do it," Corin said. Will and Darrin chuckled as they led their horses into stalls. "Oh, when you have a minute can you come by? I need you to sign these," Corin asked Darrin. His brother glanced at the papers.

"You and father already signed these," Darrin said, puzzled. "These are for Madoc, aren't they?"

Corin grimaced at the name. "Yes. He won't read anything unless it's been signed by the 'proper authorities.' Which, in his opinion, I don't count as," he said.

"I'm surprised you haven't, ah, 'talked' to him about that yet," Darrin commented.

"I could, but then he'd start citing all sorts of rules and regulations and the 'talk' wouldn't end so well," Corin replied.

Will laughed. "I should tell you that I've decided tae stay if you'll still have me," he said.

"That's the best news I've heard all week," Corin smiled. "And as 'Supreme Overlord of the Papers,' I can put you anywhere you want."

"The term is 'General of the Warbands,'" Darrin corrected.

"A detail," Corin interrupted.

"Anyway, we thought the Hawk Flight might be a good fit," Darrin said. Corin approved immediately.

"I just promoted Aeron to lieutenant at Lynwood Keep, so Flynn needs another man in his patrol. I think you and he will get along well. I'll let him know as soon as I can." Corin said. "But if you'll excuse me, my duty as 'General' calls me back."

- -

Twenty minutes later, Kara met Corin in his office. He handed her the papers for Lynwood and she stored them safely in the leather satchel that hung over her shoulder as he, with much muttering, continued to dig through the piles of paper on his desk.

"Finally. These are mostly for Liam's patrol," he said, handing her a stack of letters from the men's families. On their frequent trips to Kingscastle, Kara and her brother would pick up and deliver letters back and forth to the men who were out on patrol. She also placed the letters in her pouch before fastening it securely shut.

"Is that all, sir?" she asked.

"I hope so," Corin replied. Kara couldn't stop the light laugh that escaped her. She hadn't quite gotten used to seeing the Captain surrounded by papers and with ink stains on his fingers.

"I know it's a mess," Corin commented wryly. "Darrin keeps threatening to assign me a secretary."

"Is there any reply from Lynwood?" Kara asked.

"No, those are just the commission papers for their new officers," Corin said. "How are things between you and Kieran now?" he asked casually. Kara blew a sigh. She and her brother had an argument the week before and hadn't made up.

"I haven't talked tae him in a few days. I said we should go visit our family in Braeton. We haven't seen them in years. But he says we're both too busy and can'nae just leave. So, I've been mad and it made me blow up at Andras today."

"I wondered where that came from," Corin said.

Kara blushed. "Sorry, sir. I'll try and make it up tae him. Someone should be nice tae him," she said.

"I am nice," Corin protested with a grin and Kara laughed. The warband knew the Captain's opinion on the newest recruit. "But about Kieran, I can give you both some leave time if you want, or there's talk about holding the Festival this year. Your family could come then," Corin said.

"Thank you, sir. I'll talk tae Kieran about it," Kara said. "Good luck, sir," she said, gesturing to the desk.

"Thanks. Ride safe and I'll see you out there in a few days," Corin said.

- -

For the second time that day, Corin found himself thinking about Mera. Since the day they met in the stables, he had crossed her path more than usual. A fact he greatly attributed to his sister and mother.

He didn't deny that he enjoyed talking with her. It was refreshing to talk to someone who wasn't chasing after him because he was a prince. He had a feeling she understood him a little more than most because she had treated him when he had, well, almost died a year ago after the battle. She had guessed most of his story when she saw his scars but had not said anything about it.

His musings were interrupted by a knock on the open door of the study. He looked up to see a thin, stoop-shouldered man. He wore a scholar's robe and he clutched a satchel under his arm.

"How can I help you?" Corin asked him.

"Sire," the man bowed. "Prince Darrin assigned me to help you with all…this." He looked at the desk with something akin to horror in his eyes. Corin saw immediately he wasn't going to get rid of the man at all.

"All right, there's another desk over there," he nodded to the opposite wall. "I'm sorry, but I don't know your name."

"Gerralt, your highness," the man replied.

"Sire, there seems to be no indication of whom this is from," Gerralt said a few hours later. Corin glanced at the paper.

"Oh, that's Captain Bryn from the garrison at Carnedd," he replied.

Gerralt sniffed. "I don't see how your highness can tell. This handwriting is atrocious."

Corin knew the comment was directed at the writing in all the letters, including his.

"Gerralt, leave that one on my desk please. Bryn needs a reply soon," he said.

"That's the fourth one today that needs a 'quick reply,'" Gerralt said.

"I know," Corin said. "As you've been so kind to point out, I'm a little behind. Don't worry, it'll get done. I've already decided I'm not going out on patrol tomorrow."

Gerralt continued to sort out papers.

"Sire, it seems all this letter is lacking is a signature," he said.

"Gerralt, I told you that you can just call me 'sir.' Everyone does. Or if you want a title, 'Captain' will do just fine," Corin said patiently for perhaps the third time that morning.

Gerralt's sniff indicated what he thought of "everyone."

"Now, *Sire*, about this one," he said. Corin resisted the urge to punch a wall. It was going to be a long day.

Kieran could see the lights of Kingscastle through the dusk. Gwennyd, his gelding, sensed they were close to home and picked up his pace to a brisk trot. Kieran was content with the pace. He wanted to get home. It had been a long two weeks out on patrol and there were still reports to give to the Captain. Gwennyd nickered as he saw another horse and rider ahead of them. Kieran thought he recognized the rider and after a moment's hesitation, spurred Gwennyd to a canter to catch up.

"Andras! What are you doing out here?" Kieran asked.

"I was asked to deliver a dispatch to Dyffryn," Andras replied rather smugly.

Kieran hid a smile. "I'm glad I missed out on that assignment," he said. "Captain Einion doesn't seem tae like me. I figure maybe I talk too much, but I can'nae help it."

It seems like no one has any sort of respect around here, Andras thought.

"What are you doing out?" he asked.

"Och, I'm on my way back from my run," Kieran said. "You don't mind if we ride back in together, do you?" he asked. Andras couldn't really refuse, so he nodded. "Grand," Kieran said.

Andras would have kept up his practice of not associating with any members of the warband, but Kieran kept up a steady stream of conversation, gently pressuring answers from Andras. Before he knew it, Andras had given up almost all information about himself and his family, but Kieran freely reciprocated, going into plenty of detail about his own life. Andras wished that Kieran had not had so many adventures. It made Andras's life seem dull and unimportant in comparison. For maybe the first time, Andras found himself thinking that perhaps the warband was not as bad as he had thought.

"I've got tae leave my reports in the Captain's office. You want tae come with me tae the kitchens afterward? We've missed dinner by now," Kieran asked.

Andras stuttered. "I should get back to the barracks," he said.

"Och, you won't get in trouble if you're with me. Besides, your lieutenant should know you got sent out so you'll have a meal waiting," Kieran said.

"Are you sure?" Andras asked.

"Positive," Kieran replied cheerfully. Andras nodded again and a few minutes later they clattered into the courtyard. Two yawning stable boys took their horses and Andras followed Kieran to the barracks office. Kieran pushed open the door and was halfway to Corin's desk when a voice interrupted him.

"What are you doing in here?" Gerralt asked. Andras estimated that Kieran jumped at least a few inches into the air in shock.

"Hammer of Lleu!" Kieran yelped. "Who are you?"

Gerralt sniffed. "I'm the new secretary. Again, what are you doing?"

"Leaving my reports for the Captain," Kieran replied. He put a hand to his chest to feel his still-racing heart. "Captain might have left a warning sign," he muttered. Andras almost couldn't help himself. He found the situation funny. What was happening to him?

"Give them to me. I'll make sure he gets them in the proper order," Gerralt said officiously. Kieran looked at him warily as he took the papers out of his pouch and handed them to Gerralt.

"What are those?" Gerralt asked as Kieran took something else out of the bag.

"Letters for the families of Flynn's patrol," Kieran said. "These get left here." He laid them on Corin's desk and his tone dared Gerralt to argue with him. The secretary chose not to, sniffing in despair of the youth of the warband. Kieran backed out as if he had been confronted by a dangerous animal.

"We're doomed," Kieran stated as he closed the door behind them.

"Why? He seemed like he knew what he was doing," Andras said.

"Aye, but I think it's my destiny tae be killed by a secretary," Kieran said. "Come on, I'm starving!" He led the way to the kitchens where another surprise awaited.

"Kieran," the kitchen maid greeted him. "Oh, dear, I didn't know there would be two of you," she said as she saw Andras.

"The Captain must have forgotten," Kieran said. "But that's all right. Jenny always gives me more than enough. We can easily stretch it tae two," he said.

"I think there are still some leftovers from dinner too," the maid said. They sat down a few minutes later to a varied meal. After the day's riding, Andras found that he was hungry. Kieran unabashedly chatted with the serving girl while they ate in order to catch up on any gossip he missed while out on patrol. Andras listened as they threw names about. It seemed Kieran knew everyone in the castle. Kieran knew Andras wasn't the most popular around the warbands and, feeling sorry for him, worked him effortlessly into the conversation.

It was another hour before they left to return to the barracks. There, Andras was confronted by an angry Captain Pedr.

"Andras! Just where do you think you have been?" he shouted. Any activity in the barracks halted. Andras began to answer but the captain cut him off. "Disappearing without a word and returning well after hours? What do you think you were doing exactly?" Pedr demanded.

"Easy, Captain," Kieran cut in smoothly. "Captain Corin sent him out on a run and must have forgotten tae tell you. I met up with Andras on my way in and we've just been getting dinner," he said. Captain Pedr glared at Kieran who returned his gaze unperturbed. Captain Pedr cleared his throat.

"Very well," he said. "Continue."

"Thank you, sir," Kieran said. "Oh, and speaking of not telling people, who is that wee devil in the Captain's office?" he asked. Uproarious laughter greeted his question and even Andras smiled.

"So you've met Gerralt then?" Llewellyn asked.

"That I have!" Kieran returned. "Near scared the life out of me. Andras could tell you."

"Aye, he's been handing out threats all afternoon. Seems neither the Captain nor us have any idea of proper etiquette," Llewellyn said.

"Doesn't surprise me," Kieran said. "I saw the look in his eyes. He seemed about ready tae stab me with a quill pen, and this beautiful life would have come tae an untimely, and messy, end!"

There was helpless laughter all around.

"Seems a bit dramatic even for you, Kieran," Dylan gasped for breath.

"Och, what's life without a little exaggeration?" Kieran asked with another laugh.

"Get on with you!" Bran shook his head. Kieran bowed mockingly and turned to go. Andras stopped him.

"Thanks," was all he said.

"Careful, Andras. People might think you care," Kieran said with a merry grin and disappeared.

"You sure you're not coming, sir?" Llewellyn asked.

"Yes, and this is probably the worst decision of my life," Corin replied. Llewellyn laughed. As Corin's second-in-command in the patrol, he was leading the men back to the forest until Corin would be able to join them.

"He's quite a terror, that Gerralt," Llewellyn said. "I thought he was going to take my head as a warning to all those who don't knock."

"You should probably tell Martin before he gets here," Corin commented.

"Oh look, here he comes now," Llewellyn said. Corin half turned to see Gerralt advancing with an irritated expression on his face.

"Lleu give me strength! Get going before I change my mind," Corin said. Llewellyn laughed again and saluted as he wheeled his horse. The patrol clattered out of the courtyard and through the gate. Corin took one look at Gerralt and fervently wished he could go with them.

It seemed like days later when Corin crossed the courtyard again that afternoon. He met Mera at the doors of the stables.

"Everything all right?" he asked at her slightly confused expression.

"Yes, I suppose. I was just convinced that I wanted to go for a ride," she said.

"Isn't that odd?" Corin mused.

"What?"

"Well, I just happened to mention to a certain unnamed person that I was planning to do the same," Corin said, shooting a glance back at the castle. Mera clapped a hand to her mouth.

"Oh my...she...that's why...oh I'm so sorry!" she stammered.

"Let's just say that 'subtle' is not a trademark of the fates," Corin commented wryly. Mera giggled. It seemed they both had a very clear idea of what was happening but neither seemed to mind too much.

"Well, then, noble sir, shall we defy the fates and ride out despite this purely chance encounter?" she asked solemnly.

"Your bravery astounds me, kind lady," Corin replied, equally solemn. "That sounds like an excellent idea," he added with a grin.

They rode slowly along, talking and laughing as they got to know one another better. Mera and her brother were alike in many ways. But she was quieter and more reserved than her outgoing brother. And her gentleness offset his warrior spirit. The children in the castle loved her, often faking illnesses so that she would "treat" them. With an unfailing sense of humor she would play along with them, giving the "sick" or "injured" child a dose of medicine made mostly from sugar.

"So, what's your favorite part about being back here in the castle?" Mera asked.

"My favorite part? Probably the food," Corin said.

"The food?" Mera laughed.

"Aye, after years of not knowing when you'll get your next meal or being faced with the threat of your brother's cooking, it's nice to know you can get a decent meal when you want," Corin said.

"I suppose that's true," Mera agreed. "Is Martin's cooking really that bad?"

"It almost legendary through the warband and not in a good way."

"What about you? Can you cook?"

"I can put a meal together."

"You make that sound like a bad thing." Mera raised her eyebrow.

"Since I was in Calorin for so long, I got used to their food. I still use the spices. Just don't tell any of the cooks. I'm sure I'd get in trouble," Corin laughed.

"Did it take a lot of getting used to? Being back here?"

"I still am, a little," he admitted. Karif came flying in to take his perch on Corin's shoulder. Since Gerralt had taken up residence in the office, the hawk had vacated his usual place on the windowsill. Mera watched as Corin chided the hawk for this fact as if he were human. Karif simply chirped back at Corin and settled down on his shoulder. Corin seemed to accept this answer.

"That's as close to an apology as I'll get," he said.

Mera laughed. "Does he usually do that?"

"Not usually. Mostly he just looks smug."

"I didn't know birds could look smug."

"Trust me. If you hang around long enough, you'll see it."

Two days later, Corin bid farewell to a disapproving Gerralt and, accompanied by Will, left the castle to join his patrol.

Chapter 13

Aiden woke the next morning as the first rays of sunlight slipped in through the windows. Breakfast was subdued as the defenders cast glances at their champion. As Skive rebandaged his shoulder, Aiden met with Jamey, Tam, and Blair.

"We decided Tam and Blair will accompany you," Jamey said. "Myself, Cai, and Rona will be waiting at the doors."

"Sounds like a plan," Aiden approved. After Skive finished, Aiden followed Tam and Blair up the stairs.

"If you're fighting our battle, we'd better make you look like a Champion," Tam said. They entered the chamber where Aiden first met Laird Gòrdan. Aiden changed into fresh clothes. Black pants and a short sleeved blue tunic. He laced up the sturdy boots that had served him in Calorin. The plated brigandine was too heavy for his shoulder so he donned the plain, thick leather tunic. After he buckled on his vambraces, Tam and Blair began to apply the war paint the Clans had worn into battle since before they arrived in Braeton.

Three diagonal marks on his right cheek signified he was the third son of a Laird. An intricate spiral on his left denoted his role as Champion. One line went from his forehead down his nose and chin and there were slanted marks around his eyes. Six bands were painted in the deep blue paint around his left arm.

Three went above the wildcat tattoo and three below it. Blair painted the complex spirals and symbols on his right arm. On the back of his left hand, Tam marked the ancient rune for strength. Aiden dipped his finger into the paint and marked a letter in Calorin on his right hand. When asked what it was, he replied, "He was a friend of mine. It's tae remind me that this time I can'nae fail."

To finish, Tam marked a four pointed star at the base of Aiden's throat and traced over the same tattoo on his forearm. Aiden sharpened his remaining sword and buckled it over his right shoulder as Tam and Blair applied the woad to themselves. Aiden armed himself with his daggers as they finished. Tam drew the claymore that Aiden was to use and Blair ran his finger, coated with woad, down the blood channel on both sides.

Finally, everything was finished. Blair exited the room, leaving the brothers together.

"You ready?" Tam asked.

"As I'll ever be," Aiden replied. "Look, Tam, if everything goes wrong, you take charge after me."

"I'm praying nothing goes wrong," Tam said. "Just remember what Diarmad said when he built this place: 'In times of trouble, a champion shall rise up and Scodra shall not fall.'"

"I hope he was right," Aiden said. He pulled Tam into a hug. "It was good tae see you again, little brother," he said. Tam took a deep breath as they stepped apart and took up the claymore, carrying it as they left the room.

It was almost noon. Tam and Aiden halted at the main doors. The defenders gathered behind them, quietly wishing him luck. Looking at them, Aiden realized he was frightened. Not for himself but for what would happen to them if he were killed.

"Be careful, Aiden." Rona reached out to him.

"Sure, it's easier than it looks," he replied with a smile as he squeezed her hand. Cai and Jamey swung the doors open and, flanked by Tam and Blair, Aiden descended the stairs out into the vast compound where Adalwulf and Torsten awaited, backed by their army. Aiden took the claymore from Tam.

"Lleu help me," he whispered and stepped forward to meet his enemy. Silence fell over the Durnians and Braetons as they began to circle each other.

Torsten carried an axe in one hand and the other twirled a rope to which was attached a wicked-looking pronged hook. To Aiden's extreme disgust, Torsten was carrying Aiden's other sword across his back.

"So at last we meet," Torsten sneered.

"You miss me?" Aiden asked.

"This is the last time I will have to endure your insolent tongue!" Torsten said.

"Well then, we're even. I'm tired of seeing your ugly face," Aiden taunted.

Torsten charged with a roar. Aiden brought his sword up to block the axe and jumped to the side to avoid the flailing hook. Torsten pressed in and Aiden steadily retreated, blocking, ducking, and weaving. They circled around and around. Suddenly Torsten reversed his axe. He jumped in close and drove the handle into Aiden's injured shoulder. Aiden smashed the pommel of the claymore into Torsten's face. The Durnian reeled back, flicking out with the rope. The hook caught on Aiden's side and Torsten yanked hard. It cut through the leather and skin before coming free. A low gasp came from the defenders as Aiden stumbled a few steps and the Durnians cheered.

Ignoring the pain, Aiden attacked Torsten, forcing him to defend with the axe. Then, with an expert stroke, Aiden sheared the axe blade from its handle. Torsten threw away the ruined weapon and drew the sword, spitting out blood as he did. They closed on each other again, blades flashing as they strove back and forth across the arena. The hook flicked out again and wrapped around Aiden's left arm just above the elbow. Torsten pulled hard, embedding the hook further into Aiden's arm.

Aiden dropped the claymore and drew his sword, bringing the keen edge slashing down across the rope. They reeled away from each other. Fighting against the pain, Aiden twirled his sword, rejoicing at its familiar weight. The wound in his shoulder forgotten, Aiden charged Torsten again. They fought like demons and within the space of a few seconds Aiden had inflicted several wounds on Torsten.

The earthen courtyard was churned up as they strove. Blood flowed and mingled with the dirt. Aiden battered the sword from Torsten's grasp but staggered. Torsten grabbed an axe from an onlooking Durnian and advanced. Aiden saw Torsten thundering toward him through blurred vision. Reflexes, honed by years in the Phoenix Guard, overrode the burning pain from his wounds. He launched into a backward roll and came up on one knee, grasping the sword firmly in both hands. Torsten couldn't stop himself in time and the blade plunged through him. The axe fell from Torsten's lifeless hands. The effort of withdrawing the sword suddenly seemed too much and Aiden let go of the handle as Torsten crumpled to the ground.

Then Tam cried out a warning and Aiden turned to see Adalwulf advancing toward him, sword in hand. Aiden scrambled toward the claymore lying nearby but Adalwulf reached him sooner, kicking him savagely in the chest and slamming him to the ground. Tam and Blair drew their claymores and moved to help but were confronted by Durnians.

Aiden reached for the claymore lying to his left but Adalwulf's foot slammed into his wounded arm, breaking the hook. Aiden screamed in pain.

"I underestimated you, Aiden," Adalwulf said softly, placing his foot on Aiden's chest. "Tell me, how does it feel to know that you failed? I'll kill them all, you know. Starting with your father and brother. And then the way will be clear for the North to fall."

"I underestimated you too. You're a bigger coward than I thought! You don't even honor your own terms!" Aiden gritted.

"Oh, perhaps I did not make myself clear. You are only the victor if you survive," Adalwulf said, raising his sword. Trapped and scrabbling for a weapon, Aiden's right hand found the point of a broken arrow. He clutched the shaft and plunged it into Adalwulf's leg. The Durnian staggered back, freeing Aiden. He grabbed the claymore as Tam and Blair broke through the Durnians with help from several other warriors. Blair helped Aiden stand and half-carried him up the stairs. Jamey cut a swath from his cloak, folded it and pressed it to Aiden's side. Rona steadied him as he leaned against the wall.

"What do we do now?" she asked with a tremor in her voice. Aiden glanced at the Durnian army beginning to advance as they beat their weapons against their shields.

"Get inside. I'm afraid this might be the part where we die," he said. They had begun to move inside the doors when a warrior came dashing down the stairs.

"Wait, sir! You won't believe this!" the man gasped. Stepping outside, the warrior cupped his hands to his mouth and let lose a thunderous war cry that halted the Durnians. "Haway the Clan!"

Then, to the amazement of the defenders, it was answered.

"Haway! Canich tae Scodra!"

"That's Ranulf!" Tam cried. New hope flared in the Braetons. The Durnians had halted in confusion. Adalwulf desperately shouted orders to counterattack the new threat he could hear coming. Even so, they were caught off guard when Ranulf, Artair, and two hundred warriors painted for battle charged through the wide gates. Tam led the defenders into the battle as Rona stayed at the top of the stairs with Aiden.

Aiden saw a small group of Durnians led by Adalwulf making a determined push for the gate. He felt the old battle rage in his blood and took up the claymore before leaping down the stairs and fighting toward the gate.

To give him credit, Adalwulf was no coward. He saw plainly that he was beaten. He would return to Durna for more men and finish this as he was ordered. He gathered as many men around him as he could and made for the gate. His plans were dashed at the sight of the figure standing in the gateway.

"You're outnumbered once again, Aiden," Adalwulf said.

"I don't want tae fight you," Aiden said. "You answer tae him."

Adalwulf turned and saw Ranulf standing behind them. Aiden addressed the other Durnians. "If you boys want tae make a run for it, then Blair and I will give you a sporting chance," he said as the cold-eyed warrior stepped up beside him.

Hampered by his wounded leg and faced by the anger of Ranulf, Adalwulf didn't stand a chance. None of his men made it out of the gates alive either. Those who were not killed threw down their weapons and surrendered. Soon, it was all over. The warriors raised their shouts of victory as Ranulf mounted the steps of the fortress. All fell silent as Laird Gòrdan came out. Everyone strained to hear the words that passed between him and Ranulf. Then, Ranulf bowed to his father and they formally clasped hands. Laird Gòrdan nodded for Ranulf to continue and his son turned to the warriors.

"There is one we should be honoring. The man who began this fight and the Champion who held Scodra against all odds. Aiden!" Ranulf said.

Blair was practically holding Aiden upright but Aiden straightened as he heard Ranulf call. They slowly approached the stairs and Aiden struggled to stay erect as all eyes turned to him. He halted at the base of the stairs and gazed up at the imposing figure. Aiden knew his next actions would decide the fate of Scodra. But Ranulf shook his head when Aiden looked to him. Summoning up his remaining strength, Aiden held the claymore out across both palms and looked to Laird Gòrdan.

"Your sword, my Laird, and the blood of your enemies," he said. Gòrdan descended the stairs. As he took the sword, thunderous cheers broke out once more.

"Aiden, can you ever forgive me? I'm so sorry! For everything," Laird Gòrdan said. Aiden realized he was crying and saw the tears in his father's eyes.

"Aye, I'm sorry too," he said.

Laird Gòrdan gathered him in an embrace returned by his son. Then the world spun and Aiden felt his father steady him. Ranulf lowered him to the ground and Tam called desperately for Skive. Jamey and Blair carried him inside and laid him on a table. Skive hurried up with his pouch of medicines. He opened Aiden's tunic and pushed up the shirt to expose his injured side. Ailsa brought hot water and bandages. Skive mixed a paste and, after washing the cuts, spread it over the wound and bandaged it.

Tam propped Aiden up, half conscious, as Skive looked at his arm. The hook had broken and the prongs were still embedded in his arm. Skive pulled a small flask from his bag, uncorked it, and poured some powder into it. He handed it to Tam.

"He needs to drink all of this. Hold him down," Skive ordered the others. Tam wrapped his arm firmly around Aiden's chest as he helped Aiden drink some of the liquid. Jamey braced Aiden's shoulder as Skive began removing a prong.

Aiden's whole arm erupted in pain and he stifled a scream. Jamey and Blair pinned him down to the table as he jerked away. Women hurried the children away and Laird Gòrdan gripped the edge of the table as he watched.

"That medicine hasn't taken hold yet. Just wait!" Blair said.

"If I wait he could lose his arm!" Skive said, his normally stoic face agitated and concerned. "Give him the rest, Tam!" he said. Skive waited until Aiden had drunk. "Aiden, I'm going to do it again. Are you ready?" he asked. Aiden nodded numbly, sweat beading his forehead. It took the three men's combined strength to hold him steady as Skive pulled again.

Skive reached for the second prong. By this time the medicine had dulled some of the pain radiating from the wound. After the second prong lay on the table, Skive paused. Aiden was trembling and Tam had both his arms wrapped around his brother.

"Let me give you some more medicine," Skive said.

"No, just finish!" Aiden gritted. Skive obeyed and pulled out the final prong. Aiden shuddered as it came free and Skive began the laborious process of cleaning and stitching his arm back together. At some point, Aiden lapsed mercifully into unconsciousness.

Rona gently washed the war paint from Aiden's face and arms. He still lay on the table. Skive wanted to wait before trying to move him. Rona felt a tug on her sleeve. She looked down and saw Brannan.

"Is he gonna be all right, Aunt Rona?" he asked.

"I hope so, Brannan," she replied.

"I want tae be like him when I grow up," Brannan said.

Rona smiled. "I think he'd like that," she said. A spasm of pain flickered over Aiden's face as he moved slightly. Brannan reached out and patted Aiden's hand.

"There, there, it's gonna be all right," he whispered to the sleeping warrior.

Chapter 14

Aiden woke to a sound he had not heard since returning to Scodra: the sound of children laughing floated through the open window. He was in his own bed, warmly covered against the cool air. By the light he guessed it was about mid-morning. Of more than that he was not sure. He did not know how much time had passed since the battle. He dimly remembered waking a few times from troubled dreams but there had been a comforting presence beside him. But for now, he was alone.

He abandoned any thought of trying to sit up. He could feel the bandage around his side. Looking down, he saw heavy bandages on his arm. The fiery pain of before had quieted to a dull ache and he was very relieved to find that he could move his hand and fingers. His shoulder had also been re-bandaged and someone had washed away the woad.

The door creaked open and Tam entered.

"You're finally awake!" he said, sitting down in a chair by the bed.

"Finally? How long has it been?" Aiden asked.

"Four days," Tam replied.

"Four days!" Aiden exclaimed. "What did I miss?"

"Not much. Davy and Artair escorted the rest of the Durnians tae the border. Some of the families have returned and everyone was concerned about you," Tam told him.

"Was it really that bad?"

"For the first two days. Skive was worried until your fever broke. How do you feel now?"

"Well, considering I feel like I'm held together by bandages, I guess I'm all right," Aiden replied. "How about you?"

"Composing my latest epic tae be sung at the feast in your honor when you're finally up and about." Tam grinned.

"Are you serious?" Aiden asked apprehensively.

"Oh, yes. Father insisted."

"How is he?" Aiden tentatively asked.

"He's fine. He's talked with the captains and most of the Clansmen tae apologize. Most seem willing enough tae forgive and get back tae normal. He's promised tae pass the torc tae Ranulf by the end of the year which helped smooth things over. He's hardly left your side the past few days," Tam replied seriously.

Aiden was silent. Then he asked, "Is Jamey still here?"

"No, he had a talk with Father and he left," Tam answered. Aiden's face darkened with anger. "It's not what you think, Danny!" Tam hastily reassured him. "Father pardoned him, but Jamey said he wanted tae go back tae his house for a few days."

"Why didn't you just say so in the first place?" Aiden exclaimed, very relieved.

"You weren't exactly giving me a chance, were you?" Tam retorted with a grin as Skive entered the room.

"I hope he was already awake, Tam," Skive said, somewhat disapprovingly.

"Yes, he was," Tam said. "After the threats you were handing out, no one dared come within fifty feet of that door."

"Good," Skive said. He helped Aiden slowly sit up so that he could change the bandages. Aiden winced when he saw his arm. It was still swollen and bruised and was a mass of stitches.

"You think that's bad? You should see your chest where Adalwulf kicked you," Tam remarked.

"I think I can feel it." Aiden put his hand to his aching chest, feeling another rough bandage under his shirt.

The skittering of claws announced the arrival of Illyria. She crouched by Skive and watched the door as her tail wagged slowly.

"The young ones chase her around all day, especially after Jamey left with his hound," Skive said. Brannan burst in leading Jean and another boy.

"You're awake! Aunt Rona made us tiptoe around so you wouldn't wake up, sleepy-head!" Brannan informed Aiden as he sat down on the bed.

"Oh really? Considering the noise you savages just made, I'm very grateful," Aiden replied.

Jean giggled as she clambered onto the bed. "You're funny. I like you," she said.

"Well, I'm flattered," Aiden said.

The third youngster looked up from where he was busily stroking Illyria. "You gonna come wiv us, Tam? You promised you'd play wiv us!"

"Of course! We'll go now," Tam said. "Apparently there was a debate on how their reenactment of 'Manachan's Bard' is supposed tae turn out, so my help was enlisted. Although I think they just want me tae play the part of the captured bard," Tam explained to Aiden. The furtive smiles and giggles that were exchanged more than confirmed his guess.

"You want tae come too, Danny?" Jean asked Aiden. Aiden was a little surprised at how fast his old nickname had caught on with everyone.

"We need a horse for Manachan," Donnan chimed in. Aiden laughed.

"I would love tae, but," he lowered his voice, "I don't think Skive will let me."

"Once your arm is healed, you can go play all you want," Skive said mock-seriously.

"See? But until then, you'll just have tae come and tell me about everything," Aiden told the children. Their eyes brightened.

"I'll bring you a flower too," Jean decided.

Brannan rolled his eyes. "Come on, Tam! We already made your dungeon by the lake!" he said, grabbing Tam's arm.

"Bye, Aiden. We'll be back if Manachan decides tae rescue me." Tam looked at Brannan who smiled back disarmingly.

"Bye, Danny!" Jean and Donnan shouted as they ran out of the room followed by Illyria.

"It's a little strange tae have people who barely know you care about you so much," Aiden said, thinking about what Tam had said.

"You are their champion. They won't forget what you did for them," Skive replied.

"It sounds as if they have you tae thank as well for keeping me in one piece," Aiden said. Skive simply inclined his head. "What are you going tae do now?" Aiden asked.

"I have been given permission to remain here for as long as I desire."

"Will you?"

"Perhaps. This is a good place," Skive said. "It would be hard to move on."

Aiden silently agreed. He had forgotten how much he had missed his home.

Business that could no longer be delayed prevented Gòrdan from visiting Aiden again. Ranulf joined him for the councils and began to help him sort through the business of the Clan that had long been hindered by Adalwulf. It was as if Gòrdan saw for the first time the steady head that Ranulf had. His son knew personally many of the problems that had plagued the Clan and now brought them gently to the surface for Gòrdan to address.

Before dinner he saw Ranulf take a woman's hand and pull her in for a kiss. *Brighde*, Gòrdan remembered. They looked happy together and he was aware again of just how much he had missed. Tam entered carrying a young girl on his back and there was a small boy latched onto his leg. The warrior, Douglas, laughed and detached the lad and Blair clapped Tam on the shoulder as he swung the girl down. Gòrdan was content to sit back and watch his people through the meal. His sons laughed together over something and Artair argued with another captain. Children stole sweets instead of eating the food in front of them. Husbands and wives, long separated, sat close to one another. Sounds of hundreds of conversations filled the room.

In the midst of it all, Gòrdan glanced to his right and saw the two empty chairs. He sipped at his drink. Aiden would live, but who knew where William was? He would rebuild this family. He excused himself from the table and left the hall as someone called for a song and Tam's clear tenor voice responded. Ranulf's deeper baritone joined and more and more voices added to the music. The song followed him as he mounted the stairs and came to Aiden's room. He knocked once and entered.

The fire burned and Aiden was awake. He was propped up against the pillows, his arm in a sling. A plate of food lay mostly untouched on the chair beside the bed. He looked up as Gòrdan entered.

"Sir." He tried to push himself more upright but Gòrdan stopped him.

"May I sit?" he asked. Aiden nodded and Gòrdan placed the plate on the chest by the bed. He saw the small figurine that guarded the plane.

"You used tae play with that constantly," Gòrdan said.

Aiden smiled tiredly. "You gave it tae me. I couldn't have been more than four," he said.

"I'm surprised you remember that," Gòrdan said. They paused. "How are you feeling?"

"Tired. Skive says I'll be all right," Aiden replied. "I don't really remember much." He hesitated. "They said you stayed with me."

"Yes," Gòrdan said. "I didn't…I couldn't let you go again."

"Father, I know in the past I've said some things—" Aiden began.

"It is I who should be apologizing," Gòrdan interrupted. "I'm the one who should be asking for forgiveness."

"Father—"

"Let me finish, Aiden. I pushed you too hard and let my temper get the better of me too easily when it came tae you."

"I wasn't exactly easy on you either."

"But you shouldn't have had tae go so far before I realized—"

"Running away was probably the best thing that I could have done. It gave me a chance tae learn what I needed. Nothing good would have come out of me staying," Aiden said seriously.

"I'm sorry that it was like that," Gòrdan said. "I'm sorry for the grief and pain I have caused you. I blamed myself every day after you left. I thought for sure that I would never see you again."

Aiden rubbed at his eyes. "And here I thought you had danced for joy." His mouth quirked and a laugh escaped Gòrdan.

"What can I do tae make amends?" Gòrdan asked.

Aiden shrugged and winced. "I'll stay if you'll have me and we can try tae start again," he said.

Gòrdan smiled. "I like the sound of that," he said.

Aiden paused a moment before broaching a new topic. "Tam said you spoke with Jamey. Thank you."

"It was the very least I could do for the lad. Another of my many mistakes," Gòrdan said. Aiden shifted and sank further back into the pillows. Gòrdan saw that he was tired. "You should rest. I'm sure Tam has told you of the plans for the feast," he said.

Aiden smiled. "Of course he did. Tam never could keep a secret," he said. Gòrdan laughed lightly and moved to the door. They heard the sounds of another song as he opened it.

"What is it?" Aiden asked as he nodded toward the sound.

"It is a song of homecoming." Gòrdan recognized the tune.

"It's been so long since I've heard any of them," Aiden said. Despite his previous words, Gòrdan could see that his son was sad at all he had missed during the years he had been away.

"I'll leave the door open then," Gòrdan said.

Aiden lay back after his father left and adjusted the sling. He felt as if a burden had been lifted by their conversation. The cautious understanding laid between them now would do for a start. The song ended and Tam began a slow ballad. Aiden closed his eyes and slipped into an untroubled slumber.

- -

A few days later, Aiden slowly descended the stairs. Skive had declared him healed enough to rise. With his continued recovery, preparations had begun for the celebratory feast.

Rona was busy in the kitchens. It was a maze of activity as cooks rushed around preparing food. Her attention was distracted as she saw the head cook, a large matronly woman named Morna, greet Aiden at the doors of the kitchen.

"Master Aiden! What can I do for you?" she asked.

"Just a wee bit of food tae tide me over until dinner," Aiden replied.

"Of course!" Morna said. She led him over to a table by the wall, near the open fire. "You're in time. I just pulled your favorite out of the oven." She left and Rona watched as she brought back a plate loaded down with a steaming meat pastie and a slab of bread and cheese.

"I suppose you'll want some ale as well?" Morna asked.

"No, ma'am, just the regular. It wouldn't be the same without it," Aiden replied. Morna smiled and left again. Rona's heart irritatingly skipped a beat or two when Aiden caught sight of her and smiled. She returned the smile and moved to greet him. He still looked a little pale and his arm was held in a sling.

"Just a wee bit of food?" Rona chided him.

"I'm absolutely starving," Aiden replied. "Besides, good food helps you heal faster. It's a well-known fact. Morna used tae feed me on the frequent occasion I missed a meal," he said. Morna came back with a tankard of milk.

"Morna, I think you've only gotten better," Aiden said as he began eating. "You don't know how many times I thought about you and your creations over the years."

"It's no wonder with that strange food they have in the South. And goodness knows what that Skive has been feeding you. He and the little ones were in here the other day cooking up something horrible," Morna clucked disapprovingly. "You remember you're always welcome down here? You're too thin," Morna fretted. Aiden nodded, a pathetic look on his face. "Will you have room for dessert?" Morna asked.

"This is more food than I'm used tae, but I'll try," Aiden said.

"Oh, you poor darling!" Morna exclaimed and hurried off to get him more food.

"You should be ashamed of yourself!" Rona exclaimed. "I'm fairly sure you just lied tae her!"

"No, I just wasn't entirely truthful. Rule number one, Rona: always make friends with the cook. I've never gone hungry," Aiden said.

"Why do I believe that? You are completely hopeless," Rona said.

"Thank you," Aiden said with a smile. Morna set down another plate with an oversized slice of apple spice cake and took away Aiden's already empty plate.

"Morna, you remembered how much I love this!" Aiden said appreciatively.

"I made one specially for you," Morna said.

"For me?" Aiden's voice caught theatrically. Rona rolled her eyes.

"Any time, Aiden. And bring that younger brother of yours too. He doesn't eat near enough either," Morna said.

"And just like that, I have free reign of the kitchens again," Aiden said as Morna left.

"And how many kitchens have you talked yourself intae?" Rona asked.

"Quite a few. I'm usually hungry."

"Are you looking forward tae the feast?"

"No, I'm rather dreading it."

"But it's for you."

"Exactly," Aiden said. He pushed his chair away from the table and rose. "Do I have you completely confused yet?"

"A little. Maybe I'll understand in time," Rona replied. He flashed a quick smile before leaving the kitchens. He didn't have a definite goal in mind. All he knew was that he wanted some fresh air. He walked slowly down the familiar hallways and let the memories rush back, some good and some bad.

He eventually came to the main hall where servants moved around cleaning and preparing. Some noticed him and greeted him with smiles. Blair and Douglas came through the open doors and caught sight of him.

"Aiden!" Douglas cried and they moved toward him. "I seem tae miss everything exciting around here," Douglas said, clasping Aiden's hand.

"Next time you can hold off the bloodthirsty horde and I'll go for help," Aiden said.

"On second thought," Douglas laughed.

"Glad tae see you're up," Blair said.

"Thanks," Aiden replied. "What's been going on the past few days?"

"I've been working my fingers tae the bone," Douglas said. Blair elbowed him in the stomach.

"The only thing you've been doing is avoiding work," Blair said. "They've got the main gates fixed and any damages tae the outside of the keep have been repaired."

"Aye, except for the windows," Douglas said.

"Laird Gòrdan didn't seem too happy with how many were broken," Blair said. "I do feel a bit bad about that."

"No, you don't," Douglas said.

"You're right, it was a little funny tae see him squirm," Blair said, then checked himself. "I'm sorry, Aiden," he said. Aiden had a slight smile; he could imagine it. He waved a hand dismissively.

"It's all right for now. I'm still getting used tae being on moderately good terms with him," he said.

"Speaking of that, I guess you should know that some of the old stories about you are resurfacing," Douglas said.

"Anything good?" Aiden asked.

"I've made it my duty tae hear every one of them, so you can rest assured that no, none of them are particularly good," Douglas replied. Aiden smiled wryly.

"Good tae see some things haven't changed much around here," he said. "What about the dead?"

"They were laid tae rest the night after the battle. You missed the Lament. We all thought we might have tae play it again for you," Blair said.

"I'm thankful you didn't," Aiden replied. "I'm sorry I missed it. I would like tae visit."

"Are you up for the walk?" Douglas asked.

"Probably not, but don't tell anyone," Aiden said. He and the two warriors left the keep and headed toward the far side of the lake. It was further than it looked but Aiden was enjoying the warm, summer air too much to complain.

The burial grounds of the Clan were silent under the whispering trees. Blair and Douglas halted by newly dug graves. There were more than Aiden remembered. Blair stood in front of one. Douglas rested a hand on his shoulder.

"I see your mother's been here," he said, indicating the flowers that rested on the grave.

"Aye, and my sisters. They arrived a few days ago," Blair replied.

Aiden listened in silence. There were more tokens on the graves: memoirs to the fallen warriors from their families. He knew there was one more grave that he should visit but he couldn't bring himself to. Not yet.

Their conversation returned as they left the grounds and neared the keep. Aiden saw the figure waiting in the gateway and smiled.

"You've only been up for a few hours and you're already in trouble." Ranulf shook his head.

"What can I say? Some things never change," Aiden grinned.

Ranulf laughed. "Come on. Skive's been looking for you and you've already been tae the kitchens, I hear."

"I'm just trying to get back tae normal, that's all," Aiden said.

Ranulf shoved him lightly toward the keep. "Get on with you!"

The next day was a haze of anticipation. As the sun moved to the edge of the western sky, Clan Canich gathered at the tables set out in the open courtyard. The laden trestles were set in a wide rectangle with a fire burning in the middle. As everyone gathered, Ranulf came forward and threw a folded piece of the blue plaid into the flames. The Clan stood in silence to honor the fallen warriors and then the feast began in earnest.

As the sun finally set, torches were lit and candles on the tables sprang to life. Aiden sat at the head table with his brothers and father. Artair and the other captains sat with them. Jamey had come back to Scodra for the celebration and sat at one of the lower benches with Skive and Blair.

Aiden sat back and watched the people surrounding the tables. Everything was a picture of happiness.

"Anything wrong?" Ranulf asked him.

"No, it's just been so long since I've been part of anything like this," Aiden replied.

"Well, then, welcome home," Ranulf said. Aiden laughed infectiously.

"What are you laughing about?" Tam asked.

"Nothing. I'm just happy," Aiden said.

"It's about time!" Tam grinned and Ranulf and Aiden laughed harder.

"Oi! Tam! Are you going tae drink all night or will you give us a song?" a warrior called.

"I might, Macraith, if you're still slim enough tae dance!" Tam shouted back through the laughter. Tam vaulted over the table and took up his pipes. At the first trill, the tables were vacated as men and women filled the space between the tables with a whirling dance. Tam allowed them no rest and as soon as he finished, he began another tune. The Clanspeople breathlessly found new partners and began again. Jamey asked a blushing young woman and Blair escorted her sister into the ring. Jean and Brannan twirled each other around in a corner. Ranulf found Brighde and whirled her effortlessly into the dance. Rona danced with her brother who had returned with Ranulf and Artair.

Aiden sat by his father for he had been strictly prohibited from joining in because of his still-healing wounds. Truthfully though, he was glad to have the excuse.

"How much longer until you're free of that sling?" Laird Gòrdan asked.

"Skive hasn't told me, but hopefully not much longer. I'm not very patient with it," Aiden replied. He hated the restrictiveness of the bandages as well as the forced inactivity since he was used to riding and fighting constantly.

"I wish your mother were here tae see you again," Laird Gòrdan said.

"I would have like tae be able tae tell her good-bye at least," Aiden said.

"She'd be proud of you. Just like I am," his father said. Aiden only nodded, feeling his eyes smart. *It must be the smoke*, he told himself.

Tam played another five songs and then surrendered the bagpipes to Macraith as the dancers collapsed onto the benches. Tam took up a small, flat drum and, as Macraith began to play, he stroked time on the drum. As soon as they had the strong marching tune, Tam began to sing. The warriors joined in, stomping every third beat to the old battle song.

Song followed song and then, as the moon took its place in the sky, Tam took up the bagpipes. A woman stood and sang the Clan's Lament as he played. After the last notes faded into the night and a respectful silence was observed, Tam began to sing. To Aiden's slight discomfort, it was the retelling of the siege of Scodra, the raising of the Clan, the prominent part he had played and his fight as Champion. As Tam finished, the Clan rose and cheered their acclaim. The warriors raised their swords in a salute to Aiden.

"What are you gonna play next, Tam?" Brannan asked as it finally quieted.

"Och, give the laddie a break, ye wee terror!" Macraith said. "I bet I can out fiddle you and all the little ones, eh?" Brannan and the young children whooped in excitement as Macraith unpacked his fiddle. He began a merry reel and the children danced, effortlessly keeping time.

Tam sat down on the bench and leaned against the table. Aiden brought him a drink and sat next to him.

"How do you do it?" Aiden asked, impressed with his brother's skill.

Tam shrugged. "I don't know. I've always felt like it's a part of me," he replied. "What about you, Danny? Do you sing?"

"No, I haven't had much tae sing about," Aiden replied. "And no, you won't get me tae," he said.

Tam laughed. "We'll see," he said.

Jamey and Blair joined them. "Now that you're not playing, Tam, there's several young ladies who want tae dance with you," Jamey said, grinning.

"Och, I don't know, Jamey, you looked like you were keeping them occupied." Tam smirked. They laughed.

"Aye, I'm trying tae hide from little Jean right now. She told me I *had* tae dance with her," Jamey said.

It only took Jean a few minutes to find Jamey and Tam. The small girl ran up accompanied by Donnan.

"Tam, play 'The Frog's Reel' so Jamey and I can dance," she said.

"Right now?" Tam asked.

"Of course, silly," Donnan spoke up.

"If you can help me up, I'll play it," Tam said. Jean and Donnan grabbed his hands and pulled. Their faces twisted with effort as they tried to move Tam.

"No fair! You're too big!" Donnan muttered. Aiden tipped a wink to Jamey and, as the children pulled again, they shoved Tam forward.

"Ha! We got you up! Now you hafta play!" Jean said triumphantly. Tam conceded defeat.

"Come on, me darlin'!" Jamey said, sweeping up a giggling Jean.

"We'll make sure Tam plays it. Right, Donnan?" Blair said. He and the young boy marched Tam off to where he took up the bagpipes again. Rona came up and sat next to Aiden.

"It's not so bad, is it?" she asked.

"We must endure it," he replied, unsuccessfully attempting to keep a solemn face.

"Yes, it's a hard, terrible life you lead now, isn't it?" Rona said.

"Och, as always," he said. She nudged him sharply in the ribs. "Beautiful and cruel you are!" he exclaimed. Rona adopted a lofty look but couldn't hold it for long.

"So what now?" she asked. "No dragons tae slay or helpless maidens tae rescue?"

Aiden shrugged. "I don't know. I've got some catching up tae do though," he glanced over to where his brothers and Jamey stood.

Lit by the torches and the brilliant full moon, the feast continued long into the night.

Chapter 15

Corin absentmindedly tapped the heel of his boot against the chair as he wrote. Gerralt cleared his throat thunderously. The noise startled Corin so much that he jerked violently and broke the tip of the quill. He bit back a flow of Calorin and glared at Gerralt. Unperturbed, the secretary stared frostily back.

"Didn't your mother teach you it isn't polite to curse?" an amused voice asked.

Corin turned his glare to Martin who stood in the doorway.

"I'm going down to the training grounds. You coming?" Martin asked.

"Maybe later. I still have some reports to look over," Corin said.

"Are you a soldier or a scholar?" Martin asked. "Gerralt can take care of it. I'm sure he's fully capable."

Gerralt sniffed in agreement. That decided it for Corin. He grabbed his weapons hanging from the back of the chair and stalked from the room followed by a smiling Martin.

"Even during the war you weren't this stressed," Martin said, firing an arrow and nodding in satisfaction as it hit the center of the target.

"Gerralt's been more zealous recently with his use of 'your highness' and 'sire,'" Corin said, aiming to match Martin's shot.

"Someone actually using your titles? We can't have that, can we?" Martin said, putting an arrow into the second ring of the target.

"Shut up!" Corin replied, sending his arrow to land beside Martin's.

"Well, technically you could fire him, couldn't you?" Martin asked, shooting again.

"Yes, but as much as I hate to admit it, he keeps a good handle on things, especially when I'm gone."

"Or maybe Darrin is trying to get you to acknowledge your exalted position," Martin suggested.

"I have seriously considered it," Corin said, grimacing as his arrow landed further from Martin's than he wanted.

"You really think he'd do that?" Martin asked. Corin raised an eyebrow at him. "You're right. He would," Martin agreed. "Did you hear they're holding the Autumn Festival again this year?"

"Aye. Darrin mentioned it the other day. He wants to invite the Clans," Corin said as he released an arrow.

"This will be your first in a few years, won't it?" Martin said.

"Aye, last time we were still racing ponies," Corin said with a smile.

"Trey still wins the horse races, but Zephyr could easily beat that mare of his."

"Maybe, but as soon as that big lump of a horse smells a race he gets so excited that he wears himself out before we even start," Corin said. Martin laughed and sighted down another shaft. His next question surprised Corin.

"So, what have you done to my sister?" he asked. He hid a grin as Corin's arrow flew wide of the target.

"What?" he asked, startled.

"She mentioned you at least four times this morning," Martin said. He laughed again as Corin seemed lost for an answer. "And it's the happiest she's looked in a while."

"So...?" Corin asked questioningly.

"Of course I don't mind!" Martin said. "For some reason she seems to like you." He studied the target as he prepared to shoot again. "All right, I've given you an easy shot that you can't miss." He smirked as he stepped away.

"I'm not going to hear the end of this, am I?" Corin asked ruefully as he shot.

"Of course not!" Martin said cheerfully. "What kind of a friend would I be?"

"Gerralt, how can I help you?" Darrin asked as the secretary entered his study.

"I just need a few signatures, your highness." Gerralt presented several letters to Darrin. He looked around wistfully as he waited for the prince to finish. He missed the rich furnishings of the castle offices. The small study in the barracks contained only the bare minimum.

"How do you like your new position?" Darrin asked. Having heard his brother's rather passionate opinion, he was curious to hear what Gerralt would say.

"Getting a mule to move would be easier than getting any work done! 'I have a system,' he says! All I see are hopeless piles of letters and reports. He hardly stays long enough to get anything done!" Gerralt began somewhat irately, and then remembered whom he was talking to. "Your pardon, my lord."

Darrin waved him off. "Gerralt, he's not used to any of this and he doesn't have the greatest store of patience."

Gerralt's sniff indicated that he had noticed. "Perhaps. But if he did rush off to the forest every chance he gets and then stay for who knows how long and, not only that, but he insists on leaving with anyone who might need something, so he's hopelessly behind in the work!" Gerralt fumed politely.

"Corin might be a prince, but the Hawk Flight is who he is," Darrin told Gerralt. "Nothing will ever change that and wild horses couldn't drag him away from the men under his command."

"But all of the warbands are under his command!" Gerralt protested.

"Exactly. Once you see that, you'll understand him better," Darrin said. Gerralt sniffed. He didn't believe in "getting to know" one's obvious superiors, even if they didn't act like it.

"I've ignored you all day. What do you need?" Corin asked Darrin as he entered the study without knocking, a habit which grated on Gerralt's nerves especially since it seemed to extend to all of Corin's men. Corin stopped when he saw Gerralt. His secretary gathered up his papers and exchanged a frosty glance with Corin as he left the room.

"Don't give me that look," Corin said to Darrin. "I don't know why you assigned him to help me."

Despite himself, Gerralt stopped outside the door.

"Because he's a good influence on you," Darrin hid a smile.

"I knew it," Corin said. "But he's built my character quite enough, thanks." Darrin chuckled. "Come on, Darrin. I'm never going to be any good with all these titles. I'd be perfectly happy just being a captain."

"But when we first saw each other again you didn't want to be the captain."

"Don't change the subject. You know what I mean."

"You're one of the few people I would entrust with the job."

"Well, then, let the other person do it."

"Martin blatantly refused," Darrin said. Corin groaned in frustration. "Look, if you want I can replace Gerralt."

Outside, Gerralt held his breath as Corin paused before replying.

"No, let him stay. He manages everything well, despite the fact that we irritate each other," Corin said. Gerralt was a little surprised. He had expected to be dismissed at once. *Maybe he should find out more about the prince.* But he dismissed the thought and left. After all, there was still work to be done. In the study, Corin and Darrin had turned to another subject.

"An official messenger is being sent to Clans Gunlon and Strowen for the festival. It might be easier if you sent a messenger to Clan Dyson," Darrin said.

"We'd get there quicker," Corin commented. "Kara's in the middle of her run. I'll send Kieran."

"Have you heard anything about the state of Clan Canich?" Darrin asked. Corin shook his head.

"Brian would've told us. I asked him to keep us informed, mainly for Will's sake." Corin referred to the captain of the small force that Clan Dyson kept to patrol the border. The Clan had been an ally of the Hawk Flight in the war and so the two sides kept frequent contact.

"If anything has changed with the Clan, have Lord Dandin forward the message on," Darrin said.

"What about Clan Mavor?" Corin asked.

"Last I heard from Lord Colwyn and Clan Gunlon, there's a small war going on between Clan Mavor and the neighboring tribes across the mountains. We'll send the invitation but I don't know if they'll come," Darrin said.

"How soon do you want Kieran to leave?"

"As soon as possible," Darrin said.

Corin nodded. "I'll let him know."

As Corin stepped outside the castle, Karif swooped in to land on his shoulder. The hawk butted him gently on the cheek.

"Where've you been hiding recently?" Corin asked the bird. Karif cocked his head secretively. "Be that way then," Corin said. The hawk nipped at his ear. "I know. We'll only be here for a few more days. And you might as well come back and get used to Gerralt because he's not leaving anytime soon," Corin admonished. Karif ruffled his feathers and settled more securely on Corin's shoulder as he went to find Kieran.

The Braeton was out in an open field by the training grounds working a young horse. Corin saw them on the far side of the field. Clan Gunlon was renowned for its horse masters and, even though he was still young, Kieran was no exception. He had taken a scruffy and bad-tempered horse that no one else had wanted and had begun to train it. His expectations were more than met by the talented horse and Kieran was thoroughly enjoying the challenge it brought.

Corin put his fingers to his mouth and gave a piercing whistle. Kieran turned the horse and nudged it to a gallop. They thundered to a stop in front of Corin. Kieran jumped from the saddle and threw a salute as he greeted his captain.

"And how's the unholy terror today?" Corin asked.

"Och, as lively as ever, sir," Kieran grinned. "I decided tae name him Taran. Though Kara objected tae his having a hero's name. He only let her stay on for about five minutes the other day."

"He looks like a good runner. But other than that, I don't know what you see in him, Kieran."

"Aye, he's not much tae look at, but he's got a fire in him. He'll carry you until you both die," Kieran said. He dug an apple slice out of his pocket and gave it to Taran. The horse nipped at Kieran's hand as he finished chewing. Kieran slapped its nose. "What'd I tell you about that? I'll give you another when I'm good and ready!" he said. Taran glared balefully at Kieran but stood quietly by.

"I need you to run a message to Clan Dyson for Darrin," Corin said.

"This about the Festival, sir?"

"Aye, I said you'd get it there faster than anyone he's got," Corin said.

"You can bet your life," Kieran replied. "I could ride circles around those shabby excuses for riders."

"You leave tomorrow," Corin said.

"Grand! I've been wanting tae try Taran out on a longer run. Do I come back here, sir, or continue on my route in the forest?" Kieran asked.

"If you want to be stuck with Taran for two weeks then you can go ahead and start your run," Corin said.

"I might do that. I'm sure Gwennyd won't mind. That horse has gotten too fond of his oats," Kieran said. He rolled down his sleeves and picked up his sword that lay nearby. "Since I'm leaving a few days early, is there anything else I'll be taking, sir?"

"Not yet. I'll send any other letters or dispatches with Llewellyn when they leave."

"Staying behind again, sir?"

"For a few days."

"Och, I'm not sure how you do it, Captain."

Corin laughed. "Me either, Kieran," he said. "I heard you stood up for Andras the other day?"

"Aye, just until he learns that Captain Pedr's bark is worse than his bite," Kieran replied, rubbing Taran's forehead. "I don't think it'll be too much longer before he figures everything out."

"Do you ever have anything bad to say about people?"

"Och, I've got plenty tae say, but what's the point?"

"You're a better man than any of us."

"I'm not sure about that," Kieran said. "But if you want tae think that, then I won't stop you," he said cheekily.

Corin laughed. "Darrin will have the letter you're to take. You can get it from him when you're ready to leave."

"Yes, sir." Kieran saluted before mounting Taran again and riding back to Kingscastle.

Chapter 16

Aiden paced restlessly. Skive had just left after rebandaging his arm. The wound in his side was all but mended, but Aiden's arm seemed to refuse to heal. Aiden tugged at the sling in frustration. Skive had prohibited most activities which left Aiden little to do but prowl the fortress. He knew every inch of the wooden keep and the courtyards and he was bored. Aiden looked out the window at the forest that had done nothing but call to him for the last few days. He held a short debate with himself. What could it hurt? He could use some trouble.

Aiden took up his knives, wishing he could use his swords again. He left his cloak behind. It was the height of summer and the days were wonderfully warm. He left the room and went down to the stables. It had been almost a month since the battle and Scodra had gradually changed. More and more of the Clan had returned and the valley was bursting with life. The fields were now well tended and the compound rang with activity. Everyone seemed to know Aiden by name and often stopped him to talk.

Aiden didn't usually mind. He'd done the same in Gelion and Calorin. He enjoyed getting to know every part of the place he lived. But today, he wanted to get away. Narak's stall was empty and a stable boy stopped beside him.

"We turned him out early this morning, sir," he said. "He's in the lower paddock."

Aiden smiled. This couldn't have worked out better.

"Should I get him for you, sir?" the boy asked.

"No, that's fine," Aiden said. He took down Narak's bridle. The boy's eyes widened.

"But—" he began to protest. Aiden held a finger to his lips and winked conspiratorially. The stable boy subsided with his own grin. He and all the young lads idolized Aiden. He wouldn't say a word.

Aiden left the stables and passed unhindered through the main gates. He quickened his pace, reaching the paddocks within a few minutes. Narak was happily frolicking with another horse and playing a confusing game of tag. He halted at Aiden's whistle and neighed a loud greeting as he charged the fence. Aiden's laugh and accompanying smack sent the stallion tearing around the paddock with head and tail held high. Aiden slipped into the paddock and waited. Narak came to a stop a few feet away from Aiden and snorted in excitement. Aiden took a step and Narak danced away. Aiden dodged toward him, sending him on another exuberant gallop. Aiden waited, and the process began again. Narak seemed more than content to play and wear himself out, so Aiden happily obliged. Almost half an hour later, Aiden sat on the fence while Narak took an extended roll in the thick grass. The stallion finally stood and came up to Aiden, nuzzling him gently.

"I know. I've missed you too," Aiden said. He fed Narak some carrots taken from the stables. Narak munched contentedly. Aiden took the bridle from the fence post where he had left it and slid off the fence. Narak obligingly lowered his head and Aiden put the bridle on and brushed off Narak's back with his hand before leading him out of the paddock. Narak sniffed at Aiden's sling.

"You're going to have to go easy on me today," Aiden told him, using the bottom rung to help him mount. Narak sensed his master was not the same as usual and stepped out slowly. Aiden urged him on and entered the forest. They spent the afternoon wandering up and down paths. Aiden had spent great amounts of time in the forest as a young boy with his brothers and Jamey. It was one of the things he missed most during his time away. He finally stopped and slid down from Narak. The stallion sneezed and rubbed his nose on Aiden.

"Are you trying to give me away? These were clean clothes," Aiden reprimanded. He sat down on a fallen log and Narak nosed at the ground. Aiden brushed off his clothes as best as he could. New clothes had been made for him. He had grown used to the looser comfort of the Calorin style and had finally persuaded the seamstress to make his new wardrobe in a mix of Calorin and the northern design. He had noticed in Aredor that Corin had done the same. Aiden saw that his family didn't exactly approve, but they had respected his decision. For that, Aiden was grateful. His musings were interrupted by the sound of another horse coming down the path. He hoped he would be able to talk his way out of it. He couldn't exactly hide Narak anywhere.

Rona appeared around the bend, leading her horse. She seemed surprised to see Aiden.

"Should you be out here?" she asked.

"I'd have tae say no," Aiden replied.

She smiled. "You know, the more I hear, the less you surprise me."

"I'll take that as a compliment," Aiden grinned. "What brings you out here?"

"Skive mentioned he wanted some herbs yesterday and I told him I knew where tae find them," she explained, holding up a pouch.

"Ah, since you might possibly be talking tae Skive in the near future, would you mind…?" Aiden gestured to Narak.

Rona chuckled. "I won't say anything," she said. Aiden was relieved. "Been a bit restless, have you?"

"You could tell?"

"Oh, between the pacing, Skive's complaining, and the knife throwing, it wasn't hard," Rona said. Aiden saw he had unconsciously taken out a knife and had been tossing it with his good hand. He smiled a bit sheepishly and put the dagger away.

"Well, when you put it like that," he said. He stood and took hold of Narak's reins to join Rona on her way back to the keep.

"Have you enjoyed being back?" she asked.

"Aye, but as you noticed, I am a bit bored. There's only so much for a one-armed man tae do," Aiden said.

"I wish I had some suggestions," Rona said. She waited while Aiden turned Narak back out into the paddock.

"I'll figure something out," Aiden said, as they continued back to the fortress.

"I'm sure you will," Rona agreed.

"What's that supposed to mean?" he laughed.

"I...oh no! Here comes Skive!" Rona was interrupted. Aiden cursed lightly. The bridle was all too evident in his hand and the healer was fast approaching. Rona took off her cloak. She took the bridle from Aiden and hid it under the cloak as she draped it over her arm. Aiden was lost for words for a second.

"Aiden, what are you doing out here?" Skive asked suspiciously.

"Taking a walk," Aiden said.

"Where?" Skive asked pointedly. "And what's this?" he brushed horsehair from Aiden's sleeve.

"I admit I went tae the forest," Aiden said.

"And he held my horse for me while I gathered some of the herbs you wanted," Rona jumped in. She handed the pouch to Skive. "Did I get everything?"

Skive still looked distrustful as he looked through the pouch.

"Yes, it's all here. Thank you, Rona," he said. He left, throwing several glances back at them. Aiden waited until he was safely away.

"Thank you."

"I couldn't let our Champion get in trouble, could I?"

"I do wish people would stop calling me that," Aiden said. Rona saw he was serious and didn't press the subject.

"I'll take the bridle back tae the stables for you," she said. "And you should probably change before you get any more questions," she suggested.

"Aye, who knows if you'll be there tae get me out of the next mess," Aiden said. Rona smiled.

"Glad tae help," she said. They parted ways at the stables and Aiden hurried to change his clothes.

He was quiet at dinner and Tam noticed. "What's wrong?" he asked.

"What? Nothing," Aiden replied.

"Danny, you've barely said two words together. Something's wrong," Tam told him.

"Everyone is suddenly so perceptive around here," Aiden muttered. Laird Gòrdan heard and smiled into his drink. Every bit of his son had returned. He nodded to Captain Artair.

"Aiden, I hear something's been bothering you," Artair said.

"Why does...? Nothing's wrong with me!" Aiden protested.

"As I was saying," Artair continued. "*If* you don't have anything else tae do, I'd welcome you down at the training courts. I hear nothing but how good your sword play is."

"You don't have tae make me feel useful," Aiden warned. Artair shrugged.

"The warriors wouldn't mind seeing you down there. A Champion's input is always respected," Artair said.

"Fine," Aiden said shortly. He didn't know why it irritated him so much that everyone referred to him as the champion. Laird Gòrdan leaned closer to him.

"You'll just have tae get used tae it, Aiden," he told him in a low voice. He saw the stubborn look on his son's face. "Believe me, Braetons have long memories."

Aiden toyed with his beaker and said no more. He lay awake until late that night, wishing that Will was there. He had been closest to William. They had stood up for each other in every situation. He wondered what Will was doing and where he was. Tam had said that Will went looking for Aiden, and he wondered, not for the first time, if his brother would have come with him when he ran away. He probably would have but Aiden felt he had been better off on his own. He tossed and turned until sleep eventually found him.

He had little choice the next morning and found himself in the training courts. Artair had been right and Aiden was welcomed eagerly by the warriors, both young and old.

"Blair and Cai here have done nothing but talk about your swords," one warrior said.

"Believe me, I wish you could see them, but…" Aiden pointed to the sling.

"How much longer?" Douglas asked.

"I don't know," Aiden said. "I'm about tae just cut my arm off and save it the trouble."

"I promised Skive you wouldn't do anything rash, so wait until you leave here at least," Captain Artair said dryly.

"Yes, sir," Aiden replied through the laughter. He spent the rest of the morning in the courts during the training session. The next two weeks followed the same pattern. He took Narak out a few more times and spent most of his time at the training courts offering his advice, especially to the young warriors.

One afternoon, after most of the warriors had left, Aiden remained behind. He picked up a wooden training sword and began to go through the motions against his opponent—two thick striking posts. He quickened the pace of his blows until he heard a crack. He had broken the training sword. He threw it to the ground and hurled a knife into a nearby target with a yell of frustration. He had been injured in Calorin, of course, but there it was different. As long as he could walk and could wield a weapon, there was always something to do. Here, no one seemed to want to let Aiden do anything. *The benefits of being a Laird's son and a blasted Champion!* Aiden thought bitterly as he yanked the dagger free. Suddenly, he could take it no more. He untied the sling and threw it to the side.

He carefully moved his arm, clenching and unclenching his hand. It was still weak and hampered by the bandage, but he could use it. Aiden found another practice sword and took it up in his left hand.

"I'd ask, but maybe I don't want tae know," Artair said. Aiden turned to see him watching.

"You going tae stop me?" he challenged. Artair shook his head.

"I thought maybe I'd help," he said. Artair picked another training sword and joined Aiden in the arena. "Start with the basics," he said, taking a stance. Aiden understood and moved his sword to parry as Artair gave him a series of easy attacks to block. After only a few minutes, Aiden's arm began to ache but he pushed on relentlessly. Artair went through the attacks one more time before halting.

"Don't overdo it," he warned. "Now, let's see how good you are right-handed."

Aiden switched hands and Artair began again with faster and more complex moves. A small audience began to gather as Aiden brought a new attack to Artair. The captain saw a fresh light returning to Aiden's eyes and held nothing back. The courtyard echoed with blows as they fought. It ended suddenly when Artair's sword shattered under a blow. Aiden wiped sweat from his forehead.

"Thank you," he told Artair. The captain threw the ruined sword away.

"What for? You broke two of my training swords," he said.

"Sorry about that," Aiden said. Artair laughed.

"Feel better, do you?" he asked. Aiden felt as if a load had been taken off.

"Better than I have in weeks," he admitted. "I just don't know how I'm going tae explain this one tae Skive."

"You'd better think of something fast," Artair warned. The healer was pushing his way through the men. There was no expression on his face but Aiden knew him well enough. Aiden waited as Skive stopped directly in front of him.

"I guess I should be impressed you lasted this long," Skive said. "But if that wound worsens, it will be your own fault."

"I understand," Aiden said levelly.

"You might as well leave the sling off now. I will be around tonight to look at your arm," Skive said. Aiden nodded and Skive left.

"I never know what tae expect with that man," Artair said when he was gone.

"I'm still alive, right?" Aiden asked. Artair clapped him on the shoulder with a laugh.

"Looks like it. And it sounds like I'll see you here tomorrow for another session. You're a little slow," Artair said.

Aiden rose early a few days later. His left arm was sore but he would not complain. Finally free of the sling, he had been using his arm as much as possible. Skive didn't want to admit it, but ever since the day in the training courts, his arm had shown drastic improvement. The bandage wouldn't remain for much longer.

Aiden went down to the stables. This was one of the last things that Skive had forbidden but Aiden couldn't resist any longer. He put the bridle on Narak and led him from the stable. Narak snorted in the early dawn as Aiden leaped onto his bare back. Aiden saw the valley stretch out in front of him and he gave into the temptation. He held Narak to an easy canter for a few minutes before letting him lengthen into a gallop. The rising sun sparkled on the dew as they tore around the fields.

They circled the lake and Aiden saw another rider in the tree line ahead of them and began to rein Narak in. The stallion fought it for a moment then began to slow. He would have pulled up beside the other rider but Narak balked and reared as a fox darted in front of them. Aiden rode it and would have retained his seat if Narak had not added an exuberant buck. Aiden tumbled to the ground. He continued his fluent curse of his stallion until he saw who the rider was.

Rona had brought her horse up when she saw him fall. She caught Narak's reins.

"Are you all right?" she asked. Aiden stood and winced a little as his shoulder twinged. He had worn a short-sleeved shirt that morning and checked the bandage on his arm. He appeared to still be in one piece.

"I think so," he said. "I didn't expect tae see you out here this early." He took Narak's reins from her.

"Early morning is the best time for doing something everyone would disapprove of, isn't it?" she asked. He saw then that she was dressed in a tunic and breeches and was also riding bareback.

"I wouldn't worry about it."

"Really?" Rona sounded surprised.

"Sure," Aiden said as he mounted again. "You're pretty good with a sword, so who's going tae argue with you?"

She laughed. "If only it worked that way."

"I've been trying tae remember you from before I left," Aiden said. "I haven't had much luck."

"I wasn't born here," Rona said. "My parents died when I was about fifteen and my uncle brought me and my brothers here. We arrived only a few weeks before you left. I remember it well."

"That worries me," Aiden grinned.

"It was quite bewildering. Scodra was in an uproar for weeks," Rona said.

"So what do you do now when you're not giving intae your rebellious side?" Aiden asked.

Rona laughed. "Morna is actually my mother's cousin. She agreed tae take care of us, so I help her in the kitchens most days. Or there's always something that needs doing," Rona said. "Although, apparently you can'nae keep out of trouble," she said. She couldn't resist his smirk.

"There's nothing else for me tae do," he said. "No one seems tae want tae let me get my hands dirty."

"Well, you are a Laird's son."

"I don't look very distinguished right now, do I?" he asked. She smiled and reached over to brush off bits of bracken that clung to his tunic. He ran a hand through his hair to do the same, leaving it even more tousled than usual.

Rona checked the position of the sun. "I should get back," she said.

"Me too," Aiden said. "Do you mind if I ride back with you?" he asked. Rona shook her head and they spurred their horses on. Narak pranced a little.

"He seems very spirited," Rona commented.

"That's one word for this idiot," Aiden said. "He never knows when tae stand still. It's gotten me intae trouble more than once."

"Are you ever not in trouble?" Rona asked.

"Only when I'm asleep, and sometimes not even then," Aiden laughed with her. He wasn't sure where the next question came from but he didn't stop it.

"Would you like tae do this again?" he asked. "Obviously minus the falling."

Rona paused for a moment.

"I'd like tae. I can'nae tomorrow, but maybe the day after?" she replied.

"Sounds like a plan," Aiden agreed. They reentered the gates as the keep was beginning to stir. They hastily stabled their horses and hurried to change before being caught.

Their plans to ride were dashed by the heavy rain that began falling the next night and continued on into the early morning. Aiden still went to the stables to care for Narak. The stallion nibbled at his hay while Aiden brushed and untangled his mane. Footsteps sounded and Aiden looked up to see Rona leaning on the stall door. She reached out to Narak and the horse moved his head away.

"He's a little picky about the company he keeps," Aiden said.

"I've never seen anyone take care of his horse as much as you do," Rona commented.

"Habit," Aiden said. "We rarely let the grooms take care of our horses in Calorin."

"What's it like in Calorin?" Rona asked. "I've always wondered what the countries are like outside of Braeton."

"It's beautiful in its own way. You just have tae get used tae how flat and hot it is," Aiden said. "There aren't many trees, so I found myself missing the forest, especially when I first got there."

"Where else did you go?" Rona asked curiously.

"I've been tae Gelion and Argus. I've never been east of here though," Aiden replied.

"Argus," Rona mused. "I think that's where this came from." She loosened the leather cord around her neck and handed the necklace to Aiden. It was a rounded black stone with a swallow in mid-dive carved in relief.

"My great, great uncle was a trader, they say. He travelled throughout Cimbria and brought this back for his wife. It passed tae my mother and she gave it tae me before she died," Rona said.

"It looks Argusian," Aiden agreed. "I think this is a King's swallow. The birds live only in the Valley of the Kings."

"What's that?" Rona took the necklace back.

"It's where the Argusians bury their kings. I've never seen it. We never made it east of the river past the desert," Aiden said. "But the swallows are supposed tae be the spirits of the fallen kings that remain behind tae watch over and protect the people. I wonder how he got it. A stone like that must be valuable."

"You really think so?" Rona asked, touching it hesitantly. She wore it every day to remind her of her mother. Aiden shrugged.

"A merchant friend of mine showed me something similar once. He called it onyx. He said the Argusians would bless stones like that tae hold the memories of lost loved ones. I'm not sure I quite believe that," Aiden said.

"It's a lovely idea though," Rona said. "What were you doing in Argus?"

"What else would I be doing?" Aiden said. "Fighting a war."

"Did you win?"

"Both sides reached an agreement eventually," Aiden said. "It was probably the most miserable campaign I've ever been on. I hate even the thought of sand."

"You must have plenty of stories tae tell," Rona commented.

"Tam is trying to convince me tae tell him. But I'm afraid there's not much tae tell. It's just one battle after another," Aiden said. "That's what makes it so hard tae settle down here. It's too quiet."

"You'll get used tae it."

"Maybe." In his heart he knew he wouldn't for a long time.

The next few days were busy as several of the chieftains of the villages came to see Laird Gòrdan. Aiden's presence was required at most of the meetings and he fidgeted restlessly. Skive had finally decided to remove the bandage on his arm and Aiden longed to ride again. At supper one evening, Rona caught Aiden's glance. He made an annoyed face at her and she only smiled and shook her head back. He grinned and tried to turn his attention back to the rambling chieftain seated next to him. Rona's brother noticed the silent exchange.

"Are you sure you do not aim too high?" he asked.

"What do you mean?" she returned.

"He is the Laird's son. You help in the kitchens," her brother reminded her.

"Aiden doesn't care about that. He's just a friend," Rona told him.

"I respect him. He's a fine warrior, but I don't want tae see you hurt," Eideard said.

"He wouldn't," Rona protested.

"I'm just warning you not tae be surprised if he forgets about you," Eideard said.

Rona glanced back to the head table. Aiden wasn't as careless as Eideard might think, she was sure of it. But she wondered at her swift defense of Aiden. True, she didn't know him well but she had to admit she was quite taken by the young warrior. She knew she wasn't the only one. Aiden was handsome, outgoing, and had an irresistible air of mystery surrounding him which led to a never-ending chatter among the young women of Scodra. Rona wondered what he might say if he knew.

Out of long habit, Aiden rose early. It had been over a month since Skive had declared his arm healed. Scodra was still asleep so he dressed and went down to the stables. Narak greeted him with a quiet nicker. Aiden saddled and bridled Narak quickly as the stallion stamped his foot in anticipation.

They walked quietly out of the stables and Aiden mounted in the courtyard. The guards at the gate nodded a greeting as they swung the doors open. By now, they were used to Aiden's morning routine. Narak pulled eagerly at the bit as Aiden held him to a walk. They passed the lake and entered the forest. Aiden was spending as much time as he could re-familiarizing himself with the trails surrounding Scodra. He urged Narak into a canter.

They left the main paths and took a smaller game trail while jumping logs and splashing through a small stream. They pulled to a halt in a quiet, small valley. Aiden dismounted and sat on a rock while Narak began to graze.

Aiden opened his pouch and took out the food that Morna had left out for him. There was even an extra apple for Narak. He ate and watched the early sunlight play in the valley. He heard a faint rustle in the grass behind him. Narak half raised his head and flicked his ears toward the sound. Aiden watched the stallion as he put his head back down and continued grazing. He began slicing an apple.

"You going tae stand there all day or were you waiting for an invitation?" he suddenly asked.

Jamey smiled and moved forward to join him. He laid his bow down at his feet and Maon sat obediently beside him.

"All right, if you're so smart, how long was I standing there?" he asked. Aiden bit into an apple slice.

"About five minutes," he said. "So, how'd you find me?"

"We were out hunting and Maon picked up your trail. We figured we'd come visit a friend."

"I haven't seen you much since the feast," Aiden said.

"Sorry about that. I've been on my own for so long that I'm not used tae all the people in Scodra," Jamey said.

"It takes a while tae adjust tae new things, doesn't it?"

"Is that why you've ridden out for the past few days? Wanting some time alone?" Jamey asked. Aiden glanced sideways at him.

"Have you been following me?" he asked.

Jamey chuckled. "I spend a lot of time out here. You don't think I can'nae pick up some new tracks?"

"Fair enough. You did learn from the best," Aiden said.

"So did you," Jamey replied.

"Aye. I'm still surprised your father allowed me tae come visit," Aiden said.

"It's not like anyone could have stopped you."

"Both sides certainly tried," Aiden said. "But I think your father understood that I needed something tae do, tae get me away from home…and more trouble."

"After you ran away, your father came and visited. Och, he almost beat down the door and demanded tae know if we had done anything tae you," Jamey said. "But Father stood in his face and gave Laird Gòrdan a piece of his mind. They argued as only two angry Braetons can. Father wasn't worried about you. He knew you could take care of yourself."

"They came looking for me?"

"Aye, but you'd done a pretty good job of scrambling your trail. Will even snuck out tae find me and ask if I knew where you'd gone."

"I didn't even know where I wanted tae go. Besides away," Aiden said. "I stopped in one of Clan Gunlon's villages. An innkeeper had a map, so I looked at it and saw the Masian Sea. Then all of the sudden I knew that's what I wanted tae see. After that, I went west and then south."

"Did you find what you were looking for out there?"

"Aye. I felt free. No one knew who I was. I learned some hard lessons and finally grew up. A captain gave me the discipline I needed tae control myself," Aiden said. "I made some good friends and left a few behind." His eyes clouded as he saw again a distant unmarked grave and a name he had taken as his own.

Maon saw a rabbit venture out of the grass and he looked beseechingly at Jamey. At a quick nod from Jamey, the hound sprang away in quick pursuit, yipping excitedly. The two friends smiled at his exuberance.

"What did you do after your father died?" Aiden asked.

"I carried on as best I could. It got lonely out here sometimes. Will would occasionally come tae see how I was doing. The first year was hard, but then I found Maon, half-starved and lost. He had probably wandered off from one of the settlements. We keep each other company."

"But now you can come and go as you please," Aiden said.

"Aye. I might show up again soon. I finished all the food that Morna sent back with me nearly a week ago. I don't know how I lived off my cooking before," Jamey said and Aiden laughed.

"I always told you she was amazing," he said. "She's currently trying tae make up for all the meals I've missed over the past ten years. It's a wonder I can still move."

"You weren't joking, were you?" Jamey said, sitting back from the table. It was two days later. He had come to Scodra for a visit and Aiden had taken him to the kitchens for lunch. Or, as it turned out, a minor feast provided by Morna. Aiden put his boot against the table and tilted his chair back.

"I never joke about food," he said, tossing a nut and catching it in his mouth.

"I think I've changed my mind. I might come tae live here after all," Jamey said.

"Don't let Morna hear you. She was just saying the other day how awful it was for you tae live all alone out in the 'gloomy forest,' I think it was," Aiden said.

"I might agree," Jamey said.

Tam and Ranulf walked into the kitchens to join them.

"I told you he'd be down here," Tam said to Ranulf.

"Well, it was either here or the training courts," Ranulf said.

"All right, you've found me. Now what?" Aiden asked, tossing another nut. Tam caught it midair and ate it, ignoring Aiden's offended glare.

"Aredor's Autumn Festival is a little over a month away and they've invited the Clans," Ranulf said.

"We going?" Aiden asked.

"Father isn't, but he wants some of us tae go," Ranulf said.

"Well, I will. I've got a good friend who lives over there," Aiden said. "You going, Jamey?"

"Aye, I suppose I will. It'll give me a chance tae get out of 'the gloomy forest,'" Jamey said and they both chuckled.

"Well, then, Father wants tae talk tae you when you have a chance, Aiden," Tam said.

Aiden nodded. "Where is he?"

"In the main council room. With Neason," Tam answered with a grin.

"What's Neason doing here?" Aiden asked, disgust edging into his voice.

"He brought the message on from Clan Dyson," Ranulf replied. Aiden caught Jamey's questioning look.

"My least favorite cousin," he explained.

"He said he wanted tae see you," Ranulf said.

"Oh, I just bet he did," Aiden said. "I'll wipe that ridiculously white smile off his face too."

Tam unsuccessfully tried to stifle a burst of laughter.

"Can I come? I've been wanting tae see this for years!" Ranulf smirked.

"No, you may not!" Aiden replied. "Now, shut up, both of you!" he glared at them as he left the kitchens, followed by another burst of laughter. "I've seen wild dogs with better manners!" he muttered to himself.

Aiden met Laird Gòrdan and Neason coming toward him in the hallway.

"Well, if it isn't little Aiden!" Neason exclaimed. Aiden gritted his teeth. He had always stood shorter than his brothers but had made up for it with strength and agility. Neason, in contrast, was taller than most Braetons. He was a few years older than Aiden and had never missed a chance to push him around as children.

Aiden smiled tightly. "Neason! As condescending as ever, I see," he said. Neason ignored the remark and Laird Gòrdan hid a smile.

"I heard you were back and a Champion! I wanted tae see for myself," Neason said.

"Yes, I became a soldier. What is this world coming tae?" Aiden replied.

Ranulf interceded as he came up with Jamey. "Neason, I don't think you've ever met Jamey," he said, introducing them.

"I've heard so much about you," Jamey said. He winked at Aiden and, with a bow to Laird Gòrdan, he and Ranulf turned Neason away and walked off down the hall.

"They came just in time," Laird Gòrdan remarked.

"Please tell me he's not staying for dinner," Aiden said.

"You know he is," Laird Gòrdan said. "And aren't you two a little old tae continue childhood squabbles?" he reprimanded.

"I vividly remember him trying tae drown me," Aiden said.

"I never heard about that," Laird Gòrdan said.

"That was the summer he visited while you and Uncle went tae the Gathering," Aiden said. "Anyway, he never got in trouble."

"Both of you should try tae put that behind you," his father said.

"I'm more inclined tae throw a rock at his face," Aiden said. Laird Gòrdan chuckled.

"I trust you heard the reason for his visit?"

"Yes, sir. Tam and Ranulf just told me," Aiden said. They began walking toward Laird Gòrdan's study.

"Are you going?" the Laird asked.

"Yes, sir," Aiden replied.

"Good. I want Ranulf tae stay here. I have much tae speak with him about. I plan tae pass the torc tae him at the New Year," Gòrdan said. "I wanted you tae go. This Festival will build the friendship between the Clans and Aredor."

"I'll be on my best behavior then," Aiden said with a grin that was returned by his father.

"That's reassuring," Laird Gòrdan said. "There is one more thing. I have a feeling that William is in Aredor. Find him and let him know that his home is open tae him."

"I will, Father," Aiden said.

"The Festival is held at the end of the harvest. I already plan for Artair and a score of men tae go along. Tam is going and I believe some of the men will bring their families," Laird Gòrdan said.

"How long will we be there?" Aiden asked.

"The Festival itself lasts for a week. I will leave it tae you and Artair tae decide when tae come back," Laird Gòrdan said. They parted ways and Aiden went down to the training court behind the stables. In the months since he returned his father and he had been slowly building a new friendship. As a young boy, Aiden had built up resentment against him and he found that he had held on to it for all these years. His father was trying and Aiden could only do the same. At times, despite their best efforts, they still found themselves at odds, but the remembrance of years past helped them through. He had never hated his father and he had some fond memories of his childhood, but it would still be some time before he could completely trust him again.

Aiden strung his bow and began to shoot. His arrows fell wide of his intended marks and he muttered in frustration. He knew his arm was still weak and he shouldn't complain, but he just wanted to get back to normal. He drew a knife and sent it crashing into the target. He sent two more spinning after it. Retrieving the daggers, he repeated the process again and again as he varied his throws underhand, overhand, and to the left and right sides.

He nodded in satisfaction as his last knife smacked solidly into the center of the target.

"I'm glad you didn't know how tae do that ten years ago," Neason said behind him. Aiden was startled. He had been so focused that he hadn't heard anyone approach.

"I made do with what I had," Aiden said as he turned around. Neason gave a slight smile and rubbed his ear unconsciously.

"It still aches from time tae time," he said.

"It was just a pinecone," Aiden protested.

"A bloody big one!"

"I had saved it all winter," Aiden said with a half-smile mirrored by Neason.

"I figured I should come apologize," Neason said. Aiden eyed him up and down. He wore a short sleeved shirt under the heavy brigandine. Bracers covered his forearms, above which were two tattoos. On the left was the circle of Clan Dyson and on the right was an intricate three way spiral. Neason was the Champion of Clan Dyson.

"You're not just waiting tae jump me again?" Aiden asked suspiciously.

"Och, I doubt I could even get close enough tae," Neason said. "Besides that, just looking at you, I'm fairly sure that you could get the best of me any day."

"Don't lie. You're practically a giant compared tae me. Not tae mention that enormous claymore you're carrying," Aiden replied.

"Well, I'd definitely have less of a chance now. And I did come tae see you. We heard some stories about the fight and it's not hard tae get people around here tae talk about you," Neason said. "Truth is, when we heard how you had left, I wished I had the guts tae do something like that."

"You? I always thought you weren't scared of anything," Aiden was surprised. "And you became the Champion."

"I never felt like I really earned it," Neason said. "But you have."

"No, I'm just the idiot who thought I could hold off four hundred Durnians with fifty men. It's a miracle we made it through alive. If Ranulf hadn't come along when he did, I'd have died," Aiden said.

"We never got that version of the story," Neason said.

"Aye, you never hear how deathly afraid the 'hero' is either," Aiden said. He and Neason walked toward the target where Aiden pulled the knives free and sheathed them. Neason extended a hand and Aiden clasped it firmly.

"Come back around in a few weeks and we'll see how good you really are with that oversized rabbit skinner," Aiden said.

Neason laughed. "I'll be looking forward tae it," he said.

Aiden found Ranulf a short time later.

"How did Neason become champion?" he asked.

"He and a few other warriors were out hunting one day. It was just after the Calorins had taken control of Aredor. The story goes that twenty Calorins had crossed the border and surprised them. Neason fought them off while his companions escaped. He killed most of the patrol and, even though he was wounded, helped one of his injured warriors get away. But if you ask him, there were only twelve Calorins and the other warrior was helping him more than the other way around. There were other battles, but that one gained him the respect of the Clan," Ranulf said.

"Dyson helped the Hawk Flight in the war. Did he fight then as well?" Aiden asked.

"Aye, he was named Champion shortly after the war ended. How do you know about the Hawk Flight?" Ranulf asked. Aiden hesitated. He couldn't tell Ranulf the real reason he knew so much about the war.

"My friend that I mentioned? He commands the Hawk Flight," he said.

"You know the Hawk?" Ranulf exclaimed.

"It's a long story. But yes," Aiden said. "How do you know about him?"

"We've all heard about him, mostly from Dyson. That was just before Adalwulf came," Ranulf replied. Aiden grinned. Corin would love to hear that he was famous not only in Aredor but also through Braeton.

Laird Gòrdan watched Aiden during the evening meal. He was sitting at one of the lower tables with Blair and Jamey, listening attentively as Neason spoke. The Champion gestured with his hands as he described a battle. Neason finished and the conversation continued, punctuated by frequent bursts of laughter.

"How does he do it?" Ranulf wondered. "He hates someone in the morning and by dinner it's like they're lifelong friends. Does he have no enemies?"

"He does. But I have a feeling that they're all dead," Laird Gòrdan replied.

Chapter 17

William scanned the path. As in the weeks before, there was nothing to see. He turned and made his way back to the camp. He briefly reported to Lieutenant Flynn and joined Padrig by the fire. The smell of lunch pervaded the sheltered campsite. Will had been with the Hawk Flight for nearly a month now. He was still amazed with how quickly they had accepted him, especially as an outsider. He had moved through the training courses within a few days, passing with a high recommendation from the gruff captain. The members of Corin's patrol that had been at Kingscastle at the time had welcomed him once they saw his skill. Will still thought a large part of his reception was because the Captain had accepted him without issue.

"Anything to see?" Padrig asked. Will shook his head.

"Same as always," he replied. "You think there will be another attack?"

"The Captain seems to think so. Some Braeton brought him news that seemed to worry him. If he thinks something might happen, then we'd best stay ready," Padrig said. It was a complacent trust that Will had seen throughout the entire warband. He knew Padrig had fought in the first war, his missing finger proving it. Will knew that Aiden's return and the news of Calorin was no coincidence. There were more stories told only in the Hawk

Flight about the first war and the strangers that had helped the warband in the last great battle. He wanted to ask Corin about it but was afraid that he would get no answer.

The rest of the patrol began to trickle back into camp. Lieutenant Flynn took their reports and made quick notes on a piece of parchment. They had just begun to eat when hoof beats sounded and Kara rode into the camp. She saluted Flynn and handed him a dispatch. The men looked up expectantly as she reached into the pouch again and pulled out letters from their families. Kara finished and helped herself to some food. She came and sat next to Will.

"I'm sorry I didn't have anything for you," she said a little shyly. He was, after all, a Laird's son.

"That's all right," he said. "I'm used tae it by now."

"Has there been any news about…?" she asked.

He shook his head. He had met Brian from Clan Dyson. The captain had greeted him respectfully when he found out who Will was but was not able to tell him much about Clan Canich other than there had been a battle and Laird Gòrdan still ruled. But all Will really cared about was news of Aiden. What had become of his little brother?

"I'm sure he's fine," Kara replied to his unspoken question.

"How did you know?"

"The Captain was asking me the other day if you'd had any news about your brother," Kara admitted. "Do you think you'll hear from your family?"

"I doubt it. I'm still banished, remember? And they don't even know where I am," Will said. Kara heard the edge of sadness in his voice. She knew it was hard for Will to admit to anyone that he had been expelled from his own Clan. She couldn't imagine what that would be like. She hadn't seen her Braeton family in years, but she could still return any time she wanted.

"I'm sure things have changed by now," Kara said. "They say the Durnians are gone, so there's no reason someone couldn't come looking for you."

"Kieran was just here the other day telling me the same thing. You and he are quite the rays of sunshine, aren't you?" Will said.

"He'd like tae think he is," Kara replied. Will laughed. He didn't mind the young twins. There was a sort of understanding among them. All three of them were Braetons who had not seen their homes in a long time. And Will was just grateful to hear the brogue again. It made home finally seem closer.

Kara waited until early afternoon for Flynn to write a report for her to take back to Kingscastle. This was her last stop before heading back. She dozed off and on beside the campfire, its heat adding to the summer warmth. She let the smell of pine fill her nose and listened to the quiet noises of the forest. She had come to love Aredor possibly even more than Braeton. Of course she would never admit that to Kieran. Someone cleared his throat and she opened her eyes.

"Ian, what are you doing here?" she asked. Ian was part of Llewellyn's patrol. There had to be a good reason for him to be here.

"Catching you sleeping on the job apparently," Ian said. "You should be ashamed."

"Why? You do it all the time." She yawned.

"Horrible lies!" Ian said as he sat down next to her. "But to answer your question, Captain had some new patrol orders that he sent in with Llewellyn. I got picked to bring them."

"Kieran hasn't gotten his lazy self out here yet?" Kara asked.

"He running another message to Clan Dyson, so he'll be a bit behind," Ian said.

"You're still here, Ian?" Flynn's second-in-command asked.

"You act like you're trying to get rid of me, Trefor," Ian laughed. "I haven't told Flynn yet. You know you don't disturb him when he's writing."

Trefor only laughed.

"I heard that, lad," Flynn said as he came up. "You're smarter than you look."

Ian laughed with Kara. Everyone liked the tall lieutenant. He was very distinctive with his red hair. He usually didn't carry a sword, being more than capable with the ornate longbow and dirk he carried. Ian relayed his message and Flynn gave Kara his letter. Kara tightened Delyth's girth and Ian took his horse's reins.

"Which way are you going?" he asked. She pointed to the path she would take, yawning again.

"Stop that," Flynn ordered, stifling his own yawn. "We've still got a few more days before we can sleep in a wonderful bed again."

"I will think of you all when I get back tae Kingscastle," Kara said, smiling sweetly.

"It's a good thing you're pretty," Flynn told her.

"That's the nicest thing anyone's ever said tae me," Kara said, her voice catching a little.

"Oh, get out of here," Flynn said good-naturedly. Kara grinned and mounted. She waved to Ian who was going the opposite direction. She wished they were going the same way. She rarely got to spend much time with him or Kieran anymore. She held Delyth to an easy trot. It would take them all day and into the next to reach the castle.

- -

Kara rode in behind a group of warriors. She had greeted them and received cold nods in return. She was used to it by now. Not everyone approved of her riding with the Hawk Flight. It was the same story as she rode through the town. Several of the older women glared at her. Men's clothes were not appropriate for a young woman. But Kara saw several girls and young women looking admiringly at her and some dared to wave. She smiled and waved back, bringing more disapproval. She knew she had no reason to be ashamed. She had the blessing of the captain and the other lieutenants. That was enough for her.

A groom took her horse but she was stopped before she could go to the barracks office. Amaura saw her in the courtyard and came to greet her.

"Kara! I was hoping you'd be here soon," the princess said.

"You'll have tae hold your plans for a little while. I'm a bit dirty," Kara said.

"Not to worry, I just wanted you to help me convince Mera to have dinner with us tonight," Amaura said.

"I have tae find the Captain first, and then I'll be free," Kara said.

"Well, you won't find him in there." Amaura pointed to the barracks. "He is out walking with…" she paused for dramatic effect. "A woman."

"Our Captain? With someone?" Kara couldn't quite believe it.

"Aye, and wait till you see who it is!" Amaura seemed about to burst. She led Kara into the castle and up a flight of stairs to a window that overlooked the gardens. They both peered out and saw Corin and Mera on a path below.

"Mera?" Kara said. "They're perfect for each other!"

"That's what I thought!" Amaura exclaimed.

"So that's the real reason for dinner tonight." Kara understood now.

"Yes, I want her to talk! I must know everything!" Amaura said. Mera could be quite secretive and it killed Amaura. Laughter floated up to the window. Kara smiled a little wistfully.

"They look happy together," she said.

"Don't worry, Kara. We'll find someone for you someday," Amaura said.

"If she survives not turning in reports," a voice sounded behind them. Kara whirled around.

"Lieutenant Martin! Fancy meeting you here," she said. Martin maintained his glare for only a few more seconds.

"What are you two doing up here anyway?" he asked. Amaura pointed triumphantly out the window. Martin glanced out.

"Ah yes, our budding romantic. Who would have guessed?" he said. Kara and Amaura laughed.

"How long have you known?" Amaura asked.

"For a while. They are both an open book to the master," Martin said superiorly.

"The master?" Amaura scoffed. "I don't know why women fall for you."

"That's because they don't know me like you do," Martin grinned as he began to walk away. "Oh, and Kara, he's leaving. You'd better get down there and report before you have to tell him you were spying on him."

Kara took his advice and hurried back to the barracks. She arrived just before Corin. She knocked on the open door and entered. Gerralt looked up from his desk.

"Ah, Kara," he greeted her amiably before going back to his work. Corin eyed her skeptically as he sat down. She only smiled and shrugged slightly. She seemed to be the only person in the whole army that Gerralt didn't mind. She handed in the reports from Liam and Flynn. She answered his questions as seriously as she could. Amaura's excitement had taken over her. She still couldn't quite believe what she had seen.

"Everything all right, Kara?" Corin asked suspiciously. Kara hid her smile.

"Yes, sir. Is that all?"

"I suppose it is," Corin said. She hurried out of the room as fast as she dared. Karif landed on the open windowsill and began preening. Corin looked longingly at out the window as a fresh breeze wafted in. Gerralt cleared his throat and Corin glared at him before turning back to the endless piles of paperwork.

- -

Corin woke early the next day. It looked like a beautiful morning until he remembered what day it was. Lord Mabon was coming. He disliked the lord and knew the feeling was entirely mutual. In fact, Lord Mabon made it his sole purpose in life to argue and contradict everything Corin said.

He spent the morning out on the training fields, working the recruits for the Hawk Flight. Evan was progressing quickly and Andras had been less vocal of late. Corin thought it was probably because Andras realized he would have to work harder so that Even would not surpass him. It was making life more pleasant for all involved. After returning to the castle, Corin changed to fresh clothes and joined his father and Darrin in the courtyard to greet Lord Mabon. Karif alighted on his outstretched arm and turned somber yellow eyes to the troop of men entering the castle gates.

Corin unconsciously reverted to the silent and guarded look of the Phoenix Guard. Karif felt him stiffen and fluttered to his shoulder to better glare at the newcomers. Corin knew that the lord wasn't an enemy but Mabon still set every fiber of his being on edge.

A young girl of about four years suddenly darted out from behind the stables. Lord Mabon's horse reared in surprise and the lord cursed. Corin jumped forward and swept the girl out from under the flailing hooves. Lord Mabon brought his horse back under control and looked around angrily as if he would try to blame Corin for what happened.

King Celyn stepped forward to intervene.

"I'm sorry for that, Lord Mabon," he said. "Your journey was pleasant, I trust?"

Lord Mabon inclined his head. "Yes, your majesty. It is always a pleasure to see Kingscastle again," he said.

Corin was distracted by the girl tugging on his shoulder. "Corin, Corin," she lisped her r's to w's. "Hefin hurted hisself. Can you come?" she asked. Corin wasn't sure who she was or who Hefin was, but he would rather find out than deal with Lord Mabon. A groom caught Corin's attention.

"Prince Darrin said for you to join them as soon as you were able," he said. Corin set the girl down with a sigh of relief.

"All right, show me where," he said to the girl. She grasped two of his fingers and pulled him toward the rear of the stables. Corin heard the crying before they saw the boy. He sat at the base of one of the trees that sheltered the open pens. The boy held his arm at an awkward angle and Corin could see that it was broken. He knelt by Hefin and reached out to him. Hefin sniffed and manfully tried to stifle his tears. He would not cry in front of the warrior he idolized.

"I fell," he explained.

Corin looked up at the tree and saw the branch that had caused the accident. "You climbed higher than I did at your age," Corin said.

"Really?" Hefin sniffed again.

"Aye, I used to sneak out here and climb this tree. As I recall, it was particularly good for seeing all across the castle."

"Still is," Hefin said. Corin smiled and helped the boy up.

"Come on. Let's get you to a healer. That arm looks like it hurts." He sent the girl running off to the castle to alert a healer. Hefin leaned against Corin as they made their way toward the castle infirmary.

Mera met them at the door with the girl.

"I wasn't sure what Bronwyn was trying to tell me," she said. "Why don't you lads come in and I'll see what I can do."

Hefin dragged his feet a little and Corin saw he looked nervous.

"There's nothing to worry about," he said reassuringly. "I've been in here plenty of times."

Hefin took his hand again and they went over to a bed. Mera handed the boy a cup of medicine.

"Drink this, Hefin. It'll stop your arm from hurting so much," she said. She began to gather material to form a splint and sling after sending Bronwyn off to find their guardian. "I might need some help," she told Corin as he sat next to the boy. "Do you mind staying? I know Lord Mabon just arrived."

"I'd rather be here and I think you know it," Corin said. Mera smiled and knelt in front of Hefin.

"I'm going to set your arm back in place. Can you be brave for me?" she asked. Hefin bit his lip and nodded. Mera rolled up his sleeve on the injured arm.

"Will it hurt a lot?" Hefin asked Corin.

"It will at first," Corin told him.

"I thought you were gonna say no," Hefin said.

Corin almost laughed. "I'm always honest with my warriors." he said.

Hefin straightened. "Have you ever broked anything?"

"I once broke two of my fingers," Corin said, holding out his hand for Hefin to see the fingers that had remained slightly crooked.

"Did Mera fix them?" Hefin asked.

"No, that was before I knew Mera as a healer," Corin replied. Hefin looked like that was hard to fathom.

"I've always known you, haven't I, Mera?" he said.

"You have," Mera agreed. "And if you can believe it, I knew Corin when he was just your age," she told Hefin. The boy squinted up at Corin as if trying to imagine that.

"That must have been a long time ago," he said. Corin and Mera laughed.

"I'm not that old!" Corin protested. Mera was still laughing as she reached for Hefin's arm.

"All right, let's get this over with, Hefin," she said. Hefin allowed her to take hold of the broken arm and moved closer to Corin. Corin wrapped a steadying arm around the boy and nodded to Mera. Hefin buried his head against Corin and cried as the bones were pulled back into place.

Bronwyn charged back into the room as Mera began to wrap a bandage around Hefin's arm. She was followed by a rather breathless woman who ran to the bed as soon as she saw the boy. Corin recognized her as Lady Eira. She had lost her husband and a son in the war and now she and her remaining daughter looked after many of the orphans in the castle. Bronwyn jumped up and down beside Lady Eira.

"See! Hefin was climbing, then he fell, so I ran and ran and there was a horsie that went whoosh! And Corin came and he's a very nice person and Mera said she could help," Bronwyn was in her element trying to explain everything that had happened.

"Hefin, are you all right?" Lady Eira asked concernedly. Her ward nodded. The bitter medicine he had drunk earlier was dulling some of the pain. "What did I tell you about climbing that tree? You were supposed to take Bronwyn out for a walk, nothing more!"

"I promised I wouldn't tell," Bronwyn piped up again. Corin hid a smile. It could have been him and Amaura at that age. Lady Eira saw him and dropped a quick curtsey.

"Thank you, my lord. Bronwyn said you helped?" she said.

"Barely," Corin said. "I'm afraid I didn't quite discourage him from trying again."

"Nothing I say will anyway. You should know that," Lady Eira said. "My husband broke his arm in that tree and my son certainly tried." She turned to Mera. "What needs to be done for Hefin?"

"He can lie down here this afternoon if he wants," Mera said. "I can look after him."

Bronwyn struggled to climb onto the bed. Corin saw her intent gaze fixed on Karif who had taken up a perch on the bedpost. Karif regarded her with an aloof interest and then swiveled his head to look at the earthenware jar that Mera brought over.

"I want to see the birdie!" Bronwyn said. Lady Eira caught her breath as she saw which "birdie" Bronwyn meant. Corin lifted the young girl onto the bed beside him.

"Wait," he told her as she would have grabbed at the hawk. He extended his wrist to Karif and the hawk latched comfortably onto the vambrace. Corin crouched with the hawk in front of both children carefully showing them how to stroke its feathers.

Mera handed Hefin and Bronwyn both a sugar cube from her supply and they munched happily.

"Can he have one?" Bronwyn asked, pointing to the hawk. Corin took a cube from Mera and crumbled it in his hand. Karif swiftly cleaned the crumbs away and ruffled at his chest to get the bits that had fallen from his beak. The children giggled and Corin took another cube. He put part in each child's hand and helped them hold their hand out slowly. He clicked gently to the hawk and Karif delicately picked up the crumbs offered.

Mera and Lady Eira watched a bit breathlessly as the dangerous hooked beak came and swept above the small hands. Hefin and Bronwyn had no such worries and they laughed merrily again.

"No more or he'll get too fat to fly," Corin said. Bronwyn found this to be hilarious and rolled on the bed as she laughed.

"No more for you either," Mera reprimanded as Corin stole a sugar cube and popped it in his mouth.

"Will you get too fat?" Bronwyn asked.

"I certainly hope not," Corin said.

"Maybe we'd have to tickle him back down to size," Lady Eira said as she performed that very action on the young girl. Bronwyn shrieked with laughter as Lady Eira swept her up into her arms. "Come along, little one. We'll let Hefin rest for a while," she said. Bronwyn called out merry goodbyes as she was carried from the room. Mera made sure Hefin was comfortable on the bed before she accompanied Corin to the door.

"I had no idea you were so popular among the children," she said.

"I didn't either," Corin said. "At least I can count on someone to like me."

"Until you're old and fat," Mera said. "Or older," she amended. Her heart leapt when she saw the merry glint in his eye.

"Then Lleu help me if you think I'm old now. By the time I'm finished with the meetings with Lord Mabon today, I'll have aged again," Corin said.

Mera smiled again. "You'd better get down there while I'll still cling to the memory of this poor young lad." Corin only laughed and left the infirmary.

The midday meal was being served and Corin made it to the hall with seconds to spare. Lord Mabon nodded a distant greeting, not wishing to offend the son in front of the father.

"I half expected you not to show back up," Darrin said quietly to him.

"I thought about it," Corin replied. "Remind me again why I have to be there anyway?"

"He's one of our most important lords, Cor. We stroke his pride a little and keep him informed. He still has a large warband, so we need his men," Darrin said.

"He should give us his men anyway," Corin growled. "I've never been very good at stroking massive egos," he said. Darrin hid a smile.

"I know that a little too well," he said. Corin only glared at him.

When the meal ended, the King and many of the lords gathered in a council chamber. Lord Mabon stopped Corin just outside the door.

"Our hero returns," he said. "Saving children now? Don't you have anything better to do?"

"Maybe if you weren't so careless, I wouldn't have to," Corin replied.

"So self-righteous! But I suppose that comes from your Calorin friends," Lord Mabon sneered.

"Lord Mabon!" Martin joined them at that moment. "I heard Corin cleaned up another one of your messes today?"

The Lord's smile froze on his face.

"I should have known your faithful hound would be skulking around," he said to Corin. "Your father would be ashamed of how far you've fallen," he baited Martin.

"Don't try to fool me, Mabon. I know very well you still want the General's belt. And since I didn't see you on any of those bloodstained battlefields, I don't think it's my father who would be ashamed. Tell us again what you did during the war?" Martin smiled carelessly but he was taut with anger. Lord Mabon glared daggers at him before storming into the chamber.

"You shouldn't have gone so far, Martin," Corin said.

"He bloody well needed to hear it! My father didn't die so that the lords like Mabon could keep their seats under the Calorins!" Martin ground out.

"Are you coming in?" Corin asked.

Martin took a deep breath. "Darrin asked me to be there. Though I think I'm supposed to be a calming influence on you. Sorry if it turns out to be the other way around."

"Oh, no, I'd like Mabon to have to stare at both our faces for the next few hours."

"Have I ever told you that I quite enjoy having you as a friend?" Martin said as they entered the chamber.

Chapter 18

Aiden snuck up behind Tam. He had been successfully stalking his brother for the past ten minutes. He quickened his pace and grabbed Tam by the shoulders. He had never heard Tam curse before and his brother whirled around as Aiden nearly fell over with laughing.

"You look like you had a heart attack!" Aiden wheezed as he doubled over. Tam kicked him in the shin but he was starting to laugh too.

"Between you and Will, it's a wonder I haven't yet," Tam said.

"I'm bored. You want tae go hunting?" Aiden asked, rubbing his shin. "Oh, come on! What are you doing anyway?" he asked when Tam hesitated. "Nothing? That's what I thought," he said. "Don't be a boring bard."

"Very funny," Tam said. "How long did it take you tae come up with that?"

"Almost all morning if you can believe it," Aiden said. "You want tae come?"

"Fine, I'll come!" Tam sounded wearied, but he wasn't really doing anything and there was never a dull moment with Aiden.

"Perfect. I had them saddle your horse already."

"You weren't going tae take 'no' for an answer, were you?"

"What does 'no' mean again?" Aiden inquired innocently.

Tam rolled his eyes and they headed toward the stables. They weren't the only ones with plans that afternoon. Rona was also making her way to the stable yards. She wore breeches and held a spear, ignoring the many stares thrown her way. Aiden and Tam saw her and stopped.

"She looks determined," Aiden commented.

"It doesn't surprise me. She and Will would ride out on occasion," Tam said.

"Will?" Aiden sounded surprised.

"Aye, they were good friends before, you know, everything happened," Tam said.

"I hadn't heard anything about that," Aiden said. Tam almost thought he detected a hint of jealousy in his brother's voice.

"I'm surprised you hadn't. They were very good friends," Tam said. Aiden looked at him.

"I see what you're trying tae do," he said.

"Really? And what's that?"

"Clever. Very clever."

"Are we going hunting, because…?" Tam raised his shoulders.

"All right, let's ask her tae join us and see how you like being beaten…by a girl," Aiden said.

"By all means," Tam gestured for Aiden to continue. They met with Rona at stable doors.

"What are you doing today, Rona?" Aiden asked.

"It is my birthday today, so I'm going hunting and I'm going tae wear whatever I want." She challenged either of them to say anything.

"Perfect. We were planning tae hunt today as well. Nobody should hunt alone, should they, Tam?" Aiden asked pointedly.

"No, especially not on their birthday," Tam agreed. Rona watched them suspiciously.

"Indeed! So you should join us, Rona," Aiden said. "It would be our pleasure."

Rona agreed quickly. She had been hoping to run into Aiden again. The past few weeks had kept her busy. She did not want to admit how irresistibly charming he could be or how much she had missed talking to him. She quickly saddled her horse and strapped a bow and quiver to the saddle. Tam did the same and they left the fortress.

Tam saw another rider approaching them.

"And Jamey just happens tae be visiting today with his spear?" he asked.

"How convenient," Aiden said. "Rona, you don't mind?"

"Not at all," she said. The young woodsman was quiet but was still enjoyable company. She wondered if she should find some other women her age. Morna had been complaining the other day that she only spent time with young men. But why sit inside when you could go hunting? She spurred her horse forward into the forest with the others.

Jamey and Aiden knew the hunting runs well and they were soon in quick pursuit of a stag. It fled in terror and they lashed their steeds in quick pursuit. They lost the deer when it vanished into the shrubbery but Maon quickly raised the trail again. Aiden pulled Narak off the path and spurred him on faster to cut off the deer. He leaned low in the saddle to avoid branches and trailing vines. The stag skidded away as Aiden turned Narak in front of it. Before it made good its escape, Rona threw her spear and the stag fell onto the path. Her eyes shone triumphantly and Aiden lowered his spear.

"And what was that about *me* getting beaten by a girl?" Tam asked. Jamey laughed merrily and Aiden smiled and saluted Rona with the spear.

"Aye, but I know a good kill when I see one, Tam," he replied.

"We might have tae have another hunt tae assuage his wounded pride though," Jamey said.

"You know me too well, Jamey," Aiden said. "You might not be invited just tae give the rest of us a chance," he teased Rona. She smiled as she dismounted and retrieved her spear. Jamey called off Maon who had begun to worry at the deer's ear.

"Are we taking this back tae Scodra?" he asked. Aiden sized up the carcass.

"Sure, and I'll cook it," he said. He noticed Tam and Rona looking at him skeptically. "I happen tae have many talents, thank you."

"I'll believe that when I see it," Rona said. Jamey laughed again.

"We need tae keep her around, Danny. She certainly keeps you on your toes," he said. Rona blushed a little as the four of them laughed.

When Morna saw the meat, she claimed it as hers and set about cooking lunch for the four of them.

"You don't really think I'd let you loose in my kitchens, do you, Master Aiden?" Morna had asked. Aiden had relented with a sigh and sat down with the others to eat at the kitchen table. They kept easy conversation and Aiden entertained them with some of the stories of his time in Calorin. At one point, they were practically wiping tears away.

"You did *what?*" Tam gasped for breath.

"Not one of my finer moments, I can assure you," Aiden said, taking another drink of ale.

"Are you sure you had any of those?" Jamey asked. Aiden threw a crust of bread at him.

"I'll have you know that I became famous in that village. Never mind the fact that they lived on the far border and rarely saw outsiders," Aiden said. Rona held her side as she tried to stop laughing.

"I'm sure your friends were jealous," she said.

"So jealous that they remind me of that incident every chance they get," Aiden said cheerfully.

"Do you miss it there?" Rona asked curiously. Aiden hesitated.

"Occasionally," he admitted. "But I was the best hunter in Calorin and here I've fallen tae second best." He gestured to Rona and shook his head as they laughed again. Morna came up and swept his boots off the table.

"There's a messenger here tae see you apparently," she said. Aiden straightened in his chair as a rider wearing the green plaid of Clan Dyson came in and handed him a letter.

"The Hawk's runner gave it tae us at the border a few days ago, sir," he said. Aiden quickly read it and smiled.

"Morna, you'll make sure he gets something tae eat?" he asked and the cook nodded. "If you two will excuse us. Tammy, we need tae go talk with Father."

They found Ranulf with their father in his study.

"You were right, sir. Will is in Aredor," Aiden told Laird Gòrdan as he held up the letter.

"How did you find out?" Ranulf asked.

"I told you I have some friends there. He's been there for a few months," Aiden said. Laird Gòrdan sighed in relief.

"I'll have a letter for him before you leave for the Festival," he said. "I want you and Tam tae make sure he knows he can come back home."

The brothers exchanged a satisfied look. It would be good to be together as a family again.

"And what about you, Aiden?" Laird Gòrdan asked. Aiden was startled.

"Me?"

"You obviously need something constructive tae do," his father remarked. Aiden hesitated a moment before he noticed Tam and Ranulf trying to hide smiles.

"Really?" he pointedly asked them.

"At the rate you're going, we're not going tae have anything left tae hunt or any practice poles left in the arena," Ranulf said.

"Maybe if you'd actually let me do something around here," Aiden said. "I know I'm a Laird's son, but I can do more than strut around with swords all day long."

"There's not much tae do," Laird Gòrdan said. "We're at peace now."

"And what if the Durnians try and come back?" Aiden asked.

"They won't. They know by now that Adalwulf failed and the Clan has gathered again," Ranulf said. That seemed to be the end of the conversation so Tam and Aiden left.

"Are you all right?" Tam asked his brother.

"Aye, I'm just…I need something tae do, Tam," Aiden said.

"You've seemed more cheerful than I remember since the battle," Tam said.

"I learned a long time ago that another day you get tae live is another day tae laugh. Even if it's forced sometimes," Aiden said.

"You're not happy here?"

"No, I am. I…this isn't what I'm used tae, Tam." Aiden looked around at the wooden walls around them and suddenly felt claustrophobic. "I'll be back later," he said, and left Tam standing slightly bewildered in the halls.

Narak was still fresh enough and was always eager to run again. They galloped down a little used pathway until Aiden reined up. *Maybe Corin could help*, he thought. Narak pulled at the reins as Aiden turned him back to Scodra. They would leave for the Festival within the week and he found himself looking forward to the journey.

The morning they were to leave was misty and cool; autumn had settled in to the forest. Twenty warriors and their families waited in the courtyard and Aiden saw, to his pleasure, that Rona would also accompany them. The company waved farewells to those to remain behind and, led by Jamey and the ever faithful Maon, they left Scodra and turned onto the road to Aredor.

Chapter 19

King Celyn was surprised when he saw his youngest son in the castle library.

"It's not like you to be so studious, Corin," he said. His son smiled as he replaced a book on the shelf.

"I still don't seem to get any answers though," Corin said.

"What are you looking for?" his father asked curiously.

"Anything about Durna. I don't care much about their politics. I want to know how they fight, how they move and train. The garrison at Lynwood is practically all new, so they can't tell me anything," Corin said.

"Do you really think that the Sultaan made an alliance with the Durnians?" King Celyn asked.

"Most likely," Corin replied. "It's what I would do. The Calorins lost too many men in the first war and Aiden brought news of more unrest. The Sultaan won't have enough men for another campaign. I know how the Calorins move and think but I know almost nothing about Durna."

"I've had some dealings with them in the past, mostly over border disputes," King Celyn said. "They are some of the best foresters and trackers in the north. The Durnians are shrewd, clever warriors. It takes much for them to admit defeat. Their axes are a force to reckon with."

Corin thought over this information.

"I know that the Calorins will attack again if they gain the trust of Durna. They probably know the Hawk Flight and Lynwood Keep will be waiting if they come over the west border. The Durnians can lead them through Dunham Forest and would be able to find us more quickly than the Calorins could. What do you think we should do?" Corin asked his father. He was always grateful for the years of campaign experience his father could give him.

"As you said, the Durnians will be able to track almost anything. I would leave the horses behind and go on foot. That would reduce the risk of being found. You would be more likely to be ambushed than during the first war," King Celyn said. "Use the garrison at Lynwood to patrol the northern section of the forest. That way you have more men to spread along the border."

Corin nodded. "It's been almost three months since Aiden brought word about the Sultaan's ship. If a treaty was completed, the messenger would have to get back to Calorin and the army would begin to assemble," he mused aloud.

"That would take a number of weeks. And transport back to Durna would be no easy task," King Celyn said.

"The Durnians will know better than to begin a campaign with winter coming soon. If I were the Sultaan, I'd winter my troops in Durna and then attack in the spring," Corin said. "But there's the chance I've got it all wrong. They could attack during the Festival when our guard will be relaxed."

King Celyn understood his agitation and uncertainty. He had faced it many times before.

"Corin, the best thing you can do is keep your men prepared," he said.

"I've talked to them. They understand the need for caution and readiness. We can't afford to be caught unawares. But everything has been quiet. Even the Raiders haven't attacked the coast as frequently. Something is going to happen," Corin said.

"Speaking of your men, how is that young man you took off Tristan's hands?" King Celyn asked.

"Andras has changed little, much to my and Pedr's irritation," Corin said. "But he has made good progress with the training. I suppose I'll have to let him into the warband fairly soon."

"You're considering letting him loose in the forest?" King Celyn asked, half-jokingly.

Corin smiled. "He's good with a blade and the training comes easily to him. If only I could find a way to help him get over himself," Corin paused. "I'm hoping he'll figure out that he's not going to get special treatment once he's in the warband."

"That's going to be difficult, considering the Hawk Flight's legend. And you've trained them to be the best warband in Aredor," King Celyn pointed out. The black and green uniforms were a source of pride to their wearers and everyone recognized the distinctive hawk crest. But the warriors knew better than to abuse their status or they would answer directly to the Captain.

"We'll see," Corin said. "He's going in my patrol."

"You seem sort of grimly pleased about that," his father said.

"Well, I can't wait until he sees our highly luxurious camp for the first time," Corin laughed.

"You're leaving again soon, aren't you?"

"Yes, sir. I'll go tomorrow to meet up with my men for the last part of the patrol. Then everyone is meeting at the camp so we can determine who has leave for the Festival. Some haven't been home in over a month."

"You are coming back for the Festival, aren't you?" his father asked suspiciously.

"Yes, it's been made perfectly clear that I have to be there. I've also been ordered to see that a specific few come back too."

"Like who?"

"Martin, Will, Kieran, and Kara. Their family is coming from Clan Gunlon."

"It'll be good for them to see their relatives. And it will be good to see more of you," King Celyn said to Corin.

"Aye, I feel like I've hardly gotten a chance to actually talk with you since the dungeons," Corin agreed.

"Not the best circumstances for conversation," King Celyn said with a chuckle. "We'll have to make up for lost time at the Festival."

Corin nodded with a smile. He was looking forward to spending some more time with his father outside of councils and ceremonies. He had hero-worshipped him as a young boy, convinced that he was never wrong. He would be glad to put away conversations of supplies, tactics, and training. He had tried to spend as much time as he could with his family since the ending of the Calorin War the year before. But with his newfound responsibilities, he was hard pressed to. He knew it saddened his mother more than anyone. The Festival would give him a chance to catch up. He had missed so much during the long years he was in Calorin.

Corin was greeted joyfully by the men of his patrol when he joined them two days later.

"Don't enjoy yourself too much, Captain," Bran joked as Corin dismounted with a sigh of satisfaction.

"It's too easy not to. A whole week with no paper in sight," Corin replied. The men laughed quietly. "Anything to report?" Corin asked Llewellyn. The lieutenant shook his head.

"No, sir. Quiet as usual. But I keep feeling like something's going to happen soon."

"I told him we're still not used to the peace, but recently some of us have felt the same," Dylan spoke up.

"Aye, Flynn's been a little jumpy and Liam's been nosing at the border like a bloodhound," Bran said.

"Martin's not at ease either. You can feel it at the border. It's too quiet there," Llewellyn said. Corin listened quietly to his men. Most in the Hawk Flight were veterans of the war where their lives had depended on a feeling of danger and instinct. He trusted them all. He too had had faint stirrings of unease. He needed to spend more time with the warband.

"Tomorrow we'll head closer to the border and spend the rest of the patrol there. We'll see if there's anything new to pick up," Corin said. The men nodded in assent. As the Captain trusted them, so they trusted him. They had full confidence that he would lead them out of whatever might be coming.

The border between Durna and Aredor was marked by a strip of forest that had been cleared long ago. It was several yards wide and ran from the Grey Cliffs to the northern edge of Aredor. It had become overgrown since the invasion and looked hazardous to the eyes of the Hawk Flight. The wild brush would provide perfect cover for enemy scouts to slip unseen into Aredor.

Corin stood hidden in the trees and looked across the expanse into Durna. An owl hooted and Liam flitted back across. Corin had sent for Liam and his patrol. Liam had been a lieutenant and forester at Lynwood before the war and had trained his men to be the best trackers in the warband. Liam had been one of the first to meet Corin upon his return to Aredor and had become one of his closest friends.

"I don't see anything out of the ordinary, Corin," Liam said. "It's just game trails and animal tracks."

Corin adjusted his quiver over his shoulder.

"Still, let's start to vary the routes. We can't take any chances," Corin said. Liam nodded.

"We've all been on the lookout for different tracks or patterns, especially on the less used paths," he said, then laughed shortly. "I still wonder how much of this is me not used to the peace."

"You're not the first to say it," Corin told him. "But this is different. It's that feeling you get right before someone ambushes you. Like someone is watching you and nothing is as quiet as it seems," he said. They cast one last glance over the border and then turned away. They would take a different road back to camp where the whole warband had begun to assemble.

"We'll be making a few changes over the winter," Corin announced to the men gathered in the main caves. Over eighty men filled the cavern either sitting at the tables or leaning against the walls. "First, we'll leave the horses behind. Some will stay at Lynwood and the others will go to garrisons outside the forest. Kara and Kieran, you'll keep your horses here along with a few spare ones," he said. There were nods of understanding. It would mean longer patrols on foot, but their lives might depend on it.

"Second, the newest recruits will be taking the oath by the beginning of winter. There will be some rearranging in the patrols to ensure the proper fit. You all know what to do. Teach them everything we know," Corin said. Again, there were murmurs of agreement.

"Will there be any more recruits coming in after them, Captain?" one warrior asked.

"Not unless there is a vacancy," Corin replied. The warrior nodded. The only vacancy would come at one of their deaths.

"We'll be trying some new routes over the winter. They'll be marked on the map. And from now on we'll be constantly changing paths. Split up and vary the use of trails. Take the lesser used paths. Don't ever do anything the same way twice. Again, you all know what to do," Corin said.

"You really expecting something, Captain?" Kieran asked.

"We'll find out for sure when spring comes," Corin replied. "I don't want any word of this getting out. We don't need undue panic."

"We won't breathe a word," Llewellyn spoke for the whole warband.

"Martin, do you have that list?" Corin asked. Martin dug into his pouch and produced the paper. "I'll only send thirty of you home this time. I know it's the Festival and I wish I could give everyone leave, but we can't leave this place completely unguarded. For the rest of you, when your time comes you'll get a few extra days. It's a poor exchange but it's the best I can do," Corin said.

"We don't mind, sir, just as long as we can see our families," a warrior said stoutly. Corin read the names from the list. It was a mix from all four patrols but mostly from those that hadn't been home in a few weeks. After the men were dismissed, Will found Corin.

"I've no family in Kingstown. Let me stay behind and send one of the younger lads," Will said.

"Sorry, Will. That decision wasn't made here. I'm just passing on orders," Corin said.

"But, sir—"

"If I wasn't ordered myself to be there, I might consider it. But I'm the Captain, so you're going. You're not going to make me pull full rank on you, are you?" Corin asked.

"I might, just tae see you do it," Will replied. "But the Clans will be there. Among them I'm an outcast. I can'nae wear the plaid."

Corin understood. Among the Clans the plaid represented everything. It was their pride, their honor, and marked their tie to their Clan. To be seen without it and to be forbidden to wear it brought shame and dishonor to a Braeton.

"You are in Aredor now and everyone, even the Clans, respects the uniform you are wearing," Corin reminded him. Will nodded reluctantly. It was more than his inability to wear the plaid. He wondered if any of Clan Canich would come and what they would think of him? Would his father be there and what would he say to the son he had banished?

"Yes, sir," he replied.

Corin went to the small side cave that was separated from the main caves by a curtain. It was where he kept his belongings and slept. He began to pack his bags. They would leave the next morning to return to Kingscastle in time for the Autumn Festival to begin.

Book 2

The Autumn Raids

Chapter 1

It was midmorning when the towers of Kingscastle came into sight. Tam, used to wooden fortresses, stared in wonder at the immense stone keep and walls. Aiden rode beside him.

"It's a grand sight, isn't it?" he said. Tam nodded in silence. This was the first time he had travelled beyond Braeton, or any great distance from Scodra for that matter. Rona edged her horse up along with Jamey. By now they could see the town that surrounded two sides of the castle.

"It's so big!" she marveled.

"Wait until we actually get there," Aiden told her.

They circled the castle to enter through the main gates under the west wall. They were met in the courtyard by grooms and a captain of the guard.

"We saw you coming. Clan Strowen and Clan Gunlon arrived yesterday," the captain said. "The King and Prince Darrin are on their way to greet you."

As he spoke, the main doors swung open and King Celyn descended the steps followed by Darrin. Brannan stared wide-eyed at the imposing figure coming toward them.

"Is that a real king?" he whispered to Rona.

"Yes. See his crown?" she whispered back.

"I like the other man better. He looks nice," Brannan said.

"That must be Prince Darrin," Rona told him. Darrin caught Brannan looking at him from the corner of his eye. He turned and gave the boy a smile and a wink. Brannan smiled tentatively and waved back.

"My father sends his regrets that he couldn't come, your majesty," Aiden said to the king. "This is my younger brother, Tamhas, and Captain Artair."

"Welcome," King Celyn said. "There will be room for all of you in the castle. If there is anything you need, don't hesitate to ask," he said before moving on. Darrin moved in to greet Aiden.

"Welcome back," he said.

"Thank you, sir," Aiden said and then introduced some more of the party.

"We're expecting Corin back this afternoon," Darrin told Aiden.

"He on patrol?" Aiden asked. Darrin nodded.

"It's been quiet so far," he said.

"How long do you think it will last?" Aiden asked.

"Corin thinks they'll come in the spring," Darrin replied. "But enough for now. I'll send someone to show you to your quarters."

"Thank you," Aiden replied.

"What was that all about?" Tam asked curiously after Darrin left.

"Nothing tae worry about," Aiden said. "Just some business with the Hawk Flight and the border."

"There might be another war?" Artair fit the conversation together. Aiden looked grim.

"But we're not here for that. Get the horses taken care of and then everyone can do as they want," he said. Some handed their horses to grooms. A stable boy came forward to take Narak. Aiden saw the stallion's ears flick back warningly.

"You'd better let me take him, lad," he said. The groom willingly led Aiden inside the stables and showed him an empty stall.

Rona took her bags and, along with her sister-in-law, began to shepherd Brannan and the other young children inside. They were stopped by another woman. She was dressed in the finest clothes Rona had ever seen and wore a regal looking circlet around her forehead.

"Welcome," the woman said. "I'm Amaura," she introduced herself. Rona dropped a brief curtsey.

"My lady," she said. "I'm Rona."

"You don't have to call me that," Amaura said. "I'm just happy to see some other women here."

Rona took her sister-in-law's bag while she chased after Brannan who had decided to start exploring.

"I'm sorry about..." Rona began.

"Oh, don't worry," Amaura laughed. "It must be very exciting for him."

"It is. He didn't stop talking about it the whole way here. I'm afraid I couldn't tell him much about castles." Rona blushed slightly, wishing she didn't sound so dull. Amaura didn't even seem to notice.

"If you need anything, I'd be glad to help," she said. "But you must tell me how you did your hair!" Amaura exclaimed noticing Rona's intricate braids for the first time. Now Rona smiled. A princess was asking after her hair!

"It's simple really," she said.

"If you have the time, you must show me!" Amaura said. "Please! There's not too many other women my age around here these days. I'd love to have some girly conversation."

Rona smiled again. Amaura wasn't the only one who wanted some female companionship of her own age.

"I'd enjoy that," Rona said. "There's tae be a feast tonight?" she asked. After receiving Amaura's confirmation she continued. "Maybe we could meet before and I can show you?"

"That would be wonderful!" Amaura exclaimed. She stood aside to let Rona join her sister-in-law to finally catch the young ones and take them to their quarters.

Not long after, Aiden and Tam emerged from their room dressed in clean clothes with the plaid cloaks wrapped around their shoulders. They walked slowly through the hallways toward the main hall. Jamey and Rona joined them and they looked curiously at the tapestries adorning the walls. Each one detailed different heroes and moments in Aredor's history.

The main doors still stood open. Aiden heard a sentry call down to the captain of the guard.

"Hawk Flight coming in, sir!"

Aiden made his way to the doors as a clatter of hooves sounded in the courtyard. A familiar voice gave the dismissal order. Aiden watched as Corin dismounted and unbuckled his packs from the saddle. Two stable boys shoved each other to try and take Zephyr first. Corin instead beckoned to a younger groom. He leaned down to give instructions to the boy who took the reins and looked up hesitantly at the huge stallion that towered over him. Zephyr lowered his head and snorted gently as Corin patted him on the neck. He slung his bags over his shoulder and headed toward the door.

"Well, well! Look what the dog dragged in!" Aiden said in Calorin. Corin looked up to see him leaning against a pillar at the top of the stairs. A delighted grin spread over his face.

"You came! We hoped you would be able to!" he also reverted to Calorin. He mounted the stairs and they embraced. "So, this is you cleaned up and acting your place?" Corin said, taking in the plaid cloak.

"Aye, a look you haven't mastered yet it seems," Aiden replied with a smile. Corin laughed.

"It's hard when I keep forgetting my titles," he said.

"Well, I have a whole week to remind you in every way possible," Aiden said. A familiar cry sounded and the grey hawk darted down to join Corin.

"You're still carrying that wee bag of feathers around?" Aiden asked. Karif chirped at him. "No? You tell him what to do?" Aiden addressed the hawk. Karif cocked his head and chirped again.

"He says yes," Corin said.

Tam and the others had followed Aiden outside. He watched as his brother greeted the captain, listening in wonder as they spoke in a strange, flowing language. Aiden and the stranger looked alike in many ways. Their clothes were cut differently from those around them. The pants were looser and were tucked into the same worn boots. The sleeves of the shirts were wider and battered vambraces were buckled over all. A hawk was emblazoned on the stranger's thick leather tunic and Tam knew he carried more weapons than the daggers and curved blade hanging at his belt. Aiden caught sight of them and motioned them over.

"I brought some company with me this time," he told Corin. He introduced Tam, Rona, and Jamey saying, "This is Prince Corin, sometimes called 'the Hawk.'"

"Only on formal occasions," Corin said, shaking their hands. "And I try to avoid those."

"Still the strong, silent type, eh?" Aiden joked.

"I have no choice when you're around," Corin retorted.

"All this time and I thought you were my friend." Aiden shook his head.

"I thought we were friends back in Hannad, too," Corin said and Aiden smirked.

"I was just following orders. And I won't even mention Bayhas!" he said. It was Corin's turn to smirk.

"I was just following orders!" he mimicked.

"That's it! I'm not talking tae you. I still haven't forgiven you for that!" Aiden said lightly.

"That's harsh considering I brought you a surprise," Corin said, nodding behind him. Aiden's companions had listened to the exchange in quiet amusement and Tam followed Corin's nod. He stared in disbelief and caught Aiden's arm.

"That's Will!" he exclaimed, pointing down into the courtyard. Corin stepped aside to let them pass as Tam ran down the steps.

Will's face broke into a delighted smile as he saw Tam and practically tackled his younger brother before wrapping him in a hug. Tam finally pulled back and turned Will to face Aiden.

"Danny?" Will exclaimed.

"Hey, Will," Aiden said. "You're a sight for sore eyes!"

"Aye! It's good tae finally see you again!" Will said as they embraced. "Ten years, eh? I didn't expect you tae still be so short." His eyes twinkled merrily.

"Only because you look fatter," Aiden returned with the same sly gleam. Will laughed and hugged him again.

"I didn't expect tae see either of you here," Will said. "Adalwulf?"

"Dead," Tam answered. "Father sits on the throne again."

"We'll tell you later," Aiden said as Will was about to launch a slew of questions. "But first." He winked at Tam who took off his cloak and wrapped it around Will's shoulders. Will touched the plaid hesitantly and looked to his brothers as the full weight of the action sank in. Aiden smiled broadly and nodded once.

"He's been pardoned!" Rona exclaimed. Corin smiled as he watched the scene unfold in the courtyard.

"How long has he been here?" Jamey asked.

"Four months. I hoped he wouldn't have to stay here forever. I knew Aiden would stir things up once he got back home," Corin said.

"How long have you known Aiden?" Rona asked.

"Almost seven years. I'd do anything for him. He's saved my life more than once," Corin answered.

"He said the same thing about you," Rona said. Aiden had told them stories about his and Corin's adventures around the campfire along the journey.

"I owe him more than he knows. He taught me to trust again," Corin said.

"Will! Am I really seeing this?" Kieran said as he approached with Kara.

"Aye, you are. I can hardly believe it myself," Will replied.

"I'm so happy for you!" Kara said.

"Thanks," Will said. "These are my brothers." He introduced them. Kara looked at Aiden and a blurred memory flashed by that she had tried to forget.

"You're the one..." she began but Aiden shook his head imperceptibly. "Who visited earlier this summer." She finished instead. Then she summoned her small store of Calorin. "I understand," she said. "But I never was able to thank you."

"You're welcome," Aiden simply replied. The twins were immediately called away by relatives who had anxiously awaited their arrival.

"You going tae tell us what that was about?" Will asked.

"No, and you can'nae ask her either," Aiden said cheerfully. They made their way up the steps to where the others still stood.

"Did you know they would be here?" Will asked Corin.

"Not for certain. It was mainly Darrin's idea, especially after I might have gotten a letter from someone asking if I knew where you were," Corin said. Will noticed Aiden looked rather innocent and smiled. From what he remembered of his brother and what he had seen of Corin, they might have been cut from the same cloth.

"And speaking of Darrin, I should go give him a report before he tries to hunt me down," Corin continued.

"Can I talk to you later?" Aiden asked in Calorin before Corin walked away.

"Aye, you all right?" Corin asked in kind. He looked concerned so Aiden quickly reassured him.

"I'll tell you later," he promised. Corin disappeared into the castle and Will greeted the others.

"What are you doing running around with these lads?" he asked Rona. She hugged him with a laugh.

"Getting more trouble than I bargained for," she replied. Will smiled and clasped Jamey's hand.

"I see you're wearing the plaid," he said. "I'm glad tae see it. It was too long in the coming."

"You're not the first tae say it," Jamey replied.

"I can'nae tell you how good it is tae see all of you again!" Will said. Aiden smiled.

"Come inside and let's find a place tae catch up," he said. "We'd all like tae hear what you've been up tae."

- -

Kara trod lightly along the corridor to her chamber while humming a tune. The Festival was finally here and there were relatives to meet again. And tonight was the big banquet to begin the Festival.

She pulled her favorite dress from the wardrobe, bathed and dressed. She stood in front of the mirror and tugged the folds of the light blue dress into place. The sleeves were slashed, showing white fabric underneath and a thin belt encircled her waist. Satisfied, she turned to the painstaking process of brushing and drying her long, blonde hair. When she finally finished, she sat in the chair at the dressing table and stared at herself, completely mystified as to what to do next.

A knock sounded at the door.

"Come in," she called and Amaura entered, accompanied by Rona.

"Are you ready?" Amaura asked.

"No, I'm not!" Kara moaned. "I don't know what tae do with my hair!"

Amaura laughed.

"It's easy for you!" Kara exclaimed, turning fully around in the chair. "You look beautiful!"

Amaura was wearing a deep red dress in contrast with her dark hair which was held in place by a simple silver band encircling her forehead. A delicate flower carved from agate hung on a chain around her neck.

"Thank you," she said gracefully. "Have you met Rona?" she asked Kara.

"Not yet," Kara said, rising. "You're with Clan Canich?" She saw a small silver wildcat pin fastened at the top of Rona's neckline.

"I am. Amaura said you are from Clan Gunlon?" Rona asked in turn.

"My mother's people," Kara said. "And she'd despair of me now. How do you two manage it?" she asked. Rona wore a dark green dress, delicately chased with silver embroidery. She had pulled her dark hair back from her narrow face in several small braids which then intertwined together behind her head.

"What?" Rona asked.

"Tae look so perfect! I'm always covered in dirt and horsehair or I'm sharpening my sword instead of worrying about hair and clothes," Kara said. Amaura laughed again.

"If you did you wouldn't have time to be a runner for the Hawk Flight," she said. "Besides, I'm sure there are plenty of people who like you just the way you are, starting with the young men in the warband who'll be begging you to dance with them tomorrow."

Kara smiled.

"If any of them can recognize me," she said.

"They won't be able to by the time we're finished with you!" Amaura declared.

"Do you want help with your hair?" Rona asked.

"Yes!" Kara exclaimed fervently. She sat down in the chair and Amaura began to brush her hair as Rona pulled some ribbons from the box on the table. Rona pulled Kara's hair back in a simplified version of her own hair. She plaited two small braids together and fastened them with a white ribbon, leaving the rest of Kara's hair free to fall down her back.

"Thank you so much!" Kara said as she quickly pulled on her shoes.

Kieran knocked on the open door.

"Ma'am." He bowed to Amaura and Rona. "You finally ready?" he asked his sister.

"Yes." She smoothed her dress one last time.

"You look very nice," he complimented her.

"So do you," she returned. Kieran wore a light blue tunic to match her. His boots and belt were freshly cleaned and polished. He even kept the sleeves of the fresh white shirt rolled down for the occasion.

The four of them made their way down to the main hall and met Corin halfway.

"I almost didn't recognize you, Kara," he grinned. She swept a curtsey.

"Your highness," she smiled back. She had to admit he looked the part. He wore a high collared, dark blue tunic edged in silver thread over a white shirt. Black pants were tucked into new black boots. Light leather bracers were buckled over his forearms and a dagger hung from his belt.

"You will allow me to escort my sister, won't you, Kieran?" he asked mock-seriously as Amaura took his arm.

"Corin, where is it?" Amaura asked as they continued down the stairs.

"What?" he asked innocently.

"You know what I mean," she replied.

"I misplaced it again. It's so very clumsy of me," he said.

"It's only a simple silver circlet. It's not like you have to wear a crown or anything!" Amaura said. "Darrin is wearing his."

"That is because he's the crown prince. Besides, if anyone doesn't know who I am, Father or Darrin will give them all my titles so I don't have to wear it," Corin argued. Amaura sighed in exasperation.

"What are we going to do with you?"

"I feel like an idiot!" Aiden complained.

"Why? Because you look respectable?" Tam asked. Aiden glared at his brother as he straightened his tunic.

Tam and Will were already dressed and were making sure Aiden wore the proper clothes. He wore a high collared white shirt with blue embroidery. A black tunic with the same blue stitching running down the front and edges went over the shirt. Tam handed him black leather bracers embossed with brown leather and silver.

"This is ridiculous!" Aiden muttered as he pulled on stiff new boots. "I can barely move in all this!"

"You're the son of a Laird and you're in the place of an ambassador. You have tae look presentable for once in your life," Will said, holding out a belt to him. It was the same design as the bracers.

"I'm not wearing that," Aiden refused and took up his plain black belt instead, buckling it on with his knives. Tam pulled a brooch from his bags.

"But you're wearing this," he said.

"Why do you have all this in your packs, Tam?" Will asked.

"Father wanted tae make sure it got here," Tam replied.

"I'm beginning tae understand why," Will said. Aiden rolled his eyes and took the brooch. Two wildcats with sapphire eyes fought each other in the circle. Aiden draped the plaid cloak around his shoulders and fastened it in place. Will adjusted the plaid so that it fell in proper folds. Aiden put his last knife in his boot and straightened up.

"Are all four knives really necessary?" Tam asked.

"Yes, and I will prove it tae you," Aiden replied. "You ladies ready tae go?"

"We're not the ones who took forever tae get dressed." Will smirked and pushed the door open. Aiden straightened the tunic again and sighed, resigning himself to his fate.

"Some things never change, do they?" Will asked.

"Unfortunately," Aiden agreed. "But I'm telling you, if for some reason we're attacked tonight, I won't be of any use tae you. I couldn't fight in these clothes."

"Then it's a good thing we have nothing tae worry about," Tam said, pushing Aiden through the door.

They met Corin and the others as they reached the hall.

"Look at you!" Corin said to Aiden. "I didn't think it was actually you."

"Shut up," Aiden replied. "Help me clear something up. How many are you carrying?"

"Three. Why?" Corin asked. Aiden turned triumphantly to Tam, who raised his hands in defeat.

"Show him yours," Aiden said. Corin gave a quick flick of his wrist and a blade lay in the palm of his hand. Another twist and it was gone.

"He's been giving you another one of his lectures, hasn't he?" Corin asked Tam. They entered the hall and Corin drew Tam and Will into easy conversation. Aiden found himself by Rona.

"You look…different," she said.

"That's a good word tae describe it." Aiden chuckled.

"What do you mean?"

"I don't feel cut out for all this—these clothes and having people notice me. I guess I'm not quite used tae it."

"You'll be fine," she assured him.

"You really think so?" he raised an eyebrow.

"Yes, I do."

A bell rang, signaling the beginning of the feast. They parted ways. As head of the party from Clan Canich, Aiden had to sit at the head table with the other lords and the King and Queen. To his relief, he was seated next to Corin and Trey.

"We only have to do this once, right?" he murmured to Corin.

"Yes, I made sure of that," Corin replied softly, but Aiden could still hear the relief. Queen Elain sat next to Corin and he re-introduced his mother to Aiden.

"Aiden, perhaps you can tell me something about my son. Has he always treated that animal like a human?" she asked. Aiden glanced to see Karif perched on the back of Corin's chair.

"Honestly, ma'am, I think it's the other way around," Aiden replied with a smile and Queen Elain laughed.

"You do, eh?" Corin asked.

"You know it's true," Aiden said.

"It probably is, isn't it?" Corin admitted, offering Karif a piece of meat which was eagerly accepted.

"Trey, Martin keeps telling me I should challenge you to a race," Corin said. Trey leaned forward from the other side of Aiden.

"Sure, but you know I can beat you any day," he said lightly.

"To give myself a sporting chance, I was thinking the Chenedl," Corin replied.

"Corin! That's the most dangerous race. No one's done it in almost one hundred years!" Queen Elain exclaimed.

"Then maybe it's time someone tried it again," Corin said. "What do you say, Trey?"

Queen Elain saw the light in Trey's eyes that was mirrored in her son's. She'd seen the same look in her husband's eyes and so many other warriors and knew that nothing would deter them. Men leaned forward all along the table to hear Trey's answer.

"If no one's done it in that long, then I'm in," Trey said. "Give me a day to rest Nerys?"

"Aye, Zephyr could use a day as well," Corin agreed.

With the day settled, talk soon turned to other matters. The evening moved slowly on. Corin refilled his beaker and nodded to Aiden. When Queen Elain turned again, they were both gone.

Corin opened the door to his room and Aiden entered.

"Well, I like what you've done with the place," Aiden commented. A bed sat against the far wall and two arm chairs were placed by the fireplace. A table and chairs sat by the window and a wardrobe stood in the corner. The other prominent feature of the room was weapons. Two javelins leaned against the wall by the door. A sheathed broadsword hung horizontally on the wall above the hearth. Corin's bow and scimitar lay on the table and the hilt of a knife peeked out from under a pillow on the bed.

Aiden took off his cloak and bracers and loosened the top of his tunic as Corin moved his packs from the armchairs.

"This yours?" he asked, looking at the broadsword.

"It was supposed to be given to me when I got old enough to start training," Corin said. He took it down and handed it to Aiden.

"It doesn't look like you ever tried tae use it," Aiden said, unsheathing it.

"Martin has tried to teach me, but the scimitar is my weapon. I can't give it up. I still use the javelins instead of the heavier spears, to the disappointment of some of the lords. They still think I'm part Calorin in spite of everything," Corin said. Aiden shook his head in disgust and replaced the sword.

"So what's bothering you?" Corin asked.

"Is it that obvious?" Aiden asked. Corin shrugged.

"You looked like you were favoring your left arm earlier and I keep hearing bits and pieces of you saving Braeton from a massive invasion. And you look restless. So…?" Corin said.

"I wish you weren't so observant sometimes," Aiden said. Corin smiled as he unbuckled his vambraces and also loosened the top of his tunic.

They settled into the armchairs with beakers of ale and Aiden related the plain story of the fight for Scodra and the few events after. He pushed up his sleeve so Corin could see the new scars on his arm that crippled the lower legs of the wildcat tattoo.

"It seems like it has taken longer to heal than normal. I haven't seemed to get full strength back and I can't really train with anyone like I'm used to," he said.

"And…" Corin prompted, sensing that was not all.

"I don't know," Aiden said. "How do you do it? It's so quiet there now. I feel on edge."

"Going out on patrol helps me," Corin said. "I've gotten so used to war that now I almost can't handle this peace."

"Aye, and they don't really understand. Tam tries but…it's like…since the trouble is over, they expect me to just put aside everything I've learned and settle down. To be…someone. I just haven't figured out who yet. I'm not proud of everything I did in Calorin, but it was my life for eight years and I can't just put it away." Aiden said.

"I know," Corin said softly. "I'm supposed to be healed and able to move on and be some sort of hero. But I can't forget everything that ever happened to me. I still have the nightmares, Aiden, and how many times did you have to wake me from those?"

They fell into silence for a few moments.

"So, what now?" Aiden asked. "I feel like I'll burst if I don't find something to keep me busy."

"There might be something I can do," Corin said. "I'll have it worked out before you leave."

"Even though you won't tell me, thanks, mate," Aiden said.

"I still wake early and there's a small training courtyard that's rarely used," Corin said.

"I'll meet you there," Aiden said. "The usual?"

"The usual," Corin confirmed with a smile.

Chapter 2

Tam woke shortly after dawn. Aiden's bunk across the room was empty and neatly made. Overcome by curiosity, he rose and dressed and left in search of his brother. A sentry silently pointed him to a more secluded part of the castle grounds. The sounds of hollow blows guided him through a stone passageway that led into a courtyard. He halted inside the entrance and watched the two occupants.

Aiden and Corin wore short-sleeved shirts with arms bare of bracers. They sparred with wooden training swords in a fighting style different from anything Tam had ever seen. Aiden held two but every so often one sword would change possession and he fought with one.

Suddenly, at a sharp word from Aiden, the swords were dropped and they moved to hand-to-hand combat. Tam saw that even though the style was fast and aggressive, very few blows were actually landed with force. Corin tumbled sideways after a light strike to his ribs and came up on his feet. Aiden signaled a halt and leaned over, his hands on his knees.

"You all right?" Corin asked in Calorin. Tam took an impulsive step forward, thinking Aiden was hurt. Corin sensed the movement and gave Tam a nod as he recognized him.

"I'm fine," Aiden replied as they both regained their breath. "I didn't hit you too hard, did I?"

"I hardly felt it," Corin replied.

"Who's watching?" Aiden asked, catching a movement at the entrance.

"It's Tam. He's worried about you, Aiden," Corin said. Aiden straightened and rubbed his arm. "You want to move on?" Corin asked. "Don't overdo it. It took over three months for my arm to fully recover after the lion attack."

"I'll be fine. We can go slower," Aiden replied. "You can come and sit down, Tam," he called in Rhyddan. Tam came forward and sat on one of the benches under the overhanging roof and leaned against a pillar. Aiden and Corin went over to another bench and pulled on their short-sleeved mail coats and leather tunics. The heavy vambraces and belts were buckled on next.

Aiden withdrew his swords from their sheaths and twirled them experimentally as Corin unsheathed his scimitar. They moved to the center of the court and began again. Slowly at first and then gaining speed, it was a rhythmic pattern of blocks, thrusts, and lunges as if they had done it hundreds of times before. Tam saw that as before, blows were halted just before they hit the body or were struck with the flat of the blade.

Their faces were grim in concentration as steel hit steel in the dangerous dance. Then Aiden's sword slipped and slashed Corin's sword arm. They halted suddenly and Aiden loosed a frustrated yell in Calorin when he saw the blood.

"You all right, Hamíd?" he asked.

"Aye, it's not deep. I'll take care of it when we finish," Corin replied.

"No, we'll stop now," Aiden said.

"Do the last part again, Emeth," Corin said. "My arm will be fine."

Tam watched breathlessly as Aiden unwillingly began the attack again. They moved more slowly through the remainder of the exercise. Tam went over to them as they finished. Corin sheathed his sword and directed Tam to a pouch lying on the bench that held a few rolled bandages. Corin held his arm as Aiden took a waterskin and washed blood away from the cut. He took the bandage from Tam and wrapped it securely around Corin's arm.

"I'm sorry, Cor," Aiden said, speaking in the northern tongue.

"I might lose my arm and it's your fault," Corin replied, a smile tugging at his mouth.

"You're funny," Aiden said.

They sat down and began cleaning and sharpening their weapons while including Tam in their conversation. He watched them as they worked and joked good-naturedly. Aiden seemed more at home with Corin. But they were so alike anyway, Tam reflected: strong and dangerous. Scars from countless fights laced their bare arms. They were familiar with war and carried its burden along with their own secrets.

"We've probably missed breakfast by now," Aiden said as he finished with his swords.

"Well, I could look regally down my nose and get us something, or the cooks probably remember you," Corin said.

"That's because I'm so memorable," Aiden grinned. Corin shoved him. "I'm willing tae bet you go down there pretty frequently. You're almost as good at the pathetic face as I am," Aiden said.

"What? A respectable person like me?" Corin said. They both laughed.

"I'll meet you down there in a bit then?" Aiden said.

"Aye. Tam, you want to join us?" Corin asked. Tam nodded his agreement. Aiden left the courtyard but Tam lingered behind as Corin prepared to leave. He draped his cloak carefully over his arm to hide the bandage and blood that still remained.

"Can I ask you something, sir?" Tam asked.

"Sure." Corin nodded.

"Can you tell me what my brother was like in the South? It's just that I can'nae quite figure him," Tam said.

"I was in the Phoenix Guard with him." Corin held out his vambrace so Tam could see the insignia. "We met when we were about twenty years old. We were part of the best fighters under Lord Rishdah. Aiden was young but I think he was the best warrior among all of us. He took care of me and looked out for me when I was training. He's the best friend I could ask for."

"Why does he not want any praise for saving Scodra?" Tam asked. "And if you don't mind me saying, you don't seem tae take praise either."

"It's different for both of us. In the Guard we did so many things, some of which were sometimes considered to be impossible. But our whole purpose was to protect our lord. We lived for that and never received much recognition for it. He's just not used to it, Tam," Corin said.

"I'm just trying tae understand him better," Tam said.

"Give him some more time, Tam. It wasn't easy for me to explain myself after I returned and the war ended. It still isn't. We have to get used to being home again," Corin told him.

"Why was Corin in Calorin with you?" Tam asked Aiden after breakfast. Corin had left to meet some more guests that had arrived and Will and Jamey had joined them.

"I can'nae tell you that," Aiden said. "A man's past is his own tae keep."

"I don't even know," Will said as Tam looked to him. "Even most of the veterans of the Hawk Flight don't know much about him. Lieutenant Martin knows him the best but good luck trying tae get anything out of him."

"Resign yourself, laddie," Aiden told him. "The only way you'll ever find out is if he tells you and that will never happen."

They walked through the bustling courtyard and out to the open training fields. The fields around the castle were a buzz of color and activity. The Clans mixed easily with their Aredorian neighbors and shouts and laughter filled the air. There was a swirl of green and black and a merry young man greeted Aiden.

"I heard you came but I didn't get a chance to see you yesterday," Martin said. He and Aiden clasped hands and then Tam and Jamey were also introduced.

"Is there anyone here that you don't know?" Will asked his brother.

"I just have one of those faces," Martin said. A tall somber man appeared behind Martin.

"The kind that leaves children screaming?" he asked. Aiden greeted Trey who gave a rare smile. Tam and Jamey watched in silence born of wonder. They had heard enough from Aiden and from stories freely told in Aredor and carried to Braeton by merchants to know that they were meeting some of the heroes of the Calorin War as it had begun to be called.

"Corin and I are walking the course," Trey said to Martin. "You should be there since you are officiating."

"Fine!" Martin said. "Care to tag along?" he asked the Braetons. They all agreed. Will would have accompanied them also but he was hailed by two members of the Hawk Flight.

"So what's so special about this race?" Aiden asked. They walked with Martin behind Corin and Trey who were discussing the course with an older warrior.

"The Chenedl is the most difficult race of the Festival. The competitors race bareback around the training grounds and they must jump the obstacles specified," Martin said. They came to a fallen tree that had been dragged to the grounds for the race.

"Bareback, you say?" Jamey asked, looking over at the massive trunk.

"Aye, I don't envy them one bit!" Martin laughed. Further along, a ditch yawned across the trail.

236

"They said no one's done it in a hundred years?" Tam asked.

"It used to be run almost every Festival. But one year two warriors decided to ride it. One was killed after his horse threw him at a jump. The next year his friend ran it to honor him and no one's done it since. They still lay out the course every year though. It's a sore temptation for the younger warriors. Corin and I might have run it a few years ago if things had been different," Martin said.

"Why don't you do it now?" Aiden asked.

"I'm not nearly skilled enough to get through it. Corin and Trey are two of the best riders in Aredor. I'm more than content to watch," Martin said.

"Don't let him be so modest!" Trey called back.

"You're supposed to be paying attention up there, not eavesdropping on my conversation!" Martin yelled.

"We let you officiate the race and this is what happens," Corin called.

"Yes! I'm in charge this time, so no talking up there or you both lose!" Martin said.

"That's not even possible," Trey replied.

"There's a first time for everything," Martin warned.

They caught up to Corin and Trey at the edge of the river. The banks were steep where the river curved.

"You'll have to be careful where you jump in at this curve," the warrior was saying. "The river is shallow here. You'll go down river and come out where the bank levels down there." He pointed. "After that there's two more jumps and a straight shot to the finish. And of course there should be no one playing in the water tomorrow," he said. Martin saw where the warrior was looking.

"How'd he get all the way out here?" he sighed. "Hey, Gwilym! What are you doing?"

A young boy of seven looked up from where he was crouched by the water.

"Well, first I was chasing a rabbit, then there was a frog, then I wanted to catch a fish, then…" Gwilym continued until Martin held up his hand.

"Enough! You've been busy. You catch anything?" he asked. Gwilym shook his head. "We'll come back in a few days and do it properly," Martin said.

Gwilym brightened. "Really?"

"Really. Now come up before you get even dirtier," Martin said. Gwilym stared at the steep embankment.

"Can you help me?" he asked.

"No," Martin replied. "Find a way up."

Gwilym stared intently at the earthen wall confronting him and then used a tree root to scramble to the top where Martin relented and helped him the last few feet. Gwilym shrank against Martin's leg when he saw the strangers.

"This is Gwilym. He's my…" Martin seemed unsure of what to say.

"Martin's my uncle," the boy piped up. "And he's a friend," he pointed to the warrior. "And he's an uncle." He pointed to Corin. "And he's a grampa." Trey was last to be singled out.

"That's quite a mix of relatives you have," Aiden commented.

"Oh, I have lots more," Gwilym said.

"Really? How many?" Tam asked. Gwilym looked up at Martin.

"About twenty uncles and two aunts," Martin supplied.

"How did he manage that?" Aiden asked.

"Uncle Cor, would you mind?" Martin nodded at Gwilym. Corin understood.

"You've already seen the rest of the course, so if you'll excuse me, sir," the warrior said to Trey.

"Thanks, Ivor." Trey nodded.

"Come here, Gwilym. The best place to catch frogs is just down the river here," Corin said. Gwilym grabbed his hand and they hurried down to the river.

When Corin and Gwilym were gone, Martin began to relate the story.

"During the War, the Calorins started attacking the villages. We had the whole warband out to stop them but they finished with one small village before we got there. It was burning and he was the only one of his family alive. I pulled him out of the house and he wouldn't let go of me. He was about five years old. We took him to the settlement in the forest but it still took several days before he would let me leave him alone. He asked me if I was going to be his new father. I didn't know what to say so I became his uncle instead. After that he kind of adopted the rest of the warband and my sister," Martin said. The others listened somberly to the story as they heard Gwilym shouting as he and Corin chased after the small river creatures.

"How did you manage tae be the grandpa?" Jamey asked Trey. Martin smiled widely as Trey answered.

"Martin thought it would be funny to teach him to call me that," he said.

"I just thought Grandpa Trey had a much nicer ring to it than Uncle," Martin said as they all laughed.

"Trouble is, Gwilym saw that they all thought it was funny and picked right up on it," Trey said with a rueful smile.

"Grampa! Martin! Look what we caught!" Gwilym ran back up. "Let me show them, Uncle Cor!" he bounced up and down.

"All right, stay still and hold it like I showed you." Corin handed Gwilym the small frog he was carrying. The boy took it and proudly displayed it to his "uncle" and "grandpa" who viewed it with proper exclamations.

"Would you like to hold it?" Gwilym shyly asked Tam.

"Sure, if you don't mind?" the young Braeton crouched down and took the frog from Gwilym.

"Do you know how to catch them?" Gwilym asked Tam.

"We don't really have them where I live," Tam said.

"Where's that?"

"I live in the forest far away from here," Tam replied.

"I used to live in the forest with my Uncle Martin," Gwilym informed him.

"That's the longest he's ever talked to a stranger," Martin marveled as Tam and Gwilym chatted amicably.

"Tam can talk tae anyone, especially the little ones. They all love him," Aiden said.

Jamey had also been pulled down alongside Tam once Maon had started sniffing at the curious creature that Tam held.

"Can I keep it, Uncle Martin?" Gwilym begged. "I can put it in my room."

"That might not be a good idea," Martin said hesitantly.

"Why?" his "nephew" demanded.

"Well, Mera wouldn't like it. Aunts are kind of particular about frogs. Ask your Uncle Cor if you don't believe me," Martin said.

"Aunt Kara likes them," Gwilym pointed out.

"It takes a special kind of aunt to like them," Martin said.

"Let's go put it back by the river," Corin said. Gwilym took the frog and went back to the river with Corin.

"I hope those aren't your good clothes," Martin reprimanded Gwilym when they came back. Gwilym brushed furtively at the dirt on his clothes.

"No, Aunt Mera said I didn't have to wear them today," Gwilym said.

"Martin's more of a mother than an uncle," Corin said to the others.

"Can you give me a ride back, Grampa?" Gwilym asked Trey.

"You nearly broke my back last time," Trey said.

"I'll give you a lift if you want," Aiden offered.

"Really?" Gwilym asked.

"Sure. I've carried your fat Uncle Corin before so I think I can carry you," Aiden said. Gwilym's eyes widened at the news of this feat and he eagerly nodded. Aiden handed his swords to Corin and settled the boy on his back.

"Martin, can they be uncles?" Gwilym asked as they turned back to the castle, thoroughly taken with the Braetons.

"You'll have to ask them," Martin told him.

Upon receiving answers of assent, Gwilym decided that they would be his "far away uncles" like Trey now was, "'cept he was a grampa."

Gwilym's adopted family was hard pressed to keep straight faces at this comment.

"I'd be careful where I keep those swords, Aiden. Martin is eyeing them again," Trey warned.

"You up for a bout then, Martin?" Aiden asked. "I hear you're pretty good."

"Aye, I'm all right with my blade," Martin replied casually. "This afternoon then? I have another challenge to tend to."

"Sure. Whenever you want. I'll be ready," Aiden replied.

"Can I come watch? I never get to," Gwilym complained from his perch on Aiden's back.

"You might as well. It's the Festival, so everyone will be out watching," Martin said.

"We have to make sure our Blademaster retains his position," Corin said.

"Just as long as you or Trey never challenges me in public," Martin replied cheerfully. When they reached the castle, Aiden let Gwilym slide down from his back. Corin handed Aiden his swords.

"Softie," he said.

"You have no room tae talk, *Uncle*!" Aiden replied.

Chapter 3

Aiden watched his opponent carefully. Martin was good. He seemed to know Aiden's next move before Aiden knew it himself. Martin's face was intent as he watched the double blades and beat them back with his broadsword.

Corin watched keenly from the edge of the rough arena. Martin and Aiden were still moving slowly, feeling out each other's strengths and weaknesses.

"They won't get hurt, will they?" Mera asked anxiously. Corin looked over to see her standing beside him. "I hate it when he does this!"

Amaura and Rona were also with her and Corin noticed Rona watching the fight with slightly better hidden anxiety.

"Don't worry. You only try to beat the blade, not the opponent," Corin said. "They'll be fine."

"I still don't like it," Mera said.

The crowds of spectators called encouragement as Aiden and Martin began to move faster, sparring in earnest. Aiden pushed relentlessly, trying to find an opening but there seemed to be none. It happened suddenly: the tip of Martin's blade caught his left sword and tossed it aside. Another deft movement and his right sword was trapped against his body. He looked down to see a dagger locked against the left blade.

Aiden laughed in sheer amazement and Martin disengaged his blades.

"Incredible! No one's ever beaten me like that before!" Aiden exclaimed.

"I don't know if I could have actually finished you off like that. You won't hold it against me, will you?" Martin asked.

"How could I? It was beautiful!" Aiden said.

"Thanks," Martin smiled. "It wasn't easy. How do you manage to keep them going for so long?" he asked, thoroughly impressed now that he had faced the double swords for himself.

"I'd show you but then you'd know all my tricks." Aiden grinned, sheathing his swords and extending his hand. Martin did the same and clasped it firmly.

"You beat me fair and square, but I might try again another time," Aiden said.

"I look forward to it," Martin replied.

Aiden went over to where Corin, Trey, and his brothers stood, still shaking his head in amazement.

"He's good," he said.

"Aye. I feel fortunate to have beaten him once," Corin said.

"I've done slightly better," Trey said. "Twice for me."

They watched Martin prepare to fight his other challenger, a burly warrior from a keep in the Cymro Mountains.

"I've heard Cadoc is the best fighter in the eastern part of Aredor," Trey said.

"He looks good," Corin agreed.

"How long do you give Martin?" Trey asked.

"With Cadoc's size, about ten minutes," Corin estimated.

"How could you possibly know that?" Amaura demanded.

"Because we've done this a few times," Corin told her.

"How long did you give me?" Aiden asked curiously.

"A generous twelve minutes," Trey said.

"And?" Aiden questioned.

"Twenty," Corin replied with a grin.

They watched closely the exchange of blows between the two contestants.

"Azrahil would kill himself tae see this," Aiden said, marveling. Mera shivered seeing the open admiration in their faces at her brother's skill. She didn't understand the appeal after healing the rents made by the shining blades. She stifled an involuntary cry as Martin staggered back under a heavy blow from Cadoc.

"He's too tired tae finish! I should have waited!" Aiden said as Martin began to slowly retreat under a fresh attack from Cadoc.

"He's fine. He can fight for three days without stop," Trey reassured him.

"Aye, this is my favorite part," Corin said.

Cadoc, seeing his opponent retreating, became more confident. Martin allowed himself a slight smile when he saw a change in the pattern of the blows. Doubt crossed Cadoc's features at the sight of the smile but it was too late to change. Before Cadoc knew it, Martin stood alongside him with his blade laid across Cadoc's back.

Angry at being beaten and at seeing the triumphant light in Martin's eyes, Cadoc kicked at his opponent's leg as Martin stepped away. It caught Martin in the knee and he fell with a surprised cry. Cadoc gathered his sword and attacked. Martin barely warded off the blow and scrambled to his feet.

"Cadoc's out for blood and he's made Martin angry. This might not end well for Cadoc," Trey said worriedly to Corin. They both took a step forward. Silence had fallen over the onlookers. Aiden caught a glimpse of Martin's face. Whereas before he had been fighting with almost joy at the tests, he now moved with an even greater speed and efficiency, his eyes sparking angrily.

Cadoc's feet were suddenly swept out from under him and he fell to find his sword hand held in a viselike grip and a sword raised above him.

"Martin!" Corin barked as he saw the sword beginning to fall. Martin stopped and drew a shuddering breath. He slowly lowered the sword and tapped Cadoc's chest with the point. Cadoc let his sword fall from his hand, beaten. Martin again stepped away and, turning his back contemptuously on Cadoc, slowly limped over to Corin and Trey. He sheathed his sword with a snap, still roused and angry. Corin laid a calming hand on his arm and looked back to where Cadoc was being helped to his feet. Cadoc's angry expression faded at the warning look the Captain gave him.

Trey helped Martin limp over to a nearby bench set outside a tent. Mera hurried to him. Martin gripped the edge of the bench as Mera gently probed at his knee.

"Are you hurted, Uncle Martin?" Gwilym asked anxiously.

"It's nothing your Aunt Mera can't fix," Martin reassured him, gesturing for the boy to join him on the bench.

"I think it's all right, just swollen and bruised. You need to stay off it for a few days," Mera told her brother.

"I'm not just sitting around for a week!" Martin exclaimed.

"How are you?" Liam asked, coming up to join them.

"I might never fight again," Martin said.

"If only! And stop being so dramatic!" Mera said before consulting with the Hawk Flight's healer. Liam tested her theory himself.

"If you're trying to finish the job, just cut it off," Martin complained.

"She's right, Martin. You might stay behind from patrol for a day or so as well," Liam said.

"What? You can't make me do that!" Martin exclaimed.

"Do you want to make it worse?" Liam argued.

"Captain!" they both appealed to Corin.

"You're outnumbered, Martin. They're right and I'm not going to argue with both of them," Corin said.

"Traitor!" Martin muttered. "Fine!"

"Excuse me, your highness."

Corin turned to face the speaker, a tall man draped in the red plaid of Clan Strowen.

"Yes, my lord?" he asked.

"I would ask your lieutenant if he would be willing tae teach some of our younger lads," Laird Searc made his request. Corin turned to Martin who then nodded.

"I'd be glad to help, sir. When will they be ready?" Martin asked.

"I could not help but hear that you will have some extra time. They can be ready now if you wish," Laird Searc replied.

"How many, sir?" Martin asked.

"Five. And be warned that some of them are overly proud and arrogant," said Laird Searc.

"We'll sort that out. Anyone in particular, sir?" Martin asked.

"My son," Laird Searc replied. Martin cleared his throat awkwardly and the Braeton chuckled.

"You'd be doing me a favor," he said.

"All right, bring them over," Martin said.

"Can I watch?" Gwilym asked.

"No, I don't want you learning anything you're not supposed to," Martin said. Mera took Gwilym's hand and they left with Rona and Amaura. Laird Searc brought the young men up, led by a swaggering young Braeton.

"I'll leave you lads tae it," Laird Searc announced after catching Martin's look and leaving.

"You're supposed tae teach us? You can'nae even stand. I saw the fight," the leader sneered.

"Oh, really? What did you think?" Martin asked amiably.

"You were a fool tae let him kick you and tae turn your back on him," the young man answered.

"If you want to think that," Martin shrugged.

"I do. I also think you have nothing tae teach us," he declared. Three of his companions laughed in support.

"All right. We'll see if I do or don't. Draw your blade and if any one of you five can fairly knock me off this bench or disarm me, then you're free to go. But if not, we continue my way," Martin said, unsheathing his sword.

"You can'nae be serious!" the young Braeton exclaimed.

"Oh, I'm serious, laddie," Martin said softly. "You first. And you, go last." He pointed to the biggest boy in the group who had not laughed. Corin rested his hand against his mouth to artfully hide his smile and Aiden struggled manfully to restrain his laughter.

"This is just like Andras all over again. I couldn't stop smiling for days after Martin finished with him!" Trey whispered gleefully.

They saw another member of Clan Strowen watching in grim pleasure as Laird Searc's son struck at Martin who almost carelessly blocked the blow and sent the claymore flying.

"Next!" Martin called. Three more Braetons were also disarmed in short order. The last one came up slowly.

"Are you sure, sir?" he asked Martin hesitantly. Martin smiled up at the hulking youth.

"I might surprise you," he said.

"Come on, Guaire. The only thing you're good for is knocking things over!" Solas mocked as Guaire flushed.

"Come on, lad. Give it your best shot," Martin encouraged. He allowed Guaire a few more strokes than the others before sending the claymore to land in the ground beside Solas's foot.

"Is that good enough for you boys?" Martin stared levelly at the young Braetons who nodded awkwardly. The warrior of Clan Strowen that had been watching came up.

"Martin," the man greeted him briefly.

"Eornan," Martin nodded.

"I saw you fight. It was a cowardly hit you took. I came at Laird Searc's request tae offer any help you need," Eornan said.

"Perfect. Do you mind using a claymore today?" Martin asked.

"That's Strowen's champion," Tam told the others quietly, looking in awe at the tall, somber man. His eyes were as keen as the falcon of his Clan. Instead of a claymore, he carried a strange looking blade. A long black handle flowed into a blade that curved slightly at its tip.

"Aiden, would you join us as well?" Martin asked.

"You're the one the story is about?" Guaire asked, staring at Aiden. Aiden nodded to him.

"Aye, I'll come. I'll have tae borrow a claymore," he told Martin.

"I have an extra," Eornan said.

"You'll make us fight two champions?" one of the new students exclaimed.

"I won. We do it my way," Martin told him. "And you're not flailing away at anyone yet. We've got some work to do."

"Trey, it looks like Darrin and Tristan want us," Corin said, seeing his brother wave him over. "Martin, I'll send yours down."

"You have a claymore?" Guaire asked in surprise.

"A Blademaster should be able to use other blades besides his own," Martin said. "Come on, Guaire, you can be my crutch. We're going somewhere out of the way where there's a lovely spot for me to sit and watch you work."

Guaire grinned and helped Martin to stand and limp toward another part of the training grounds. Eornan wordlessly jerked his head after them, indicating the other students should follow with him and Aiden.

Tristan had just arrived at Kingscastle and he and Trey left to discuss some of the affairs of Castle Martel. There were some other new arrivals that Darrin took Corin to meet. The brothers entered the great hall and went to join the rest of their family who gathered with the visitors in front of the dais.

"Uncle Maldwyn!" Darrin greeted them first.

"Darrin!" Their uncle clasped his hand heartily. Maldwyn saw Corin standing slightly behind Darrin. "Well, I said I wouldn't believe it until I saw it. You are alive after all!"

"Hello, Uncle," Corin said. "It's been a long time."

"Too long, lad," Maldwyn said as he hugged him.

"We've missed you, Corin," his aunt said, also embracing him.

"They say that you are 'the Hawk.' So we have you to thank for all this." His uncle gestured around them. Corin shifted awkwardly.

"People seem to forget that I had a little help," he said.

"You do the stories justice, lad," Maldwyn said. He turned back to his sister and brother-in-law.

"He said they fled to Cyndor after the mountain keeps were taken. They returned to Cair Esgair only a few months ago," Darrin filled Corin in quietly. They had found that many of the mountain forts had been taken after their garrisons had fled further into the mountains or into Cyndor.

"It's a good thing we waited to regarrison the keep then," Corin said.

"Aye, from what Uncle Maldwyn said, most of their men escaped with them, so the Cair has a full company," Darrin replied.

"Good. That saves us fifty men that we can put somewhere else," Corin said.

"Aye, Cadfael could use some more men. It's close enough to the coast if we have a problem with the Raiders," Darrin mused.

"Enough talk of business. It's the Festival and you boys promised," Queen Elain reprimanded.

"Sorry," they said, not very contritely.

"They take after you, don't they, Celyn?" Maldwyn chuckled.

"Darrin?" a young woman said breathlessly as she approached with Amaura.

"Rhian?" Darrin exclaimed. She ran to him and he took her hands.

"Oh, I heard you were alive, but it's so good to see you!" she exclaimed.

"What happened to you?" Darrin asked.

"Father made Mother and me leave Caer Benllech when the Calorins got too close. We were to go to Cyndor. I wanted to wait and tell you but we hadn't heard anything for weeks. We met with your uncle and went with them," Rhian said.

"I wish I had known where you were. I would have come," Darrin said.

Amaura came to stand by Corin.

"They were going to get married. But then the Calorins came," she said. It was the only explanation Corin needed as they watched Darrin and Rhian reunite.

"There's someone I want you to meet," Darrin said. He brought Rhian over to his siblings. "My brother, Corin."

"I'm so happy to finally meet you," Rhian said warmly, taking his hand. "Darrin used to tell me so much about you!"

"I hope he didn't bore you too much," Corin said with a grin. Rhian laughed.

"I only heard the best," she said. "And it seems that we still hear about you."

"You really shouldn't believe everything you hear," Corin said. Rhian smiled.

"I'll keep that in mind," she said. Darrin again took her hand and she smiled up at him. Amaura took Corin's arm.

"Kara is about to race Kieran. I told her I would be there, so you can come with me," she said.

"Well, let's go. I told both of them I'd watch. The winner gets an extra day of leave," Corin said.

"We'll see you later. I'm so glad you're back, Rhian," Amaura said.

As Amaura and Corin left the hall, she let out a sigh of contentment.

"Oh, this makes me so happy!" she said and Corin smiled.

"They do seem happy together," he agreed.

"Did he ever tell you about her?" asked Amaura.

"No, but I know what it's like to not talk about someone you think you won't ever see again," Corin replied. Amaura briefly tightened her hold on his arm. She had always felt that she would see her brother again and couldn't imagine what Corin had gone through.

"Mera is going to be there," she said.

"Really?" Corin sounded disinterested.

"Oh, come on! You like her, don't you?" Amaura prodded him.

"Maybe I do, but I don't see her that often despite your and Mother's efforts," said Corin as he tugged her hair. Amaura was unabashed.

"Well then you should talk to her now," she said.

"Despite what you would like to think, I don't need 'someone special' right now. I just got my family back," Corin said, putting his arm around her. *But it was more than that,* he thought. Something was coming.

They walked out the main gates and through the town to the open grounds where farmers and craftsmen displayed their wares. Further along, various competitions were being held where warriors tested their skill against one another. Horse races were constantly run. Most of Aredor's warbands were mounted and there were few foot soldiers. These races had always been the biggest part of the Festival for there was no poor horseman in Aredor.

"Captain!" Kieran greeted Corin.

"A few of our cousins wanted tae race as well, sir," Kara said. "Is that all right?"

"It's your race," Corin said. "If one of you wins, you still get the extra day."

The twins grinned.

"Grand. They think they can beat Kara. I was going tae let her win but since we can still get that day..." said Kieran. Kara shoved him.

"Just for that, I will beat you," she said. Two young Braetons walked up with their horses. They were slightly older than Kara and Kieran and wore the purple plaid of Clan Gunlon.

"You sure you want tae race, Kara?" one asked.

"Are you sure you want tae?" Kara retorted as her cousin laughed. The four riders tightened their girths and Kara and Kieran shortened their stirrups. The Braetons removed their cloaks and mounted. The twins, dressed similarly in breeches and shirts with sleeves rolled up to the elbows, also mounted.

Members of the Hawk Flight had gathered and they called encouragement to their riders as they went to the starting line. The horses shifted in excitement as they saw the dirt track.

"Captain, will you give the signal?" Kieran asked. He and Kara saw Corin step forward and they gently touched their horses with their heel. Their mounts' ears turned back toward them in expectation. Corin put his fingers to his mouth and gave a piercing whistle that rose on two notes. The horses sprang away, obscured at first by a cloud of dust.

The onlookers soon caught sight of the riders again. The four horses were running evenly together. When they came around the last bend of the track toward the finish, a nod of understanding passed between Kara and Kieran. They eased up into the stirrups and their horses began to pull ahead. When their cousins began to try and come even with them again, the twins tugged on the reins to move their horses in front of the others. The race was now between the twins and they put all their effort into beating each other. In the end, Kieran barely won, coming ahead by a nose length. Their cousins were not far behind.

The four riders dismounted and congratulated Kieran with no hard feelings.

"Och, you've finally beaten us, Kara," her cousin said.

She smiled. "I always used tae tell you that I would one day."

"So you did," he said. "Congratulations tae you and that wee horse of yours."

"Thanks, Micheil. Since I beat you, do I get a dance tonight?" Kara asked.

"Sure you do. And if you're as good as you used tae be, then maybe more than one," Micheil replied.

As he began to lead his horse away it spooked suddenly. Delyth danced nervously. As Kara tried to pull him away he dodged forward and, caught off guard, she stumbled backward into Tam. He steadied her and she brought Delyth to a standstill.

"I'm sorry," she said as she turned to him.

"That's all right," he replied. "You're pretty good."

"Thanks," she said. "My brother and I spent the war outrunning Calorins so we know a bit about racing." She loosened Delyth's girth.

"If you don't mind my asking, how did you become part of the warband, being a Braeton…?" Tam asked.

"And a girl?" Kara finished for him with a laugh. "Our father was Aredorian but we were raised in Braeton. He and Kieran were here visiting some of his family when the Calorins invaded. They never came back and I convinced an old warrior tae give me some training. When I was seventeen, I came looking for them. The warband found me instead and the Captain let me stay on as a runner."

"Did you fight as well?" Tam asked.

"Only when I had tae. The Captain tried tae keep both of us away from it and I'm very glad he did," she said somberly.

"You still ride with them, don't you?" he asked.

"Aye, it's our family now. But most outside the warband don't approve," she said. "I think it's mostly because I dress like a boy," she said with a grin. Tam laughed.

"Do you get much trouble?" he asked.

"Och, I can handle the women who don't think it's appropriate for a young woman tae spend her time with a warband. As for the warriors in the other warbands, most don't think I belong and try and make things difficult. I usually try and settle it when I can. If not, then they have tae face the Captain or any of the Hawk Flight," said Kara.

"Does that happen often?" he asked.

"Not as often as it used tae," she replied. "The lads in the Hawk Flight take care of me and make sure I'm all right. I'm sure it's strange tae anyone outside of the warband, but the way they see it, I helped the best I could during the war. And I haven't left," she finished.

"I don't think I know anyone quite like you," said Tam.

"Anyone as crazy?" Kara laughed, but she blushed slightly. "I don't usually talk tae anyone about it. Usually the young warriors are trying tae prove that they're better than me."

"Kara! Why'd you let that worthless brother of yours beat you today?" a warrior of the Hawk Flight called as he passed.

"Even a girl can'nae win all the time!" she called back, laughing with the warrior. She turned back to Tam.

"There's the dancing tonight down in the town square. Are you going?" she asked breathlessly.

"Aye, I'll be there. They asked me if I'd play," replied Tam.

"You're a bard?" Kara asked in surprise.

"I haven't earned the name yet. Maybe one day," he said.

"Well, I'll see you tonight then," she said. He nodded and Kara led her horse away.

- -

"How are your new students?" Corin asked Martin at dinner.

"Sore and humbled," Martin replied cheerfully. They were seated at one of the lower tables with Trey, Aiden, and Will.

"They're not the only ones who'll be a bit sore. I can barely lift my arm right now," Aiden said.

"Too much technique?" asked Corin with a grin.

"Way too much crammed intae a few hours," Aiden replied. "Reminds me why I gave up the bloody great thing."

"You working them again tomorrow?" Trey asked Martin.

"No, I'll only need to give them one more day. Eornan is training them in Braeton so they don't really need my help anyway," Martin said.

The meal began to finish and everyone started to leave the castle hall and go down into the town in preparation for the dancing.

"I'm starting to think this might be the best thing that's ever happened to me," Martin said as he stood, favoring his injured leg.

"We'll still know how to find you by following the trail of fainting, heartbroken women," Trey told him. Martin laughed sarcastically.

"But before you know it, I'll be the only bachelor around here," Martin remarked innocently. Will smothered a grin as Corin and Trey shot glares at Martin.

"Do you dance?" Aiden asked Corin.

"Amaura made me learn. Be grateful you don't have a sister," Corin replied as they followed the others out.

The square was brightly lit with lanterns as the last light faded from the western sky. The wide square was already filled with dancers as the music played. Musicians from Aredor and Braeton and even a travelling group of players from Cyndor traded places, never letting the music falter.

Aiden saw Corin and Amaura join the dancers. Will, Trey, and Jamey also found partners. He saw Rona nearby. He held out his hand. She took it with shining eyes and he drew her into the dance.

"I didn't know you danced," she said as the song finished.

"Not very well. It's been a while," he admitted.

"It's not too hard," she said.

"Then should we give this next one a try?" he asked, matching her smile.

Trey claimed Amaura and Corin asked Mera and was shyly accepted. Kara whirled by with one of the young men of the Hawk Flight. There was finally a pause in the music and Rona and Aiden left the crowd to sit on the benches that lined the outside of the square.

"What do you think of all this?" Aiden asked her.

"I don't know. It's so different from Scodra," Rona said. "But I'm glad I came. You?"

"Aye, me too."

"I'll be glad tae go back though. I've never been away from Scodra for so long. I don't know how you did it."

"When I first left, I thought I would never go back."

"Why?"

"Anger drives you further than you know."

"And is it still there, this anger?"

"It's hard tae let go of, but it has faded with time. And now that I have come back, I hope I'll never feel it again," Aiden said. Rona slowly reached over and took his hand. He let it stay there.

"There doesn't seem tae be a need for it anymore," Rona said. Aiden smiled. Now that he had made peace with his father, there was no need for the anger that had once filled him. He looked to the young woman sitting next to him.

"No, there isn't," he said.

Tam found Kara as she was escorted back by a partner.

"Are you claimed for this next dance?" he asked.

She shook her head. "Not yet," she said. They stepped into the dance. It was a slower tune, allowing them some conversation.

"You have no shortage of partners," Tam commented.

"I noticed you don't either," Kara replied. "What do you think of the Festival?"

"There's always something new tae see," Tam said. "I've never traveled much before."

"I hadn't either before I left Braeton. It was like I never realized how big the world was outside the boundaries of my village."

"Do you like Aredor?"

"I've seen almost every part of it. It is a beautiful country. I don't regret coming here," she said. The dance ended and they withdrew to the benches. They took two mugs of ale from the servers who circled the square. Kara sat on a table and rested her feet on the bench as Tam joined her.

"Have you ever seen a Festival before?' he asked.

"No, this is my first," she said. "What is Scodra like?" she asked. They took turns telling each other of their lives. Tam asked about Will's time in Aredor and she was curious to hear the tale of the battle at Scodra that had been circulating among the Clans.

"There you are!" they were interrupted some time later by Kieran and Ian. "We wondered where you'd gone off tae," Kieran said.

"Just resting my feet a moment," Kara replied. She introduced Tam and Ian. "He's Will's younger brother," she said.

"Then it's a pleasure to meet you," Ian clasped Tam's hand. "He's a welcome relief especially since I usually have to deal with these two," he said to Tam.

"What a friend," Kieran said. "Tam, did you know that Kara is the best rider around here? Except for me, of course."

"And Kieran is the most annoying twin anyone could have," Kara said.

"I'll drink to that," Ian said. Kieran frowned at him.

"You'll do anything for a drink," he told Ian. Ian shrugged.

"Will I be able to have another dance later, Kara?" he asked.

"Sure, if you get me some more ale," she bargained.

"And you think I'd do anything for a drink?" Ian turned to Kieran. Tam was laughing and Kara smiled. A merry reel was struck up by a fiddler from Clan Strowen. Kieran grabbed Kara's hand and pulled her down from the table.

"Come on! I'm really good at this one," he said.

"Ha! You wish!" Kara said.

"A challenge then?" Kieran asked.

"Is it a challenge if you know I'm going tae win?" Kara returned. Kieran made no reply as he whisked her into the dance. They staggered back a few minutes later and Kara collapsed on the bench.

"You might not get that dance later, Ian," she said, fanning her face.

"I've never quite managed tae master that one," Tam said.

"Neither has Kieran apparently," Kara said. Kieran flopped onto the bench beside her.

"It's not fair that it speeds up at the end," he said. Kara laughed.

"Are you playing later, Tam?" she asked.

"We'll see," Tam said. "I've never played for this many people before."

"Please? Ian's never heard a bard play before," she said. "You'll be wonderful."

"It looks like I'm about tae get my chance," Tam remarked, seeing Blair and Will coming toward them.

"Come on, Tam! Canich is calling for you!" Will said.

"No excuses! We have tae show them that only the best come from Canich!" Blair said. Tam pulled a face as they escorted him away.

"He seems like a nice enough fellow," Kieran commented.

"Yes, he is," Kara agreed thoughtfully. Ian and Kieran exchanged a knowing glance.

"What?" Kara demanded.

"Oh, nothing. You two just looked like you've made good friends," Ian remarked. "I promise I'm not jealous."

"Stop it. It's nothing like that!" Kara protested.

"I'm sure you'll be wonderful!" Kieran mimicked, fluttering his eyes.

"Shut up!" Kara pushed him off the bench. Ian obligingly helped him to his feet. They simply smirked as they backed away.

"Boys!" Kara muttered to herself.

Chapter 4

The next morning the castle and all its guests were caught up in anticipation for the race. All activity was halted as midday approached. The crowds that had gathered at the training grounds parted as Corin and Trey walked to the starting line. Kara and Kieran followed leading their horses. Zephyr held his head high, snorting and dancing in excitement. Trey's mare, Nerys, arched her neck and pranced alongside Kara.

Martin was already there with an excited Gwilym. The king and queen were seated on a raised platform. Mera and Amaura pushed up beside Martin.

"Please be careful!" Amaura begged both of the riders.

"You shouldn't worry so much, Maurie," Corin told her.

"I shouldn't worry when you insist on trying to kill yourself?" Amaura exclaimed. Kara and Kieran handed the horses to Corin and Trey. They both leapt easily onto the horses' bare backs. Corin nudged Zephyr forward and the stallion reared. Corin rode it and turned him in a quick circle. Nerys backed away and Trey turned her on the forehand before pushing her sideways to the start line. Karif flew down to land on Corin's arm for a moment before Corin sent him flying off with a quick word. Gwilym would have run forward with Martin but Liam caught him and swung him up onto his shoulders.

"You ready?" Martin asked the riders. Receiving nods from them both, he drew his sword and brought it down in a flashing arc. The crowds cheered as the horses bolted to a quick gallop and took the first jump together.

Aiden saw Mera anxiously clasping her hands. He knew there was something different about Corin these days.

"He'll be all right, you know. He's one of the best riders I've seen and Zephyr will take care of him," he told her. Mera smiled nervously at him.

"Martin keeps telling me that," she said.

Tam stood with Kara and Kieran as they watched the race. The twins were following it intently.

"Captain is falling a bit behind," Kara said anxiously.

"No, he's just cautious of the next jump," Kieran said as Zephyr cleared the obstacle with room to spare just behind Trey. "They're coming tae the river now."

"I hope they're careful. It's a steep bank," Kara said, shielding her eyes to watch as the riders suddenly seemed to vanish into the ground. All eyes turned to the bend of the river where they would reappear. A minute passed and then another. Voices murmured uneasily.

"Do you think something's happened?" Tam asked.

"I don't know," Kieran replied.

"Martin?" Amaura asked nervously. "Where are they?"

"Give them another minute," Martin replied, hiding his own sudden anxiety.

"There they are!" a voice shouted. Cheers rang out as Corin and Trey emerged from the river, still racing side by side.

Martin hurried to the finish line as they began the last leg of the race. Trey took the last jump behind Zephyr but quickly drew even again over the open ground. Corin and Trey crossed the line together. More cheers erupted as they slowed their horses and came to a stop.

"What happened?" Martin demanded. Trey was soaking wet and Corin's clothes and face were streaked with mud.

"It was steeper than we first thought," Trey said as he and Corin laughed. They saluted the king and queen who both looked very relieved that the race was over.

"Martin, declare a winner," King Celyn said.

"A tie, your majesty," Martin replied. The men of the Hawk Flight and Castle Martel applauded boisterously.

"Are you hurt?" Mera asked Corin as he slid down from Zephyr.

"Just some scrapes and bruises. Nothing life threatening," Corin replied. "I told you we'd be fine."

Mera smiled as Karif flew in and gently butted Corin's cheek.

"I'm not the only one who didn't quite believe you," she said.

"He can be quite a fussy ball of feathers sometimes," Corin said and Karif chirped.

"Did you win, Grampa?" Gwilym asked as Liam set him back down.

"Not this time. Uncle Cor and I tied," Trey explained.

"Oh, but I thought someone was always supposed to win." Gwilym was confused.

"I see you've been giving him another lesson," Mera said to Martin who only grinned in response.

"You're gonna have to take a bath, Uncle Cor!" Gwilym laughed gleefully.

"Oh, really?" Corin said, scooping him up and tickling him. Gwilym giggled helplessly while begging to be put down. Corin instead swung him onto Zephyr's back. The big stallion turned his head to look at the small burden he now carried.

"Hello, Zephyr," Gwilym said. The stallion snorted gently and Corin handed Gwilym the reins.

"Just like Grandpa Trey showed you," he said. Gwilym's face scrunched in concentration as he wrapped his hands around the reins. Corin stood back and Zephyr stepped slowly and carefully away. Gwilym turned Zephyr in a circle, stopping by the king and queen as they began to descend the platform.

"Hello, my majesties!" he said cheerfully.

"How are you today, Gwilym?" Queen Elain asked with a smile.

"I'm good. I'm riding Zephyr. See?"

"I do. You must be getting quite big," King Celyn said.

"Oh, yes. Uncle Martin says I'm starting to grow like a weed," Gwilym said solemnly.

"I tell him it's 'your majesty' at least twice a day!" Martin shrugged hopelessly.

"Stop being such a mother," Trey told him.

"Gwilym, you want to ride him back to the stables for me?" Corin asked. The boy straightened importantly. Corin put a hand on the reins as he walked with Zephyr. Trey and Nerys followed alongside. Queen Elain watched them leave and saw Corin and Trey stopping to talk to their men, many of whom were also "uncles."

"Sometimes I pity that boy for having lost his family like he did. But I also believe he is as good for this new family as they are for him," she said to her husband.

"Aye, he reminds us all what we fight for," King Celyn replied.

The dancing continued that night in the town. Aiden again accompanied Rona. They drew to the side and a man addressed Aiden.

"Excuse me. Do you know where I might find Lord Trey? They said he'd be here," the man said. Aiden quickly took in the man's stained uniform and hurried manner and pointed him to the other edge of the square where Trey was with Amaura. The warrior thanked him and moved off. Aiden watched him go, a faint unease stirring. The feeling heightened as Trey and the man began to talk intently. Trey stopped and gave a quick whistle. Corin excused himself from Laird Dandin and joined them. Aiden knew the look that came over Corin's face.

"I'll be right back," he told Rona and threaded his way toward them. Martin had also seen the messenger and he joined Aiden as they caught up with Corin and Trey. They had drawn Darrin and King Celyn apart with Tristan.

"My men decided to keep on their regular patrol to the estuary where I was to rejoin them," Trey said. "But they ran into a large force of Raiders." He gestured to his lieutenant to continue.

"Three ships, sire. Maybe more on the way," he said.

"My men are pinned down on the coast. But in their current position they are also holding the Raiders from striking further inland," Trey said.

"That part of the coast is mostly unguarded by outposts. The few that are there are mostly manned by farmers," Darrin said.

"Let me take my deugain," Corin said.

"Why not the Hawk Flight?" King Celyn asked.

"I need them ready to defend the forest border," Corin replied.

"Because last time there was a Raider strike this large was just before the Calorin invasion," King Celyn remembered. "How soon can you leave, Corin?"

"I'll find Bedwyr now. We'll ride with first light," Corin said.

"Thank you, sire," Trey said to King Celyn.

"I'll get back to Castle Martel as fast as I can and muster the warband if needed," Tristan said.

"Don't voice this about too much," King Celyn cautioned. They were all reminded of the celebration around them. The men nodded in agreement and disbanded.

"Corin, I'll go with you," Aiden said.

"You're not leaving me behind either," Martin said.

"Martin, your leg needs to rest and, Aiden, you're here in the place of a Clan Lord. I can't ask either of you to come," Corin said.

"Captain Artair and Tam can take care of things for a few days and I never asked," Aiden said. "I can add two more blades."

"I can ride and I don't need my leg to draw a bow. I'd just follow you anyway," Martin argued. Corin hesitated for a long moment.

"All right," he decided. "Martin, find Liam for me? I need to talk to him after I see Bedwyr."

Martin threw him a salute and hurried off.

"Thanks, Cor," Aiden said.

"You might regret this later," Corin warned. "But it will be good to have you there."

Rona had followed Aiden and now stood with Mera and Amaura.

"What's happening?" Rona asked.

"I don't know. But's it's not good at all," Amaura replied anxiously. She caught Darrin and pressed for an explanation.

"It's just a quick trip to the coast to make sure all is in order," Darrin said.

"You're lying," Amaura said. Darrin only looked at her. "It's Raiders, isn't it?" she asked. "How bad?"

"We're not sure yet. Corin is taking his men. They'll be gone a few days. Amaura, don't say much to anyone," he cautioned. She nodded.

"It's bad, isn't it?" Rona asked when Darrin had left.

"Yes, it is," Amaura replied.

Aiden found Will and Tam and explained everything.

"Are you mad, Danny?" Will exclaimed. "You're just going tae leave?"

"Yes. Corin's like a brother tae me and while there's a battle tae fight, I'm going tae be there at his side," Aiden said.

"Fair enough. But do you expect me tae let our brother go off alone?" Will asked.

"I want tae go too," Tam put in.

"Both of you?" Aiden exclaimed. "But I can'nae grant that! Father would have my head!"

"We can worry about Father later. Let's go talk tae the man in charge. I am still part of the Hawk Flight," Will said.

"This was their idea!" Aiden protested to Corin.

"So, you three think it's a good idea for me to take the Chieftain's sons to a battle they really have no part in?" Corin asked, slightly incredulous.

"Corin, I don't feel like I've earned a place in the Hawk Flight. I've barely drawn steel since taking the oath," Will said.

"I can vouch for Tam. He can handle himself in a fight," Aiden said.

"If Captain Artair consents to this, then you two be ready to ride tomorrow," Corin said to Will and Tam.

Aiden had less difficulty with Captain Artair than he imagined.

"We have our warriors that can be added tae the Aredorian force," Artair said.

"No, they don't want tae involve the Clans," Aiden said. "But I don't know how that will work if the three of us are going."

"Just make sure all of you come back safely, or Laird Gòrdan will come for me after he finishes with you," Artair said. "I wish you would allow the rest of us tae come."

"Aye, I'm sorry tae leave you here," Aiden said.

"I know well what it is tae want tae fight for friends and brothers. You will bring more honor tae Clan Canich," Artair said.

"I hope I can," Aiden replied, struck by his words. "We'll be back in a few days."

The courtyard was dark in the early morning. Corin's personal command of forty men from the King's warbands waited in the courtyard. Aiden wore his chainmail coat under a plain tunic. He left the plaid behind and instead wore his black cloak. He had found a javelin in the armory that suited him better than the heavy spears of the northmen. Tam was dressed similarly to him and Will wore the uniform of the Hawk Flight. Like the others, they all carried extra provisions and quivers. The Aredorian warriors sat quietly on their steeds; rounded shields hung over their backs and spears rested in their hands. Finally, Corin emerged, giving some last orders to Kara. Kieran was riding with the warband and Kara would follow after.

"After three days, I want you to join us with any news," Corin said.

"Aye, sir. And if all is quiet?"

"Come anyway. We may want another runner," Corin said.

"Good luck, sir," Kara said. "I'll see you in a few days," she said to Kieran.

"Give Aunt Una my love," he said.

"I will unless she starts giving me another lecture," Kara said and her twin laughed.

Amaura had also risen early.

"Be safe." She hugged Corin.

"We'll be back soon," he promised. He mounted Zephyr and Karif found his perch. Corin took his javelin from Bedwyr, his captain, and another warrior unfurled their standard: a black banner on which a silver hawk flew. As part of the warband, Corin and his men wore the grey and blue uniforms, but their cloaks were clasped with rounded brooches in which a hawk stretched its wings.

Trey was last to mount. He suddenly kissed Amaura, leaving her momentarily speechless. He wheeled his horse and followed Corin from the castle. Aiden saw Rona at the top of the steps. He gave her a smile before riding out.

Amaura and Rona hurried up the wall steps to join Mera who already stood there.

"Are you all right, Mera?" Amaura asked.

"No! He let Martin go! And they both claimed it would be better than if Martin stayed," Mera said.

"He wouldn't know what to do if he were left behind," Amaura said. "Instead they must leave again, to fight and gain glory and not care if they are wounded. They cannot even stay to celebrate what peace we have." She wrapped her cloak tighter around her. Rona watched the warband disappear. The rising sun marked the tips of the spears and she suddenly felt an ache in her heart.

"Do you always watch them ride away?" she asked.

"Yes, and it is too often," Amaura replied.

"They will come back, won't they?" Rona was seized by a momentary panic. Mera took her arm.

"By Lleu's help, they will," she said. They all exchanged the same look of anguish at the uncertainty that the men might not ride back. Meanwhile, the men that they loved rode with bright eyes to find if their fate awaited them on the sands of Aredor's coast.

Chapter 5

They rode all day and into the night, only stopping to rest and water the horses. The miles flew by and by mid-morning of the next day they had reached the coast. Corin called a halt and sent two scouts to find the Raiders. They returned an hour later with news.

"Nearly two hundred Raiders, sir. They've got our lads pinned down by some rocks and surrounded," one reported to Corin.

"And we saw another ship out on the horizon, sir. It was too far to tell if it's a Raider," the other said.

"How far away are we?" Corin asked.

"About a mile, sir," came the reply.

The deugain covered the distance quickly. They saw the enemy force surrounding large outcroppings.

"Hadyn! Why didn't you tell me it was Rufus?" Trey snapped to his lieutenant.

"Sorry, sir. Captain Alun said I shouldn't," Hadyn replied.

"Trey?" Corin questioned.

"*Captain* Rufus commands these ships. He has taunted us for two seasons now. His only purpose in life seems to be to make others suffer. His crew is all the same. I've seen the people they've killed. He knows these are my men and so he won't leave until I and all of them are dead," Trey said.

"Well then, let's go meet him," Corin said. "Split in half. Trey, take command, the rest go with me. Hit them hard and if anything goes wrong, get to the rocks. Aiden, you and Martin are with me. Will and Tam, go with Trey. Move out!" he ordered.

The deugain split and readied their spears. They charged at a shouted command. The Raiders, being a seafaring people and not fond of horses, were thrown into momentary fear and panic. The Aredorians passed through their ranks and turned again only to find the Raiders finally marshaled against them. The warriors set their shields in place and charged again, but the superior numbers of the Raiders began to tell and the deugain fell back to the rocks.

"Put the horses behind the rocks!" Trey's captain shouted as he and his men poured arrows into an advancing Raider force.

Aiden pulled Narak through an opening between two rocks and found that what had looked like a solid outcropping was riddled with alcoves and passages that could easily shelter all their horses. He left Narak sanding obediently and ran back out. Corin and Trey were already talking with Captain Alun.

"They surprised us. We saw the ships but they were already on land and waiting for us. We were driven here and, as you can see, there is no easy way out," Captain Alun said.

His men had pushed the sand into higher dunes. Their rectangular shields had been driven into the sand and shorn up, forming a short barricade between them and the Raiders. The pirates had surrounded the rocks on all sides, making any attempt at escape dangerous.

"How are you on supplies?" Trey asked.

"Low. We've been here for five days and we're almost out of water. The horses have hardly had any," Alun said.

"We brought extra. Lieutenant Harri will distribute extra supplies as needed," Corin said. He began to place his men around the shield wall. Aiden and Martin were posted next to each other.

"Where are the rest of your lads?" one of Trey's men asked beside them.

"We can't be getting you Sharks out of trouble all the time," Martin joked, then turned serious. "The Captain thought they might be needed on the border." The Hawk Flight frequently met Trey's men and they were on familiar terms with each other. Trey's deugain had come to be called the "sharks" in part because of their fighting ability and also because of the crest of Castle Martel emblazoned on their red tunics.

"Aye, we've worried about that these few days. I was surprised to see you and the Captain here," the warrior said, ducking as an arrow flew by and sending one off in return.

"I think he might have actually pulled rank." Martin and the man chuckled. "As for me, I didn't want to miss the opportunity for a guaranteed fight."

"Lieutenant Hadyn brought you just in time," the warrior said. Many of the Martel deugain were wounded and most, having been relieved by Corin's men, had fallen into an exhausted slumber.

Aiden looked out at the enemy force. Their triremes were anchored just offshore, the black hulls gleaming dully in the sunlight. The Raiders seemed well supplied with arrows and provisions. Pushed back against the rocks and with the sea to their side, the Aredorians were well and truly trapped.

"I've never seen so many gloomy young women all at once," Queen Elain declared. Rona, Amaura, and Mera sat despondently at the table, only picking at their food.

"How long do you think they're going to be gone this time?" Amaura asked her mother.

"Not as long as you seem to think it will be," Queen Elain said. "Trey never stays away long and my son and that young Aiden will be all right," she said knowingly. Rona and Mera blushed and protested weakly. Queen Elain only smiled.

"You girls seem to forget that I've been watching young people for a long time," she said. "I also know that sitting around won't make time go any faster. Go! You're young and free! Don't waste it!"

Kara came up to their table.

"The Clans are holding a feast out on the field. Do you three want tae come? I can promise good food and endless dance partners," she said, enacting a previously devised plan between her and the queen.

"Yes! It would do you good," Queen Elain said when they hesitated.

"Don't make me go alone!" Kara pleaded.

"Well..." Mera began to relent.

"Perfect!" Kara exclaimed. "It starts in an hour. And don't worry about getting all dressed up, there won't be many seats." She danced away before any protests could be made. Rona saw that the queen had also retreated.

"I guess we're going?" she said.

"With not much of a choice," Amaura said.

"I'll tell Gwilym that he can come. He's been pestering me about it for the last two days. Both he and that nephew of yours, Rona," said Mera.

"He and Brannan together? That sounds like a dangerous mix," Rona commented.

"Aye, I get worried when I can't see them. I forget how much energy he has until Martin leaves," Mera said. The mention of the absent brother brought back thoughts of the others who were gone and melancholy sighs.

An hour later, Kara met them in the main hall. She wore the purple plaid of Clan Gunlon over a plain dress. She escorted them down to the open fields where Clans Gunlon and Dyson had encamped. The smells of cooking food wafted through the air. Fires and torches were lit everywhere one looked. Next to the tables were freshly broached barrels of ale. Hundreds of voices chattering all at once were broken suddenly by a song or the quick skirl of bagpipes and drums. The Clans' plaids were colorfully intermixed with the bright colors of the Aredorians.

Gwilym quickly ran off into the crowd with Brannan. Rona and Mera waited in the lines to get plates laden with food while Kara and Amaura brought beakers of dark ale. All four sat down on a blanket close by Kara's relatives and several members of Clan Canich. They ate with their hands and laughed with the wild energy that had infused the encampment.

The bard of Clan Dyson jumped up and shouted over the noise, "Up on your feet now and we'll show the stars how we dance!"

Rona and Kara whooped and jumped to their feet before finding partners and starting the spinning, stomping dance. Mera and Amaura watched, laughing and clapping in time. After the dance finished, Kara found some of her cousins and brought them over. The men helped Mera and Amaura to their feet and taught them the steps to the next dance. They soon found that there were plenty of partners willing to teach them the dances loved by the Clans.

Much later, they all sat down on the blanket with fresh mugs in their hands to listen to Strowen's bard sing.

"Is it always like this when the Clans meet?" Mera asked, watching the people.

"Aye, even when the occasion is not so joyful," Rona said.

"I find it hard to believe that a Braeton could be sad," Amaura said and Rona laughed.

"It's long been said that when we're angry we want a fight, when we're happy we want a dance, and when we're sad we want a ballad," Rona said.

Amaura lay back on her elbows and looked up at the stars.

"I wish it would never end." she sighed.

"It is beautiful," Kara agreed softly. "Kieran will be sorry he missed it."

"When do you leave for the coast?" Rona asked.

"Tomorrow morning," Kara replied.

"Will it be over when you get there?" Rona asked.

"Probably not," Kara replied cheerfully. "It hardly ever is. I always manage tae catch the ending."

"When will you be back?" Mera asked.

"I'm not sure." Kara shrugged. "I could come back with them or the Captain might send me on tae the forest. The patrols will be starting again since the Festival ends tomorrow," she said.

"I guess I'm staying until they get back," Rona said.

"You must come and visit here again," Amaura said.

"I'd like that," Rona said. "Maybe in the spring you can come tae our season's feast."

"It wouldn't be too hard for me tae take letters. I can give them tae one of Clan Dyson's runners," Kara offered.

"You could do that?" Amaura asked.

"Sure. Captain wouldn't mind as long as I can make my run in the usual time. We have messages for the Clan sometimes," Kara said.

"Since the trouble at Scodra is gone, there might be someone willing tae go tae Clan Dyson for letters," Rona said.

"It doesn't sound like it will be too much trouble," Mera said. "Thank you, Kara."

"You're welcome," Kara replied. "But I must say goodnight. It's late and if I drink any more, Delyth won't be happy with me tomorrow." She laughed.

"Be careful, Kara," Amaura said.

"Do you have enough supplies?" Mera asked.

"Aye, Lieutenant Liam made sure my bag was well stocked with everything before he left," Kara replied. She had been learning the basics of caring for the wounded from both Liam and Mera. The warband would most likely need more healing supplies by the time she got there. She walked slowly back to the castle, sad to leave the festivities, but happy to depart the next morning to join the warband.

Chapter 6

Aiden took a sparing sip from his waterskin. The days had been mercifully cool due to the movement of autumn toward winter. He took a glance over the barricade to where the Raiders waited as they had the past four days. The enemy's ranks had been thinned since the warband had arrived but they still outnumbered the northerners. Aside from the occasional sorties at one another, the two sides had remained apart and exchanged arrows.

"It's about time for them to start again, isn't it?" the warrior beside him commented.

"Aye, they should have finished lunch by now," Aiden agreed.

"Just about the time we should be getting ours," the warrior said, watching the path of an arrow as it flew toward them. He moved aside and the arrow thudded into the ground. Aiden picked it up and fitted it to his bow. He sighted carefully, loosed, and watched a Raider fall as it found its mark.

"How are you holding up?" he asked Tam who was positioned beside him.

"I'm all right," Tam replied steadily. "The only battles I'm in seem tae be sieges."

"Aye, but this time, we were the help," Aiden said.

"You need to get out more, lad," the warrior addressed Tam. "These sieges are one thing but a cavalry charge or an ambush? Those are what really get the blood flowing."

Tam listened as his brother and the warrior traded stories, looking completely at ease as they loosed their arrows. He clenched his hand to steady it before drawing a shaft of his own.

All activity was halted that afternoon as a figure strode forward under a white flag.

"Rufus," Trey spat as he recognized the figure. Corin and Martin joined him at the barricade.

"I want to speak with Lord Trey," Rufus called mockingly.

"What do you want?" Trey shouted back.

"To tell you that you will finally pay for what you did to me!" Rufus said, touching the bandage he wore over his left eye. Trey smiled for the first time.

"How is your eye doing, by the way? I'll meet you in single combat and finish the job!" Trey said.

"I don't think so. I like you where you are," Rufus said. "Is that the famed Hawk with you?" he asked. "I've long wanted to meet him. I know some people who do nothing but talk about you."

"Is that so?" Corin asked. "And who might these people be?" He exchanged a look with Martin and Trey. They didn't like the way the conversation was going.

"Friends you will have the honor of meeting very soon," Rufus said. "Too bad I will have a chance to kill you before they do."

"Looks like you were right, Cor," Martin said under his breath.

"Come spring there will be no one to stop me from sailing these waters," Rufus laughed.

"You seem very confident in that, Rufus," Trey said.

"I have every reason to be. I'll kill you and your Sharks and then where will your precious castle and dimwitted brother be?" Rufus mocked. Martin grabbed Trey's arm to hold him back.

"You haven't killed us yet," Corin pointed out.

"I want to take my time. I'm not getting paid for speed," Rufus said. He was enjoying seeing how helpless Trey was. The Aredorian haunted his every move during the raiding season and was responsible for his missing eye. Rufus wanted a long and satisfying end to his revenge.

"I'll kill him slowly," Trey swore. "You will curse the day you were born!" he shouted to Rufus.

"Maybe one day, but it won't be you that will make me," Rufus jeered. Trey was halfway up the barricade before Martin caught him.

"I will strangle you if I have to," Martin threatened him. "He's just a braggart, Trey. You'll get your chance soon."

Rufus had retreated when he saw Trey move. Trey broke free from Martin's hold.

"One way or another I will meet him in combat before this is over," he told Corin.

"You'd better hurry," Martin said to Corin as Trey stalked away.

"I know. I don't like what Rufus said at all. We need to get out of here," said Corin.

- -

Martin joined Aiden as night fell.

"We have a plan yet?" Aiden asked him.

"Not that I know of. Corin's trying but we don't have the best amount of maneuverability here," Martin said.

"Aye, we might be here a while longer," Aiden said. He could see no clear way out of the situation.

"It might not be as long as you think," Martin said. "He's got that look."

Aiden saw Corin coming toward them. He crouched beside them.

"Listen for a minute and tell me if you hear anything," he instructed in a low voice. Martin and Aiden sat up straighter and leaned toward the barricade. The waning moon and stars shed little light on the beach. The Raider's campfires and the few torches of the northerners flickered brightly in the darkness.

For a moment all Aiden heard was the endless crash of the waves and the movement of a horse by the rocks. The short moan of one of the wounded men broke the stillness. Then another noise, barely audible, sounded in the darkness. Martin stiffened as he heard it too.

"Bedwyr heard something on the north side too," Corin said.

"Someone just drew a blade," Aiden whispered.

"Trey has alerted the line. You think you could give us a light, Aiden?" Corin asked. Aiden cut two strips of cloth from his tunic and bound them around two arrowheads. Corin held a small branch of driftwood to a torch.

"Everything quiet, Captain?" he called loudly.

"Nothing out of place, sir," Trey called back.

Corin nodded to Aiden. He quickly laid one of his shafts on the bow and stuck the point into the small flame. It burst to life and he fired straight out into the night. He sent the other arrow further to the left. The quick light gave them what they needed to see. It glanced on dark figures and drawn blades. Corin gave a sharp call and any spare torches were lit and thrust along the barrier.

The Raiders, startled for a moment by the sudden lights, sprang up and rushed the barricade. Aiden dropped his bow and drew his swords, wishing desperately for more light as a Raider jumped over the dune at him.

The defenders fought frantically as more than one torch was knocked over and sputtered weakly in the sand. Then the enemy faded back into the darkness, leaving them breathless and bewildered. For the remainder of the night the defenders looked longingly to the east, willing the dawn to come sooner.

The sun finally came and they were able to see the result of the attack.

"Ten dead. Only two were ours," Trey reported. "We used the last of the wood too."

Corin listened silently. He had hoped to avoid the situation they now found themselves in. He had racked his brain for any solution, but he had no plan. Kieran interrupted his thoughts.

"Rider coming in, sir," he called.

The whole warband had seen a disturbance along the Raider line. A lone rider broke through.

"It's Kara," Trey said. They watched with bated breath as the enemy began to give chase. Kara swung Delyth along the water line. As arrows began to fly, she kicked free of the stirrups and slid to the side, clinging to the saddle and keeping Delyth between her and the Raiders. Delyth heard Kieran's guiding whistle and put on an extra burst of speed, plowing through the sand. He gathered himself and jumped over the shored defenses, knocking Kara loose as he landed and slid to a stop.

Kieran grabbed the horse and hurried it to the rocks as Kara breathlessly scrambled to her feet and the defenders drove away the pursuing Raiders.

"Any news?" Corin asked.

"No, sir. The border is still clear," Kara replied.

"Good," Corin said in relief. "Did you get hurt coming in?"

"No, sir. The sand made for a softer landing than I'm used tae," she replied.

"See to the wounded. The Martel healer was killed several days ago," Corin said. Kara saluted and made her way over to the shelter of the rocks where the more seriously wounded lay. Corin watched her go, feeling the hint of a plan tugging at his mind. He quickly found Lieutenant Hadyn.

"How did you get out to give us the message?" he asked.

"The Raiders have any exits on the other side of the rocks guarded so I swam out. I went down the coast about half a mile and found a horse," the lieutenant said. Corin left him and crouched by a rock near the water's edge.

This is probably one of the worst ideas I've ever come up with, he reflected. *Even during the War.* He stared out over the water. This might take quite a bit of convincing on his part. He took a quick glance back. The Raiders were lighting new fires. No attack would come any time soon. The Aredorians settled down and were pairing off to watch and sleep. Those on watch cast discreet glances his way, hoping the Captain had a way out.

Corin returned his gaze to the sea, knowing all too well the trust riding on him. It had been hard transitioning from the South where he had taken orders for years and then coming home and having to learn how to give them. He had put forth highly doubtful plans with a forced show of confidence and they were accepted without question. He felt like he had been lying to everyone for three and a half years.

I can't do this, he thought. Unconsciously, his hand went to his pouch and he pulled out a small block of wood and began carving. Darrin, his father, and the whole warband trusted him, but he knew there were several lords waiting for him to fail. *They aren't the only ones,* he thought.

Aiden watched him as he shaped the piece of wood. Corin had done it in Calorin to pass time. Aiden knew the look on his face. He abandoned any thought of sleep and pushed aside his cloak. Will silently watched him join Corin by the water.

"You're not regretting leaving, are you?" Aiden asked, squatting down behind him.

"Do you?" Corin asked.

"Halfway through the siege of Scodra I was wondering why I left Calorin," Aiden replied with a faint smile. A small seabird hopped boldly in and stole a wood shaving before being chased away by Karif.

"So, is there a plan yet?" Aiden questioned.

"Do you think I can come up with something that will get us all out of here?" Corin asked in return.

"Yes," Aiden replied simply. Corin laughed shortly.

"You and sixty other men. What if I fail?"

"You won't. Doesn't history prove otherwise?" Aiden asked.

"When did that mean anything?" Corin asked. "How do you know I'm any different from the broken, beaten slave you found seven years ago?"

"You talk more," Aiden replied.

"Because people believe I might have something worth saying. They believe that if Aredor is attacked, the Hawk will come in and save them. I don't even deserve that name," Corin said, watching Karif toss and peck at a piece of wood.

"Remember at Janzori when you came up with that half-brained idea and Azrahil agreed tae it?" Aiden asked and Corin nodded. "I was halfway up that wall when I realized why. It was because you had enough courage tae stand up and try even though it looked like we wouldn't make it. I realized then that I would follow you through an ocean of fire and back even if you thought we couldn't make it. You're the strongest person I know. When I first saw you, I knew that if I was in your place, I would be dead. You don't give up, Cor, and that's why these men believe you can get them out of here."

"Thanks," was all Corin could say as he half-turned to look at Aiden. He saw by the look in Aiden's eyes that he meant every word and that was all he needed. Corin took a short breath. "But you might regret that when I tell you what I have in mind right now," he said. Aiden grinned.

"Let's hear it!"

A long moment of silence greeted Corin after he finished outlining the plan.

"Sounds good to me," Martin said. Aiden saw that Martin, like himself, was ready to trust Corin implicitly. Trey paused for a moment longer, thinking it over again.

"So, you're saying we swim the horses down the coast in order to outflank them?" he asked.

"Aye, the Raiders have us surrounded on all sides except the water. They fear the horses, so we should use it to our advantage. It will be dark tonight with the moon all but gone so we should be able to get past the ships unseen," Corin said.

Trey looked to his captain.

"It's risky, but I like it," Alun said. "How far down the coast are we going, sir?" he asked Corin.

"You know these waters better than I do," Corin said. Alun nodded thoughtfully.

"About a quarter mile east there are some more rocks like these. We can come in behind those. It should be far enough to stay hidden from the Raiders. It won't take more than a quarter hour to swim it. But we'll be more than ready to get out of the water by then," he said.

"Bedwyr?" Corin looked to his commander. The quiet captain nodded.

"Aye, I think it will work. We have sixty men able to fight," he said.

"Trey, I want you and Captain Alun to lead the men down the coast. Bedwyr, help Alun divide the men, then gather everyone together so we can tell them," Corin ordered. The two captains saluted and left together.

"You sure about this one, Cor?" Trey asked quietly.

"Didn't I tell you never to ask me that?" Corin returned.

"Aye, but I am just the same," Trey said.

"There's a great amount of risk, but I don't see any other way," Corin said.

"Then let's make sure it works. I'm ready to go home," Trey said.

"Aye, all I have to do now is make sure everyone else agrees," Corin said.

Aiden slipped away to find Captain Alun.

"If there's still room, I'd like tae volunteer, sir," he said. The tall, somber captain looked him up and down.

"You know what's involved or you wouldn't be volunteering," he stated.

"Yes, sir," Aiden replied.

"Permission granted. Lord Trey and I will be talking it over with everyone after Prince Corin announces it," Captain Alun said.

"Thank you, sir," Aiden said and rejoined Will.

"You've looked busy," his brother commented. "What's going on?"

"You'll find out in a minute," Aiden promised.

A short whistle gained everyone's attention. They gathered in the center of the circle with the exception of a few guards. Corin took a deep breath and began.

"As you all know, we have no visible way out of here. But…" he had every man's full attention. "We're dividing in half. Lord Trey will lead half of you down the coast tonight by swimming your horses past the ships and about a quarter mile east. At dawn the rest of you will ride with me. The plan is to be able to outflank the enemy. They'll have nowhere to run but the water," he completed. "Captain Alun and Captain Bedwyr have divided you out. If any man feels like he cannot discharge his part, I'll not think less of him," Corin said.

"And miss the chance to tell the story of how we sent the Raiders packing? No, sir!" one of the Sharks called. "I'm going, right, Captain?"

"Aye, you are, Cefin," Captain Alun replied. Corin saw that the rest of the warbands seemed to be in agreement with Cefin.

"Then read out the rest of the names, Captain, and let's get ready," he said.

"Odd how your name got called for this," Will remarked casually to Aiden.

"It is, isn't it?" Aiden replied.

"Still need tae be in the middle of everything, eh?" Will asked.

Aiden grinned. "I can'nae help it," he said. "Besides, I like tae swim."

"Och, get out of here before I throw you in myself," Will said, smiling.

Aiden left him and went to join the other men gathering with Trey and Alun. They were a mixture of both the Kingscastle and Martel warbands.

"We'll leave the saddles behind. We can't afford to weigh the horses down any more than necessary. Leave your chain mail and any extra weapons behind, take only what you need," Trey said. "We'll be using the sealskin bags to carry weapons. Those of you who came with the Captain, my men staying behind have contributed their bags. They can hold your swords and keep some clothes dry to change as soon as you make it out of the water. Any questions?"

There was a chorus of "No, sirs!" and then at a nod from Trey, they disbanded. Aiden found his packs and pulled out some fresh clothes and stowed two of his knives and the mail coat away. Placing his bow and quiver with the bags, he unsaddled Narak and set the saddle on the blanket on the sand. Darkness was falling fast as he carefully put his weapons in the bag and fastened it securely shut before slinging it across his chest.

"Be careful," Tam said.

"I will," Aiden said. He was also leaving his leather tunic behind, so he would have almost no protection in the morning. "I'll see you tomorrow," he said before leading Narak away. The other men had begun to gather along the water line with their horses.

"You ever done anything like this before?" Aiden asked one of the Sharks.

"Not besides to train, and never in the dark," the warrior replied.

"That's reassuring," Aiden said wryly, bringing a chuckle from the warrior. Corin joined them in the fading light.

"You look more nervous than we do," Aiden told him in Calorin, seeing through his forced air of calm. Corin simply shot him a glare.

"I figured we'd wait for an hour or so until they've settled down for the night," Trey said.

"Did you find their sentries on the other side of the rocks?" Corin asked.

"Aye, Captain Alun has appointed a few of the lads to go take care of them shortly," Trey replied. Corin nodded. "Get out of here, Cor, before you start pacing!"

"You stay behind next time!" Corin retorted as those within earshot stifled smiles.

"Good luck tomorrow, sir," the warrior beside Aiden said to Corin.

"And to you. I'll see you all tomorrow," Corin replied before leaving.

Aiden settled in to wait, striving to calm his racing pulse. Finally the whispered alert came and the force began to move.

"I'm going first," Captain Alun said. "Since Aiden volunteered, he goes next. Five minutes between each man. Remember, only a quarter mile down. I'll try and have some sort of light set out to guide you in."

Muffled "Yes, sirs," were the only response. The Captain mounted his horse and urged it forward into the surf. Within a few moments he was lost in the darkness. Five minutes seemed like an eternity to Aiden before Trey nodded to him. He mounted Narak. The stallion walked into the water, throwing his head as the cold water swirled around his legs. He tried to step over the incoming surf until a reassuring pat came from his master. Aiden felt Narak strain against the waves as they moved into deeper water.

When he judged they were far enough out, he slid from Narak's back, increasing the stallion's buoyancy. He kept a hand on the reins as he swam alongside his horse and tugged Narak around to swim parallel to the coast. They swam gamely while fighting against the bitterly cold waves that pushed and pulled at them.

No alert was given from the triremes as they passed. The minutes passed agonizingly slowly as they moved down the coast. Finally Aiden saw a brief pinprick of light to his left. He pulled on the reins to turn Narak toward the shore. The surf pushed them in and, when Aiden felt Narak's hooves touch the ground, he pulled himself back onto the stallion.

Captain Alun held the torch aloft as they splashed onto the shore. He grabbed Narak's reins as Aiden dismounted, numb from cold.

"Change your clothes, lad, or you'll freeze. Then help me build a fire. There's just enough driftwood lying around," the captain ordered. Aiden complied as fast as he could, stumbling about in the darkness until the pile of driftwood flared weakly to life. He waited by Captain Alun as the men came singly to shore. Last of all came Trey.

"Everyone make it?" he asked, wiping water from his face.

"Aye, sir. We're all accounted for," Alun replied. "You'd best get changed. It's not long until dawn."

Corin waited patiently. The night had passed quietly. It wouldn't be long now before it was time to move. He felt the nervous tug at his gut that always came before a battle. A seagull squawked from the rocks as the eastern sky began to lighten imperceptibly. The sleeping warriors began to stir. Martin slid in beside him.

"You ready?" he asked.

"Aye, I didn't sleep at all last night," Corin replied.

"I would attempt to lecture you, but I didn't either," Martin said.

Faint sounds of horses shifting, girths being tightened, and weapons being checked began to echo. Martin and Corin rose and found their horses. Shields were moved and the sand smoothed out and the warriors rode single file out of their defenses. The Raiders fell back in surprise as they saw the approaching line of horses and the circle around the Aredorians was broken. Kara watched them ride out. She was waiting with the wounded. She saw Kieran with Tam and silently wished them both luck.

Riding behind Will, Tam watched as the Raider camp erupted into a puzzled activity as they saw more riders come from the east. Captain Rufus laid about with his sword, driving his men to prepare a defense. The Raider force was driven together as the Aredorians joined ranks. The hairs on the back of Tam's neck rose as Martin stood in his stirrups and sounded the eerie wolf howl. It echoed across the lonely coast and was answered as Karif dove from the sky to land on Corin's arm. Steel was drawn on both battles lines. Corin brought his scimitar down in a great, flashing arc and they charged.

Kara made her way through the aftermath, tending to the wounded as best she could.

"Rufus got away!" Trey shouted angrily as the longboats filled with escaped Raiders fled to the triremes after the northerners' horses carried them to victory. The sails were spread and oars began to move, taking the pirates out of reach. Martin attempted to calm Trey as the ships made off with his enemy. Aiden found Tam looking a little dazedly around him.

"You all right?" Aiden asked.

"I think so," Tam replied, taking a bloody hand away from his arm. Will ran over as Aiden helped Tam sit down. He ripped open the sleeve to look at the wound.

"It doesn't look bad, Tam," Aiden said. Aiden took a bandage from Will and wrapped it firmly around Tam's arm. "That will stop the bleeding for now. We'll get Kara tae look at it as soon as possible," he said. Tam nodded as they helped him to his feet.

It took most of the day to finish with the battleground. There were a few Raider prisoners taken who were allowed to care for their dead. Riders were sent to Castle Martel and to Kingscastle with news of the victory. Kara watched Kieran ride off before turning to Corin.

"Are you hurt, sir?" she asked.

"I see Liam passed on his nagging habits to you," Corin commented.

"And he wasn't lying about your evasiveness either," Kara said. "I mean that respectfully, of course," she said. Corin couldn't hide his smile.

"Of course you do," he said. "I'm fine for now. Go see to Tam. I want him and his brothers back in one piece. The last thing I need right now is an angry Clan coming after me."

The Raiders had used several of the remaining longboats to build a pyre by the water's edge on which they placed their dead companions. The sun was low in the sky when they lit it. The Aredorians gathered together and watched, having already lain their fallen to rest in a single grave not far from the beach.

Only Tam stood at the water's edge just beyond the reach of the incoming waves that were tinted red by the setting sun. Then softly, he began to sing. The words echoed over the silent coast.

"What's he doing?" Corin asked Aiden.

"He's singing the dead tae Heaven's Halls," Aiden replied quietly, struck by the haunting melody.

"It's not Rhyddan," Martin said.

"No, it's the old language of the Clans. None but the bards know it now," Will replied.

"Do you think it works, sir?" one of the young warriors asked. He had lost a close friend in the fighting. Will looked over at his drawn face.

"Aye, lad. I think it does," he said and the young man wiped a tear from his face.

- -

The next morning the prisoners boarded the last longboat, loaded with some supplies, and pushed out to sea.

"That's more of a chance than they ever gave their victims," Trey ground out angrily as he watched them go.

"Aye, but would you have given the order to kill them?" Corin asked. Trey simply shook his head.

"We've been here too long. Let's go home," he said.

Chapter 7

"They're back!" Amaura announced excitedly. Rona and Mera hurried to join her as she ran outside to the courtyard. They were joined by other families anxiously scanning the ranks of warriors who rode in through the gates.

"Where's Corin? And Trey?" Amaura asked Martin as she suddenly filled with panic.

"Trey went with his men back to Castle Martel to report to Tristan," Martin explained.

"And Corin?" she demanded.

"We lost a few men. He and Captain Bedwyr are telling their families," Martin told her.

"I'm glad you're safe," Rona said to Aiden as he dismounted.

"I told you we'd be fine," he replied. "And I usually try not tae lie too badly."

Rona laughed, still amazed at how happy she was to see him alive and well. They were interrupted by Laird Dandin.

"I hope you don't mind the intrusion, ma'am, but might I speak with Aiden?" he asked. Rona dropped a curtsey to the Laird and left.

"I know you just got back, lad, but I'm thinking this might be the only chance before my Clan leaves today," Dandin said.

"I'm at your disposal, my laird," Aiden said, his interest thoroughly piqued.

"Corin had mentioned tae me that you might be looking for something tae keep busy. We keep a regular patrol on our borders along Aredor and Durna, especially now that there might be another war. I'm offering you a place in one of the patrols," Laird Dandin said.

"Under what conditions, sir?"

"A patrol goes out for two weeks. Right now we have three patrols, so you would have time tae go home in between," Laird Dandin told him. Aiden thought it over for a long minute.

"What if trouble should come back tae Scodra?" he asked.

"You'd be free tae go, unbound by any oath as a Laird's son and member of another Clan," Laird Dandin said. Aiden looked over to his brothers who waited for him.

"I don't know yet, sir," he said.

"I understand, Aiden. I will be visiting Scodra by the first month of winter. There were once strong ties between our Clans that I would see reestablished. You can give me an answer then," Dandin said.

"You've made me a generous offer," Aiden said, bowing respectfully.

"I'll see you in a month then," Dandin said.

"Yes, sir," Aiden replied.

"What were you two talking about?" Will asked, his curiosity mirrored in Tam's face.

"I'll tell you on the way home," Aiden said.

"Then I think I need tae talk tae you both," Will said.

"About what?" Aiden asked.

"I don't think I'm going with you. At least not yet," Will said.

"What do you mean?" Tam asked.

"I read Father's letter and I know he wants me home, but I feel like I owe it tae Corin tae stay for at least a year. I already spoke with him about it," Will said.

"And?" Aiden asked.

"He wanted me tae go home but I told him I'd stay through the spring at least. They might be needing some extra help by then," Will said. "He's giving me a few weeks leave, so I'll be there at the New Year when Ranulf takes the torc."

"That's not too far away," Aiden said.

"Laird Dandin offered you a place in the Clan's patrol, didn't he?" Will asked.

"Aye, he did," Aiden affirmed.

"Are you taking it?" Tam asked, slightly shocked at the news.

"I don't know yet, Tam. I need tae think it over," Aiden replied.

Clan Canich spent one more day at Kingscastle before preparing to return home.

"Did Lord Dandin talk to you?" Corin asked Aiden.

"Aye, I don't what I'll do yet. Will said he's staying," Aiden said.

"I told him he was free to go if he wanted. You and I both know how hard that separation can be," Corin said.

"Aye, we'll see what the winter brings," Aiden said. "It was good tae see you again, Cor."

"You too, Aiden."

Farewells were said, and between Tam and Kara there was a shy promise to write. Before Clan Dyson had left, a system had been worked out to transmit letters from Clan Canich to Dyson and on to the Hawk Flight.

With the departure of the Clans, life in Aredor slowly settled back to its normal routine. A few days later, the Hawk Flight gathered together at the caves where the newest recruits took the final oath. Corin divided them among the patrols, sending Ian to Martin's patrol with Evan and keeping Andras in his patrol. As he stepped out from the caves and into the open air, Corin felt a sudden chill. Somewhere on the plains of Braeton, Aiden felt it too.

"Anything to report?" the man asked.

"No, sir. We've seen no fresh tracks or movement in over a month," the forester replied. "It's like the Aredorians have disappeared."

"I trust your men haven't revealed themselves?" the man asked.

"No, sir. We Durnians have the greatest skill in the forest. There's no chance the Aredorians have seen us," the forester said.

"You had better be right. We can't afford any mistakes. The Hawk Flight and their captain must be taken by surprise and wiped out," the man said.

"They say he's like a ghost," the forester said.

"No, he's human enough. My predecessor was too careless and now I will have the honor of killing the Hawk myself!" The man's eyes gleamed in anticipation.

"When will your troops arrive from Calorin?" the forester asked.

"Soon. By the first thaw we will begin to move. With you and your men to guide us through the forest, we will be unstoppable!"

Book 3

Battle for Aredor

Chapter 1

Aiden wrapped his cloak more tightly around him against the frigid winter air. He again scanned the forest as he waited. It was nearly an hour later when he finally saw movement through the trees. A solitary figure leading a horse emerged onto the path.

"I wondered when you were finally going tae show up," he said. Will released the hilt of his sword as Aiden pushed back his hood.

"Danny! How did you know I'd be coming this way?" he asked as they embraced.

"Well, I might have written tae a certain friend of mine..." Aiden said with a grin.

"The pair of you!" Will shook his head.

"I can'nae accompany my own brother home?" Aiden asked.

"I hope you have a horse because I won't wait for you," Will said.

"Aye, I left Narak just up the path," Aiden said.

"I thought you'd still be on patrol," Will said as they continued walking.

"It just ended and I got permission from the captain tae wait here on the border for you," Aiden said. He had decided to join the patrols of Clan Dyson. After much discussion and some arguing with his father and Ranulf, he had given Laird Dandin his answer. In the end it was the pirate Rufus's words that swayed him. He knew there would be a war in Aredor soon and he wanted to do his part to help Corin.

"I'm glad you did, brother," Will said.

"Don't tell me you're nervous!" Aiden said teasingly.

"It's been almost three years. Don't act like you weren't worried when you came back!" Will returned.

"Scared stiff actually," Aiden said, untethering Narak. "How are things in Aredor?"

"Quiet. No sign of anything. But Corin still has us on full alert," Will replied.

"Aye, same here. Although I am starting tae regret joining a patrol in the middle of winter," Aiden said.

"It's bloody freezing! Why are we still standing here?" Will said. They both mounted their horses and spurred them on to a brisk trot.

A few days later they paused at the top of Scodra valley. Narak whinnied as he recognized the end of their journey.

"Come on, I'll race you down," Aiden challenged. The horses plunged down the snowy slope, slowing to a canter as they drew near the open gates of Scodra. Shouts went up from the guards as they recognized Aiden and Will. Their family came out of the keep as they rode in and halted at the foot of the steps.

Ranulf and Tam were the first to greet Will in a joyful reunion. They stood back with Aiden as Laird Gòrdan came down the stairs to meet his son. Quiet words were exchanged between them and finally an embrace. Aiden felt a nudge at his hand. He looked down to see Illyria. He reached down to stoke her ears. The huge dog had taken to following him around when he was home on leave. Almost unknowingly, he had started talking to her when they were alone as the dog was more than content to sit and listen. Illyria licked his hand before padding away again.

"Did you hear that Skive is leaving Scodra?" Ranulf asked.

"No, where's he going?" Aiden asked in surprise.

"He's not moving far. Father gave him a piece of land in the forest. Jamey says it's not far from him. He's helping Skive build a house," Ranulf replied.

"Why'd he decide tae leave?" Aiden asked. Ranulf shrugged.

"Probably tae stop you from stealing his dog," he said. "You'll have tae ask him yourself."

The foreigner was not at dinner but Aiden was fully occupied. Still not entirely comfortable with sitting at the head table, he would often move down and join Blair and Douglas. More often too, the warriors would come by and greet him, especially those who were at Scodra during the siege. And Captain Artair would always find time to ask about his patrol. It was moments like these, seated in the warm hall and surrounded by friends, that he almost regretted joining the forest patrol. But he couldn't deny the freedom he felt every time he rode out.

After the meal ended he went to his room and began to reclean and inspect his gear as he did after every patrol. There was a knock on the door and Ranulf entered. Aiden took his boot off the wooden chair and shoved it toward him. Ranulf turned the chair around and sat down as Aiden continued sharpening his sword.

"Danny, while you were gone, Father and I began talking with Artair and some of the other captains. Canich has not had a champion in years. The Clan needs a champion and we want it tae be you," Ranulf said. Aiden paused momentarily, then continued working on his sword. Ranulf waited patiently until Aiden put down the whetstone and began polishing the blade.

"Why me?" he asked.

"Have you forgotten what you did for Scodra?"

"No, it's just…I don't think I'm the right one."

"Why, Aiden?" Ranulf asked curiously. Aiden paused before answering.

"I know I have the skill, Davy, I just don't think I have the heart," he said. "I've turned and run from so much in my life. Do you know me well enough now tae believe I won't do it again?" he looked up to meet Ranulf's gaze. Ranulf saw that his younger brother still felt lost and he began to understand.

"Is that why you haven't spoken tae Rona since you've been back?" he asked. Aiden nodded wordlessly. He had slowly begun to realize after the Autumn Festival that he was falling in love with the young woman.

"It was anger that drove me away, Davy. I can control it better now, but it's still there. I'm afraid that I'll hurt someone because of it. I've made my peace with Father, but I can'nae forget the way I felt for so long after I left," Aiden said.

"But that's in the past, Danny. You can'nae hold ontae it forever," Ranulf said.

"No, but some wounds take longer tae heal than others."

"Aye, and Adalwulf left heavy scars among the Clan. Everyone respects you for what you did, Aiden. You stayed and fought when no one else would."

"You would have too, Davy," Aiden interrupted. Ranulf smiled.

"Aye, but it took someone more than me tae start the fight. Despite what you may think, you do have the heart of a Champion," Ranulf said. Aiden again met his steady gaze.

"When do you need an answer?" he asked.

"I take the torc in four days. That's when we need a decision," Ranulf replied. Aiden nodded pensively. Ranulf rose and left the room. Aiden put his swords away and leaned back in the armchair. He had been afraid that something like this would happen. The position of Champion was a high one within the Clan. He did not feel ready for the burden of its responsibility and felt as if he would fail and bring disgrace to the Clan. He rose and went to the window. The moon shone softly down through the tree that grew by the opening. Aiden looked down at his old escape route from the keep. He had no reason to run anymore but the gnarled branches tempted him as they once did. A muffled knock distracted him. He smiled as he heard it come through the wall from Will's room beside his.

"If you can still open it, you can come in," he called. There was a faint click and Will pushed part of the wall open.

"I don't think that was our old password," he said.

"You never used it much anyway," Aiden replied with a grin as he turned to face Will. Years before, they had discovered the secret panel connecting their rooms. There was also a narrow passageway between the walls, but it ended sharply and they never found the way to the rest of it. But the panel had remained their jealously guarded secret.

"It got too long and complicated after a while," Will said with a smile. He leaned against the wall. "I figured you might want tae talk."

"Were you listening?" Aiden asked.

"No, Father and Davy told me earlier."

"Why don't they make you Champion?"

"I have been gone for a few years."

"It's not like I've been here," Aiden replied, sitting against the table. "I just don't know if I can do it."

"I think I might understand why," Will said.

"You do?" Aiden asked in surprise.

"You seem tae forget who my captain is," Will said. Aiden smiled faintly. He knew Corin still struggled like him.

"Everyone must think we're two of the strangest people they've ever met," he said.

"I won't deny that," Will said lightly. Aiden smiled again.

"There is one person I wish I could talk tae," he said.

"Mother," Will guessed. Aiden nodded.

"She always listened," he said, feeling a quick pang of sorrow when he thought of her. She had always found him and comforted him after he and his father argued. She never stopped trying to bring peace between them.

"She always knew you'd come back," Will said.

"I wish it would've been sooner. I miss her," Aiden said. Will agreed quietly.

"It was partly for her that I decided I would try and find you again," he said.

"What do you think she would say right now?" Aiden asked and Will paused for a long moment.

"I think she would tell you tae stop trying tae hide and tae accept who you are as a Laird's son and as a warrior. You ran from it once and I think you're still trying tae. Stop, Danny, and let yourself come home," Will said. Aiden made no reply. He could almost hear his mother through Will's words. "And she'd tell you not tae let Rona slip away."

"You too?" Aiden asked with a rueful grin.

"I'm not blind, Danny. Don't lose her or you'll regret it forever."

"I know. But I'd rather take one decision at a time."

"Aye, well, I'd offer more advice but I feel like I should start charging you for it."

"You've done enough damage already," Aiden replied. "Thanks, Will."

Will only nodded and withdrew to his room. Aiden blew a heavy sigh as he felt his life changing irreversibly.

Aiden went to the forest the next day. It had been weeks since he had last seen Jamey and he also wanted to find Skive. Jamey was not at his house and Aiden followed the tracks down a path until he heard the noise of axes against wood. Maon barked a greeting as Aiden entered a new clearing. Jamey and Skive looked up and Illyria bounded forward to nuzzle Aiden's hand.

"You found us," Jamey said.

"You act like it would have been hard tae," Aiden returned. Jamey laughed, setting the axe down and coming to greet him.

"You two have been busy," Aiden commented. Felled trees lay on one side of the clearing and Jamey and Skive worked to break them apart. The stumps would remain until the ground thawed enough to remove them.

"It is slow going," Skive said.

"You need some extra hands?" Aiden asked. Jamey looked to Skive, who nodded. Despite the chill air, Aiden took off his cloak and put it on a stump. He joined in as Skive directed.

"You could have as much help as you wanted if you asked," Aiden told Skive as he took an axe and began to remove branches from the wide trunks.

"A man should build his own house. I am grateful to your father for his hospitality, but I want a more private place of my own," Skive replied. Aiden agreed. The hall seemed crowded, especially in the winter.

"So, you're planning on staying then," Aiden said.

"Aye. You and I are both alike in that we have wandered far from our homes. But unlike you, I cannot go back," Skive said.

"Do you miss it?" Aiden asked, helping Skive drag branches away to a new pile.

"More than I can tell."

"Would you go back if you could?" Aiden asked. Skive looked at him.

"I think you know the answer. Why do you ask these questions?"

"I… things are turning out differently than I thought they would if I came back."

"There are rumors that you would become Champion."

"I don't know yet."

"You would make a great champion," Skive told him. The only sound was Jamey splitting another log. Illyria growled as Maon became too playful and bit her tail.

"Rona seems lonely of late," Skive commented. Aiden stopped.

"Does everyone have an opinion on Rona?" he asked a little sharply.

"What bothers you so much about it?" Skive asked. "Why do you hold back?"

"Say I become Champion. What would become of her if something happened tae me?" Aiden asked.

"A warrior knows the risks of going to battle. She does too. There is something else?" Skive asked. Aiden wished he wasn't so perceptive.

"The stories say I was born under a red star," Aiden said.

"And so you bear the battle-wrath," Skive finished. "I can see it in the way you fight."

"It's true," Aiden said. "It used tae overwhelm me in battle and I would not be stopped. I finally learned tae control it but I can always feel it lurking, waiting tae come. I feel like I'd only hurt her."

"You've never hurt anyone you care about because of it, Aiden," Jamey interrupted. Aiden half-turned to see him standing behind them.

"But it has still caused their deaths," Aiden said. There was a sadness in his voice that Jamey had never heard before.

"The battle-wrath does not run as strongly in my veins. My wife did not fear it. She only knew that I would protect her," Skive said. "The Clan looks to you to do the same. I do not think that Rona will be frightened of anything."

"Do you think I should become Champion?" Aiden asked both of them.

"I can think of no one better," Jamey said.

"You think you cannot, but nothing could be further from the truth. You can lead the warriors of this Clan to glory," Skive said.

"I hope I can do one fraction of what this Clan expects of me," Aiden said. The conversation was ended and they turned back to work. Aiden was grateful to stay busy. He had too much to think over.

The next morning he rose early and walked to the far side of the frozen lake. The only sound was his footsteps crunching softly in the snow. Two stone pillars engraved with a wildcat fighting a raven marked his destination.

He passed through the pillars to the burial place of the Clan. The silence seemed magnified among the graves. He crouched and brushed snow away from the stone that marked his mother's resting place.

"I don't know what tae do this time," he said softly. But Will had been right. He had hidden his tattoos while he was gone, not even showing them to Corin. He had always been afraid of being found out for who he really was. "I don't know why I still am," he said. "I came back, Mother. I'm home now, so what's stopping me?"

He realized that it was the thought of having to stay. Once he took the responsibility he would no longer be able to leave if he needed...or wanted. He looked down at the gravestone. A lily was carved into the surface around the Clan's emblem. *How many more graves would he kneel in front of?* He saw Dillon's grave not far away. They were surrounded by many more. Some stones cracked and crumbled with age and others were so old that the stones had vanished.

"Stop running," Will had told him. He never understood how he came to his decision crouching there in the frozen graveyard, but he knew he would take his place in the Clan.

He stood stiffly. He almost laughed as he saw a figure on horseback riding by the lakeshore.

"Will was right on both counts, Mother. I think you'd like her." He left the silent stones and strode toward the figure.

Two days later, Ranulf stood before the Clan as Laird with his new bride beside him. Aiden knelt before him, dressed for battle. Placing his weapons at Ranulf's feet, he swore the ancient oath of the Champion: to protect and serve his Laird and to uphold the Clan with strength and honor.

Ranulf placed a simple bronze torc around his neck and slid a bronze armband onto his bare right arm above the new spiral tattoo. Brighde fastened a plaid cloak of the finest make around his shoulders.

The celebration was a wild affair as representatives from the other four Clans mixed with Canich. The champions of Strowen, Mavor, Gunlon, and Dyson welcomed Aiden into their midst.

He had managed to persuade both his father and Laird Dandin to allow him to continue with the patrol from Clan Dyson. They had reluctantly agreed with the condition that if no trouble came to the North in the next few months, he would return to Scodra. He accepted the decision with some relief. He was still not yet ready to settle down for good. Almost a week later, Aiden again accompanied Will back to the border, bidding him farewell before they each disappeared back into the forest.

Chapter 2

Gerralt made his way across the courtyard, clutching a bundle of papers as he sidestepped puddles of melting snow. Even though it was early morning, the barracks were already alive with activity. He pushed open the door to the office and halted in surprise. Corin was already there. He was slouched forward on the desk, head pillowed on his arms, asleep.

Gerralt paused, uncertain of whether to wake him or not. He set his papers down on his desk. His chair squeaked against a floor stone as he moved it and Corin came awake. He closed the book that had been in his hand and rubbed his eyes tiredly.

"Morning," he mumbled when he saw Gerralt. The secretary returned it with his customary "Good morning, sire," and then, seeing the flickering stub of candle, asked, "Have you been here long?"

"I was having trouble sleeping last night, so I thought I'd come down and get some of this taken care of. I felt a little guilty for not doing any of it yesterday," Corin said. Gerralt sniffed, still taken a bit off guard. Corin shoved a stack of papers toward him. "These are finished," he said. "I've had no trouble going through this. Thanks for keeping it organized."

Gerralt didn't hear the usual note of impatient sarcasm and stammered a quick "You're welcome, sire," as he took the papers.

Corin took up his quill pen and began to work again. Gerralt saw the pensive look on his face and asked a question that surprised them both.

"Is everything all right, sire?"

"What?" Corin's head flew up.

"It's just...you look troubled and you said you couldn't sleep," Gerralt explained himself.

"Oh, I um...there are some memories that always come back this time of year," Corin said. Remembering Castimir's death and seeing the season change had brought on an increased restlessness. Gerralt looked back to his work as Corin began to write again. Almost an hour passed in silence before Corin laid down his pen and rubbed at the ink stain on his fingers. Gerralt still worked patiently on. Over the winter they had developed a grudging respect for one another, but Corin still knew almost nothing about him.

"Why did you choose to be a scholar, Gerralt?'" he asked. His assistant paused.

"I wasn't at first," he admitted. "I served in the King's warband for almost two years."

It was the last thing Corin expected. He leaned back in his chair. "What happened?" he asked.

"My first battle. It was on the coast against the Raiders. I realized then that I could never be a warrior and I asked to be discharged." He looked away from Corin. "You must think me weak."

"No. It takes plenty of courage to realize you aren't meant for something," Corin said. "Besides, we can't all be warriors. Someone has to keep delinquent princes like me in line." He was glad to see a faint smile flash across Gerralt's face. "I wish I could remember you. That must have been when I was still here," Corin said.

"Aye, it was. And I remember you, sire," Gerralt said.

"Probably because I made sure everyone knew who I was," Corin said with a grin. "It might be a good thing I disappeared. I would've ended up an extremely arrogant prince and you would find me even more insufferable."

"I don't find you insufferable," Gerralt protested, then unbelievably added, "on rare occasions."

Corin burst out laughing and startled Karif. Gerralt smiled, relaxing for the first time since taking the position.

"I guess we can get along then," Corin said.

"It looks that way, *sir,*" Gerralt replied. Not long after, Corin was called away to meet his brother and father.

"I know you just returned two days ago and have 'forgotten' about the Lords' meeting tomorrow," his father said.

"I knew there was a reason I needed to stay out longer." Corin grimaced. As the lords had returned to their lands or as others had been appointed, it seemed that more than one could not forgive him for spending half his life in Calorin and for the obvious influence it had wrought in his behavior. It didn't matter that he had used that knowledge and training to save Aredor.

"Speaking of, when do you expect...?" King Celyn asked meaningfully.

"Almost any day. It's thawing quickly," Corin replied somberly.

"I sent messengers to the Lords midwinter informing them of the situation. You will have to give a full report tomorrow," King Celyn said.

"Please tell me anything else!" Corin groaned. Darrin smiled.

"I have just the thing. I wanted to tell you earlier, but Rhian and I are going to be married."

Corin pulled him into a hug. "Congratulations! When?"

"Hopefully in a month's time," Darrin replied.

"There will be another change at that time I wanted to speak to both of you about," King Celyn said. His sons turned their full attention to him. "Aredor's kings have long been able to lead the warbands into battle. Something I am no longer able to do," he said.

"But, Father!" Darrin protested.

"No," King Celyn interrupted. "If we are faced with another war, Aredor needs the strongest leader she can have. You're ready, Darrin."

"How do you know?" Darrin asked.

"Because I've watched you, both of you, and I know this is not a mistake," King Celyn said. "And, Corin, it's time for you to take the General's belt."

Corin tried to protest but Darrin stopped him.

"There's no one else I'd rather have at my side as General than you," he said.

"One day I'll have a good comeback for that one," Corin said. King Celyn chuckled.

"I want to be there when you do," he said.

"It'll be creative, I'm sure," Corin grinned.

"You want to think it over at the training grounds? I'm riding Frithun down there now," Darrin said.

"You're saying you want a rematch?" Corin asked. Earlier in the winter he had beaten Darrin in the exercises with the spear. Their father laughed.

"I used to be the master of that course," he said.

"Then come down with us," Darrin said.

"No, it's been too long," King Celyn protested.

"Come on, Father. We'll go easy on you," Corin challenged. His father replied with the same sparkle in his eyes.

"All right, but I'm warning you—I used to make grown men cry. I'll see you both in the stables in ten minutes."

Feeling like young boys again, the brothers hurried to change and raced down to the stables but arrived behind their father.

"Already falling behind, I see," he said mock-severely.

As they rode to the grounds, their stallions snorted anxiously, feeling the scent of spring in the chilly air. Their arrival caused a stir of excitement among the warriors. Due to a troublesome old leg wound, King Celyn was a rare sight at the training grounds. His sons gladly fell behind him as men stopped and greeted the king respectfully. The somber old captain, who had survived the war and many campaigns with the king, greeted them at the spear run.

"Here to give the young lads a lesson or two, sire?" he asked.

"Hoping to, Pedr," King Celyn replied.

The spear run was several yards wide and the wooden fences marking its edges stretched straight on for nearly sixty yards. Stuffed targets mounted on slender poles were scattered down the run at the end of which stood a large, round target. As an added challenge, the ground was soaked by the melting snow and churned to mud by the passing of countless hooves through the day. All three of them selected spears from the rack by the run.

"Youngest first." King Celyn indicated Corin.

"Hit every other target," Pedr instructed. "Finish with the center of the final target."

Corin moved Zephyr back several yards from the beginning while testing the weight of the spear. At the captain's nod, he began. He completed the course cleanly, but Zephyr bolted beyond the target before Corin could rein him back in.

"You have to be in control as you finish," Pedr lectured him as if he were a beginner. Darrin rode next but his horse slipped and swerved in the mud before he could hit the final target.

"Riding like a novice." Captain Pedr shook his head. King Celyn rode the course perfectly.

Again and again they rode the course hitting the targets as Pedr instructed or as they were set out. Despite his earlier protestations, King Celyn was still a master of the spear and his sons fell behind. More and more warriors joined Pedr, drinking in their display of skill.

"I wish I could have seen him in battle," Corin said to Darrin, watching their father ride again.

"It was a thing of beauty, lad," Pedr said as he heard Corin.

"It was incredible," Darrin agreed. King Celyn rode slowly back.

"That's it for me, Pedr. But I think the boys can do one more," he said.

"Will you be giving them the course, sir?" Pedr asked.

"Aye, but there's not much they need to work on," said King Celyn. "Darrin, do you remember how you beat Ivor several years ago?"

"Aye, I think so, Father," Darrin said.

"Don't worry, sire," Pedr smiled broadly for the first time. "I remember that course like it was yesterday."

It was set up quickly and Darrin carefully chose a spear. He raced down the course, stabbing and knocking down the targets with sure aim until there was only one target left. He threw the spear into the ground beyond it, and then swung down from the saddle. Still holding onto the pommel, he kicked the last target, ran a step beside Frithun before vaulting into the saddle again. He grabbed the spear, twisted it, and rammed it with deadly force into the final target. He cantered back to loud cheers led by Corin and King Celyn. Then the king turned to Corin.

"You do well with the spear, son, but let's see what you can do with the javelin," he challenged. Corin smiled in agreement. He had been training with the Aredorian spear but his true skill was with the lighter Calorin weapon.

"Aye, Captain! Show them how you took down those Argusians during the raids!" Llewellyn called. Pedr nodded in agreement.

"Set it up then," Corin said. Celyn's eyes widened and there were quiet mutterings from the men as over fifteen targets were set up.

"Did you see this?" Celyn asked Darrin.

"No, I was leading a separate attack at the time. But this is one of the Hawk Flight's favorite stories," Darrin replied.

Corin moved Zephyr to the line and drove him forward with a cry. He swung the javelin at the base of the first two targets, snapping their poles. He hefted the javelin with ease, twisting it around himself to stab at multiple targets set to the sides as he passed. He came toward two targets set side by side. Corin pulled hard on the reins, causing Zephyr to rear and strike one with his hooves while Corin left the javelin embedded in the other target. Corin drew his scimitar and spurred Zephyr away, slashing through the two remaining targets before halting his horse perfectly at the end of the run.

There was brief moment of silence before the men of the Hawk Flight began cheering him. They were quickly joined by many others. Corin turned and walked Zephyr back as Karif flew in to perch on his shoulder. King Celyn watched in silence. He had never seen his son in battle, but he knew he had just seen the Hawk. Corin's face was expressionless as he made it back and his hands gripped the reins tightly. Pedr saw it and went up to him.

"Are you all right, Captain?" he asked quietly.

"Aye, I just don't remember it as fondly," Corin replied. For a moment he had been back in the burning village exacting retribution for the deaths of his countrymen.

"Corin, my father used to tell me that the moment you do, you cease to be a warrior and become nothing more than a savage who kills for pleasure," King Celyn said. Corin reached down and rubbed Zephyr's neck as he tried to calm his racing pulse.

"That gets more impressive every time, Captain!" Llewellyn said.

"Maybe, Llewy, but I think you gave me fifteen too many targets," Corin replied. Men laughed. They knew how war stories became exaggerated with time, especially in Llewellyn's case. King Celyn watched his sons talk with their men and Captain Pedr came to stand by his horse.

"I think you'll be putting Aredor into good hands, sire," he said. King Celyn nodded.

"Aye, Pedr. I watched the men's faces when they rode. We should not fear for the future," King Celyn said. Pedr nodded in silent agreement.

"If you don't mind, I'll take the long way back," Corin said as they prepared to ride back to the castle. Neither Darrin nor his father argued so he spurred Zephyr away.

"He's fine," Darrin reassured King Celyn. "It's something about this time of year. He's never told me though." But as warriors, they thought they had a fairly good idea.

Corin rode at a steady canter, reveling as the wind swirled around them. Karif soared overhead. They stopped by the river and Corin dismounted. It was quiet and peaceful and had become one of his places of refuge from the castle.

The water had begun to free itself from its cover of ice. He brushed snow from a rock and sat down. Zephyr philosophically pawed at the ground until he found fresh grass to graze on. Karif flitted in and out as he pleased. Corin took out his half-carved block of wood and began to work on it, keeping his mind occupied on the task.

Time passed slowly and the tension inside him eased as he worked. Karif landed in front of him and chirped. Corin became aware of hoof beats coming toward them. He looked up to see a familiar rider. Zephyr whinnied as he recognized Mera's gelding.

"What are you doing?" she called.

"Hiding," he replied.

"From what?" she asked with a light laugh.

"The usual," Corin said. Mera knew that this did not include her. They had sought each other out over the winter and begun to know each other well.

"Then may I join you?" she asked. Corin nodded and rose to help her as she descended the bank. Mera spread her cloak over a rock before sitting.

"Everything all right?" she asked. Corin smiled. Mera had always been able to read him, despite everything he tried.

"Yes and no," he replied.

"Thanks for being so clear," she said.

"I try," he replied with another smile.

"What is that?" she pointed curiously to the object he held in his hand. He ran the knife over it again, smoothing the last edge before handing it to her. Mera turned the carving over in her hands, studying it intently. It was a fish, but not one she had ever seen.

"It's called a dolphin," he explained. "I saw one once when I was coming home before the War. Some of the Gelion merchants carry it on their flag."

"It's beautiful," Mera said. She remembered she had seen another carving like it. "You made Gwilym's horse, didn't you?"

"Aye. He wouldn't rest until he got one," Corin said.

"I didn't know you carved," Mera said.

"I started in Calorin. It helps to pass time or to keep my mind busy," Corin said. Mera fell silent for a moment, understanding the meaning of his words. She ran a finger over the smooth back of the dolphin.

"What are you going to do with this?" she asked. Corin shrugged.

"I don't know yet. Most of the younger children know I do it, so they pester me for a carving. But this one's not spoken for yet," he said.

"May I keep it?" Mera asked.

"If you want it," Corin replied. Her fingers closed over the carving.

"Gwilym says you're taking him down to see the yearlings?" Mera said.

"Tomorrow, if I'm still alive after the Lords' meeting," he said. Mera laughed quickly again, a sound he had come to love. "But, unfortunately, I still have some reports to look over and I've already been gone much longer than I promised Gerralt I would be."

They both stood reluctantly. Mera chose to continue her ride, watching wistfully as Corin cantered back to the castle and trying for what seemed the hundredth time to discern her true feelings for him.

Corin caught the sympathetic look that Tristan and then his Uncle Maldwyn gave him. He had just finished giving a full report on the movement of the Hawk Flight and the nearing possibility of another attack whereupon the room had burst into loud conversations. After several outraged questions, Captain Haul of Lynwood Keep admitted to being fully aware of it.

"How much were you going to withhold from us?" Lord Mabon questioned Corin who artfully deflected the question to his father.

"I did not see need to cause panic through the country over an event that may or may not occur," King Celyn replied.

"You would wait until the Calorins are cutting our throats in our houses?" Lord Siarls put in. "How do we know any of this information is correct?"

"Prince Corin trusts the source implicitly," King Celyn said, pointedly giving Corin his title.

"Oh, the other northerner who seems to prefer the Calorins over his own country?" Lord Siarls directed it to Corin.

"I would hardly say that since he was just named Champion of Clan Canich," Corin shot back. He tapped the arm of his chair impatiently.

"But nothing that comes from the South can be trusted," Lord Siarls said to Corin. The room tensed and Corin's eyes narrowed dangerously. The Lords Mabon and Siarls always seemed to try and cause trouble for him but neither had ever gone that far before. They were two of several lords that had been allowed to rule their lands under the Calorins only because of the richness of their holdings. Darrin gave Corin a warning look which Corin chose to ignore.

"If that is the case, my lord, then maybe you can explain to me how you, out of the men in this room, retained hold of your lands during the war?" Corin asked, his voice deathly calm. Lord Siarls choked with anger.

"You have no right...!" he stammered.

"Explain to me why the Calorins left you on your seat while I fought against those who desecrated our country. Explain why my men died while you paid tribute to the Calorins!" Corin's voice rose in anger. Lord Siarls flew from his seat and Corin rose to meet him.

"You know nothing of what happened!" Siarls shouted. His blood nearly froze when he looked into Corin's face.

"And you know nothing of me," Corin replied quietly. Lord Siarls had no reply. He reclaimed his seat and, after a brief moment, Lord Maldwyn asked after the defenses of Lynwood Keep as if nothing had happened. Since Aiden had brought word of the Sultaan's plans the summer before, the garrison had been steadily increased, leaving them well able to assist the Hawk Flight if necessary.

Lord Mabon would have questioned the preparations for an attack again, but Darrin cut him off.

"Raiders hinted at it last autumn. Lord Trey can also attest to this," he said. Lord Mabon opened his mouth to argue the honesty of the Raiders but one look at Corin killed any questions he would have raised. Corin spoke only as needed and his anger slowly faded by the time the meeting finished in the early afternoon.

Gwilym was waiting for him outside the council room and bouncing from one foot to the other in impatience.

"Are you finally doned, Uncle Cor?" he asked.

"Yes, you little wretch!" Corin replied.

"Your Uncle Cor might need a drink before you go," Tristan said.

"Are you thirsty?" Gwilym asked Corin.

"No," he told the boy. "I'll be fine as long as I don't have to see him for a while," Corin told Tristan. Gwilym listened carefully.

"Someone annoying you, Uncle Cor? Why don't you chop 'em in half with your sword?" he asked.

"What *do* you, Martin, and Trey teach him exactly?" Tristan asked Corin.

"Oh, lots of stuff," Gwilym answered.

"I'm sure they do," his Uncle Tris agreed. "Has your Uncle Cor taught you how to play nice with others?" he asked. Corin laughed sarcastically. Gwilym's impatience won through and he grabbed Corin's hand, dragging him away while informing him that Aunt Mera was also accompanying them.

The yearlings were kept in a large pasture by the training grounds. They were walking through the town when Corin heard someone behind them. He turned to see Llewellyn running toward them.

"Captain! There's a rider coming in full speed. It looks like Martin!" he gasped.

Gwilym took Mera's hand as Corin and Llewellyn raced back to the castle. He didn't understand why Corin looked so frightened to see his Uncle Martin.

Gerralt heard the shouts and pounding feet as Martin burst into the office. Martin dropped a few words in Calorin.

"Where's Corin?" he demanded. Gerralt felt sudden panic and could only state the obvious.

"He's not here."

Martin repeated his first words and ran out again, shouting for someone to find the Captain. Gerralt followed him out into the courtyard. A groom held a lathered horse and the men of the Hawk Flight had begun to gather. Martin headed toward the castle steps when a shout stopped him. He waited for Corin and Llewellyn to join him. They held a quick conference and Corin re-questioned Martin before both of them tore up the stairs into the keep. Llewellyn went over to the men.

"Start packing, lads. We're leaving in two hours."

"You are sure about this, Lieutenant?" King Celyn asked. The council had gathered back together.

"Yes, sire. Lieutenant Liam and his patrol found the tracks two days ago. They were well covered, but enough for a large force. And yesterday we saw their campsite. Almost a hundred Calorins and Durnians," Martin reported.

"Only a hundred? Is this the massive invasion we have heard so much about? Why didn't the fearless Hawk Flight attack?" Lord Siarls sneered. Martin treated him to a pitying glance.

"*If* I'd been allowed to finish, Lieutenant Flynn also saw a second strike force further down the border. And just because we can't see them does not mean there aren't more Durnians out there. My lord, we aren't stupid. Even twenty men of the Hawk Flight are no match for a force arrayed like that," Martin said.

"What do you mean 'arrayed like that?'" Tristan asked. He and Darrin looked concerned. Having fought with the Hawk Flight in the War they knew well that twenty men could have wreaked havoc on the enemy force.

"They've set up traps and snares around the camp. And they carry a banner depicting a hawk pierced with a javelin. They will hunt us relentlessly and this will soon become bloodier than the first war," Martin said. The room was deathly silent. Then King Celyn stirred.

"The fight has come to you first, General." He formally named Corin to the position. "What are your plans?"

"I leave immediately for the forest. Captain Haul, I'm coming to Lynwood as soon as I've met with my entire warband," Corin said. Captain Haul nodded. He would leave as soon as he could to prepare the Keep for war. "I'll send Kieran to alert the Clans. Our warbands are still sadly depleted and we will need their help long before this is over," Corin continued. "And, your majesty, it would be best to begin preparations for the defense of this castle. We'll hold them in the forest as long as we can, but I can make no promises."

King Celyn agreed.

"My lords, return to your lands and prepare for the worst. Make sure your men are ready to ride at any time to wherever they are most needed," he ordered.

"Captain, with your permission, I'll send Trey and his deugain to help. They can hold the border to the south," Tristan said to Corin.

"If you can spare them, they will be more than welcome," Corin said in relief. Trey and his Sharks would be an invaluable addition to his force. They were named after the silent, lethal killers of the sea for a reason.

"I'll pull the men from the inland garrisons to prepare for an attack from the sea," Tristan said. King Celyn approved and would have kept discussing the matter but he saw that Corin was impatient to be away.

"General, rejoin your men. A full report on the warbands here will be sent to you. I also expect reports from you as often as possible," he reminded his son.

"Yes, sire," Corin replied. He and Martin bowed respectfully and left the room.

"Martin, I want you to stay here for at least a day," Corin said. Martin immediately began to protest, but Corin cut him off. "No, you're tired. Rest and spend some time with Gwilym and your sister."

"I'm coming back with you, Corin," Martin said.

"Martin, can you tell me when you'll be back here or if any of us will make it home?" Corin stopped him and Martin finally relented.

"Fine. But I'm leaving first thing tomorrow morning," Martin said.

"I fully expect you to," Corin replied.

They found Kieran who had heard the news, along with the rest of Corin's patrol, from Llewellyn.

"You really tweaked the Sultaan's whiskers, didn't you, Captain?" Kieran said.

"Looks that way, Kieran," Corin replied.

"But at least you don't have to face Balkor this time," Martin said.

"I would rather see him again because at least I know him. I don't know who we face this time," Corin said.

"Well, I see them at a disadvantage too, sir. They know who they're up against," Kieran said. Corin and Martin smiled slowly.

"So they do. Let's go remind them then," Corin said. "Kieran, meet me in my office in half an hour. I'll have the message for the Clans ready."

They split up and Corin hurried to his room where he changed to the black and green uniform of his warband and packed. He was finished in a matter of minutes and slung his packs and bow and quiver over his shoulder and ran to the barracks. Gerralt looked up as he came in. He said nothing as Corin grabbed parchment and quill and began to write. Kieran entered as he folded and sealed the letter.

"Take this to Clan Dyson. If you see Captain Brian, tell him I'll want to talk with him in a few days. Ask if they'll send this on to Clan Gunlon and the other Clans if they see fit," Corin instructed him.

"Anything else, Captain?" Kieran asked.

"Are you fully equipped?" Corin asked, looking over the young man's weapons and packs.

"Yes, sir. I've also got anything Kara might need," Kieran replied.

"Good. And, Kieran, be careful and smart about how you ride. It's twice as dangerous as it was in the last war. Make sure Kara understands that as well," Corin said.

"I will, Captain," Kieran replied seriously. "I'll see you out there, sir. Good hunting."

Corin nodded and Kieran ran out of the barracks, leapt onto his horse, and galloped away.

"It's started, hasn't it?" Gerralt asked. Corin looked over at him.

"Yes, it has," he replied quietly. He turned back to a second letter he had begun to write.

"Gerralt, I don't know when I'll be back again. If there's anything important, send it out with Kara or Kieran when they come in. I'll see what I can do about it. Or you can just forge my signature or find someone else to sign," Corin said.

"But, sir—" Gerralt began to protest before Corin interrupted with more instructions.

"Anything that comes in from now on Darrin will probably want to see. It will be reports on garrisons and their preparations. Captain Iwan or Pedr can help you with any of it." He finished his letter and folded it carefully. He shouldered his packs and handed the letter to Gerralt. "Would you give this to Mera for me?" he asked.

"I will, sir," Gerralt said. "And, Captain…be careful."

Corin paused at the door.

"I will. Thank you, Gerralt." And then he was gone.

The courtyard was filled with families bidding the men good-bye. His men began to mount when they saw him. He arranged his packs on the saddle before going up the steps to bid farewell to his own family. Queen Elain and Amaura were on the verge of tears as he hugged them. Gwilym pushed forward and latched onto his waist.

"Why do you have to go?" he asked. Corin knelt in front of him.

"Do you remember what Martin and I told you we did when we lived in the forest?" he asked the boy.

"You said you had to keep everyone safe," Gwilym said in a low voice.

"Exactly. And that's what we have to do again. We'll be back before you know it," Corin said. Gwilym nodded as he scuffed his boot against the stones. He gave Corin a quick hug before running back to Martin. Corin stood.

"I'll hold your patrol at camp until you get there," he told Martin.

Finally all farewells were said and Corin mounted. Mera was nowhere to be seen but he knew his letter would get to her. Karif hovered above them as they rode out. Corin didn't look back; he was now focused on the task ahead.

That night Mera sat in her room, clutching Corin's letter. She was crying uncontrollably, but it was a mixture of sorrow and joy. He was gone, maybe forever, but he loved her.

It was dawn when Corin and his men arrived at the caves. The Hawk Flight was awake and assembled when they entered. Flynn and Liam had new reports to give. Corin spread the warband's unique map of the forest on the table in his side cave. It was divided into six square parts with a dizzying array of lines of it. Red lines marked the river and waterways and red squares marked any permanent camps they maintained. Blue lines defined the well-known paths and black lines delineated the Hawk Flight's favorite tracks. Liam picked up several small wooden blocks.

"They have camps here and here," he said, placing the pegs where he indicated.

"We've picked up new tracks since two days ago," Flynn said.

"Either of you moved on them?" Corin asked.

"No, sir," Liam replied. "They haven't moved from their camps yet."

"They can't stay there forever. But they may be meant to keep our attention focused on them," Corin said. "Trey is coming in and will cover here." he pointed to the two squares at the left of the map. "Flynn and Liam, keep a watch on those camps and the surrounding paths. Don't attack yet. Let them get comfortable and then we'll strike. Ioan," he addressed Martin's second-in-command. "Martin should be here by tonight. Leave tomorrow and run a quick patrol along the border and try and see where they came over. I'm leaving for Lynwood to arrange for them to send men out and then to the border to meet with Brian," he finished.

"When can we let them know we're here?" Flynn asked.

"If they haven't moved by tomorrow night, find a way around their defenses and send them a message," Corin said. "They won't leave if we ask them, so we'll start this war on our own terms."

Chapter 3

Aiden pushed Narak on faster. He was anxious to get home again. The patrol had been quiet but it was a deceptive calm. The whole forest seemed to be waiting. And they had been assigned a new commander. Aiden had yet to hear the reason. It was the man's first command and he showed it. The rest of the patrol shared Aiden's low opinion of the man.

He came to the mouth of the valley and stopped, taking in the view as if he would never see it again. Snow still covered the ground but it dripped from the trees as the sun began to put out more and more heat with the onset of spring. Smoke rose lazily from the houses and farmers walked the fields and planned for the first plowing. Narak descended the road, slopping through the mud and melting snow.

As always, the gates stood open and Aiden waved in response to the shouts of welcome. Since becoming Champion, he felt more and more guilty every time he left but no one begrudged him yet. Narak submitted to being led away by a stable boy. Cormac, who served as steward, met him inside the hall.

"We have some visitors, sir. Some cousins of yours from the one of the outer villages. Everyone is out on the hunt right now," Cormac told him.

"When do you expect them back?" Aiden asked.

"Soon," Cormac said. "I've never known a Braeton tae be late for a meal."

Aiden smiled and left for his room. The evening meal was fast approaching and he needed to change. He buckled one of his swords around his waist and put his knives in place. He knew he was supposed to wear it, but he could rarely bring himself to put on the bronze torc. He left it in the room, arranging his cloak so Ranulf wouldn't notice the torc was missing until too late.

Rona was conveniently waiting for him as he came downstairs.

"Greetings, Sir Champion." She swept an elaborate curtsey. He in turn gave an exaggerated bow.

"I'm honored that the warrior woman deigns speak tae me," he said.

"Yes, you should be," she replied and tried for an aloof look which, as usual, sent them both into unrestrained laughter. She reached up and arranged the folds of his cloak more neatly.

"How much longer do you think you'll be able tae get away with this before your brother notices?" she asked.

"Should I feel bad?" Aiden asked in return. "Because I don't really. Anyway, you're the one who suggested it," he lightly accused.

"Treachery!" she exclaimed. "You would betray me like that?" her eyes widened theatrically. He grinned mischievously.

"Yes, and there is no way tae stop it!" he announced.

"I see I underestimated you," Rona said.

"You really shouldn't, especially when he thinks he's so clever," Ranulf said as he approached. Aiden couldn't stop his smirk even though his brother had noticed his ploy.

"But I'm not the real mastermind," Aiden protested.

"You snitch!" Rona exclaimed and punched his arm.

"I gave you fair warning," Aiden reminded her and was rewarded with another, somewhat gentler, blow.

"That's the last time I help you with nefarious plans tae shirk your duties," Rona informed him imperiously.

During the exchange Ranulf saw wild merriment building in their eyes and faces.

"I'll let you get away with it for one more night." He relented only because they looked so happy together. He, along with the rest of the Clan, wished they would finally admit it to themselves and each other.

"Thanks, Davy!" Aiden gasped.

"Now, *if* you can pull yourself together, we do have some guests who are rather anxious tae see you," Ranulf said with the beginnings of a smile. Aiden tried to compose himself by adopting the bored, somewhat aloof, look perfected as a member of the Phoenix Guard.

"Perfect," Ranulf said drily which only served to thwart Aiden's attempts.

The main hall was filled with noise and activity as the rest of the hunting party arrived. Aiden and Ranulf pushed through and Aiden greeted cousins and friends he had not seen since he was very young. There was Rorie, uncharacteristically blonde; Diarmad, easy going and about Aiden's own age. He remembered Diarmad as the peacekeeper among his aunt's family. Then there was Fiona, their sister, and her husband. Neither Aiden's aunt nor uncle had come, a reoccurring illness to blame. But Aiden had thought that there was another cousin: the youngest boy. Diarmad answered his unspoken question by gesturing to a young man standing apart. He came forward reluctantly, keeping his right arm hidden in the folds of his cloak. Aiden wondered at this and obviously the young man had not joined the hunt. Diarmad put an arm around his brother's shoulders.

"You remember Kenneth," he said. Kenneth made no move to shake hands as he stared coldly at the floor. Rorie looked slightly uncomfortable and a flash of sadness crossed Fiona's face. Kenneth glared angrily at Diarmad as his brother nudged him meaningfully. In that moment the cloak moved and Aiden saw Kenneth's deformed right hand. He hid any surprise or sympathy he felt and extended his left hand.

"Hope you don't mind. I prefer tae use my left hand," Aiden said easily. Everyone looked surprised, not the least of whom was Kenneth. He hesitantly clasped Aiden's hand and gave him a quick look of gratitude.

"I won't keep you standing here any longer. The meal is almost ready and I know I'm starving," Aiden said. The group broke apart as everyone hurried to change from their hunting clothes.

Any meal among the Clans was never quiet and that night, especially with visitors, was no exception. Aiden sat at the head table with his family and cousins, recalling visits when they were younger. Most of them involved Will, Rorie, and Aiden. Even Kenneth smiled amidst the uproarious laughter. It was late when they finally left the table. Diarmad caught up to Aiden in the hallway.

"Aiden, I just wanted tae say thanks for the way you handled Kenneth," he said.

"It can'nae be easy for him," Aiden commented.

"Aye, it's not. I'm surprised he even came at all," Diarmad said.

"Can I ask how it happened? He was still so young when I last saw you. I don't remember much about him," Aiden said.

"He was born with it," Diarmad said. "And because of it, he keeps tae himself most of the time. Especially after getting bullied when he was younger." Aiden shook his head, angry at the cruelty of people. "I stopped it whenever I could, but he told me he didn't need me tae protect him. But he never learned tae fight," Diarmad said.

"Never?" Aiden asked in surprise.

"I think Kenny's always felt that Father is disappointed with him because he'll never be a warrior. It seems Kenneth is stubbornly trying tae prove him right," Diarmad said. Neither he nor Aiden could follow Kenneth's bitter reasoning. After bidding goodnight to Diarmad, Aiden resolved to find his youngest cousin the next day.

The next morning found him at the training courts with Artair. The captain often had him help with the young trainees to ensure that they didn't get too over confident. Accordingly, Aiden handed out several crushing defeats before explaining how he did it to the crestfallen boys. After Captain Artair dismissed his students, Aiden was surprised to see Rona enter the court.

"My next victim," Artair said.

Aiden remembered Rona telling him that it was the captain who had taken over her training after Will had shown her the basics. She was dressed in a shirt and breeches and carried her sword and brigandine. Her hair was pulled back in a single braid. He wasn't able to admire the sight much longer as his own sparring partner arrived behind her. His and Blair's bout did not last long before they were interrupted by Maon. The hound bounded across the courtyard toward Aiden, barking joyously. Aiden barely had time to toss his swords away as Maon promptly became entangled in his legs, sending them both sprawling.

"Jamey!" Aiden yelled as Maon licked his face. The young woodsman ran up breathlessly.

"Sorry, Danny. He caught your scent and I couldn't stop him," he explained.

"You want tae do something about it?" Aiden gasped as Maon decided to sit on top of him.

"I don't know, Danny. He looks pretty comfortable," Blair said as he tried to control his laughter. Aiden managed to shove the gangly hound off and sat up whereupon Maon began to lick his face again. Aiden scratched Maon's ears and the licking ceased only because the dog flopped across his lap. Aiden threw his hands up in the air.

"Would you do something about this, Jamey?" he implored his friend.

"It's not my fault he likes you!" Jamey replied.

"I question your training methods," Aiden said, trying to move Maon. Jamey relented and whistled. Aiden leaned back to avoid the wagging tail as Maon sprang up to join his master. Aiden quickly stood before Maon decided to ignore Jamey again.

"Everything all right over there?" Artair called, his voice suspiciously serious.

"Yes, Captain!" Aiden replied. "And I would suggest tae your student that she keep her arm a little higher as she lunges," he said. Rona glared at Aiden as the captain turned thoughtfully toward her. Blair handed Aiden his swords as Artair had Rona perform a sequence. Suddenly Aiden couldn't resist.

"That's it!" he called as Rona lunged. "Now, distribute your weight tae your back foot as you pivot away. Perfect! Keep your swing a little higher!"

Rona stopped and let the claymore drop.

"Captain, will you stop him or can I?" she asked, her lips pursed in slight irritation.

"He's not bothering me," Artair shrugged, mentally berating himself for not pushing Rona harder like Aiden said. Rona turned to Aiden.

"Anything else?" she asked levelly. Aiden actually had several more suggestions to help, but he wisely refrained for a brief moment.

"Did you need anything else?" he asked innocently.

"Maybe your charming tongue on a platter if you keep it up," she said sweetly. Aiden spread his hands in defense.

"Then can I suggest that you tighten your undercut when you do that?" he asked. An irritated smile began to form on Rona's face.

"I'll see what I can do," she said, advancing toward him. He backed away, not so sure she wouldn't do it as she began to swing the claymore with a wicked grin. He considered running before Jamey grabbed him from behind.

"I'll hold him," Jamey offered.

"Thank you, Jamey. It's good tae know that there is still a decent man around," she said.

"I'm not getting intae this," Blair said as Aiden looked to him for some sort of assistance.

"Traitors! The pair of you!" Aiden said.

"It would be quieter around here, wouldn't it?" Jamey remarked to Rona.

"I tend tae agree," Artair said. "Go ahead, Rona, as long as you keep your arm up and tighten that swing."

Rona threw up her hands in exasperation but not without a laugh.

"Dare I ask what savagery is going on?" Skive asked.

"Rona is about tae go on a tongue-cutting rampage," Blair said.

"Apparently only as long as I do it with proper technique," Rona said wryly. "Which someday, sir, you will show me," she prodded Aiden in the chest. "Or I will carry through," she warned.

"Better you than me," Artair said.

"All right! I won't critique...as much...out loud," Aiden gradually added. Again there was an exasperated smile on Rona's face.

"You are hopeless, you know," she said. Aiden smiled and her heart melted.

"I try," he said. "I swear I'll leave you alone...for now." He began to leave. "Ranulf wanted me for something," he gave a vague explanation. But in reality he had seen Kenneth walk by the courts and he wanted to follow.

Aiden left the fortress around a loose log in the walls that no one had ever seemed to find before now. He soon saw he was not the only one following Kenneth. Illyria silently stalked along his trail. Kenneth paused to allow the dog to catch up, then stopped when he saw Aiden.

"I don't need any sympathy from you," Kenneth said, reaching to stroke Illyria's head.

"I wasn't planning on giving any," Aiden returned. "You found my old escape route from the keep. I wanted tae see if you followed my other old trails too."

Kenneth was slightly taken aback.

"Is this one of them?" he pointed to the faint track they stood on.

"Aye, one of my favorites. You find my fort yet?" Aiden asked with a smile. Kenneth shook his head. "Come on, I'll show you." Aiden turned Kenneth up the path again. "You seem tae be pretty good with animals," he tried to start a conversation. Kenneth only shrugged. "She doesn't follow many people." Aiden gestured to Illyria, who paced by Kenneth's side.

"They don't seem tae care that I'm different. They…"

"Listen?" Aiden suggested and Kenneth nodded.

"Here it is!" Aiden announced grandly although Kenneth could see nothing at first. Then he turned his gaze upward and saw planks of wood nailed between three trees that grew close together. Aiden pulled on a trailing ivy strand.

"Will and Jamey helped me build it," Aiden said. "It was a good place tae come meditate on the injustices of the world."

"Injustices? You?" Kenneth asked with disbelief evident in his voice.

"Well, my best friend was banished when I was thirteen and I was convinced my father hated me, so what do you think?" Aiden asked. Kenneth allowed it with a shrug.

"At least you know your father never hated you," he said. "Mine does. He thinks I'm useless because I'm different."

"Do you know that for certain?" Aiden asked.

"You don't know what it's like being different from everyone else!" Kenneth exclaimed. Aiden almost laughed.

"Maybe I do," he said. "I've traveled, and for one thing, as soon as you cross the border everyone thinks your accent is a little funny."

Kenneth was still not convinced.

"In Gelion, there were several boys who thought they could push me around. Mind you, I'm still considered short in Gelion and I looked markedly different from everyone there. I told them off and they could barely understand me…until I punched one of them in the face," he reminisced almost fondly.

"Have you been talking with Diarmad about me standing up for myself?" Kenneth asked suspiciously.

"My point is, different doesn't mean useless," Aiden said. "Calorin was a bit of a different story. I was armed and dangerous by then but I still needed some help getting out of the trouble I always seem tae walk intae."

"And what's your point there?" Kenneth asked.

"No one's perfect, I suppose," Aiden said. Kenneth was unsure of what to say. No one had ever sought him out to talk like this before. Illyria nuzzled his hand, gently reminding him that he had stopped the rhythmic stroking.

"So what do you on your walks in the forest?" Aiden asked. Kenneth gradually found himself opening up.

"Whatever I want. Sometimes I explore new trails or just sit and watch what happens around me. Mostly I..." he paused. "I draw."

"You draw?" Aiden asked. Kenneth reached into the leather satchel he carried and pulled out a piece of paper that he handed hesitantly to Aiden. It was a depiction of Illyria. She had treed a squirrel and it chattered down angrily at her. Aiden glanced from the paper to the dog. Kenneth had captured her perfectly.

"That's amazing, Kenneth," Aiden said. The young man flushed slightly. He took the paper back and returned it to the satchel. "You're pretty good with both your hands," Aiden said, noticing that Kenneth had used his right hand to open the bag. Kenneth looked down at both his hands.

"I guess you would say that I'm not entirely useless then," he said. Aiden smiled faintly.

"I had a friend who once tended tae think the way you do about yourself," he said.

"What happened tae him?" Kenneth asked.

"He learned tae fight and now, let me see if I get this right, is leading Aredor's best warband," Aiden said. Kenneth's jaw dropped.

"You know the Hawk?" he exclaimed. Aiden mildly restrained his laughter. That would never get old. He needed to convince Corin to visit.

"Yes, I do. Ask Tam or Jamey if you don't believe me," he said.

Illyria ran off down the path and they followed as Kenneth pressed for more information.

"What did you mean before?" he asked.

"About Corin? Sorry, I'm not in the habit of telling other people's stories. Especially his," Aiden said.

"Why not?" Kenneth was practically begging.

"Well, if we let everyone know our whole stories, we would appear as mere mortals," Aiden replied mock seriously and Kenneth laughed.

"So what about me? I don't think I'll be joining forces with heroic outlaws or taking over your job as Champion with this." Kenneth raised his hand.

"I think you could pull off the bitter, yet determined, freedom fighter," Aiden said. "Or there's always piracy."

"Piracy?" Kenneth raised an eyebrow.

"Sure, just cut off your hand and replace it with a blade of some sort. It'll be grand," Aiden said. Kenneth couldn't help his smile.

"As appealing as cutting my hand off sounds, I think I'll pass," he said.

"We'll have tae work on that sense of adventure," Aiden said. Kenneth smiled again.

"What would you suggest?" he asked, surprised with himself. He had never allowed anyone to try and get to know him.

"Ever try knife fighting?" Aiden asked.

"I can'nae say that I have," Kenneth replied.

"I'll teach you then. It's easy...once you've practiced for a while," Aiden added.

"I'm so glad you decided tae add that," Kenneth said drily.

"I always tell the truth!" Aiden protested with a smile. "Though I usually find myself leaving out the most important bits."

"That I believe," Kenneth said.

Illyria bounded forward to meet Skive who walked by the shores of the lake.

"You should show him that drawing," Aiden urged Kenneth. The young man paused.

"I don't know. I don't show most people," he said but Aiden convinced him. Skive held the picture and stroked his beard as he studied it. Kenneth watched him anxiously.

"It's good," Skive said gruffly, looking down at Illyria who thumped her tail on the ground as he tickled her chin. "Tell me, if I told you what somebody looked like, could you draw them?" Skive asked.

"I think I could," Kenneth replied.

"Would you accompany me?" Skive asked. Aiden left them with a smile.

Diarmad was worried at dinner. Kenneth had not yet made an appearance. He had specifically spoken to his brother about this before they arrived.

"Relax! He's not avoiding us yet," Aiden told him.

"You seem sure of that," Diarmad said nervously. Rorie leaned over to whisper something to Diarmad.

"Would you trust me?" Aiden said. Diarmad would have replied but he was staring in what could be called shock. Kenneth had entered the hall, but his cloak was gone, his sleeves were rolled up, and he held a scroll.

"Sorry I'm late. I tried," he apologized to Diarmad as he slid into his chair.

"I didn't realize Skive was such a slave driver," Aiden said.

"Oh, I finished the sketch early this afternoon," Kenneth said. "But thanks tae you, somehow the young ones found out and he requested a picture." He pointed down to Brannan. Kenneth handed the scroll to Tam. "How did I do?" he asked. Tam studied the picture of a warrior entangled in a ferocious battle with a snarling dragon.

"It's exactly how the song describes it. Plus some of Brannan's specifications, I see," Tam handed it back with a smile.

"He was very particular about the wings," Kenneth smiled.

The rest of his family was dumfounded and they only stared at Kenneth. Aiden refilled Diarmad's beaker of ale.

"You look like you could use this," Aiden spluttered with laughter.

The next day, Aiden found Kenneth sitting on a flat rock by the lake. He had a tablet across his knees and he was drawing. Illyria basked in the sun at his feet as Skive sat nearby.

"How many people think you're crazy now?" Aiden asked.

"My whole family. Thank you for that," Kenneth replied with a trace of a smile.

"I thought Diarmad was going tae die of shock," Aiden said.

"He almost did." Kenneth gently smudged a line.

"May I?" Aiden asked Skive. He nodded and Aiden crouched by Kenneth, watching as he redrew the rough sketch of a woman and a young girl.

"She's beautiful," Aiden told Skive.

"She was," Skive agreed, staring out over the lake as Kenneth brought his wife and daughter back for him.

"I have something for you too," Kenneth handed Aiden a picture. It was Rona. She looked out at him with the mildly irritated smile that he loved.

"You trying tae state the obvious along with everyone else?" Aiden asked. Kenneth smiled as he finally looked at him.

"Think of it as revenge and thanks," Kenneth said.

"You should reconsider piracy," Aiden said. "Thanks." He carefully folded the picture and left. He saw Rona circling the lake with her horse. She caught sight of him and hurried to catch up as he waited.

"So, what did you do tae Kenneth?" she asked.

"Everyone is asking me that suddenly," Aiden said.

"I don't know many people who would do that," she said.

"All I did was talk with him," he replied.

"Maybe, but people listen when you talk," Rona said.

"I don't think I'm that good," Aiden said. Rona didn't press him.

"What's this?" she asked, taking the picture. Aiden held his breath as she opened it. "Do I really look like this?" she asked, a light flush spreading across her cheeks. He took it from her.

"No, you're more beautiful," he said. Her eyes shone gently. He knew that if he didn't now, he never would. He put an arm around her, drawing her close, and kissed her. She threw her arms around him and kissed him back. Skive chose that moment to look up.

"Finally," he said. Kenneth heard and smiled.

But happiness never lasted long for Aiden and this time it was shorter than ever. The evening meal that night was interrupted. People looked up as Cormac brought two men in green plaid up to the main table. Aiden stood quickly.

"Conall? What are you doing here?" he asked his partner in the patrol.

"It's started, Aiden. Laird Dandin is sending all the patrols out," Conall said. Aiden swallowed hard. Another war. But he decided quickly.

"It won't take me long tae pack," he said, but Conall forestalled him.

"Hold on, Danny," he said. "Laird Dandin told me tae give you a choice. The Durnians are in on it. Who knows if they'll spread their attacks past Aredor. You might be needed here."

Aiden stopped. He looked to Ranulf. The entire hall was silent, straining to hear.

"It's your decision, Danny," Ranulf said.

"Me and the lads understand, Aiden. Canich is your first responsibility," Conall said. Aiden leaned forward on the table. He saw Rona tensely regarding him. He looked away.

"I'm going," he said in a low, clear voice. "It will be safe enough here. The Durnians will be focusing their strength on Aredor first. But, Ranulf, they'll need the help of all the Clans soon enough. You'd best start preparing. It's only a matter of time."

His brother nodded. Aiden glanced around at the now solemn faces around him and searched for Rona again, but she had disappeared.

"When do we leave, Conall?" Aiden asked.

"When you're ready," Conall said. "We'll meet the rest of the lads on the border."

Ranulf interjected before Aiden could speak.

"Leave at first light tomorrow. You'll have a chance tae rest your horses and you can travel faster by day," he said. Aiden and Conall nodded their agreement. His appetite gone, Aiden excused himself. His father followed him out of the hall.

"Are you sure, Aiden?" Gòrdan asked.

"Yes," Aiden replied. "This isn't just Dyson's war or the Aredorians'. They aren't ready for this attack. The Calorins will turn tae Braeton soon enough. I'm just getting tae the fight quicker."

"The Aredorians defeated the Calorins once before. Surely they can again?" Gòrdan said. His son smiled almost sadly.

"The Calorins almost never have tae attack a second time. And if they do, they hold nothing back. They spare nothing and no one. I know and so I know how this can end," Aiden said.

"Then go, for it sounds as if you must," Gòrdan said. "Ranulf will have the Clan ready for the call."

Aiden packed his bags and inspected his weapons meticulously. He sat awake all night, staring at the flame of the candle. He was going to war again. He had fought Calorins plenty of times but what had changed was who and what he was fighting for. It was now his home and his family at stake. It was time to see how good a warrior he really was.

The outline of the tree by his window became clearer and he knew it was time to leave. He shouldered his packs and closed the door to his room.

"Aiden." A quiet voice stopped him in the hallway. Rona wrapped her cloak more tightly around herself against the chill air. She looked at him standing so strong in the hall. His plaid lay rolled at the bottom of the bag and he had donned the heavy black Calorin cloak which gave him a foreboding look in the dim light of the torches.

"Do you have tae go?" she asked.

"You know I have tae," he replied. Her face was pale and she had obviously been crying.

"But why now?" she said. "Just when…Aiden, I love you. What if you don't come back?"

"I'm like bad luck. I always turn up again," he said, attempting a smile.

"Aiden, I'm serious," Rona said. He wiped a fresh tear from her cheek.

"I've found my home," he said. "I'll find a way back." She stepped into his arms and buried her face in his chest.

"When will I see you again?" she asked against new tears.

"The Gathering is in less than two months," Aiden said. "War or no war, the Clans will hold it. As Champion I have tae be there. If it's safe, come then."

Hope stirred in Rona. Only two months!

"You'll be there?" she demanded looking up at him. He smiled.

"I'll be there," he said, holding her close again. "See me again before I leave?" he asked and she nodded. He joined Conall and his companion in the hall for a light breakfast. Tam met him in the stables as he saddled Narak.

"What's worrying you?" Aiden asked his younger brother, seeing he wasn't sure what to say.

"It's Kara," Tam admitted. "I know she rode with the Hawk Flight in the first war, but...she'll be all right, won't she?"

Aiden was usually the one who delivered their letters back and forth and saw that Tam's concern was for more than a friend.

"I'm not going tae lie, Tam. It's dangerous and she knows it. But I also know that Corin wouldn't send her out if she couldn't make it back," Aiden said.

"Is that supposed tae help?" Tam asked.

"Keep writing, Tam. Give her something tae focus on besides war. That will help," Aiden said. He led Narak out of the stall.

"Should I be worried about you?" Tam asked.

"Me? Just who do you think you're talking tae?" Aiden said. Tam smiled.

"That's why I think I should be concerned," he said and Aiden smiled.

"I'll be fine. Take care of yourself, Tam," he said.

"You too, brother," Tam replied as they embraced.

Much of the Clan had also risen to see their Champion off. He said quick farewells to Blair and Douglas. Skive gave him a nod and Artair clasped his hand, expressing a deep regret that he would not be going along. His cousins wished him luck and Brannan waved cheerfully, not fully understanding why this was different from the other times Aiden had ridden away. Aiden managed to fend off Maon as he bid farewell to Jamey and finally Ranulf and his father. Only Rona was left and she came shyly forward.

"Be careful," she said.

"Sure, surviving a war is easier than it looks," he said and she finally smiled.

"You said something like that tae me before," she said.

"And everything worked out, didn't it?" he said.

"I suppose so," Rona said. He kissed her again before mounting. She blushed as the Clan watched with smiles of satisfaction. Aiden gave one last wave as he and Conall wheeled their horses and spurred through the gate.

Chapter 4

Corin lay hidden in the forest along with the rest of his patrol. It had only been two weeks and already it was hard going. The Durnians proved to be sly adversaries and under their protection the Calorins were no longer easy targets to hit. Traps were laid in seemingly random areas of the forest. Failure to see them had cost two members of the warband a hand and several fingers. But Flynn had begun to notice a pattern to where to Durnians laid them and Martin and his men had shown themselves increasingly adept at disabling and resetting the snares.

A bird whistle announced the approach of an enemy patrol. Faint rustles marked the Durnian advance scouts and the tramp of feet announced the rest of their force. Calorins and Durnians marched in a tight column. Corin scanned them intently. He had yet to see the army's commander. A Durnian was in command of this patrol and he suddenly halted his men, perhaps sensing an attack. His fears were realized when one of the scouts reeled away from his hiding place clutching a stomach wound. In the Durnian's brief moment of confusion, Corin gave his signal.

The Hawk Flight had enough of a surprise to hold an advantage. As the enemy tried to retreat, they were herded by well-placed arrows on either side through the forest to where Martin and his men waited to spring another trap. The Hawk

Flight would not kill the few survivors who surrendered even though it meant returning foes to the field. The enemy fled and the Hawk Flight disappeared again, counting one small victory.

- -

"How is this possible?" the Calorin general fumed after driving the survivors from his tent. "How do they continually best our men?"

Askel, the Durnian commander, shrugged.

"We send them running just as often," he pointed out.

"Yes, but where are the bodies? We have an increasing number of dead, but from all reports I am to assume the Hawk has lost none of his men."

"They are not invincible. I myself wounded one but yesterday," Askel said.

"I don't want wounds! I want bodies! I want his head!" the Calorin shouted. "Your men were supposed to be the best but they can give us almost no warning. Our camps are attacked and half the time your precious traps are turned against us! This will change!" He drew his sword. "I go out with my men tomorrow. I want to meet the Hawk and spill his blood!"

- -

Two days later saw Corin at the border. The Braetons had seen a large force out and had sent for the Hawk Flight. The Braetons waited patiently as they stood or crouched in a loose semicircle in the clearing. A signal sounded and their lookout dropped lightly from a tree. Aiden looked up expectantly and saw Corin's familiar figure leading his men in.

Silent nods of greeting were exchanged between both groups as their captains spoke quickly. Aiden was thankful that Brian was there. That meant they would accompany the Aredorians. Fearghas, the captain of his patrol, would have found some cautious way out of it. Fearghas had been assigned to the patrol because he had experience with the Durnians. But as far as Aiden could tell, that was where experience of any kind ended.

"Finally!" Conall said in an undertone. "We're going tae do more than politely guard the border."

"Your manners did need a bit of work, so maybe it's a good thing we've stayed here," a man named Nichol suggested quietly.

"Then I'll politely make you pay for that," Conall said. "Right after I'm done wiping that smile off Danny's face."

Aiden and Nichol only smiled wider, thrilled as Conall was to finally see some fighting. They quickly formed up and Corin dropped back by Aiden.

"I didn't expect you to be here," Corin said.

"And miss a chance tae see your miserable face? I thought you knew me better," Aiden returned.

"Unfortunately I do," Corin replied with a quick smile. "Why do you look so ridiculously cheerful?"

"Why wouldn't I be? Out for a stroll with the famous Hawk…" Aiden said.

"Before I hurt you, I need you and Conall to do some scouting," Corin said.

"I'm flattered you would ask me," Aiden said.

"Don't be. It's purely sentimental. You used to be the best," Corin replied. Aiden smirked.

"Yes, sir!" he said. "Or, I forget, is it 'your highness' or 'general' these days?"

"Go, or I will hurt you," Corin said, his mood successfully lightened as Aiden and Conall disappeared to scout ahead.

The two forces met in open battle on a wide path. The Calorin watched the melee until he found the figure he was looking for. He drew his scimitar and waded into the battle. Corin found himself confronted by a new adversary. The Calorin fought with devastating skill and efficiency and stayed even with Corin with a smile. Then Corin was attacked from the side by a Durnian. He fought both his assailants, forcing aside any desperation he felt as he was pushed back. Karif brought him a brief reprieve by diving in and clawing the Durnian's face. A burning pain rent Corin's sword arm and his scimitar was sent flying from his loosened grip. The Calorin smiled at the blood on his sword.

"So you are human after all," he said. Corin drew a knife to fend off a fresh attack. The Calorin was disappointed when he could not overcome Corin even though he was wounded and armed only with a dagger. Corin was grabbed from behind but his attacker crumpled to the ground with a knife in his back. Knocked off balance, Corin was helpless as the Calorin general swung his sword. It was blocked by Aiden's blade and the Calorin's smile faded as Aiden attacked. Aiden battered him back, finally sending him running with the rest of his men and a wound of his own.

The greater numbers of Aredorians and Braetons gave them success but the Hawk Flight had paid the first price. One of their number lay dead and another was severely wounded. Corin regained his feet and retrieved his sword.

"Thanks," he said to Aiden. "I owe you...again."

"Don't mention it. Ever," Aiden replied, sheathing his swords. "Let me dress that."

"He's good," Corin said as Aiden wound a bandage around his arm.

"He's all right," Aiden said. "Once you fight him man-tae-man, he's not as good."

"Even so," Corin mused.

"I don't ever remember you worrying like this," Aiden said.

"And I don't remember you being so cheerful. What's with you?" Corin asked.

"I'm not sure what you mean," Aiden replied a little too quickly. Corin suddenly smiled.

"Invite me to the wedding, would you?" he asked. Aiden smiled himself.

"Wrap up this war and we'll see," he said. Corin looked over to where his men were placing the body on a rough bier.

"Aye, if this war will ever end," Corin said softly.

"It will. And, Corin, I'm glad tae be on your side this time," Aiden said.

"I'm glad you're back," Corin replied.

A call went out and the Braetons regrouped. A few minutes later the path was deserted and the birds began to sing again.

Corin stared at the blank piece of paper in front of him. He had finished the letter to the dead warrior's family only to have Liam arrive to tell him that he had to write another. He put it away and tried to compile a report for his father. The task only irritated him. They had not received anything from Kingscastle and so he had not heard from Mera. He had tried to tell himself that there was a chance for a reply when he sent the report in with Kara but it didn't help. He wished he had had time to tell her personally instead of pouring it all into a short letter.

Again, he pushed the thought from his head. He had to finish, the dead had to be buried, and there was another patrol to be run. Two days later when Kara returned from Kingscastle, she almost shyly handed Corin another letter. He slowly opened it.

It began *"Dearest Corin"* in Mera's flowing script. He heard the lookout calling for him. He scanned quickly to the end. It finished *"with all my love"* and that was enough.

Chapter 5

Aiden tossed his knife rhythmically. It was a quiet day. He and Conall were about to switch guard duty when Conall whistled from his lookout position. A rider was approaching. Aiden stood from his hidden position on the ground to intercept Kieran. The young rider dismounted as Conall descended from the platform in the tree.

"How do you keep those hidden in winter?" Kieran asked, looking up at the platform.

"They're moveable," Conall said. "It comes in handy. We just moved them all yesterday."

"I still prefer the ground," Kieran said.

"And you live in the forest?" Aiden said.

"Maybe there's a reason I'm the runner. Though Lieutenant Liam claims I'm still as loud as the Calorins," Kieran said cheerfully. Aiden and Conall grinned.

"You can take him in, Danny. Just make sure tae come back and relieve me," Conall said. Aiden nodded and led Kieran in a rather tortuous route to their camp.

He found his packs as Kieran handed the dispatches to Captain Brian. Among the letters that had arrived the day before from Clan Canich was one for Kara from Tam.

"Can you give this tae your sister?" Aiden asked. "I didn't know when she'd come this way." He handed the letter to Kieran as they made their way out of the camp.

"Aye, and can I ask you a question, sir? I hope you won't find me too bold," Kieran said and Aiden gestured for him to continue. "I wanted tae ask about your brother."

"He was concerned about her when he heard the news," Aiden said.

"That's all very well, but not many people outside the Hawk Flight understand or approve of what she does."

"Tam is a good man. He wouldn't try and talk her out of what she's doing here. I think he really cares about her."

"I know she thinks about him," Kieran said. "It's just that she's my only family left. I want her protected and happy."

"Then she's lucky tae have you as a brother," Aiden said.

"But what if something happens tae me?" Kieran asked, troubled. Aiden clapped him on the shoulder.

"What could happen tae you? I thought you were the best!" he said.

"Well, I wouldn't deny it," Kieran grinned as he mounted.

"Off you go!" Aiden smiled. "Tell that lazy captain of yours tae send some trouble this way."

"I will, sir," Kieran replied, setting spurs to his horse. Aiden settled in for another afternoon of sentry duty.

Their peaceful routine was rudely interrupted a few days later when the Calorins launched several repeated attack against the Braetons. Outright attacks turned to deadly games of cat and mouse as the Braetons matched their woodcraft against the Durnians. Soon there was no peace left in Dunham Forest as the Northerners resisted. To the south, Trey and his deugain formed an almost impenetrable barrier. Calorins and Durnians alike refused to go there and face the "dark ones," for Trey and his men, having fought the Raiders all their lives, subscribed to a harsher form of justice than the other warbands. Day followed day, each survived as the previous one. For that time, the Aredorians held.

One night, well after midnight, Martin and his men arrived at the caves. The torches were lit as Corin's men tended to their wounds sustained earlier that day. Martin found Corin in his chamber.

"They're holding at Anaer stream for now," Martin said.

"Good. We lost ground today," Corin said tiredly. "They're past the twisted oaks now." He moved a peg on the map to the position of the new Calorin camp. Martin rubbed the pommel of his sword worriedly.

"You heard from Liam or Flynn recently?" he asked.

"Kara and Kieran are both out on a run right now," Corin replied. "I should know by tomorrow afternoon, or later today," he amended, sitting down on the camp stool. The mention of the next day triggered something in Martin's mind.

"Isn't the wedding tonight?" he asked.

Corin stared blankly at him for a moment, then said, "I had completely forgotten!"

"Obviously. But you're going," Martin replied.

"We're a bit busy here at the moment, don't you think, Martin?" Corin asked.

"Cor, your brother is getting married and inheriting the crown. You need to be there to swear fealty and take the General's belt," Martin said.

"How did you know about the belt?" Corin asked. Martin rummaged in his pouch before pulling out a letter.

"Apparently your brother doesn't quite trust you." He put the paper on the table. "Here, the oath you need to know. Memorize it and find some clean clothes. I'll be back in an hour with horses for you and an escort. You're going," Martin said.

"Martin, I just can't leave!" Corin tried protesting.

"Leave right after the ceremony to come back if you have to. Corin, you need to be there. The people and Lords need to see you there in support of the King. Sometimes it doesn't matter if there's a war being fought," Martin successfully argued. "Besides, this wedding will help keep people's spirits up."

True to his word, Martin had two horses saddled and ready in as close to an hour as he could. Corin found the cleanest clothes in his pack and changed. He chose Andras to accompany him and they mounted in the early dawn.

"We'll hold here until you get back," Martin said.

"Do whatever you think is necessary," Corin told him.

"Do you know the oath?" Martin asked.

"Aye, something about punishing annoying, insubordinate lieutenants," Corin said.

"Corin!" Martin exclaimed in exasperation and Andras hid a faint smile.

"Relax! I know it," Corin said. "Are you going to let me leave? You're worse than my mother."

"Yes, leave! Before I kill you!" Martin said.

They spurred away, riding a confusing trail away from the caves and finally setting a steady pace for Kingscastle. They changed horses several times and rode into the castle courtyard by early evening. Grooms rushed to take their horses and Corin and Andras ran up the castle steps.

"Just in time, sir," one of the guards said as they swung the doors open. Darrin met them at the entrance of the great hall.

"You made it!" he was relieved.

"Barely," Corin said. "We have time to change?" he asked.

"No, you have about a minute to spare," Darrin said.

"Fine. Andras, you can go find your family. I'll let you know when we leave," Corin said. Andras saluted and left.

"I'm surprised to see him here," Darrin commented.

"I don't think anyone would recognize him from a few months ago," Corin said. "But you can hear about this later. You have to go get married!"

They entered the hall and Corin slipped along the side of the crowd to the front where his family stood. Amaura felt a light tug on her hair and turned to see her brother.

"Corin! You're—"

"Filthy!" her mother interjected.

"Hello, Mother. I just got here. Sorry," Corin said.

"I'm surprised to see you here. Is it wise to leave?" his father asked in a low voice.

"Martin threatened mutiny," Corin said lightly. "He can handle things until tomorrow morning."

"You're not staying?" Amaura was disappointed.

"I can't. You know I don't like parties," Corin said, but his look promised his father a report later. Amaura could only smile. Her brother would never tell her how bad it was in the forest.

The crowd was drawn on either side of the hall, leaving clear the path to the dais where Darrin now stood. All heads turned as Rhian entered escorted by Maldwyn, her guardian since her family's death in the first war.

"She's beautiful!" Amaura breathed. Rhian's wardrobe was severely limited after fleeing the country and having no home of her own to return to. So Queen Elain and her sister-in-law had taken matters into their own hands. Rhian wore a dress of pure white. Gold thread was stitched around the neckline and chased elegantly down the bodice and trailing skirt. Around her neck was clasped a necklace with a single pearl, carefully wrought around with gold. Her hair was simply pulled away from her face and the rest fell over her shoulders.

But Corin was not looking at her. Mera was standing opposite him. She turned suddenly and caught sight of him and her face broke into a joyful smile. They hardly turned their attention away as Maldwyn performed the marriage ceremony and Darrin and Rhian spoke the unchanging vows to one another.

Then King Celyn came forward and in a solemn ceremony, crowned Darrin as Aredor's new king. Darrin was handed a new crown and placed it on the head of his queen. They took their place on the thrones and after the cheers finally died away, Maldwyn called for the oaths of fealty to be spoken. Corin came forward. He knelt with unsheathed sword and, looking unwaveringly at Darrin, recited the pledge to his king. Lord Celyn watched the contrast between his sons. Darrin was resplendent in his finest clothes, white and gold to match Rhian and his sword was buckled by a gold-wrought belt. And Corin: his clothes were patched and stained by dirt and blood. The bright blade that glittered in his hands attested to his trade.

That's how it would ever be, Celyn thought. *Darrin, the king, and Corin, the warrior. They could conquer worlds,* he thought, seeing the complete devotion and dedication to each other in their faces.

Corin stood and sheathed his sword. Darrin stood also.

"You're not out of this yet, brother," Darrin said. He signaled and a young boy came forward bearing a silver circlet.

"Please tell me that's not—" Corin said.

"Do you mind kneeling again?" Darrin asked.

"Yes," Corin replied.

"This won't take long," Darrin said. Corin knelt. There was no arguing.

"I hate you," he said.

"Of course you do," Darrin said amiably, then raising his voice so it echoed to the furthest corners of the hall, he declared, "Until such time as I have a son to succeed me as heir, I name Corin, Celyn's son and my brother, as my successor." He placed the circlet on Corin's head. Corin felt like a noose was being placed around his neck. "I also name him to be General of my warbands and bearer of the rights and duties therein," Darrin said. Corin rose and Rhian came forward holding the General's belt that had been newly made for Corin. The thick leather was embossed with the wolves of the warbands and was lined with gold that merged into the golden buckle. Corin removed his cloak and Darrin buckled it across his chest.

"I would say thanks, but I feel ridiculous," Corin said. Rhian reached up and straightened the belt over his shoulder.

"Oh, I wouldn't. It livens up your outfit quite nicely," she said. Corin and Darrin tried hard to restrain their laughter and preserve the dignity of the moment for everyone in the hall. Corin had come to know his new sister-in-law over the months since the Autumn Festival. She was calm and steady, with a quick humor. She held the grace of a queen and was a perfect match to Darrin.

She gave them her brilliant smile and returned to her seat. Corin stood to the right of Darrin as he also sat back down and received the fealty of the lords of Aredor and the recognition of the Lairds of Braeton. When all was finally finished there came the call to the feast. Before following, Corin gave a brief report to the new King, his father, and several of the lords including Tristan. Darrin persuaded Corin to remain for at least part of the feast. So he stayed, eating and talking, but time weighed heavily on him. Andras saw his signal from the high table and went to prepare fresh horses. Corin slipped away and went to his room where he left the circlet and belt.

He was crossing the empty hall when he was stopped by Darrin. "You were just going to leave?" Darrin asked.

"I was thinking about it," Corin replied.

"I'm glad you came."

"You should thank Martin."

"I'll make sure to when everyone gets safely back," Darrin said.

"We're trying," Corin said somberly.

"Be careful, Cor," Darrin said, hugging him.

"I hope I get a good-bye as well." Rhian joined them.

"I would hug you, but I'm sure every woman here would kill me if I got your dress dirty," Corin said. Rhian laughed, taking his hand.

"Thank you for coming. I know it must be hard," she said.

"I wouldn't have missed it," Corin said. "Congratulations to both of you." She reached up and kissed his cheek.

"Be careful," she said.

"I will," he replied. They watched him leave the hall.

"He'll be fine, won't he?" Rhian looked up at her husband.

"Don't worry about him or the war tonight," Darrin told her. She rested her head on his shoulder.

"But you will," she said.

"I always do," he replied.

Corin heard someone call his name. He saw Mera standing at the entrance to the gardens. He joined her and they stepped outside.

"You're not hurt, are you?" she asked.

"I'm fine." He smiled. "I've missed you."

"And I, you," she said. "Corin, this war…when will you come back?" her eyes glistened with unshed tears of uncertainty. Hardly knowing what he was doing, he kissed her.

"Soon," he whispered and turned to leave but she caught his hand and kissed him again before disappearing into the castle.

The courtyard was dimly lit by the flickering torches and the cloud-crossed moon, but Andras could have sworn that Corin was smiling as they mounted and rode from the castle. But back in the forest there was little to smile about. The enemy was slowly forcing the Hawk Flight back and every step was precious.

Attacks on the Braetons ceased. The Calorin general wished to focus his forces on the obstinate Aredorians. He would cut the Hawk Flight off from Lynwood Keep and the border. They would force the Northerners from the forest and begin the attack on the rest of Aredor.

All grew quiet on the border. The Braetons patrolled it anxiously, searching for anything. The riders rarely came and even the paths from Lynwood were quiet. But they knew their orders from the Laird. They could not cross the border into Aredor without permission. They would wait and conserve their own strength against an invasive attack from the Calorin armies. Aiden grew restless. The forest was silent, reflecting the brooding, pensive feeling in his heart. As the time for the Gathering drew near, he wished less and less to go.

Chapter 6

Reports sat unread in front of Corin. It had been two weeks since the wedding and it felt like an age. They had lost more ground and Lynwood Keep was slowly being barred to them. Five new graves were dug in the clearing at the caves. Then, the caves themselves were discovered by the Calorins. Liam and his patrol barely escaped the attack. That was almost a week ago and since then the patrols had been constantly on the move.

Trey and his men had not seen the enemy for days and he wanted to move his line forward.

"Tell him to move but don't overreach. They might be trying to draw him out," Corin said to Kara. She only nodded. She and Kieran did not get much rest. Their rides had become fraught with danger at every turn. She had only just escaped capture and certain death on her way to report to Corin. They were all slowly being worn down. She rode off and Corin's and Liam's patrols joined ranks. Another enemy force had been sighted, another fight was planned.

But their luck turned again and they were ambushed. The force they were to attack was only a decoy. Flames sprang up to encircle them. The Calorins and Durnians trapped with them fought mercilessly and others outside the fire contributed their arrows. Corin marshaled his men, ever thankful for their control in the most severe circumstances. Daring the flames and the enemy on the other side, they leapt through. Liam quickly counted as burning clothes were extinguished. They had lost two to the first flames but one other was missing.

"Where's Corin?" Liam asked. A figure darted back across the fire and Llewellyn shouted after Andras. For seconds there was nothing except the crackle and roar as the fire ate at anything in its path.

Corin was fighting when he was attacked from behind. There was a spear across his neck, crushing and choking him. He flailed against his assailant, growing weaker and weaker. Suddenly all went slack. Someone grabbed his arm and yelled at him to run. He did and they burst across the fire.

Andras fell to his knees, coughing and choking against the smoke. Corin lay deathly still for a moment and then he, too, was coughing, trying to force air back into his lungs. Liam steadied him until he could breathe. Ian helped Andras up as they stumbled away from the spreading fire.

"We'll go back to the caves," Corin said.

"Captain, we can't! The Calorins will have left a guard," Llewellyn protested.

"Aye, but that's the last place they'll expect us to go," Corin said. "There's too many wounded here. We'll recall the patrols and plan our next move." He sheathed his sword that he had somehow kept hold of and they left with the fire still raging behind them.

Any sentries left by the Calorins at the caves were quickly and silently disposed of and the Hawk Flight filed in. Torches were lit and wounds and burns tended to. Martin and his men arrived soon after. They had seen the smoke from the forest fires and had come to investigate when they met the messenger.

Another day passed and Corin grew uneasy. There had been no word or sign of Kieran or of Flynn's patrol. Finally he called Liam and some of their men and they set out toward Lynwood Keep. Rain was falling steadily, a welcome relief from an unusually warm spring. Corin winced slightly as Karif's talons tightened on his shoulder. The hawk's head swiveled suddenly and Corin held up his hand to halt the men. A second later he heard what the hawk had. A faint moan came from somewhere off the path.

They hurried toward it and were confronted by one of the worst sights of the war. Kieran lay in a bloody clearing. His horse was pierced with javelins and three Calorins lay dead. Kieran was sprawled there with only the same faint gasp marking him as alive.

Corin and Liam ran to him as the others hurried to make sure they were alone. The young man was barely recognizable as blood congealed around multiple wounds. He tried to speak when he saw Corin but the cuts on his face and blood in his mouth prevented it.

"Easy, Kieran!" Corin said, wiping some of the blood away. He looked back to Liam who only shook his head. There was nothing he could do; Kieran was dying. "Kieran, what do they know?" Corin asked desperately. Kieran managed to smile and shake his head. They had gotten nothing from him. He tried to lift his hand and Corin took the bloodstained paper from him. Kieran sighed in relief and died. Corin closed the young rider's eyes and tucked the paper away.

They found branches and, foregoing the rain, used their cloaks to make a bier. They stripped his possessions from the saddle and placed them alongside Kieran. The rain disguised tears on some of the warriors' faces as they carried him back to the caves.

By terrible design, Kara arrived at the caves shortly after they did. She pushed through the crowd and saw her brother lying on the bier covered by his bloody cloak.

"No!" she cried as she rushed to him. "Liam, do something!" it was a desperate cry. "Liam!"

Liam pulled her away.

"I couldn't, Kara. He's gone," Liam said. She struggled against him.

"No! You didn't try!" she cried.

"We were too late. I'm sorry, Kara," Liam said.

"Kieran!" was all she could say until Ian came and took her from Liam. Ian had been the twins' closest friend in the warband since the beginning and he could only stare in numb shock at Kieran's body as Kara clung tightly to him. Hardened warriors turned away from the scene. Kieran's death was felt keenly by all. Behind the captain, he had the most unbelievable luck. He knew everything about each warrior and every man felt like they had lost their oldest friend. Corin gave orders for the grave to be dug and the body to be prepared for burial in a stony voice. While they waited he spoke to his Lieutenants.

"The letter Kieran gave me was from Flynn. The Durnians drove them back to Lynwood. The Keep is now under siege. Kieran must have only just gotten out. We're withdrawing." The officers nodded somberly. There were too many wounded. The Hawk Flight could no longer hold back the tide. "But first. Liam and Llewellyn, find the Calorin," Corin ordered.

"Why?" Martin asked.

"You saw Kieran's body. It wasn't torture or an honest fight that killed him. They had him outnumbered and…" he stopped. "The Calorin didn't want information. He toyed with Kieran before leaving him to bleed out and die. This man does not care about his own men either. He'll sacrifice them until he has razed Aredor for his people to rebuild. He needs to know that he is not leaving Aredor alive." Corin's eyes were as hard as his voice.

- -

The rain had stopped as the warband gathered in the silent clearing. Kieran's body was placed in the ground with his sword and messenger's pouch. Kara spread the plaid of Clan Gunlon over him and cast a handful of dirt into the grave. It was slowly filled in as Corin spoke the necessary words. Then he took a spear with Kieran's name carved into it and rammed it into the fresh dirt that enclosed Kieran to mark his place.

Men filed away until only Kara was left. Her first sobs broke and she knelt at the foot of the grave, hugging herself and sobbing helplessly. After a time she felt someone's arms around her. She let them pull her up and she buried her head on their shoulder until she could weep no more. Eventually she raised her head to see the Captain and not Ian as she had expected. She withdrew and would have apologized until she saw his eyes were bright with tears he never let fall.

"I'm sorry, Kara," he said. She wiped her sleeve across her face. She thought she saw more than grief in his face.

"You know I don't blame you for this, Captain!" she blurted.

"I'm still responsible. I shouldn't have let either of you stay in the first war. You were too young and now...he shouldn't have died like this!" Corin said.

"It's war, Captain. We might all die. I know and so did he," Kara said. "And now I have no family left." She fought back new tears.

"So maybe you should go." Corin's words shocked her. "You stayed for your brother and I don't want the same thing to happen to you. You don't have to stay if you don't want to," he said. Kara looked at the grave.

"I can'nae leave," she said. "He would never abandon the warband and neither can I. You're already short a runner and this is the life I know. Besides," she tried for a smile. "Now I'm the best you've got."

Corin stood and helped her to her feet.

"You're sure?" he asked and she nodded.

"What are my orders, sir?" she asked.

"I need you to ride back to Trey. Tell him to withdraw," he said.

"Yes, sir," she said. "And, Captain, if I don't make it back, make sure that Calorin suffers."

Corin sent men to get their horses from the garrisons outside the forest. Bags were packed along with any provisions left in the caves. Corin sat for a moment on the ledge in his room. He was tired. All he wanted to do was rest. But there was too much to still be done. There was a knock and Andras entered at his call.

"You wanted to see me, sir?" he asked somewhat nervously. His last personal interview with the Captain hadn't gone so well.

"Yes. I hear that I need to thank you for saving my life," Corin said. Andras wasn't sure what to say.

"You don't owe me for anything!" Andras blurted. "I know I was horrible before, but when I came here I changed. I saw men who would willingly sacrifice themselves for you and after returning from battle again and again, I knew I could only do the same," he said and looked down at the floor in slight embarrassment.

"Then it appears I have even more to thank you for," Corin said. "Now, can you do something for me?"

"Anything, Captain."

"I'm sending the wounded out tonight. I'll need you to go along and carry a message for King Darrin telling him to prepare the warbands to meet us. I'll be there in a few days," Corin said.

"You want me to take the message?" Andras asked. A smile tugged at Corin's mouth.

"Well, since you've proved you will literally go through fire for me, I think I can trust you with this," he said. "One piece of advice; avoid any lords that might be there and try to see Darrin alone. I would never willingly inflict them on anyone."

Andras had to smile finally. The Captain could be quite opinionated about certain of Aredor's lords and his warband was sure to hear those sentiments. Corin went over to the camp table and picked up the letter he had prepared for Darrin and handed it to Andras.

"If you should get attacked on the way, you ride immediately for Kingscastle and don't stop for anything," Corin said.

"Yes, sir," Andras replied, tucking the letter safely away.

The first part of the warband was riding away as Liam and Llewellyn returned with no more to say than "We found him, Captain."

The Calorin general was riding through the forest backed by his army. He smiled in contentment. They were advancing and all was working the way it should. He almost didn't see the first tendril of smoke from either side of the path. The Calorin drew his scimitar awaiting the certain ambush. Even so he was taken aback by the dark figure that appeared through the haze. He saw the grey hawk and smiled.

"So we meet again, Hawk," he said. "I must say, you quite live up to the theatrical expectations."

"It seems unfair that you know so much about me," Corin said. The Calorin smiled.

"It *is* time we met formally," he said. "I am General Samir, trusted General of the Sultaan and the man who will kill you."

"Impressive." Corin sounded bored. "The last man to tell me that stood in your place. He is dead and his ashes scattered to the winds."

General Samir sneered.

"Balkor was a fool. He should have killed you long ago. Oh yes, I know that you were his slave before he stupidly let you go. And I will find out where you went after your release and who helped and sheltered you. I will cut it out of you myself!" he said.

"Again, you will not be the first to fail," was the reply, angering the Calorin.

"You've seen me. Now show me a face so that I may know who to look for on the battlefield," Samir said. Corin slowly pushed his hood back.

"Then know me, Samir. I am Corin, Celyn's son, King's General and Captain of the Hawk Flight. Prepare yourself for death. We will meet again," Corin said. Samir heard the cold certainty in Corin's voice and felt a chill of fear. Corin took a step back and vanished into the smoke. Seconds later, Samir heard the sounds of multiple hoof beats fleeing but he had no voice to order a pursuit.

Two days later they emerged from the forest to find an army awaiting them.

Chapter 7

The Gathering of the Clans had been held for hundreds of years ever since the bloodiest war of Braeton. There were at that time, six Clans who would not find peace among themselves over a long-forgot cause. Then, on a bloody field, the last member of Clan Taskel was hewn down by the Champion of Clan Dyson and the war was ended. On that field, the five remaining Lairds formed a pact. The following year they and their champions would meet again in peace. Despite the hatred between them, no man dared break the oath sworn in blood on the last blade of Clan Taskel. They met that year and every two years after, always with the Laird and Champion to show that they meant to uphold the peace for no Clan would go to war without a Champion or Laird.

Braeton was divided into five parts. Clan Canich went to the forest alongside their ally, Clan Dyson. Clan Strowen withdrew to the mountains, all but wiped out for they had sided with Clan Taskel. Clan Mavor also took their troubles to the mountains for its members had fought for each side and the Clan was sorely divided. Clan Gunlon, the last to enter the war, had also sided with Taskel and Strowen against the combined might of Dyson and Canich. They took to the plains, content to rebuild and raise the horses they loved.

The war was all but forgotten now, but the Clans kept the ancient custom to renew their old pledges of friendship to one another. It lasted for a week and was well attended by each of the Clan's warriors. The old battlefield lay across both Dyson's and Gunlon's lands not ten miles from the border of Aredor, for when kings had first risen in that country, the Clans ceded them land with the peace treaty that brought the nations together for the first time.

Rona paced impatiently. Since she had fought at the siege of Scodra she was accorded status as a warrior, but it was not uncommon for some women to come with the Clans to a Gathering. For the thousandth time, she looked to the southwest. The first official day of the Gathering was the next day and Aiden had not arrived yet. His last letter had been nearly two weeks ago.

Then, calls went up from the edge of the field. Clan Dyson had finally arrived. She hurried through the tents, watching the rows of horsemen in green plaid until she found her rider. He rode at the rear—a lonely swirl of blue among Clan Dyson.

Neason rode beside Aiden. They had been part of the last group to join the Clan.

"Looks like someone's been waiting for you," Neason said as Aiden caught sight of Rona.

"You know, I should probably go find Ranulf," Aiden said.

"Aye, that's probably best. I was going tae leave you back here. I have tae keep up appearances and ride in with Laird Dandin," Neason replied in the same serious tone as Aiden.

"Laird Dandin would understand. It *is* a pressing matter," Aiden said.

"Most definitely. I'll be sure tae let him know," Neason said as they both urged their horses out of the line. Aiden spurred Narak to a gallop, closing the distance to Rona. Narak checked with a rear and Aiden dismounted only to be thrown back a step or two as Rona ran into his arms.

"You made it!" she exclaimed.

"Of course! I told you I would," he said, pulling her in for a kiss. Rona felt a nudge on her arm and saw Narak.

"Did you think I would forget you?" she asked, taking a lump of sugar out of the pocket of her dress. Aiden watched in slight disbelief as Narak graciously accepted it.

"I think it's official," he said.

"What?"

"I'm in love with you. My horse likes you," he said. Rona could barely kiss him again as she laughed.

"Come, Sir Champion! Laird Ranulf awaits," she said.

Ranulf had also anxiously awaited the arrival of Aiden. As a new lord, he could not afford for his Champion to be missing for any part of the Gathering. He felt almost weak with relief when he saw Aiden and Rona coming in hand-in-hand.

"Glad you could make it," Ranulf said.

"I missed you too, Davy," Aiden replied.

"How has it been?" Ranulf asked.

"Too quiet for weeks."

"Any word from Will?"

Aiden shook his head. He, too, was worried about their brother but Corin would have found some way to tell him if something had happened. He tried to use this to reassure Ranulf but his brother didn't share the same level of trust in Corin that Aiden did.

"Do you think they'll call for the Clans?" Ranulf asked.

"I think it would be for the best if they did, but we've heard nothing," Aiden said. "I'm sure Laird Dandin will discuss it with everyone. Braeton has tae be ready for war either way."

Rona listened in silence. The thought of war made her uneasy but she knew she would pick up her blade and fight alongside Aiden. There was nothing else she could do. Aiden felt her grip tighten momentarily in his hand and he changed the subject. Ranulf showed him to his tent. Rona and his brother left as Aiden picketed Narak nearby. The tent flap was decorated with the spiral of the Champion. Aiden didn't see why he needed his own tent but he was sure Ranulf could give him a lengthy explanation detailing how important he was supposed to be.

Inside on the camp bed, there was a pack with fresh clothes. The other "necessary" items of the Champion were also thoughtfully included. Aiden changed and joined the others for dinner around the campfire. He tried to avoid talking about the war in Aredor. He had found it harder than he thought it would be to fight the Calorins after living among them for eight years. He knew that no one could understand that, especially after hearing of the cruel brutality with which the Calorin General directed his men.

When the meal ended, he and Tam left together.

"What exactly am I supposed tae do here?" Aiden asked. "I've never been tae a Gathering and I still don't know what a Champion is supposed tae do. And don't sigh heavily."

Tam did before answering.

"As Champion you represent the Clan's army. You are here tae support the Laird and tae show the other Clans that Canich has no intention of bringing an army against them while they are away from their lands," Tam said.

"So what do I do for a week?" Aiden asked.

"I'm not sure. You may have tae accompany Ranulf whenever he meets with the other Lairds," Tam said. "But don't worry. I'm sure you'll have plenty of time tae spend with Rona."

Aiden shoved him. "Shut up!"

The next morning the five Lairds and their Champions met in the open tent that stood in the center of the camp. The banner of each Clan was hung behind the chairs of the Lairds. The bard of Clan Dyson came forward carrying a bundle of grey plaid and laid it on the table. He un-wrapped the sword of the warrior of Clan Taskel. Clan Dyson had kept the weapon for three hundred years in memory of the Clan they had destroyed. The Lairds swore again their oath of peace and friendship over the weapon and the Champions met, leaving behind their weapons. After the ceremony, Aiden went to the table.

"May I?" he asked the bard. The man nodded and Aiden lifted up the blade. It had been cared for, but still showed its age. It was not elaborate and was made of a style different from the claymores now used by the Clans. There was a cut on the hilt, perhaps where he had tried to block the final blow.

"What was his name?" Aiden asked as Clan Strowen's bard joined them. Strowen still sang of their old ally.

"No one knew him," the bard said. "Perhaps one of the greatest men in our history and all we have is his sword."

"Aye. Even the grave has been lost, but we stand over it still. These low hills are burial mounds and even the land tries tae hide the tragedy of this plain," Dyson's bard said.

"But as long as we remember, it is enough," Aiden said. Strowen's bard glanced at him keenly.

"You know more of war than many of the men here," he said.

"Aye, and what will be left of me one day? A piece of metal and a plot of ground? I will be remembered for a time for my acts of war but he will always be remembered for bringing peace," Aiden said.

"Perhaps, but your name is already in the songs. Metal corrodes, but songs will outlast the stars," the bard said.

"You honor me more than you should." Aiden handed the sword back. It would remain on the table for the duration of the Gathering, unguarded, for no one would steal the weapon and bring war back to Braeton.

"Time will tell," the bard said. "But deeds of war are long remembered. One day the ghosts of Clan Taskel and its warrior will be willfully forgotten and war will find this field once more. Peace can last days or hundreds of years but men will find a way tae break it again." And Aiden knew he spoke the bitter truth.

But outside the tent the sun shone brilliantly to dispel the dust of old memories and the dark of the future. Aiden buckled on his weapons again. Warriors met for displays of skill or strength and Marcas, the burly Champion of Clan Mavor, was calling him for a bout.

Corin shielded his eyes against the sun. The Calorin's army was still set in place. They hadn't moved since yesterday. The armies had spent the past week engaging in small pitched battles. The enemy now occupied the small village but all its inhabitants had long been evacuated. Many other towns, villages, and farms lay deserted as their people fled from the invaders.

"Captain Bedwyr, take command here and hold unless they decided to move," Corin ordered. "The King will arrive this afternoon and will decide our next action."

Bedwyr nodded. "Aye, sire," he said. Corin turned Zephyr back to camp. There was not much he could do but wait for Darrin.

When King Darrin arrived he was met by Martin. He dismounted and asked, "Where's Corin?"

"Hopefully asleep. He seems to be trying to kill himself of exhaustion," Martin replied. "Captain Bedwyr is out on the front lines. I'll go get Corin for you."

"No, I'll go myself," Darrin said. He gave orders to Lord Meical to quarter the men in the camp. Martin remained behind to give the Lord and Darrin's captain the report on the fight.

The guard outside Corin's tent saluted and stood aside as Darrin entered. Corin was asleep and even then he looked tired.

His brother had the unusual propensity to fall asleep whenever he wanted but it looked like he had just collapsed onto the bed. The tent even lacked his usual neatness. *He must be exhausted*, Darrin thought. But even then, waking Corin could be dangerous. Among the Hawk Flight, straws were drawn to see who got the job. Darrin gingerly approached Corin, shaking his shoulder and calling him. Corin came slowly awake and sat up when he saw Darrin.

"You're here! Sorry, I told Martin to wake me before," Corin said.

"It's all right. You look like you could use a couple more hours," Darrin said.

"Try a few more days," Corin yawned. He bent over to re-lace his boot before rising. "Did Martin tell you anything?"

"No, I thought I'd get a full report from my general," Darrin said. "But first, happy birthday."

"Thanks." Corin smiled. "You bring me anything?"

"A hundred and fifty more men and the provisions you asked for," Darrin replied.

"Oh, you shouldn't have," Corin said. Darrin smiled.

"What news here?" he asked.

"From scouts' reports, the Calorins are focusing all their strength here. We haven't heard or seen them spread. They'll want to take Kingscastle first. We've heard nothing from Lynwood. The Durnians have the way through the forest well-guarded. With the men you've brought, we have nearly a thousand men here," Corin finished.

"And them?" Darrin asked.

"Their numbers have increased to almost five thousand," Corin said. "Any word from Tristan?"

"He's pulled men from the coastal garrisons and some of the mountain keeps. They've seen a few ships but there have been no attacks. Trey and his men are at Kingscastle to help reinforce," Darrin said.

"How many more men can we muster?" Corin asked.

"Not many," Darrin replied somberly. "Most of the garrisons are empty by now. We have about six hundred men at Kingscastle now."

"So this is our army?" Corin pulled on his mail coat and leather tunic. "You know, just once, I would like to be evenly matched against my enemy." He turned to Darrin who almost laughed at the irritation in his brother's voice.

"I thought you told me once that everything was more fun against big odds?" Darrin said.

"I was younger then."

"That was two years ago."

"I'm older now, aren't I?" Corin finally smiled a little. The guard pulled back the flap.

"Sir, the lords have gathered," he said. Corin buckled on the General's belt and his weapons and they left the tent.

"How are you and Lord Siarls managing?" Darrin asked.

"We're tolerating each other," Corin said.

"I'm so proud of you sometimes," Darrin said.

"I won't dignify that with an answer," Corin replied as Darrin laughed.

They met the officers in an open tent. An air of exhaustion pervaded the company. Darrin was given reports on the men and new plans were laid. For the first time in weeks, the Aredorians went on the offensive. What remained of the Hawk Flight, under the joint command of Martin and Liam, drove a tight wedge into the enemy's ranks. They were soon reinforced as Corin and his deugain, along with Lord Siarls and his men, slammed into the left flank.

General Samir sat calmly on his horse and directed a counterattack. He saw the hawk flying over the Aredorians and smiled thinly.

He would enjoy killing the man who singlehandedly kept all of Aredor's hopes alive. He would have ridden forward to finish it then but a messenger stopped him. A fresh attack was coming from the opposite flank. He rode away to oversee their defensive line. Samir saw an imposing figure leading the attack on a grey stallion. There was a glint of solid gold across his chest and around his head. *The King!* Samir thought. But this was no old man as he had expected. Samir fumed quietly. He had been told that the King was infirm and would remain behind. Instead, here was a young man and where a King led, the people would follow. His campaign had just become harder. He now had another enemy to contend with. Still, he would take down the Hawk first. With him gone, the King would falter. The smile returned. He would still be victorious.

The armies withdrew from one another in the late afternoon. But that night was the last rest the Aredorians could take. General Samir retaliated the next morning and the attacks were unceasing. Another week crept by and Darrin found Corin.

"We have to withdraw," he said. Corin didn't have the strength to reply so he only nodded. "I received a letter from Father saying some of the mountain lords have come to Kingscastle."

"I'm sure we have Uncle to thank for that," Corin said. "Is the castle prepared?"

"Yes. We'll leave tonight," Darrin said.

"Take the army. I'll stay behind with a rearguard. We can give them one last surprise in the morning," Corin said. He said no more and that night the main army withdrew. The next morning General Samir looked out. The Aredorian camp was full of shouting and men were pulling down tents as horses whinnied.

"Shall we let them go, General?" his captain asked.

"No, prepare the cavalry to charge," Samir said.

"But, sir, they are leaving!" the captain protested. Samir smiled.

"You know what your trouble is, Jubair? You would show mercy," he said.

Askel, the Durnian commander, came to join them, breakfast in hand.

"Maybe you should listen, Samir," Askel said.

"Silence, you fool! What do you know of wars?" Samir shouted. He would have his triumph. Askel shrugged.

"Have your charge then. But I do not think it wise," he said.

"I don't care what you think! You are here under my command to do as I see fit," Samir said. Askel shrugged. He did not remember the terms of treaty that way, but he had no love for the Calorins or Aredorians. He would see Samir humbled and there would be no cost to his own men.

The Calorin cavalry prepared their lines and Samir joined them. They charged, reveling in the glory of hundreds of hoof beats. The camp gave the appearance of panic that gave way to ordered movement. *Too ordered,* Samir realized. He saw a cloaked figure standing fearlessly, the hawk perched on his wrist. Rage filled Samir and he kicked his horse on. His men had no choice but to follow.

Corin gave the order and his bowmen stood forward. But Samir would not give up, even as the Aredorians retreated and his men found the spears planted among the tents. Corin and his men mounted their horses and he gave one last order. Fire arrows were released and found the oil soaked tents. The Aredorians galloped away, leaving the Calorins surrounded by flames.

Chapter 8

They rode into Kingscastle a day later after another ambush on a Durnian advance guard. Zephyr's proud head drooped as a groom led him away. Martin came down the steps to meet Corin.

"King Darrin has called a council," he said. "It's about to begin."

Karif fluttered down to Corin's shoulder as they went inside.

"What's the final report on the warband?" Corin asked. Since leaving the forest he had taken charge of the army and turned over command of the Hawk Flight. But his first concern was always for his warband.

"We've lost twenty men in total and most of the lads are wounded in some way. Twelve of them won't be able to fight and…" Martin paused for a moment. "Llewellyn took a spear to his leg on the last day."

"Where is he?" Corin asked.

"Infirmary. Liam took care of him. I don't know if Liam's left there since we got back," Martin said.

"Have you slept?" Corin asked. Martin nodded.

"I just woke up so don't worry about me. When was the last time you rested?" he asked. Corin shrugged.

"There hasn't been much time," he said.

"Someone could have taken command for a few hours," Martin said.

"Like who?" Corin asked.

"Bedwyr is fully capable and if you weren't so stubborn and would take care of yourself—"

"If you weren't so concerned and annoying—" Corin interrupted.

"Someone has to take care of you, Cor."

"I'm fine," Corin replied, but his hand gripped the banister as they mounted the stairs. Martin refrained from replying only because they had arrived at the council room doors.

Corin sat at the table after giving his report. He only half-listened to the talk as he strove to stay awake. Finally he took out his knife and tossed it, catching and flipping it again—a trick learned from Nicar to stay awake during the late night watches. Those who noticed looked slightly nervous as they debated sending a messenger to the Clans.

"They came in the last war. Surely they will not want to come again!" one lord protested.

"This war affects them too. If we fall, then the Calorins will turn to Braeton," Darrin said. "The Clans will want to stop them."

"And what will we have to give in order to repay them?" another lord demanded.

"Which would you rather have? Your coffers or your life?" Lord Maldwyn asked. "I, for one, would pay anything to keep our country free."

"But we seemed to have fought the Calorins well," a young lord who had fought with the army said hesitantly.

"Aye, you held them for weeks. Do we need help from those Braetons?" Lord Mabon asked.

Thump! Corin's knife embedded itself in the table.

"We have hundreds, they have thousands!" Corin shouted. His thin patience was shattered. "We held them for weeks, but do you even know at what cost? We need more men!"

"Are there no more men to muster?" Lord Siarls asked quietly. Lord Mabon looked angry at the defection of his old compatriot.

"The mountain keeps stand empty. Those lords not here are at Castle Martel," Lord Maldwyn said.

"What of the other garrisons?" Lord Daffyd asked.

"We've emptied as many as we can," Darrin said.

"And what of the others?" Lord Mabon asked.

"Held by farmers we trained to fight," Darrin replied.

"Then call them," Lord Mabon said.

"For what? To get slaughtered? If they die then who will plant the fields or tend the forges and mills? They will be our last defense and we have already taken their sons. Aredor has nothing left to give. We are too weak to fight this war on our own. We need help," Corin said. One by one the lords nodded. They could not argue the harsh truth.

"How long do we have?" his uncle asked.

"Tonight at the latest," Corin said. The council ended soon after. Darrin sent for the best riders. They came and so did one more. Kara hesitantly knocked on the door and was given admittance. She came forward nervously in the presence of the lords, some of whom were surprised to see her. However, she ignored the arrogant looks of the other riders, none of whom served in the warband. She saw Corin's approving nod and forced the words out.

"Have you chosen yet, sire?" she asked, barely remembering the formality in time.

"No, and what argument would you make for yourself?" Darrin asked. Kara cleared her throat.

"This is a year of the Gathering, sir. I know where it will be held. All the Clans will be there and as a member of Clan Gunlon I will have the right tae speak tae the Lairds. And, sir," she said, greatly daring, "I know I can make it there, and so do you." Darrin smiled slightly.

"But she's just a girl!" one of the lords protested.

"Aye, but she and her brother saved the war for us before, more than once," Trey spoke up.

"I trust her. She can make it," Corin said. Kara smiled. That was the highest praise from the captain. It also seemed to be enough for some of the men in the room. Only Darrin remained.

"Please, sire. For my brother," she said. Darrin finally nodded. He had heard of Kieran's death and understood the desire Kara had to complete the task.

"How long will you need?" he asked.

"I can leave within the hour, sir. I'll need tae find a fresh horse and…tae say good-bye," Kara said.

The room emptied until only Darrin and Corin remained with her.

"Do you know what horse you'll take?" Corin asked.

"No, sir. I've nearly run Delyth and Gwennyd intae the ground," Kara said.

"How long will it take you to get there?" Darrin asked.

"I'm figuring nearly two days," Kara said. She pointed to the map on the table. "The Gathering is held here and most everything in between will be patrolled by Calorins."

"I'd let you take Zephyr but he needs a few days' rest before he could make a run like that," Corin said.

"Ride Frithun," Darrin offered. "He's fresh enough and he can outrun anything with you."

Kara knew Darrin's horse was one of the best in the stables, but asked, "Are you sure, sir?"

"Aye, but hurry before I change my mind," Darrin said.

"What needs to be done now?" Corin asked after Kara left.

"You need to sit back down and eat. And then you are sleeping for as long as possible," Darrin said.

"I'm—"

"No, you're not. When was the last time you ate, or slept for more than two hours at a time?" Darrin interrupted and Corin couldn't answer. "You're exhausted, Cor. Your leg gets worse when you're tired and you can hardly walk or stay upright right now."

Corin could again make no reply. "Come on. Sit down and I'll have something sent up from the kitchens," Darrin said.

Corin didn't argue and sat down, leaning wearily on the table. As Darrin left the room he saw Mera.

"I heard he was back. How is he?" she asked.

"He needs rest and a hot meal. He'd be all right in a few days if there wasn't another battle to fight," Darrin said.

"May I see him?" Mera asked, blushing slightly. Darrin only nodded and stood aside. It was one of the worst kept secrets among the women but he was glad. His brother couldn't have chosen better.

Corin barely looked up as Mera sat beside him.

"You didn't leave with the others?" he asked. Most of the women and children in the castle had left with the townspeople, putting a safe distance between them and the approaching enemy.

"I couldn't. There was too much I could do here," she said. Seeing him like that almost frightened her and she slipped her hand into his.

"I'm glad you stayed," he said simply. A serving maid entered with a tray of food.

"Can I bring you anything else, sir?" she asked. Corin glanced at the laden tray.

"I'm sure I have enough here," he said. "Is there a famine coming that I don't know about?"

The girl giggled.

"And Miss Jenny wanted to send more," she said.

"Be sure to thank her for me," Corin said. "How is your brother doing?"

"He's doing well, thanks to Miss Mera," she said. "And Catrin wanted to thank you for sending that letter."

"How is she?" Corin asked.

"As well as can be expected with two little ones and her husband gone. I'll tell her you asked," she said, dropping a curtsey.

"I should go, sir. Miss Jenny would never forgive me if I let your food get cold!"

"Do you know all the servants?" Mera asked curiously.

"Almost," Corin said with a slight smile. "But I'm sure that's not proper."

"Since when have you cared about that?" Mera smiled back as she released his hand so he could eat. "Gwilym has been asking about you incessantly since Martin and Trey got here. He drew pictures for all of you after taking over your office," Mera said.

"He what? What did Gerralt do?" Corin asked.

"I'm not sure he knew how to react." Mera laughed lightly. "But Gwilym wouldn't stop talking so he had to let him stay."

Corin laughed, picturing the scene.

"Oh, and you might check the desk drawers for a baby squirrel," Mera added.

"A…what?" Corin set his beaker down before drinking. Mera related the long, complicated story involving Gwilym and how the squirrel had taken up residence in the office. Corin laughed for the first time in weeks. But his burdens came rushing back as he finished eating and one of the guards told him that Kara was about to leave.

He went down to the courtyard and joined Darrin. Frithun was led from the stable and brought to Kara. He lowered his head and took in her scent as she rubbed his forehead. She tightened the girth and quickly recited the message back to Darrin. Warriors had begun to gather unobtrusively. They had heard the news; she was the last hope for Aredor. Frithun stood taller than Delyth and Corin gave Kara a leg up into the saddle; he held the reins as she settled in.

"You'll be fine," he reassured her.

"Maybe, but I'm just scared stiff. I don't know if I can," she admitted.

"You've never let us down, Kara," Corin reminded her.

"I know. But I keep thinking about Kieran," Kara said.

"Don't," Corin replied. "Don't think about anything but the task ahead."

Kara nodded, taking the reins in a trembling grip. He reached up and steadied her hands.

"When you get there, if you need any help with anything, find Aiden. He'll know what to do," Corin said. Kara took a deep breath.

"Ride safe," Darrin said. "And, Kara? I do want my horse back." She finally smiled.

"Aye, sir. We'll see you in a few days," she said.

The portcullis was raised and the gates swung open. She touched her heels to Frithun's sides and he stepped gracefully forward. They rode through the empty town as the stallion's hooves echoed off the paved road. There was a dull *boom!* as the gates closed. She spurred to a canter, racing away from the feeling of doom that had settled over the castle and town.

Corin went up to the infirmary. Mera and Liam were there and, to his surprise, Andras was as well. The young warrior was helping to assist another one of the healers. Corin greeted the men who were awake. Llewellyn was sitting up and Corin went over to him.

"I leave you alone for a few days and look what happens," Corin said.

"Thank you for realizing that this is your fault," Llewellyn said. They both smiled.

"How's the leg?" Corin asked.

"I'm surprised I have one left," Llewellyn said.

"Aye, unfortunately he's going to be here for a few weeks," Liam said.

"I'll be nice so long as I can walk like you promised," Llewellyn said. "Or what, Andras?"

"He'll crawl after you and kill you with a crutch," Andras supplied.

"I knew I liked that lad," Llewellyn said.

"Charming," Liam said. Corin smiled.

"I'm so glad you all understand each other," Corin said. "Oh, and Liam? You look terrible. You are hereby ordered to sleep for the next few hours." He wouldn't let Liam protest, calling over a healer. "Take care of him and make sure he doesn't get up without Lieutenant Martin's or my permission. Drug him if you have to."

"Drug me? After everything we've been through?" Liam asked.

"I can't help it. I'm a general now and the power has gone to my head," Corin replied. Liam couldn't help a smile as the healer made him sit down.

"I'll say," Llewellyn muttered.

"And Andras? Make sure he behaves. You have my permission to tie him down if you have to." Corin pointed down to Llewellyn.

"Aye, sir," Andras smiled.

"So much for thinking we were friends," Llewellyn said.

"Aye, well, I'm about to leave before my brother finds me and provides me with an armed escort and more orders to go rest," Corin said. Llewellyn and those around chuckled.

He barely made it to his room, scarcely managing to take off his weapons before collapsing into the armchair where he slept. Hours later, Martin entered his room with Andras.

"Aren't you going to wake him up, sir?" Andras asked.

"Not if I want to keep my hand," Martin replied. "We'll do it the easy way." He went over to the bed, took a pillow and threw it at Corin.

"There are easier ways you know," Corin grumbled, pulling the pillow from his face.

"Stop trying to kill me every time I try and I'll consider it," Martin said.

"I said 'sorry.'" Corin opened his eyes.

"Get up, lazy. You've slept for a shocking six whole hours. Company's coming." Martin went to the wardrobe and pulled out fresh clothes. Corin kicked off his boots and shrugged out of the mail coat, groaning as he did.

"You know better than to sleep in that," Martin said.

"I swear it's like listening to my mother," Corin complained with a smile.

"Make sure to wash behind your ears." Martin smiled benevolently. Corin complimented him in Calorin as he limped to the adjacent room where hot water waited. While he washed and changed, Martin and Andras began to clean and polish his gear.

Corin soon rejoined them, sitting on the edge of the bed and rewrapping wounds with fresh bandages. They had brought food with them and Corin packed meat and cheese in between slices of bread and began to eat while sharpening his blades.

Andras watched out of the corner of his eye, not sure how to act. The captain was sitting barefoot on the bed. After spending months in the warband, Andras had thought that he had figured the captain out, but there was always another side to see. He turned his attention back to the General's belt, polishing it carefully.

Martin caught the look and almost laughed. To those that knew him well, Corin had opened up so much since his return from Calorin. He was almost talkative and actually let emotions show. He was also better at not slipping back into Calorin if angry or agitated. But almost no one in the warband had seen him as relaxed as he was now. This time he laughed quietly.

"I think you've almost shocked him, Cor," he said. Andras looked up a little sheepishly and Corin glanced his way.

"Sorry," Corin said uncontritely. "I never got the rulebook for fearless leaders. Just don't tell anybody." Andras could see a faint twinkle in Corin's eye, something that had been missing for weeks.

"I'm sure I have a copy somewhere, sir," Andras said daringly. Both Corin and Martin burst out laughing.

"I knew there was a reason we let you stay," Martin said.

Martin began to hand Corin the cleaned gear. After thoroughly inspecting each piece and brushing invisible dust flecks away,

Corin was satisfied and pulled the last buckle into place. Martin reached out and straightened the general's belt.

"You know, I never felt like I earned this," Corin said. "You'd make a better general. I know you still have your father's belt."

Martin smiled a little sadly.

"No, Darrin and your father both asked me, but after what happened in the war...I'm happier where I am."

Corin understood. Martin's father had been the King's General but was brutally killed in the Calorin invasion. King Celyn had given Martin the position. He had only held it for a few weeks before the army was destroyed. After that, Martin had been reluctant to take command of any sort.

Andras watched quietly. He had learned that if you listened you could find out a person's past. And he could not understand after hearing some of the men talking about the war how they could be so cheerful still, especially Lieutenant Martin. But no one ever seemed to know anything about the Captain.

Corin picked up his cloak and they left the room. The castle hummed with activity as warriors hurried back and forth to various duties or grabbed a meal if they had time. Andras left to join the rest of the Hawk Flight that sat around a table. Men from Trey's deugain mingled freely with them. Trey himself was also at the table, leaning his chair back and resting his boots on the table. He was sharpening his favorite dirk as he talked with Liam.

"Look who decided to grace us with his presence," Trey said, seeing Corin. Corin spread his hand in apology.

"When did you get here?" he asked.

"A few days ago. I heard about Kieran," Trey said.

"We were able to give him a full burial," Corin said.

"Good. I had Gerralt put his name on the Hawk Flight's scroll," Trey said.

"Gerralt is still around? I thought he would have left," Corin said in surprise. Martin came up behind Trey and tugged on the chair, ignoring Trey's curse as he felt himself falling.

"Aye, apparently he's partially responsible for Gwilym also still being here," Martin said pushing Trey's chair back on all fours.

"Where is Gwilym now?" Corin asked. This was the last place he wanted the young boy. Trey waited until Martin sat down before tilting his chair again.

"Hiding from all of us," Trey said. "And it's too late to send him away now."

"Don't worry though. He knows exactly what to do when the fighting starts," Martin said.

"Good. Have either of you seen Darrin?" Corin asked Liam and Trey.

"I'm right here," Darrin answered as he approached.

"What news?" Corin asked.

"Samir and his men are still a few miles out. It doesn't look like they're leaving much behind them," Darrin said. Men who heard this muttered quiet curses. Samir was keeping his promise to lay waste to Aredor and they could hardly afford to rebuild when the country was still recovering from the first war. Corin looked at his brother. He was dressed for battle and the gold circlet around his brow declared his rule of Aredor. Seeing Darrin's anger at Samir's destruction brought Corin a faint hope that they could hold out against the powerful enemy. With the Calorins and Durnians drawing ever nearer, men were ordered to the walls.

The Hawk Flight and Corin's deugain took the west wall above the main gate. Trey and his Sharks were stationed on the south wall along with the mountain lords. Darrin paced the east and the north walls, making sure the other lords were positioned. More archers manned the turrets and towers of the keep that rose silently behind them.

"General, I have been appointed to help you hold the gate," a familiar voice said. Corin turned in surprise to see his father. Lord Celyn smiled. "I might be getting old, but I'm not infirm yet. I can still fight for my home."

"It will be honor, sir, to finally fight by your side," Corin said.

"Something long overdue," Celyn said. "What are my orders?"

Corin hesitated for a moment, not sure if he could give orders to his father but he said, "Place your men at the northwest corner. Send any archers to reinforce the tower," Corin said.

"Yes, sir," Celyn replied, then he leaned in closer. "Try not to enjoy this too much." Corin caught the gleam in his father's blue eyes and smiled.

"General." Captain Pedr bowed respectfully before following Lord Celyn.

It was not long before they heard the tramp of thousands of feet. The neighing of horses echoed in the still air. Corin's standard flew bravely beside the wolf of Aredor. The sun set, torches were lit on the walls, and they waited.

Chapter 9

Aiden squinted as he watched the path of his opponent's spear. Logan, Clan Gunlon's Champion, smiled and indicated it was Aiden's turn. Seeing how far Logan had cast made Aiden regret being talked into the contest the night before. Blair brought Aiden his javelin. Logan eyed it critically. It was smaller than the standard spears used by the northmen. There was open speculation among the spectators, many of whom had never seen a javelin, about whether Aiden could match such a throw. Even many of Clan Canich shook their heads.

Aiden stepped behind the starting mark, ran a few steps, and threw. As it was, the javelin only landed a few inches behind Logan's spear.

"Not bad," Logan graciously admitted. He was a master of the spear and, whether on foot or mounted, he could not be overcome.

"Seems a bit flimsy," Marcas, the Champion of Clan Mavor, commented as he handled the javelin. Marcas was not as tall as other men but he could easily be twice as strong. He looked as thick as a tree, but then he had to be in order to wield the battle-axe strapped to his back.

"Everything looks flimsy when you hold it," Eornan commented drily. "Except your ale mug."

Marcas laughed with the others. His strength was legendary through the Clans as was his fondness for ale.

"Ah, Eornan, so good tae see you. That merry face of yours makes me want tae dance a jig," Marcas replied. Clan Strowen's Champion's mouth twitched, the closest he ever got to a smile. The laughter continued. Logan, Marcas, and Eornan had been Champions for years and were well known by each other and the Clans.

Marcas handed the javelin back to Aiden.

"Is Captain Artair still pottering around?" Marcas asked him in an overly loud voice. At Aiden's nod he continued. "Then tell him that I demand another round of our wrestling match from the last Gathering. He cheated."

"Tell me yourself, you great windbag!" Artair pushed forward.

"I will then. You cheated, you horrible excuse for a Captain!" Marcas declared.

"I cheated? A baby could've beaten you!" Artair snorted contemptuously. They proceeded to throw insults at one another and Aiden could see it was part of a well-rehearsed routine.

"How long have they been doing this?" Aiden asked Logan.

"Since they were young lads at their first Gathering," Logan replied, listening in amusement. "They get more creative over the years."

At length, Neason was imperiously called to oversee the match and both contestants stripped to the waist. The crowd parted to allow some of the Lairds through.

"I wouldn't have missed this for anything," Laird Finley whispered to Aiden. "Marcas, you slender shadow of a Champion, do your Clan proud!" he shouted. As if that were their signal, the other spectators added their own shouts. At long last Neason declared a winner.

"Betrayed by my own pupil," Marcas said ruefully of Neason as Artair helped him up.

"That fair enough for you?" Artair asked.

"Sadly, it almost was," Marcas replied. "Don't forget, it's your turn tae challenge at the next Gathering."

"Sure, and I have two years tae think up a grievance against you," Artair said.

"Make sure it's a good one then," Marcas said.

"I will. Cheating indeed!" Artair snorted.

That night at dinner, the Clans mixed freely. Marcas and Artair sat next to each other regaling a wide audience with outrageous tales as ale flowed freely. Rona sat next to Aiden and handed him a plate of food.

"This looks good," he commented, handing her a mug.

"It should be. I helped make it. Tell me what you think." She sipped at her drink. Aiden took a bite of food, then paused. "Well?" Rona was suddenly concerned.

"Maybe you should stick tae fighting," he said. Rona stared at him for a moment.

"Why you…!"

Aiden clapped a hand over his mouth to stop himself from spitting out food as he started laughing. Rona pursed her lips.

"I'm sorry! It's delicious! It really is," Aiden said. Rona relented. She couldn't ever be angry with him. "When will you ever learn?"

"One day, I will pay you back," Rona threatened, but she was smiling.

"All right, I'll make it up tae you. I'll cook tomorrow," Aiden said.

"I still have my doubts about that," Rona told him.

"You don't think I can?" Aiden challenged.

"Let him, Rona," a woman joined in. "See if he's worth keeping. Logan here would burn a salad if I let him try."

"Och, you give me too much credit, my dear," the Champion said, leaning to kiss the woman. "Aiden, this is my wife, Mairi."

Mairi reached over to clasp his hand and Aiden was surprised to feel the strength in her hand. "Mairi is one of the best warriors in Clan Gunlon," Logan said proudly.

"And now you give me too much credit, darling," Mairi replied. "He only says that because we've been fighting each other since we could walk." She leaned forward as if confiding in Aiden and Rona.

"Aye, we only married tae do it more conveniently," Logan said.

"Shush!" Mairi laughed and kissed him again. Aiden and Rona smiled and she slipped her hand into his. They set their empty plates down and Rona leaned against his shoulder as Aiden stole another kiss. They heard one of the bards begin to sing as the flames of the campfire jumped and crackled into the peaceful, perfect night.

The next day Aiden, along with Tam, Logan, and several other warriors, went out hunting. There was never any complaint for fresh meat and the forest wasn't far away. They were riding back to the Gathering grounds after a successful morning when Aiden reined in his horse. One of the hunting hounds pricked his ears and turned south. Aiden could hear the thunder of hooves and then Logan saw the riders.

"Look!" he pointed. Aiden could see a grey horse galloping gamely as its rider kicked it on. Four more riders followed and sun glinted off pointed helmets.

"Calorins!" Aiden shouted to the others and spurred Narak forward. He heard the others follow.

"Spread out!" Logan called, setting his spear. The lead rider pulled the grey horse to pass between them. Tam and the rider recognized each other and they reined up while the others made short work of the pursuing Calorins.

"Kara, what are you doing here?" Tam asked.

"I…" she tried to catch her breath. Then she saw Aiden. "Corin sent me. I have tae speak with the Lairds!"

"Just a minute, lass. Who are you?" Logan asked. She saw his purple plaid and the tattoos.

"My name is Kara, Ewein's daughter and a member of Clan Gunlon. I serve the Hawk Flight and bear a message from King Darrin of Aredor," Kara said. Logan nodded. He had never met her but he knew of the young Clan members who served in Aredor.

"The Lairds are meeting right now. Let's waste no more time," Logan said.

Activity ceased as they rode into the encampment. Men stared at the sweat-coated stallion and his bedraggled young rider. As Kara dismounted, her legs nearly gave way beneath her but Tam was there to steady her.

"How long have you been riding?" he asked.

"Nearly two days," Kara said. "I thought I had lost the Calorins in the forest last night but they found me again at the border."

"Wait," Logan said before they began the short walk to the Laird's tent. He unbuckled Kara's bracer and rolled up the sleeve. "So no man can dispute your right tae be here," he said.

Kara had almost forgotten about the six pointed star tattoo of the Clan on her left forearm. The Lairds would hear her. As they entered the tent, Laird Dandin stood.

"Kara?" he exclaimed.

"My Laird," she replied with a bow. The other Champions entered the tent as was their right. Kara suddenly faltered. How could she speak before the Lairds and Champions, the best among the Clans? There was a reassuring touch on her arm and she looked to see Aiden. He nodded encouragingly. He had helped her before. She saw Tam and then she found her voice.

"My Lairds, King Darrin sent me with a message. Calorin and Durna have united against us. Their attacks began in early spring and we have gradually retreated before them. A force, five thousand strong, marches on Kingscastle and ships were sighted off our coasts four days ago. Our strength is not enough tae counter them. We ask for the aid of the Clans. Any assistance you would be willing tae send we will welcome, and we will repay you how we may."

There was silence in the tent as she finished. Then Laird Dandin spoke.

"Kara, find somewhere tae rest. We need some time tae discuss this," he said. Aiden looked to Tam who understood and led Kara from the tent.

"What do you think they will decide?" Kara asked.

"Och, I don't think Danny will give them much of a choice," Tam said.

"I hope it won't take long," Kara said anxiously.

"Are you hungry?" Tam asked. Kara's eyes widened as she finally realized that she was. He took her to the cook tent where she devoured the food set in front of her. Rona met them as they left the tent.

"I just wanted tae make sure you were all right," she said to Kara. "From what I've been hearing, the whole Calorin army was chasing you."

"I'm still in one piece for now," Kara replied, trying for a smile.

"Tam, let me steal her," Rona said. "Kara, you look like you could use a wash."

"That sounds wonderful!" Kara said gratefully. Rona led Kara to her tent and fetched a bucket of water. Kara washed her face and neck and Rona brushed and rebraided her hair.

"I wish I had some clothes you could use," Rona said regretfully.

"Och, I've been dreaming of clean clothes and a hot bath for weeks!" Kara said.

"Well, you look a little more human now," Rona said, using a cloth to brush some dirt from Kara's clothes.

"Thank you," Kara said.

"Ready? We don't want tae keep Tam waiting," Rona said slyly. Kara began to blush.

"Do you really think he likes me?" she asked.

"Och, sure and *no one* can tell," Rona said. "And what about you?"

"I don't know. I just feel so different around him. Like someone finally sees *me*," Kara said.

"I know. I never felt that way until I met Aiden," Rona agreed. "It's kind of wonderful, isn't it?"

Kara smiled happily.

"But do you think I look all right?" she glanced down at her clothes.

"You picked a fine time tae worry about your appearance, Kara," Rona said. "I don't think he cares!" And she pushed the young woman out of the tent.

"Let's talk about this before we go rushing off anywhere," Laird Searc of Clan Strowen said, seeing Laird Dandin about to speak.

"They need help," Laird Dandin said.

"I know. But we have tae think of our own people," Laird Searc replied. "Durna can spare men tae invade Braeton. And if we're away..." he let the thought hang.

"Aye, he's right. You and Ranulf would be fighting first," Laird Finley said. "As it is, Canich's already fought the Durnians and we've been tussling with the Enladi tribes across the mountains. I left most of the Clan at home so I can'nae offer that many warriors," he continued.

"Och, the Durnians can only think of one thing at a time," Laird Dandin scoffed. "If they do invade, it will have tae be with the Calorins or they'll be facing a war with their allies."

"You seem confident of that," Laird Searc commented.

"If I learned anything from the last war, it's that the Calorins are a wee bit selfish when it comes tae invading people's lives. If they're in an alliance with Durna, then I can bet that one of their own men is in charge. The Calorins are still looking tae take over the North and if the Durnians try tae take any land without them, the Calorins will be even less friendly," Laird Dandin said. "What say you, Colwyn?" he looked to the Laird of Clan Gunlon.

"Aye, sounds about right," Laird Colwyn said. "They'll take Aredor and come for us."

"It's already been two days since Kara left. How do we know the Aredorians are still alive?" Ranulf asked.

"If the Hawk is still alive, then so is Aredor," Laird Colwyn said.

"But they say he came from Calorin. How do we know he didn't bring them himself?" Laird Finley asked.

Aiden tried to remind himself that most of the points the Lairds raised were valid, but he seethed with impatience. Corin needed help and Lleu only knew where Will was.

"You've never met him, so I'll excuse you for that once, Finley," Laird Dandin said calmly. "Now, I'm going. Clan Dyson has already fought in this war and we will again."

"We will too. I'd see this settled before war comes tae Braeton," Laird Searc said. Laird Colwyn also voiced his assent. Clan Gunlon had fought with the Aredorians in the first war and they would not abandon the northmen this time. Aiden looked to Ranulf who had yet to speak. He knew this wasn't a light decision, but he hoped his brother would see.

"Clan Canich will also go," Laird Ranulf said and Aiden sighed in relief. "My brother William fights with the Hawk Flight and we would be proud tae fight alongside them. Besides that, I think my Champion is going no matter what I say," he said wryly and there were light laughs. Aiden smiled himself. His brother knew him well.

"Well, Finley?" Laird Dandin asked. The Laird of the Boar sighed.

"You all raise compelling arguments, so Clan Mavor will join you, but only because I'd never hear the end of it," Laird Finley said.

"Sure, Chief. You've been wanting tae go ever since you heard the message," Marcas said.

"Maybe that's true, but I had tae do a wee bit of arguing, didn't I?" Laird Finley said and the other Lairds had to agree. Finley, as any good Braeton, loved to argue but he was also never one to turn down a fight. "I have near six hundred men with me now," Laird Finley said.

"Aye, same for me," Ranulf said. The three other Lairds had brought nearly the same number with them.

"Call the lass back in then," Laird Searc said. Aiden offered to go and hurried from the tent. He saw Kara and Tam waiting nearby. Kara quickly rose when she saw him.

"What did they decide?" she asked breathlessly.

"All five Clans will go," Aiden said. "But the Lairds want tae talk tae you again."

Kara and Tam followed Aiden into the tent.

"Perhaps you can tell us more about what we're up against," Laird Colwyn said to Kara.

"As King Darrin said, the Calorins and Durnians have formed an alliance and our defenses are stretched thin. There are perhaps sixteen hundred men at Kingscastle. Any other warriors are at Castle Martel on the coast. Lynwood Keep has been under siege for the last few weeks. At least, the last we heard," Kara faltered. "That's where Will is, my Laird," she said to Ranulf. She heard a sharp intake of breath from Tam who stood behind her and Aiden looked as if he were estimating how hard it would be to mount a one-man assault on the Keep.

"I'll send tae the Clan tae muster more men. They can follow and take the Keep," Laird Dandin said.

"Aye, I'll do the same," Laird Colwyn said. "We're the closest Clans, but I suggest the rest of you send tae your Clans tae be ready in case."

The council was done as the Lairds agreed to leave by first light the next morning.

"I'll give you an escort home tae your family," Laird Colwyn said to Kara.

"No," came her sudden refusal. "I'm sorry, my Laird, but I'm going with you," she said. She faced the men staring at her and plunged ahead. "I've ridden for the Hawk Flight for four years and I'm bound tae return tae them. And…the Calorins killed my brother. Someone should be there tae fight in his name," she said.

"Well said, lass," Eornan said.

"Aye, if Eornan agrees then I'll have her along," Marcas said.

"I'm sorry about Kieran. He was a good man," Laird Dandin said.

"Thank you, my Laird," Kara said quietly.

"He'll be honored among Clan Gunlon," Laird Colwyn said. Kara could only nod her thanks again, overcome with emotion.

"Let's tell the lads and waste no more time," Laird Finley said after a respectful pause.

The Lairds and their Champions left the tent and soon the encampment was thrown into activity. Messengers were dispatched to all the Clans and fires were stoked as blacksmiths prepared for a long night's work.

- -

The sun was setting when Rona found Aiden. He was carefully cleaning and oiling Narak's saddle and bridle.

"I want tae come with you," Rona said.

"No." He shook his head.

"Why? You let me fight at Scodra!"

"And I would have spared you that."

"Is it because I'm a woman? Kara is going!" Rona argued.

"It's different for her," he said.

"I don't care! I've watched you ride away too many times. You try tae protect everyone else but who will look after you?"

"I don't need anyone tae look after me, Rona. Believe me," Aiden said sharply.

"I won't lose you because of your pride. I can fight and I'm coming with you!" she said. Aiden caught her hand and stood.

"I ride so you don't have tae see war! I've fought enough battles tae know it is the last place for you. Have you ever looked out over a field and seen the dead? Your friends, your brothers? Do you know how hard it is?" he was almost shouting. A tear trickled down her cheek. "Rona," he said more gently. "I've fought other men's battles for years and never had anything of my own tae return tae. Not until now. So I'm asking you tae stay behind because if anything happened tae you..." He couldn't finish.

"I understand," she said and walked away. Aiden didn't call her back and he hoped she would stay behind.

Men snatched what sleep they could before rising well before dawn. Horses were packed with only the necessary supplies. Kara saddled Frithun. She had hardly slept at all, wrung with nervous anticipation. Tam joined her with his horse. They rode with Clan Canich as lines of men and horses formed. Aiden had looked for Rona but she was nowhere to be found. Her tent was neatly folded and her horse and belongings had disappeared. He hoped that meant she had returned to Scodra but no one seemed to know if she had. He tried not to worry. She could take care of herself.

Horns echoed in the early morning and the army began to move. Kingscastle was more than a day and a half's journey and Aiden prayed that they would make it in time. They made camp that night and scouts reported as the Lairds made their battle plan. Aiden watched Kara and Tam talking on the other side of the fire and wondered again where Rona was. He thought he had seen her that afternoon riding with Clan Mavor but he was probably mistaken.

The camp was filled with quiet conversation as each man thought about the next day. They rose early again and the warriors painted themselves for battle. Each Clan used the color of their plaid: a savage red for Strowen, blue for Canich, green for Dyson, dark purple for Gunlon, and brown for Mavor.

Aiden applied the woad as it had been for his fight with Torsten. Mairi, who always rode with her husband, helped Kara with the war paint of Clan Gunlon. She again mounted beside Tam, his features also transformed by the woad. The Braetons rode out again, an intimidating sight. They saw none of the enemy. They rode on and began to taste smoke in the air. Finally they came to Kingscastle.

An army camped outside its walls. Smoke billowed from the towers and keep. A ram thudded against the gates adding to the clamor of battle. But above all flew the blue wolf standard. The Aredorians still stood.

Chapter 10

The defenders spent an anxious night, watching fires spring up in the town below. There were shouts and dull explosions as buildings were destroyed. In the light of morning, the Durnians rolled forward massive catapults. They used the masonry from the fallen houses to begin a barrage against the castle. Calorin archers stepped forward as siege ladders were carried toward the walls. The sun beat down upon the beleaguered defenders and Samir did not halt the attack even as the sun sank. Finally, at midnight, the enemy retreated. Weary defenders sagged at their posts. The seriously wounded were carried from the walls. The great hall was turned into an infirmary and the healers worked tirelessly.

Corin and Darrin paced the parapets, looking over damages to the walls and quietly encouraging the men. Lord Celyn watched approvingly as his sons brought fresh confidence wherever they walked. A horn rang out at dawn and in the dim light they could see a small party coming toward the walls.

"Can't they bloody well let us enjoy a sunrise?" Martin grumbled.

"I don't see a white flag, do you?" Corin asked hopefully. "Where's Flynn?"

"Lynwood," Liam reminded him.

"Why do I never have my best archer when I need him?" Corin complained.

"You can't shoot anyone, Cor, they have a flag up now," Darrin said.

"Oh, and look! It's everyone's favorite psychotic warlord," Martin said, catching a glimpse of Samir in the midst of his guard.

"You two are so pleasant when you haven't eaten or slept for hours," Darrin commented. He passed along orders to the men on the other walls to be on guard. It would be the perfect time for an ambush.

"I seek an audience with the esteemed King of this land!" Samir shouted, sarcasm heavy in his voice.

"You should start talking like that, Corin," Liam said.

"It would make you more intimidating," Martin sagely agreed. Corin stifled laughter as Darrin replied to Samir.

"I am the King. What would you say?" he asked.

"Haven't you Aredorians had enough? Realize that you cannot resist the Sultaan forever," Samir said.

"You'd think *they* would have had enough by now," Martin grumbled.

"You cannot win. And this will be worse than the war before!" Samir said.

"And yet here we are," Darrin said.

"Indeed," Samir said. "But I feel that I have the advantage."

"Lleu's Hands! Does he ever stop?" Corin muttered. "Just shoot him!"

"An advantage?" Darrin asked, ignoring Corin.

"Look at your situation. I will win this war. But turn over the Hawk to me and I will consider sparing some of you," Samir said. "The Hawk and I are very much alike and I have much I would discuss with him."

Corin laughed outright.

"A tempting deal, Samir. How long did it take you to come up with that?" Corin asked.

"Then it is true when they say the arrogance of the Aredorians will never fade," Samir said. "But think, Corin, you know

396

everything I have said is true. Would you really stand helpless while your men fall around you?"

"Do you want me dead, Samir?" Corin asked. He signaled behind the battlements to one of his men who slowly laid an arrow on his bow. "I would choose your next move carefully," Corin said. "If your man down there even thinks about shooting, you're crow meat."

The Durnian hiding among the houses froze and Samir cursed the arrow that was now pointed at his heart.

"I will kill you, Hawk! It will be more painful than anything Balkor ever did! You will burn!" Samir screamed.

"Then what are you waiting for? Do it!" Corin shouted. "But I promise you that my death won't make a difference. As long as one man still stands here, you will not win."

"You have just sealed your death!" Samir said.

"And so have you," Corin said coldly. Samir wheeled his horse and galloped away with his men.

"I couldn't have said it better myself." Darrin clapped his brother on the shoulder and then began to shout orders as the enemy began their advance.

The catapults began again. More siege ladders were thrown against the walls and the defenders pushed them down as they were able to. Darrin strove to hold the east wall against a force of axe-wielding berserkers from Durna. Trey stood over a wounded Lord Siarls while he and his Sharks held the south wall from all comers. Martin's blade danced in his hands and Corin came like a deadly whirlwind as the Calorins threatened to overwhelm the western wall.

Liam steadied Lord Celyn as the wall shuddered again. The catapults had hurled their power against the northwest corner and tower the day before and were now continuing.

"Will it hold?" Liam shouted.

"Not forever," Lord Celyn replied grimly. Corin ran up.

"Liam, we need archers!" He raised his voice above the tumult as he pointed down into the town. The Durnians, master craftsmen, had built a steel-tipped ram and covered it with a protective roof. They were now wheeling it toward the gates. Corin looked to his father.

"You and your men protect the archers," he said and was gone. Liam collected as many men as he could in the confusion to try and stop the advancing ram while Lord Celyn and his men protected them from the enemy who still poured over the wall.

At sunset, the attacks mysteriously stopped. Men collapsed exhausted where they stood. Corin slid down against the battlement and, before he knew it, fell asleep. Darrin came looking for him some time later and thought him dead but a panicked shake woke him. Corin saw his brother kneeling by him and tried to stand but every muscle protested. For the first time in a long while, he felt like giving up.

"I don't know if I can keep going," he said to Darrin.

"Don't say that, Cor," Darrin said.

"Darrin, I've fought to survive for years. I'm tired. I just want to stop. Besides, it only matters if you're here," Corin said.

"Corin," Darrin laid a hand on his shoulder. "I might lead this country but you are its soul. You give the hope of another day to everyone, including me."

"How? Why me?" Corin asked.

"Because you are still alive," Darrin said. Corin understood what he meant. By all rights he should have died years ago but something refused to let him. "If nothing else, Cor, I need you because I can't do this on my own," Darrin said.

"Then let's see if we can make another dawn," Corin said. Darrin smiled and helped pull him to his feet. In the fading light, they walked the battlements. The dead and wounded lay everywhere. The catapults had torn gaping holes in the northern walls and the tower was beginning to crumble. Those who could, rested, and took the food brought up to them. The ram was too well protected from the archers, its covering even repelling fire arrows. The west gates were battered but held for the moment.

In the new torchlight, the defenders looked like ghosts with red-rimmed eyes and faces pale from exhaustion. They rested while they could, knowing another attack was not far away. Two hours after sunset, Askel came to General Samir.

"Everything is ready," he said. Samir did not smile.

"Burn them," he said.

A warrior cried a warning as the first fireball arced toward the castle. It landed in the courtyard, breaking and spreading its fire. More and more came—giant boulders soaked with oil and set ablaze. They hit the weakened walls, tearing more ragged holes. Some hit the store houses. Servants and the reserve forces rushed to save the food stores. The northern tower was struck and set on fire as a boulder destroyed it. There were screams as rubble fell onto the defenders, crushing some and wounding more.

Corin ran to help and a smaller fireball struck in front of him. It broke, sending fragment and flame everywhere. Some hit him, engulfing his sleeve with fire. He desperately tried to smother it with his cloak. He peeled what was left of his sleeve away from his burned arm, stifling a cry as he did. Everywhere he looked there was fire. He remembered Samir's words. *"You will burn!"* How could they fight this new battle?

A moan distracted him and he saw a man trapped under the fallen stones. Ignoring his arm, he worked to pull the man out. Others came to join him, risking the crumbling, burning tower. Corin saw his father lying on the parapet. He crawled toward him, avoiding another burning missile. Lord Celyn jerked back to consciousness under his ministrations but he refused to leave the walls. Liam rushed over when he saw Corin's arm. The vambrace was intact but everything above was a blistering red. The anger Corin felt at seeing the limp body of a warrior of the Hawk Flight overrode the pain as Liam inspected his arm.

"This looks bad, Corin, you should—"

"No, just put a bandage on it. I'm not leaving this wall," Corin interrupted grimly. Liam wordlessly did as he was ordered. Corin saw the panic in the faces around him but Liam finished and looked trustingly at him. Corin forced himself to stand calmly even as he exposed himself to the enemy missiles.

The courtyard was a scene of chaos. He saw Darrin on the south wall illuminated by the fire, establishing an orderly convoy to take the wounded down to the Keep.

"My lord," Corin said to his father. "There is a well not far from the walls. Get this fire out."

Lord Celyn nodded in understanding and began to give orders as Corin ran down the wall steps. There were several wells throughout the castle grounds and Corin gradually sorted out the confusion, organizing bucket lines to save as many buildings as possible. The stables were still intact but the grooms had their hands full with the panicked animals inside. The roof of one of the barracks had caved in. Even some of the keep was ablaze. Corin helped a wounded man inside the castle and was met by Gerralt. The scribe had his old broadsword buckled around his waist.

"Gerralt!" Corin greeted him. Gerralt hitched up his sword belt.

"You look surprised, Captain," he said.

"Can you still use that?" Corin asked, gesturing to the weapon.

"If I have to," Gerralt replied. He glanced outside. "It looks like they might have destroyed my office, so rest assured, I'm ready to do my part," he said. Corin laughed as he wiped soot from his face. He caught sight of Mera tearing fresh bandages. She glanced up and smiled at him. Gerralt saw his gaze. "For what it's worth, sire, if anything happens, I will guard her with my life," he said seriously.

"Thank you, Gerralt." Corin pressed his shoulder before returning to the battle.

Another dawn came through the smoke. The fires had finally been reduced to smoldering embers. General Samir ate his breakfast and smiled. Kingscastle was a smoking ruin. The town around it had not escaped either. Fires still burned there and he could hear houses collapsing upon themselves. Captain Askel joined him.

"An impressive display last night," Samir complimented him.

"Shall we begin again?" Askel asked.

"No, not yet. I will allow them to rest before I completely destroy them," Samir said.

As it was, the Aredorians gained three precious hours of sleep and rest. There was hardly a single warrior awake. If Samir had known that, his victory would have been assured, but when he rode forward he saw warriors lining the walls and a dark figure stood beneath the tattered standards. A hawk shrieked defiantly as it came to perch on the figure's outstretched arm. Samir felt a slight chill. *They would not die!* The King came to stand by the figure; the sunlight glinted coldly off his drawn blade. They were ready. Samir found his voice and ordered the attack.

The enemy pressed hard and the weary defenders were ready to crumble when unfamiliar horns cut across the noise. Men turned and saw the rows of horsemen to the north. The Clans had come!

Chapter 11

Aiden tightened his grip on his javelin as he stared at the destruction. The Champions took their places by their Lairds as the horns rang out. Ranks closed and one single horn blew a high, piercing note. Horses were spurred forward, gathering speed and tearing toward the army waiting outside the town. Aiden felt the rush and his blood rose as he gave voice to his savage war cry.

Corin heard it even on the walls. The enemy hesitated in their attack and then turned to do battle with the new adversary on the open plains. Corin saw the way open up before him and he sprang down the steps calling for a horse. Tired though they were, his men followed without hesitation. The gates were opened and the abandoned ram was pushed from the way. Trey and his deugain joined with Corin and Darrin as they rode from the castle. Men grasped the tattered standards of the wolf and the hawk and the flags bravely flew as they rode.

Samir was still in shock at the sudden appearance of the Clans but the panicked shouts of his captain brought him back to the present and he ordered a counterattack. His cavalry was preparing to come behind the Braetons when the Aredorians slammed into them with white hot fury.

Laird Finley led his Clan against the Durnian crossbowmen who were wreaking untold damage against the horsemen. Clan

Canich joined the Aredorians and Corin and Aiden met again on the field of battle. Clan Strowen wove among the catapults, driving Durnians before them. Clan Gunlon and Clan Dyson circled the castle, taking on the enemy that still surrounded it.

As the Northern force became spread out, Samir drew together his army that remained on the plain, still several thousand strong. The Braetons and Aredorians drew their line in front of the city. Darrin rode to meet a new force from the castle led by Lord Maldwyn and they took the right flank. But Calorins that had hidden in the town drove the force in two. Clan Gunlon and Clan Dyson came from either side to join their allies.

Clan Canich still remained with Corin and his men. The battle light still shone in the Braetons' eyes but Corin saw his men begin to waver at the sight of the force that awaited them. But he had forgotten his wounds and his exhaustion.

"Don't give up!" he shouted. "Don't you give up on me! We have fought for too long to stop now. Today we end this! Today we win our freedom once and for all! They did not beat us before and they will not now! Fight with me again and let us prove that we will keep what is ours!"

Martin felt a chill as he listened. It was how he had always imagined the heroes of old. The odds never seemed impossible with Corin. Aiden spurred Narak up beside Corin and saluted him with his sword.

"Lead the way then," he said. Aiden had seen the same light in Ranulf's eyes. The Clan would follow. Trey lifted his sword and his men raised their war cry. The Hawk Flight loosed the wolf cry as Corin turned.

Across the field, Darrin saw Corin and heard the cry.

"We follow you, my Laird," Laird Colwyn said to Darrin.

"Prepare the charge," Darrin ordered. Horns sounded again and, from both sides of the field, the Northerners charged.

Aiden stayed at Corin's side as they plunged into battle but in the melee he was driven away. Narak slipped on the bloody ground and Aiden was thrown. He rolled quickly to his feet and moved into the ground fighting. Then he saw a sight that nearly stopped his heart—an all too familiar figure was fighting a few yards away. It was Rona. She was dressed in men's clothing, her face painted with woad. He ran to her, killing a Calorin that was approaching her from behind.

"Rona!" he shouted. She didn't turn as she fought a Durnian.

"Fancy meeting you here!" she replied. He set his back against hers as more enemies came at them.

"I thought I told you tae stay behind!" he said.

"You asked, and last I checked I can do whatever I want!" Rona shouted, parrying a sword blow.

"Rona!" he was exasperated.

"Shut up! We can argue later!" she replied. They soon had no extra breath for talking as their foe pressed heavy around them. They gained a welcome respite when a small mounted force from Clan Strowen swirled around them and drove away the Calorins. But just as Aiden was about to turn, he felt Rona stumble against him with a strangled cry. Time seemed to freeze as he looked to see a sword protruding from her stomach and the triumphant face of a Calorin. He heard his cry as he swung his sword and the Calorin disappeared. He looked down and saw Rona half kneeling at his feet. She had pulled the sword out and pressed her hand against the wound. He picked her up and carried her to the shelter of a nearby supply wagon. She bit her lip as he set her down.

"Did you want tae argue now?" she asked.

"Shh!" he told her, using her plaid to try and stop the blood.

"Aiden, how bad?" she asked shakily. He didn't meet her gaze as he refolded the soaked cloth. She reached up and turned his face toward her. "Aiden?"

"You'll be fine." His voice caught.

"You're a terrible liar," she said. "Stay with me?" her voice shook.

"I would never leave you," he said. She closed her eyes, feeling his strong arms holding her. Tears clouded her vision.

"Aiden, remember that this was my decision. I wanted tae come," she said.

"Why?" he asked.

"Because I love you and I want tae stay by your side through everything. And you do need someone tae look after you," she said.

"You know how much you irritate me sometimes?" he asked. She smiled.

"I wish I could tell you tae move on after I...die, but I'm feeling very selfish right now," she said. Aiden smiled through his tears.

"As if I could ever forget you," he said. "You are the first and only person I will ever love." He leaned down and kissed her gently. She smiled.

"I'll be waiting for you," she whispered and kissed him again. "Good-bye."

"I love you so much," he told her and she was smiling as her eyes closed for the last time. He felt frozen as he held her. How could she be gone?

Gradually the noise of battle found him again. He saw a Braeton warrior struck down and a young Aredorian fighting for his life. He looked back down at Rona and laid her gently on the ground. He placed her sword by her and spread his plaid over her. He stood, took up his swords and reentered the battle.

Andras lay on the ground, seeing his death blow falling when the sword was tossed away and a savage-looking Braeton warrior took on his opponent. Aiden felt the familiar anger of the berserker tug at him and in his grief he did not fight it. A wordless cry ripped from his throat as he charged heedlessly into battle.

Long hours later, the battle was ended. Corin and Darrin stood together on the blood-soaked field. They were victorious. Some Durnians and Calorins had surrendered but the rest that survived had fled. The Northerners gave no chase; the terrible cost of their victory lay on the ground around them. A grey horse and its rider picked their way toward the brothers. Kara had taken the wolf standard as its bearer fell and had carried it through the battle. She dismounted and handed it to Darrin.

"This belongs tae you, sire," she said, then turned to Corin and saluted. "Reporting for duty, Captain."

He pulled her into a hug.

"You had me worried for a little while," he said.

"I haven't let you down yet," she replied, feeling a great sense of relief now that the battle was finally over.

"No, you haven't." Corin smiled. "I'm glad you're back safely."

"Thank you, sir," she said.

Corin was about to speak again when he saw Ian running toward them. A cold hand clutched Corin's heart as Ian struggled to speak.

"Captain...you have to come..." he stammered.

"Who?" Corin asked, deathly calm.

"Lieutenant Martin," Ian said.

"Where?" Corin gripped his shoulder. Ian led Corin across the field at a run and Corin saw. Martin was sitting against Trey and Corin could see the broken haft of a spear protruding from his back. Liam also knelt beside Martin, the look on his face telling the bitter truth; Martin was dying. Martin looked up as Corin knelt in front of him.

"You came," Martin said raggedly. "And don't say anything, Cor. You know as well as I do."

"Martin, you can't...What will I do?" Corin asked. He felt only terrible panic.

"You've got these two." Martin indicated Liam and Trey. He began coughing. "Trey?" he gasped.

"I'm here, Martin," Trey said as he steadied him. Martin took a knife from his belt.

"I want Gwilym to have this. It's been passed down my family from father to son for generations," Martin said. "I need you three to take care of him. Tell him I'm sorry I had to leave. I know I promised."

"We will," Trey assured him as he took the knife.

"Corin, look after Mera for me. I know how much you care about each other," Martin continued. "Bury me in the forest with the others. And I want Ian to take my place. He's a good lad."

"Any more demands?" Corin asked.

"You won't let me die in peace, will you?" Martin smiled.

"What kind of a friend would I be?" Corin smiled sadly.

"Look after these two idiots for me, Lio," Martin said to Liam, who clasped his hand wordlessly. "Trey." Martin couldn't turn his head to look back. "Take care of yourself. You know you're the reason I made it to today," he said. "Just promise me."

"I will," Trey said, his voice trembling. He picked up Martin's sword and laid it across his lap. Martin's hand fumbled as he reached for his blade. Corin caught Martin's hand and wrapped it securely around the hilt. Martin smiled again.

"I don't want to be seeing any of you anytime soon," he said. Then he reached behind himself, grasped the spear, and wrenched it from his body. Trey held him as he stiffened in pain. Then he relaxed against Trey and was gone.

Corin bowed his head and his shoulders shook with grief. Tears tracked clean paths down Trey's cheeks as he held Martin's body and Liam closed his eyes against the numb anguish. Slowly, the Hawk Flight took the body, laid it on a stretcher, and bore it back to Kingscastle.

"Go with him," Corin said hoarsely to Liam and Trey who wordlessly obeyed. Corin joined Darrin to order the clearing of the field.

Ranulf and Tam walked through the carnage looking for their brother. Tam saw Aiden standing some distance away with his back to them. He held a scimitar in one hand while the other hung limp at his side.

"Tam, wait!" Ranulf said as Tam ran toward their brother. He had seen the bodies surrounding him. Ranulf shoved Tam away as Aiden turned and swung the sword. Ranulf managed to stop it and stared into his brother's burning eyes.

"Aiden!" he shouted, and again as Aiden blinked and shook his head as if to clear it. Ranulf caught him as he dropped the sword and almost collapsed.

"Tam, I'm sorry!" Aiden gasped as pain, so long ignored, came rushing back. His brothers helped him walk toward the castle. They passed the spot where Rona lay and Aiden stopped. Tam saw the plaid and, leaving them, walked over to it. He recognized Aiden's brooch on the cloth and folded it back. Ranulf gasped in shock when he saw Rona. Aiden was looking away and Ranulf felt him shivering. He wrapped his cloak around Aiden.

"I'm sorry, Danny," he whispered, but Aiden made no reply.

A healer met them at the doors of Kingscastle and quickly led them to a room filled with beds. She bandaged Aiden's many wounds and gave him a draft for the fever that was overtaking him. He closed his eyes and knew no more.

Corin trudged wearily toward the castle leading Zephyr. He had found the horse wandering the field as Darrin sent him back to rest. A familiar whinny sounded behind them and Zephyr raised his head as Narak trotted up, riderless. Corin caught the reins. *Where was Aiden?* he thought. He hadn't seen him after the last charge. *Had something happened to him too?* He couldn't bear the thought. Corin led both horses through the town. He would find some of the Clan and see if they knew anything of their Champion. But his plans were dashed as soon as he walked into the castle.

"Sir, Lord Trey wanted to see you," a warrior said and led Corin down a corridor. Trey sat on a bench in the hall and Gwilym was with him. The boy was clinging tightly to Trey in shock. Corin sat down with them.

"What happened?" Corin asked quietly.

"He saw…I guess he saw me and followed us. Then he saw Martin and just started screaming. I could hardly get him to calm down," Trey replied. Corin leaned forward, putting his head in his hands. He hadn't known how they were going to break the news to Gwilym or…

"Where's Mera?" he asked.

"Inside," Trey said. "Go on, I'll take care of him."

Corin rose and went to the room further down the hall. It was bare of any ornament, being the place where the dead were laid until their burial. The dead of the Hawk Flight lay beside each other and Mera stood by one. He touched her gently on the arm and led her from the room. Fresh tears escaped her eyes and she huddled against him as he wrapped comforting arms around her.

"Trey said you both were with him when he died," she said.

"Yes," Corin said.

"Did he say anything?" she asked.

"Just to teach Gwilym how to flirt with all the girls," Corin said after a long moment. Mera had to smile.

"No, he didn't," she said. "You wouldn't know how to do that anyway." She wiped tears away.

"He just wanted someone to look after Gwilym and you," Corin said.

"Gwilym!" Mera exclaimed.

"Trey is with him right now. Don't worry," Corin told her.

"Thank you," she said but felt him tense as she laid her hand on his arm. "Corin!" she cried, looking him over. "How are you even standing right now? Come with me!" she commanded.

The hall was filled with wounded from the battle but there was some space in the infirmary. He pulled off the mail coat with difficulty and sat down on the bed as she bustled around him.

"Take care of me indeed! He knew very well it's going to be the other way around," she muttered to herself and he smiled, gratefully complying with her next order to rest, and slept until Ian came to wake him several hours later.

He hurried to change into new clothes, finding to his relief that the pain from his burned arm had settled down to a dull throb. He joined Darrin and the Braeton lords for a council. Some had rested but the war paint still remained as it would until their enemies were finally defeated. Plans were made to send out patrols the next morning to search for survivors and places were found for the Clans to stay.

"Your turn to sleep, Darrin," Corin said when the meeting ended. "I'll organize a wall guard."

"We need to send a messenger to the coast," Darrin said.

"Go on. I'll find someone," Corin assured him. Darrin stumbled off and Corin found Gerralt to help him for the next few hours. They compiled casualty lists and took stock of the food supplies that had survived the fires. Every chance he got, Corin looked around for Aiden. He knew some of Clan Canich was scouting and he hoped Aiden was with them. But Tam had led the patrol and he reported to Corin.

"Where's Aiden?" Corin asked after Tam finished.

"He was hurt but he will recover in time," Tam said. Corin knew Tam wasn't telling him everything but more reports were coming in and Tam disappeared.

Corin met Darrin the next morning as Corin prepared to lead the first patrol out.

"A runner from Lynwood came in last night," Corin told him. "They held out long enough for some of Clan Dyson to come."

"Where are you headed?" Darrin asked.

"We'll go south and then sweep up toward the forest," Corin said. "The boys at the Keep are already out scouting the woods. We can send the next patrol north and then into the forest."

"Sounds good," Darrin said. "I'll send them out in about an hour."

Corin saluted and led his patrol from the castle. It was a mixed array of the Clans and Aredorians. They encountered a few small bands of Calorins and Durnians who chose to fight instead of flee. They buried the bodies and returned to Kingscastle by late afternoon. They saw the freshly dug burial mounds from across the training grounds which reminded Corin of his own bitter duty.

"I want to take the Hawk Flight to Dunham Forest tomorrow. The dead need to rest," Corin said to Darrin. His brother nodded somberly. The warband had its own ceremony to perform for their fallen. Mera found him as he left.

"Trey has gone out on patrol and Gwilym won't come out of Martin's room," she said. "Liam is still busy with the wounded. He'll hardly rest himself."

"I'll go," Corin replied to the unspoken question. He went to the familiar door and tried the handle. It was locked so he rapped gently on the door.

"Go away!" a muffled voice cried.

"Gwily, it's Uncle Cor. Can I come in?" Corin asked. There was a pause, then a bolt slid back and he could hear Gwilym running back to the bed. He was curled up on the bed, clutching Martin's knife in its sheath. Corin sat beside him. Gwilym sniffled in the silence.

"It's not fair! He promised he would stay!" he said miserably.

"I know," Corin said. "But sometimes those promises are hard to keep."

"Why'd he have to go?" Gwilym swiped tears away. Corin searched for an answer.

"Do you remember your parents?" he asked.

"A little bit," Gwilym said.

"He wanted them to know how you were doing, so he decided to go find them," Corin said. "And he thought your sister might want an uncle."

Gwilym pondered the statement.

"Will he ever come back?" he asked.

"No, but you'll be able to find him one day," Corin said. "And as long as you carry that knife, you'll have a part of him."

Gwilym clutched it harder.

"You won't go away with him, will you, Uncle Cor?" Gwilym asked, a note of terror in his voice.

"No, Trey and Liam and I will be around for a long time because we promised Uncle Martin we would," Corin said, his throat tightening as he spoke. But Gwilym was finally reassured and fell asleep. Corin took one of Martin's cloaks and covered the young boy with it before leaving the room.

Chapter 12

Early the next morning, the Hawk Flight rode out. The dead had been carefully placed in wagons. Even the wounded were going, refusing to stay behind while their brothers were laid to rest. Trey and Gwilym also rode with them. "The lad should see the Lieutenant buried," many of the warband had said, and so Gwilym had come. They rode all day without stopping. Gwilym was tired but, wide-eyed in the company of the men, he would not complain. They reached the caves by late that afternoon. Flynn and his men awaited them, also bearing their dead.

Graves were dug and the bodies buried in silence and spears were planted to mark their place. Martin was not buried in the clearing with the others. Corin had chosen a place by the caves overlooking the sunken valley. They lowered Martin's body into the grave. He had been dressed in the uniform of the Hawk Flight and his father's belt that he had worn for a time as General was across his chest. Trey placed Martin's sword over him and Corin put a grey hawk feather with it. Then they both took a handful of dirt and cast it into the grave, saying their last goodbyes. Gwilym did the same and Trey barely heard the words "Good-bye, Father." He turned away as the rest of the warband filed by, doing the same and bidding farewell to another brother.

When the grave was filled in and the spear set, the warband went inside the caves, each taking their place at the tables set in the main cavern. Beakers of cold stream water were set at each place though many stood empty. Corin took his place at the head table. Gwilym stood with him and Trey took Martin's place. Corin lay a scroll on the table in front of him.

"This paper might hold their names but we will always keep them in our hearts. We know each one and it is our duty to remember. Others may forget, the spears may rot, but we place new ones. We carry on the task that they have finished. Let us remember until we see them again." Gwilym watched solemnly as Corin began to call the names of the dead and the man by the empty place answered "Here," raising their beaker and toasting the missing warrior. The list was long; they had lost almost half of the warband. When Corin came to the last name "Martin, son of Deiniol," his voice faltered but, before Trey or Liam could reply, a small voice answered. Every man standing drank to their dead Lieutenant. After a brief silence, Corin spoke again.

"Before he died, Lieutenant Martin named his successor. At first I was surprised at his choice but then I realized that he chose well. I would honor his last request. Ian," he called. Ian came forward, a look of shock on his face. Corin handed him the silver hawk feather of a lieutenant.

"But, Captain," Ian protested. "I can't...I'm not ready!"

"Ian, I spoke with every man in the patrol and they all agreed with Lieutenant Martin. As I said, I couldn't have chosen better myself," Corin told him.

Men murmured quiet congratulations to Ian as they left the cave to return to their horses. Andras helped Evan limp out. Evan had been wounded on the walls and Andras was the one that had found him. They said nothing to each other, still struck by the somber ritual they had witnessed. But there was a quiet friendship growing between them. Evan's confidence had grown and both he and Andras had become hardened warriors over the past few months. Andras helped Evan to mount. Trey passed by at that moment and gave them both a nod. It was the respect one warrior gave to another.

Trey and Gwilym began the journey back to Kingscastle with the wounded while Corin led the rest on one final patrol. They made camp at sunset, eating and resting. Corin woke before dawn. Unable to sleep again he rose and walked some distance from the camp. A small stream gurgled and he came to stand by it. The setting moon cast shadows through the trees and in the distance a wolf howled to his companions. The scimitar felt heavy in Corin's hands and he dropped it. He sank down against a tree as he began to weep.

He wept for Martin. He wept for the men who had died. For the widows and orphans created by war. For those he had killed and those he couldn't save. For Castimir. For the destruction wreaked by war. He wept for Gwilym who had lost another part of his family. He wept until he could no more.

Karif landed on the sheath of the fallen sword. Corin looked up and saw that the dawn had come. He listened in silence as the birds began their song to greet the new day. He let it comfort him as it had since he had come back to Aredor. After a long moment he rose and washed the traces of tears from his face. He took up his sword and returned to camp.

They arrived at Kingscastle later that day and Laird Dandin came in as Corin finished his report to Darrin.

"Now that the dead have been laid tae rest, we will play them tae Lleu's Halls. The Clans will all be there and we would have you and your men there as well," Laird Dandin said to them.

"We would be honored," Darrin said. "Who will do it?"

"The Bards chose Tam," Laird Dandin said. "It will begin at sundown."

He left and Corin was finally free to find Aiden.

Chapter 13

Aiden woke the day after the battle, taking a long moment to orient himself. Beds filled with wounded men lined the walls beside him but he had no clear memory of coming there. His body ached under numerous bandages and his right hand was held in a heavy splint. He couldn't remember how that had happened either. There was one moment that he could recall with horrifying clarity: Rona lying in his arms—dead.

Why her? he thought angrily. *Hadn't enough people in his life died already?* He seemed to bring death wherever he went. He couldn't move and he didn't want to. The most precious thing in his life was now gone. The grief pounded away at him as he lay there in a haze. Sleep brought little relief. The next day was worse.

Ranulf came to see him and Aiden would not speak any more than the necessary answers. Ranulf did not speak of her and Aiden was grateful. The day passed as the one before it. Aiden barely noticed as someone changed the bandages. None of the Clan came. They were busy or Ranulf kept them away. Aiden didn't care. He didn't want to see anyone. He shut out the world and slept.

When he finally awoke, he saw that it was morning again. The light seemed clearer than it had before and he sat up slowly. He heard footsteps and saw Will coming toward him.

"Shirking work as usual, I see," Will said, sitting in the chair by the bed.

"Old habits die hard," Aiden replied, finding his voice again.

"You don't look half as bad as Tam made it out tae be," Will said.

"Shouldn't you know by now that he still exaggerates everything?" Aiden asked. Will chuckled. "When did you get here?"

"Late last night," Will replied. "Corin should be back sometime soon."

Corin. Aiden felt a little guilty. *How was he?* He had looked terrible during the battle and Aiden felt a faint twinge of worry.

"I heard Kara went and got the Clans from the Gathering. I assume Rona was there. How is she?" Will asked. Aiden froze. He would have to tell Will.

"She's dead," he said.

"What?" Will stared in disbelief. Haltingly, Aiden told him what happened, feeling again the terrible pain like a knife twisting in his heart.

"Danny, I'm sorry. I know you…"

"I loved her, Will. And she's gone," Aiden said bitterly. "What do I do now?"

"Well, you can'nae stay here forever, Aiden. I don't think she'd let you," Will said. "When was the last time you ate?" he asked. Aiden shrugged.

"Too long ago," a woman said. He recognized Mera. He saw from her stricken face that she had also heard the news. But she offered no sympathy, seeing he didn't want it.

"That settles it, then. I'll go and find you something," Will said. He left before Aiden could protest.

"Let him. He's worried about you," Mera said.

"I guess I am a little hungry," Aiden said.

"That's a good sign." Mera smiled. "How's your hand feeling?"

"I don't even know what happened," Aiden admitted.

"It's broken. You took a hard blow to your hand but I'm hoping it will heal completely. Just don't try to use it," she said.

"I'll try and remember that," he said.

"Good, and by tomorrow you should be able to get up and walk around a bit. It would do you good," Mera said. He didn't miss the hint in her voice. She left and Will returned soon after. Aiden was hungrier than he thought and ate quickly as he and Will engaged in aimless conversation. He finished and looked to his brother.

"Will, I know she was your friend too, and I'm sorry." Aiden swallowed hard. Will nodded wordlessly.

"We'll remember her properly when the time is right," he said.

When his brother left, Aiden slept again.

He woke to the sound of several voices. Corin was in the room talking with several of the men. They laughed over something and then Corin saw that he was awake. He left them and sat in the chair.

"Sorry if we woke you," he said. Aiden shook his head, pushing himself upright.

"I was beginning tae think you had forgotten me," Aiden said.

"I've been trying to come for several days," Corin said.

"Well, I hope you know that I'm deeply offended," Aiden said and Corin smiled.

"How are you doing?" he asked.

"I could feel better," Aiden replied.

Corin paused for a moment, then said, "Aiden, Mera told me about...Rona. I'm sorry."

"Everyone keeps saying that but it won't bring her back!" Aiden snapped, his anger at her death flaring again.

"You can't act like you're the only one here who's lost someone," Corin replied, an edge to his voice.

"And what do you expect me to do?" Aiden was almost shouting.

"There are still people here who care about you and you can't sit here and shut them out. Hard as it is, you have to accept it.

Death comes every day and we can't stop it!" Corin replied, his own temper fraying.

"You sound like Azrahil!" Aiden sneered.

"And you think I don't know what it feels like to lose someone?" Corin shouted. The room was frozen in silence as they glared at each other. Then Corin spoke. "The Clans' ceremony is tonight. Tam is playing the Lament. You should be there." His voice was tight as he turned and left.

Aiden felt a pang of remorse as he watched Corin go, realizing that they had never argued like that before.

"I think you know him well enough to not let that lie for long," a man said beside Aiden.

"What do you mean?" Aiden turned.

"You were arguing in Calorin and the captain usually doesn't do that. And if you are who I think you are, then you both need your closest friend right about now," the man said.

"Who are you?" Aiden asked.

"Let's just say I've been with the warband almost since the beginning," he said meaningfully. Aiden saw that the man had recognized him from his involvement in the first war.

"What happened?" Aiden asked quietly.

"You should ask him yourself." And the warrior would say no more.

Someone had left Aiden's bag and weapons by the bed and, as evening drew near, he dressed in clean clothes, fumbling with only one good hand. Finally finished, he limped slowly from the room and through the castle to the courtyard. Already tired, he leaned against one of the pillars by the main doors.

The courtyard and walls were full of Clan warriors and Aredorian soldiers, standing silently. Only the west wall stood empty. When it was time, Tam mounted the steps, carrying the bagpipes. He was dressed simply, bearing no sword or armor. A white cloak was clasped around his shoulders. As the sun began to set, he raised the bagpipes and began to play.

It was a wildly haunting melody, giving voice to the sorrow and loss. The Laments of each of the five Clans were twined into it, honoring each man that had fallen. Those that listened wept as Tam played and the sun set over the graves of friends and comrades. Tears streaked Tam's face, for he alone saw them: a long line of warriors passing into the sun on their journey beyond the world. Aiden stood dry-eyed as the music washed over him and softened his heart. She was at peace now but it would be a long time before he could be. The final notes lingered as the last edge of the sun dropped below the horizon. Men dispersed in silence and Aiden waited for Corin. Corin didn't see Aiden in the dim light until he spoke.

"Corin." Aiden stepped toward him as Corin stopped. "Look, I'm sorry," Aiden said.

"I'm not blameless either, so forget what I said," Corin said.

"No, most of it was true. I just can'nae figure out how tae go on," Aiden said quietly. He saw the same look in Corin's eyes. "Who?" he asked somberly.

"We buried Martin yesterday," Corin replied.

"I'm so sorry, Cor. He was a good man," Aiden said. He had seen how close Martin and Corin were and he had enjoyed the lieutenant's company.

"One of the best," Corin agreed. Torches were lit around them as the guard began to change.

"Zayd's spear! You look awful, Corin," Aiden said. He hadn't noticed much earlier that day. Corin smiled tiredly.

"You're one to talk," he said. "Do you need help getting back?"

"No, I'll make Tam help me. I should talk tae him. I've been avoiding him too," Aiden said.

"All right. And, Aiden, if you need anything…" Corin said. Aiden nodded.

"Thanks," he said.

Corin disappeared inside. Tam saw Aiden and came up the steps.

"Should you even be out here?" Tam asked.

"You know how well I follow orders," Aiden replied.

"You going tae be all right?" Tam asked.

"It will take a while," Aiden said

"Here," Tam reached into his pouch. "I took this before we buried her. I thought you might like tae have it." He handed Aiden Rona's necklace. He had never seen her without it. He ran his thumb over the carved swallow, remembering what he had told her that day in the stables. He held it tightly as if he could hold a part of her again.

"Thank you," he said.

He dreamed of her that night: perfect and alive.

"You going tae lie there for the rest of your life?" She smiled teasingly.

"Why you?" he asked.

"Och, I already told you why," she said.

"What if I can'nae go on?" he asked.

"You will or I'll haunt you until you hate me and beg me tae leave." *She smiled merrily.*

He wanted to laugh, but couldn't yet.

"Oh, come on, Aiden!" she was exasperated. "You're making me depressed and I'm dead."

"Rona," he said.

"Good-bye, my love," she said and turned and faded away.

Chapter 14

Darrin entered Corin's room and threw open the curtains. There was a muffled yell from the bed as sunlight flooded the room.

"There had better be a very good reason for this!" Corin said.

"You've been in here for almost two days," Darrin said.

"People need to sleep," Corin returned.

"You say that every time and you have. Come on. We have some visitors who want to meet you," Darrin said. Corin groaned as he rolled over.

"Tell them I'm not here."

"Too late, and I brought food," Darrin said. His brother sat up.

"I hate you for knowing me so well," Corin said. Darrin smiled as Corin rose and limped to the table. Darrin sat with him as he began to eat.

"Who's coming?" Corin asked.

"Some Calorin and Raider ships attacked the coast. Tristan said another ship came out of nowhere and took on the Raiders. The captain wants to meet us," Darrin told him.

"Is Tris here?" Corin asked.

"No, he sent them with an escort. And Trey said he wants to leave soon," Darrin said.

"How's Gwilym?" Corin asked.

"About as well as can be expected," Darrin said. "Kara and Tam have helped keep him occupied."

"What about the Clans?"

"They plan to leave sometime next week," Darrin said.

"How will we be able to repay them?" Corin asked somberly.

"I don't know. But we'll worry about that another time. You don't get to ask any more questions, Cor. How are you doing?" Darrin asked. Corin leaned back in the chair.

"I'm holding up," he replied. "Don't worry about me, Darrin."

"No, I will."

"Fine," Corin said. "I just...why him?" he asked.

"I wish I could tell you. He's going to be missed."

"I know. I'll figure out a way to move on eventually."

"Is there anything I can do?" his brother asked.

"Just tell me what needs to be done," Corin said.

"Clean up. You have about half an hour before the audience with the captain," Darrin said.

"I guess that means I should hurry," Corin said.

"Please do." Darrin grinned and left.

Aiden slowly walked the halls. Mera and Liam had practically shoved him out of the infirmary. He could feel his body healing but he was frustrated with how slowly he had to move. For now, he had no particular goal in mind. They had wanted him to find a new place to sit for a few hours and get some fresh air but he didn't want to sit still any longer because his mind would wander back to her.

He had navigated a flight of stairs which he had been told would take him to the main floors when a noise stopped him. It was a rhythmic tapping coming from a corridor. He heard a small sniffle and decided to investigate. The hall was dimly lit but he soon made out a lonely figure sitting on a bench.

"Can I sit down with you?" he asked the young boy and received a nod. "You're Gwilym, right?" he received another nod. "Do you remember me?"

"I think so." Gwilym raised his head.

"My name is Aiden, but most people call me Danny. You can if you want," Aiden said. Gwilym was silent but Aiden kept talking. "That's quite a knife you have there," he said.

"It's my Uncle Martin's," Gwilym spoke up. Then he looked back to the dagger in his lap. "He's gone."

Despite his own grief, Aiden's heart went out to the boy.

"May I see it?" he asked. Gwilym passed it to him and he unsheathed the blade, turning it over as he inspected it. "This is a good blade. I can see why he wanted you tae have it. A warrior always needs a good knife," Aiden said.

"I'm not a warrior. I'm only seven," Gwilym said.

"You will be one day. Come here and I'll show you how a warrior wears it," Aiden said. Gwilym stood eagerly and Aiden fastened the dagger to the boy's belt.

"It's kind of heavy," Gwilym said doubtfully.

"You'll get used tae it," Aiden told him.

"Are you a warrior?" Gwilym asked.

"Aye, but I got hurt."

"Did Aunt Mera fix you up?"

"She did. But she can'nae fix everything."

"What do you mean?" Gwilym was confused.

"Well, someone I knew very well got hurt and they…had tae leave," Aiden said.

"Like Uncle Martin?" Gwilym asked and Aiden nodded. Gwilym sniffled again and Aiden was suddenly eager to see the sun.

"I bet you know your way around the castle," he said. Gwilym nodded proudly.

"My uncles showed me every secret way and shortcut," he said.

"Perfect. How would you like tae help me get tae the stables?" Aiden asked.

"I'm not supposed to go in without a grownup," Gwilym said.

"Oh, I'm sure they'll let two warriors like us in. Truth is, I might need a little help. Think you're up for it?" Aiden asked seriously. Gwilym straightened importantly.

"Yes, sir!" he gave Aiden his best salute. Then, taking his hand, Gwilym set off.

The guards at the doors greeted them as they passed and Gwilym barely stopped to wave. Aiden paused at the entrance to the stables to ask a groom about his horse when a familiar neigh sounded.

"No need. I think I can find him," Aiden said. "But one more thing." He lowered his voice. "Is Lieutenant Martin's horse here?"

"Aye, sir. Third row over, five stalls down. His usual spot," the groom replied.

Aiden and Gwilym entered the stables and were guided by the noise to Narak's stall. A groom stood outside the door attempting to replace the water bucket. But every time he approached, Narak pinned his ears back and neighed a warning.

"I'll take care of him while you do that," Aiden told the stable hand. The man watched in disbelief as Aiden entered the stall and Narak nickered gently. Aiden moved the stallion back as the groom changed the water as fast as he could. Narak snuffled as Aiden talked to him in Calorin. The stallion searched him for treats but was disappointed.

"You talk funny, just like Uncle Cor," Gwilym said, peering over the stall door.

"Our horses don't know Rhyddan, so we have tae speak differently tae them." Aiden left the stall and leaned on the door. Narak had calmed down and was investigating the new water bucket.

"He looks funny," Gwilym said as he watched the spotted stallion.

"Your Uncle Cor always told me that I looked a little like Narak," Aiden said and Gwilym giggled.

"You want to see my horse?" he asked.

"I would love tae," Aiden replied.

An old gelding was proudly displayed and promises to watch the next riding lesson were given. Aiden guided him toward the stall where Martin's horse was kept. The brown stallion recognized Gwilym and put his head over the door to greet them. They spent some time at the stall while Gwilym expounded upon the horse's many attributes. Martin's name was brought up throughout but Gwilym only became more cheerful. Of course, after the topic was exhausted, Zephyr had to be visited and Gwilym began again.

Aiden provided a rapt audience while also surprising Gwilym with his knowledge of Zephyr. They finally made their way back to the castle, Gwilym still importantly fulfilling his role to help Aiden. They entered behind the strangest person they had ever seen.

Corin descended the stairs with a few minutes to spare. He couldn't believe it had been five days since the battle. A change had come over the castle since then. The feeling of exhaustion had left. The hall had been cleared of the wounded for the infirmaries were now able to hold them. Rubble had been cleared from the courtyard and the town. Carts of stone had begun to arrive from the quarries near the mountains to repair the damaged walls and towers. The Clans camped on the training grounds, assisting with patrols that were still being sent out. The townspeople and refugees from the castle had not yet returned. There had been no sign of the remnants of the invading army but the northmen did not dare hope that they were gone for good.

When Corin arrived in the hall, several lords and a few of the Clan leaders were there. Corin stood by Darrin's throne after greeting them.

"It's amazing what difference soap and water makes," Darrin murmured to him.

"I'm still a little tired," Corin replied.

"You'll survive."

"You are so uncaring."

Darrin only smiled, turning his attention to the doors which were swinging open. Despite all of his training, Corin gaped at the figure that approached. The man was tall but walked with a slight bowlegged stride. His clothes were a wild array from every country of Cimbria. He wore orange pants and a red shirt cut after the style of Calorin. Tall black boots from Argus were decorated with gold tassels to match the gold fish-scale mail coat common to Gelion. A yellow cap adorned with an Argusian ostrich feather perched on his head and a blue cape dyed in the vats of Cyndor billowed behind him. Four men followed, dressed after the same fashion but with subtler colors.

Corin recovered in time as the outlandish stranger and his entourage halted before the throne. One of the men, the only other to wear the golden mail, stepped forward.

"Your majesty, may I present Captain Pierre-Rodrigo, the dragon-slayer and captain of the vessel *Sting-ray*," he said. Captain Pierre-Rodrigo removed his cap and gave a flourishing bow.

"It is an honor to finally traverse this fabled country," he said. He and his companion's voices carried the accent of Gelion. At first no one knew how to react, but Darrin, seeing the serious faces of the visitors, continued in the same vein.

"You are welcome here. I have heard of your exploits on the coast that aided us," he said. Captain Pierre-Rodrigo returned the cap to his head.

"It was indeed a disgraceful thing, those ships making war in *my* sea," he said. "They had to be stopped!"

Darrin rose and descended the steps with Corin.

"This is my brother, Prince Corin, called the Hawk," Darrin introduced him. Pierre-Rodrigo stopped in the middle of another elaborate bow and looked up eagerly.

"The Hawk!" he exclaimed, then paused. "Iago!" he said imperiously. "You have lied to me! He is but a man!" he said. "You shall be keelhauled forthwith for this travesty!"

"Aye, aye, sir," Iago, the man who had introduced him, replied, apparently unconcerned. Now standing closer to the captain, Corin saw a strange light in the man's eyes. Pierre-Rodrigo was completely mad!

"I'm sorry for any deception practiced upon you," Corin said.

"I fully accept," Pierre-Rodrigo bowed. "You should not tolerate such gross deceit wrought on your name," he told Corin. "I will gladly keelhaul any offenders."

Corin wanted to laugh.

"Thank you for your generous offer, but I prefer to deal with this in my own way," Corin said.

"I shall leave it in your capable hands," the captain said, then stopped. "You, sah!" he pointed at Trey. "Are you not that great and noble Lord Tristan who gave us hospitality at the sea?" he asked.

"No, Captain," Iago put in. "Lord Tristan remained on the coast. This must be his brother."

Trey stepped forward and introduced himself.

"Ah, I see you are a man of few words. You would be an invaluable addition to my crew where there is ceaseless conversation that grates heavily upon me," Pierre-Rodrigo said. This time there was a change on his followers' faces. The hints of smiles suggested that the captain provided much of the ceaseless conversation. "What say you? Will you join my crew?" Pierre-Rodrigo asked Trey.

"I might need some time to think it over," Trey said.

"Can you dance?" Pierre-Rodrigo asked.

"Can I...what?" Trey sounded confused. In answer, the crazed captain began to twirl him around the floor. Corin never thought he could die from laughing but he came close watching Trey's helpless and confused face. Pierre-Rodrigo released him and Trey edged quickly away.

"You are lacking in some necessary skills but would still be welcome," the captain informed him.

"I still need some time," Trey said.

Darrin came forward and introduced the captain to the other lords in the hall.

"What is happening and why is Trey hiding behind you?" Liam asked in a low voice as he came to join Corin.

"I'm not really sure," Corin replied, still trying to regain any sort of composure while Trey glared at him. Liam was not the only one with questions. Aiden and Gwilym made their way up the hall to join them. Gwilym ran forward when he saw Corin. His uncle hugged him and gave him a look to ensure to best behavior. Aiden nodded a greeting to Corin and Corin only shrugged when he saw the look Aiden shot at Pierre-Rodrigo.

The lords were not sure how to respond to the captain, but he was again distracted when he saw the new arrivals.

"You sah!" he pointed at Liam. "Iago! Is he not the one?" he asked.

"If you say he is, Captain," Iago replied.

"He is indeed! The seer I have been seeking for years!" Pierre-Rodrigo exclaimed. He advanced toward Liam who looked nervous. "My dreams decreed I would find you. You must tell me what you know about my future!"

"Well…you…should tell me who you are…so I know that… you are the one," Liam began hesitantly.

"Yes! I am Pierre-Rodrigo. I slew the dragon!"

"The…the dragon…yes…then there is no doubt…is there?" Liam glanced to Corin and Trey for support but, as before, they were as helpless as he was. "What do you want?" Liam asked.

"You can foresee my future. Tell me what I will do!" Pierre-Rodrigo said earnestly.

"Foreseeing will take some time…obviously…so you might have to wait," Liam said.

"Of course! I would not dream of imposing upon you!" the captain said. Despite his plight, Liam exchanged the same look with Corin and Trey. Martin would have loved this.

Apparently forgetting his intention not to impose, Pierre-Rodrigo took Liam's arm.

"Iago, arrange for lodging. I must consult with the seer," he announced. Liam had no choice but to accompany him and one of the men from the hall. Once they were safely gone, Iago addressed Darrin.

"Would we be able to take lodging here, Your Majesty?" he asked.

"Yes, it would be no trouble to find a place for your party," Darrin said. "How long will you be staying?"

Iago shrugged.

"As long as the captain wishes. But I will urge against a long stay. He needs to get back to the sea." Iago said.

"Is he...?" Darrin hesitantly began.

"He has not always been like that. And my name has not always been Iago. Years ago, we were apprenticed together on a merchant ship. A falling spar struck him on the head in a storm. When he finally woke, he declared himself to be Pierre-Rodrigo. When we made it back to Gelion, his father didn't know what to do with him, so he gave Cleto his own ship. I guess he didn't think Cleto would actually try to sail it. As for me, I couldn't leave him as he was, so I went along and became Iago. We picked up a crew along the way. I don't think any of them mind him," Iago said.

"You get used to it," Amato, a crewman said. "Anyone who ever tries to take advantage of him sorely regrets it if they are still alive. We have a good life under him so I do not complain. And dancing is a new requirement," he told Trey.

"He doesn't remember anything before the accident, but don't treat him any differently than you already have. He can have many different moods," Iago warned.

Word spread of the strange visitors and the hall was filled that night at the evening meal as everyone tried to get a glimpse.

"How come you're called the 'dragon slayer' when dragons don't exist?" Gwilym boldly asked.

"Horror! The country's greatest warrior doubts their existence!" Pierre-Rodrigo exclaimed. "Come, I will prove it!"

Gwilym came to stand by the chair and the sea captain pulled off the chain around his neck. The whitened tooth of some great animal hung from the chain.

"I took this after I killed him," Pierre-Rodrigo said. Gwilym stared wide-eyed at the irrefutable proof in front of him. He touched it hesitantly and it took little prodding from him for the captain to launch into the tale.

Aiden sat further down with his brothers, barely touching his food.

"It's not just Canich that's asking about you. The other Clans worry too," Ranulf said. "The camp isn't far from the castle. You should come."

Aiden hardly looked up.

"Maybe," he said.

"Danny, you can'nae stay here forever," Will said.

"What do you want? Me tae pretend nothing happened?" Aiden shot back.

"No, but you can'nae shut us out," Will said patiently. Aiden avoided looking at them.

"Fine, I'll try," he said. Will and Ranulf exchanged a relieved look and let the subject lie.

After dinner, Corin and Trey cornered Liam.

"So, you're a seer now?" Trey asked.

"Very funny. You have to help me!" Liam turned to Corin.

"Why?" Corin asked.

"I spent all afternoon reciting every scrap of verse or prophecy I could remember from songs and stories. I even had to pretend to have a vision! And now, I'm a full-fledged member of the crew!" Liam exclaimed.

"Did he make you dance?" Trey asked.

"What? No, you know I can't," Liam replied.

"You don't want to go with them?" Corin asked as seriously as he could.

"I love it when you try and be funny," Liam said. "You have to help me! I will be crazier than him within a week!" He sounded desperate.

"All right, I'll try and talk to him," Corin said.

"You better or I will kill you," Liam said seriously.

Chapter 15

Aiden was woken the next morning by Gwilym.

"Can you come with me to the stables again? Everyone is busy," he said. Aiden, surprisingly, was not irritated by this.

"Just let me get dressed. You can hand me my boots," he said.

"Do you need your swords too?" Gwilym asked when Aiden was ready.

"No," Aiden said.

"I thought warriors always carried their sword," Gwilym said. Aiden looked at his weapons. He had avoided them since the battle; a bitter taste remained in his mouth as he remembered how he had gone berserk. Gwilym was wearing Martin's dagger like Aiden had showed him.

"How about I take a knife, just like you?" Aiden asked. Gwilym nodded and Aiden picked up a dagger and put it into his belt. Then, out of force of habit, he took the others.

"Why do you have so many?" Gwilym asked.

"Sometimes several daggers are better than a sword," Aiden said. "When you're older I'll show you."

"Promise?" Gwilym exclaimed, his eyes shining. Aiden saw the return of life to the boy and felt the same thing stir inside.

They visited the horses again and then Aiden allowed Gwilym to convince him to go down to the river and see the frogs. They stayed on the banks until lunchtime. As they started to leave the river, Aiden saw the tents of the Clans.

"Gwilym, can you get back tae the castle by yourself?" he asked.

"Yes, but where are you going?" the boy asked.

"Tae see the Clans," Aiden said.

"Can I come?" Gwilym asked.

"Not this time," Aiden said gently. Gwilym looked crestfallen so Aiden said, "When I get back, I'll show you how tae clean the knife."

Successfully cheered, Gwilym ran off and Aiden slowly walked to the camp. Will and Blair were the first to greet him.

"We weren't expecting you for a few more days," Blair said.

"You know healers, they're always trying tae get rid of you," Aiden said and Blair chuckled. More warriors joined them. "I feel fine," he told them. Neason came and clasped his hand.

"I guess you can see that no one was worried," Neason said. Aiden smiled.

"You of all people should know you can'nae get rid of me very easily," he said. Neason laughed heartily.

"I'm glad you're back," he said. Others expressed the same sentiment and Aiden wondered, not for the first time, at the amount of people among the Clans who cared about him. It was still new to him and he felt an amount of happiness return as his people joined him. He should not have neglected it this long.

He ate with the Clan, greeting the Lairds as they passed by. Aiden saw that no one knew about Rona and he was grateful there would be no barrier to their easy conversation. But that relief was destroyed as the meal finished and a warrior from Clan Canich approached and Aiden knew him: Eideard, Rona's brother.

"Now you come!" he spat. Aiden was silent.

"Eideard! What are you saying?" Blair was shocked.

"It's your fault!" Eideard shouted. "She's dead because of you!"

There was stricken silence among the warriors.

"Danny?" Blair turned to him in bewilderment. Aiden finally stood.

"Rona's dead," he said.

"Is that all you have tae say?" Eideard sneered.

"I didn't want her tae come! I tried tae make her stay," Aiden replied.

"Not too hard apparently. You didn't protect her!" Eideard said.

"I tried!" Aiden shouted. Will placed a hand on his arm.

"If you want someone tae blame, then blame me," Mairi, Logan's wife, said. She was on the verge of tears. "She came tae me and I told her the reason I follow Logan. I never discouraged her from going tae battle. She would have listened tae me!" Mairi said.

"You don't know that," Aiden said.

"Coward! You would hide behind women instead of admitting your fault!" Eideard snarled.

"If you want tae blame me then go ahead!" Aiden shouted. "Just remember it was her choice come! I would exchange places with her if I could, but she's gone!"

Will again held him back. Eideard spat at his feet before another warrior shoved him away and took him from the scene.

"He'll regret that," Blair vowed.

"No. He has every right," Aiden said before he, too, walked away.

Gwilym found him immediately as he returned to the castle. Aiden took him to the armory where they sat on a bench and he began to show the boy the basics of caring for a weapon.

"I didn't expect to see either of you here," Corin said. They had not heard as he entered the room.

"Look, Uncle Cor!" Gwilym held the knife up proudly. Corin took the dagger and inspected it carefully.

"Good work, Gwily," he said.

"Danny showed me how," Gwilym told him.

"I hope you don't mind," Aiden said.

"No, he was going to have to learn soon and I haven't had much time," Corin said. "Gwilym, maybe you and Aiden can help me pick out a new javelin."

"Did yours broke?" Gwilym asked.

"Break," Corin corrected. "And, yes, it did. It was my favorite one too."

"You always say that," Gwilym said, running over to the rack of short spears.

"Observant, isn't he?" Aiden said. Corin smiled.

"Thanks for looking after him," he said.

"I think we're both helping each other out," Aiden said. Corin agreed, watching Gwilym "help" as he and Aiden pointed out the finer points of the javelin to the boy. They left some time later, Corin with a new spear in hand.

"You going somewhere?" Aiden asked him.

"Samir is still alive and tomorrow we're providing him and the other prisoners with an escort to the coast. Our new friends agreed to make sure they get back to Calorin," Corin said.

"You're leaving?" Gwilym asked.

"Only for a few days," Corin said. "Grandpa Trey is going too, but do you want to go visit him in a few months?" he asked and received an eager reply. Gwilym had long been promised a trip to the sea. He ran off again and Corin was called away. Aiden was not alone long when Ranulf came to find him.

"I heard what happened earlier," Ranulf said. "I will speak tae Eideard."

"Don't punish him, Davy. He's grieving," Aiden said. "I would have done the same in his place."

"Perhaps, but you will have tae face him again. Grieving or not, he insulted the Champion. It cannot be ignored," Ranulf said.

"Why does everything have tae be so blasted important?" Aiden growled.

"Danny," Ranulf said patiently. "We leave within the week. This will be settled before then."

Aiden only nodded, feeling an old restlessness come upon him.

"Where's Tam? I haven't seen him much," he said, trying to ignore it.

"He's been spending time with Kara. I barely see him myself," Ranulf said.

"Should I be expecting a new sister sometime soon?" Aiden smiled.

"I think you might," Ranulf said, also smiling.

"I'll have tae find him tomorrow. I'm sure Will and I have enough stories tae embarrass both of them. I've let myself get terribly behind on this," Aiden said and, as he and Ranulf laughed, his brother was glad to see a light returning to Aiden's eyes.

The next morning, Aiden rose early. Horses stood ready in the courtyard. Corin and the Hawk Flight waited for the rest of the escort. Captain Pierre-Rodrigo made a dashing entrance followed by his men. Despite Corin finally convincing the captain to let Liam stay, he wanted one last conference with his "seer."

"I wish you could come," Corin said to Aiden.

"Aye, but I wouldn't be of much use with this." Aiden lifted his broken hand.

"We should be back before the Clans leave," Corin said.

"Take as long as you need tae make sure he never makes it back," Aiden said, watching Samir and the other prisoners being brought down the steps.

"I doubt he will. You know how much the Sultaan likes failure," Corin said.

There were not many prisoners as most of the Calorins had not allowed themselves to be taken alive. They were mounted under the heavy guard of Corin's and Trey's men. Samir was one of the last and, knowing well what awaited him in Calorin, he broke his bonds and snatched the scimitar from Corin's belt.

"You will die with me!" he snarled, advancing toward Corin.

Corin avoided the blade, but Samir moved too close for him to use the javelin. There was another rasp of steel and a voice shouted at Corin. He obeyed and ducked to the side. Captain Pierre-Rodrigo parried with his long blade and seconds later, Samir's headless body crumpled to the ground. The courtyard was silent. The incident had happened too quickly. Aiden helped Corin to his feet.

"You're getting slow in your old age," he told Corin. Others stared at Samir's body. Trey shrugged.

"That's fine by me," he said.

"Iago, find a sack," Pierre-Rodrigo commanded. "My lord, I am sorry for spilling blood here," he said to Darrin.

"I should thank you instead for saving my brother's life," Darrin said.

Captain Pierre-Rodrigo handed the scimitar to Corin.

"You owe me nothing. Give me one of the grey hawk feathers I believe you would leave for the Calorins," he said. For a moment, he appeared perfectly sane. Corin sheathed his scimitar and handed him the feather. Iago returned with a burlap bag and placed the head in it.

"I will deliver these to the Sultaan myself. It will be a message he cannot ignore," Pierre-Rodrigo said. Then he sheathed his sword and the dragon-slayer returned. "Why do we delay?" he asked. "Our voyage is long and tides do not wait."

The rest of the Northmen mounted and rode from the castle. The body was buried and the castle returned to life. Aiden went to the Braeton camp to face a stiff Eideard. Eventually a sort of understanding was reached between them but Aiden found no peace. He spent more time with his brothers and they had hope for the future as he appeared to be returning to his old self.

But somehow rejoining the Braetons refreshened his loss. He saw his brothers' worry and hid his sorrow. The thought of going back to Scodra filled him with dread. There, everything would remind him of her. He couldn't go back. Not yet. And he couldn't stay here either. He saw the burial mounds every day and knew her grave was also there. That knowledge haunted him every night.

Will found him one afternoon sitting by the river.

"I can'nae go back," Aiden said.

"What do you mean, Danny?" Will asked.

"I thought it would be different this time."

"What?" Will pressed.

"Everywhere I go, I leave a grave. They all died because of me," Aiden said. "I can'nae stay."

"You can'nae run again," Will said.

"That's what I do, Will! I run every time!"

"Danny."

"No, you don't know anything about me!" Aiden exclaimed. "You want tae know what I did? I fought for the Calorins. I was here when they invaded the first time. I did nothing tae help Corin. He was going tae die and a Calorin helped save him while I did almost nothing! I didn't even fight for him! I forgot my Clan for years and I betrayed my people in that war. I don't belong here and I'm no Champion!" he shouted.

"Danny."

"Don't call me that!"

"Fine. I've heard enough about the first war tae piece it together. You were no coward. Kara owes her life tae you," Will said.

"That can'nae erase anything," Aiden said.

"I'm not saying it will," his brother said. "And despite what you want, you are the Champion and you can'nae leave the Clan."

Aiden stared stonily at the ground. Will sighed.

"At least talk tae Ranulf," he said. Aiden nodded but his mind was made up. He avoided Corin that night and packed his bags. He sharpened his blades and folded away the plaid. He left the room well before dawn, filling his bag with food from the kitchens, and then went to the stables. Narak greeted him eagerly as he began to saddle him. Aiden suddenly froze.

"You must think I'm stupid," Corin said.

"You here to stop me?" Aiden asked, abandoning his brogue.

"I thought I might talk first," Corin said. "I take it Ranulf doesn't know."

"No." Aiden tightened the girth.

"Well?" Corin prodded.

"I can't," Aiden said. "I see her everywhere."

"And you think leaving will help?" Corin asked.

"It might!" Aiden snapped, then relented. "Maybe I need to think it will."

"Azrahil stopped you last time," Corin said.

"You ever try telling him 'no?'"

"Aiden."

"I know," Aiden said. He tightened the last buckle on the bridle. "Where are you planning on going?"

"I've never been east," Aiden said. "So, are you going to stop me?"

"I feel like you won't listen, so I came to say good-bye and to give you this." Corin handed him a pouch. "I 'borrowed' all this from Liam and Mera," he said.

"Thanks." Aiden fastened it to the saddle. He was strong enough to ride but his wounds were not fully healed. "Can you...?"

"Yes, I'll try and calm Ranulf after he finds out," Corin said.

"Thanks, Cor. You've always understood me better than anyone."

"Aye, but I think you're a bit of an idiot right now."

"I know. I'll be back in a year, at the most."

"You'd better get going if you want any kind of head start," Corin said, opening the door. Aiden led Narak from the stall.

"Good-bye, Corin," he said.

"Be careful, Aiden," Corin replied. He walked with Aiden to the main gates where the Braeton mounted.

"I'll be back," Aiden promised. Corin watched him ride away, a dark figure against the lightening sky, and wished he could go with him.

- -

Ranulf, naturally, was furious when he found out. But in the end he was forced to listen to Corin. The Clans left soon after with new oaths of friendship between them and Aredor. A treaty was signed between the two countries, promising to aid one another in times of future strife. The refugees were slowly returning to Kingscastle under the leadership of Queen Rhian and Lady Elain and Amaura, and life began to return to normal.

Only faint rumors returned to Durna of the war and in Calorin, the Sultaan paled with fear when he saw what Captain Pierre-Rodrigo brought. In the court, a lord and his guards almost smiled when they saw the grey hawk feather.

Corin walked the walls, watching the sun set. He heard footsteps behind him and saw Mera. Karif fluttered to the battlements to join them.

"So, what now, Hawk?" she asked with a smile.

"Hope this peace can last," he said.

"Do you think it will?" she asked.

"Maybe. Gerralt's been rather merciless in the push to get me to catch up on paperwork," Corin said.

"That's not what I meant," Mera said. Corin smiled.

"I know." He kissed her. "But as long as you're here I'll do whatever I can to keep that hope."

Chapter 16

One year later, a rider crossed the Cymro Mountains into Aredor. It took several days before the familiar towers of Kingscastle came into sight. It had been a hard year for Aredor. The war had caused the neglect of many fields and the Calorins had destroyed more. The winter was a lean one but already the green fields promised an abundant harvest.

Aiden rode through the gates and marked the changes. The walls and towers had been completely repaired. New storehouses and barracks had been built and over everything was the feeling of peace.

Mera was the one who greeted him.

"I don't think Corin was expecting you for a few more days," she said.

"Where is he?" he asked.

"Lynwood Keep for an inspection and then he'll be making a visit in the forest." She smiled. It reminded Aiden of the duty he had yet to perform. At his request, Mera took him to the training grounds. The mounds were covered with grass and only stones engraved with Clan symbols marked their purpose. One grave was set apart and Aiden stopped by it.

"Tam said one of your Clan drew the design and requested it be carved on her stone. His name was Kenneth," Mera said.

"Tam was here?" Aiden asked.

"To visit Kara and to ask after you," Mera replied. Aiden made no reply and she left him to himself.

He crouched by the stone. It bore a lily whose stem wrapped around a four-pointed star and underneath was her name with the same swallow as on the necklace he wore under his shirt.

"Hello again," he said. "It's been a year and I don't miss you as much. I guess you would say that's good. You'd also tell me tae quit moping around a grave and get back tae Scodra." He smiled. "I guess I'll finally listen." He stood. "Good-bye, Rona."

Corin returned the next day and joyfully greeted Aiden. He was glad to see that Aiden was calmer and returned to his old mood. But there was still an air of sadness he carried with him. Aiden recounted his adventures over dinner.

"I assisted with a bit of an uprising against a lord in Cyndor for a few months and then headed tae sea again. I met up with none other than Captain Pierre-Rodrigo who recruited me for his next quest. We sailed past Terminus and...we fought a dragon," Aiden said.

"What? I thought they didn't exist!" Corin exclaimed.

"Neither did I. But if you sail far enough east, you'll find them," Aiden said. "Then I went tae Calorin, visited some old friends, and I'm back."

"How are things in Calorin?" Corin asked.

"No one's really changed. I said I would pass on greetings," Aiden said. "The Sultaan is dead. Apparently your present really affected him."

Corin smiled grimly.

"And now?" he asked.

"The son took over. He didn't sound nearly as ambitious as his illustrious father, so I don't think you'll have anything tae worry about," Aiden said. "How are things here?"

"Quiet. Even the Raiders are staying away. We're trying to rebuild the warbands but it will be years before they're back to the old strength," Corin said.

"Well, I wouldn't worry. I hear your name everywhere I go in Cimbria. It'll be years before anyone dreams of attacking Aredor," Aiden said.

He left the next morning, turning north once again and crossing the border. He travelled quickly, pushing toward the forest. Two days later, he emerged at the top of the valley. Tendrils of smoke rose from the houses inside the walls. Sun glinted off the lake and he could hear children as they played. He spurred Narak forward. Men and women looked up in the fields as he passed, shouting as they recognized him. Some ran ahead to the fortress. The gates were open in welcome and his family awaited him. He let the peace of the valley fill him. He was finally home.

Epilogue

Corin and Mera were married a few months later. They had six children who would leave a legacy as great as their father. Karif and his descendants served Corin and the heirs of the Hawk Flight for generations after. Aiden never married, staying true to the memory of Rona. He never left the Clan again and became one of the greatest Champions Clan Canich or Braeton had ever known. He was a frequent visitor to Aredor to see his friends and stop at Rona's grave.

Tam and Kara also married after she left the warband the next year. Tam became accounted as one of the great Bards and sang songs of Aredor and Braeton. William married a daughter of Clan Canich and they lived their days in the peace of the Scodra valley. When he died, his name was accorded a place on the scrolls of the Hawk Flight.

Trey and Amaura married and lived by the sea where Trey built a small fleet of warships with the help of Pierre-Rodrigo—a frequent visitor after the war. Tristan wed the dark-haired daughter of a coastal lord, adding new strength to the line of Martel. Andras eventually left the warband, taking his father's chair in the fief and ruling well into old age. Evan followed him and became the leader of the deugain, serving Andras faithfully until he met his death on a Raider's sword.

Gwilym grew under the care of his uncles and with their training became a Blademaster, perhaps even greater than Martin himself.

Years later, they died.

Aiden and some of Clan Canich rode to the aid of Clan Mavor against the Enladi tribes that had pushed harder and harder at the border over the years. His party was ambushed near a mountain pass. All the Braetons were killed but Aiden held the narrow corridor until the tribes fled in fear. When the rest of the Clans arrived, they found him lying with the fallen. A wildcat rose from its place by his body where it had protected him from scavengers, and padded away. Tam played the Lament for him and after, never played again. Corin was there, also mourning the death of his wife the year before.

Not long after, Argusians and Raiders together made an attack on Aredor's coast. The Aredorians held firm and soundly defeated them but Corin was mortally wounded. After the battle, Corin found Darrin, who was also dying. Corin sat beside him and whispered, "Wait for me."

Darrin smiled and Corin leaned against the wheel of a chariot. His vision clouded and he saw ghostly figures waiting. Aiden and Martin smiled and Castimir beckoned. Liam and Ahmed stood with them and, best of all, was Mera. The last thing he saw was a grey hawk flying free above the field.

Trey found them and he was joined by their sons who would rule Aredor and the Hawk Flight as bravely as their fathers had.

When Liam died, he was buried in the forest across from Martin at the entrance to the valley. There, they passed into legend as the guardians of the Hawk Flight.

Corin and Aiden were held as the greatest heroes the North had ever known and, while wars troubled the North long after they died, their descendants rose up and did not fail.